THROUGH THE HEART

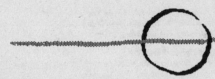

Richard Grant

SPECTRA ™

BANTAM BOOKS

New York • Toronto • London • Sydney • Auckland

THROUGH THE HEART
A Bantam Spectra Book / January 1992

ISBN 0-553-29320-6

Published simultaneously in the United States and Canada

Bantam Books are published by Bantam Books, a division of
Bantam Doubleday Dell Publishing Group, Inc. Its trademark,
consisting of the words "Bantam Books" and the portrayal of a
rooster, is Registered in U.S. Patent and Trademark Office and in
other countries. Marca Registrada. Bantam Books, 666 Fifth
Avenue, New York, New York 10103.

PRINTED IN THE UNITED STATES OF AMERICA

OPM   0 9 8 7 6 5 4 3 2 1

Praise for Richard Grant

THROUGH THE HEART

"A steampunk galley slave coming of age on an earthbound generational ship lumbering across a post-holocaust America— Grant has reinvented all the high legends of SF, bringing back the magic we felt when we first read *A Canticle for Leibowitz*." —TERRY BISSON

"*Through the Heart* is a fascinating journey through the strange lost lands of the future, wonderfully detailed and filled with unforgettable characters. To read it is to be captivated." —PAT CADIGAN

RUMORS OF SPRING

"A rare and marvelous tale." —LOS ANGELES DAILY NEWS

"Wry, hilarious, and human, *Rumors of Spring* is a joy." —SAN FRANCISCO EXAMINER

"Like all good myths, *Rumors of Spring* is rooted in a rich soil of realism. It is a wise and compassionate tale, filled with empathy for the human condition." —PHILADELPHIA DAILY NEWS

"A warm near-future fantasy . . . ably demonstrates [Grant's] abilities as a storyteller in what might be called the modern Ray Bradbury school of fantasy . . . richly detailed characters and a plentiful collection of humorous sidelights." —AUSTIN AMERICAN-STATESMAN

VIEWS FROM THE OLDEST HOUSE

"[Grant is] a daring and fearless writer, one possessing uncommon ambition, talent, and literacy." —WASHINGTON POST BOOK WORLD

"The borders of reality and fantasy collide in this kaleidoscopic foray into magical realism. . . . Highly recommended." —LIBRARY JOURNAL

"It ought to be used as a yardstick for all future works of speculative fiction. It is a grand and eloquent tale, a masterpiece." —NEW PATHWAYS

Other books by Richard Grant

RUMORS OF SPRING

SARABAND OF LOST TIME

VIEWS FROM THE OLDEST HOUSE

THROUGH
THE
HEART

FLY SOUTH

When their wagon broke down at the Oasis, Kem was traded by his family for a scavenged motor and a set of high-grade tools. The rest of the wagons blew eastward on the autumn wind. Kem stood at the edge of the Oasis the first few mornings, watching his father crawl in and out of the engine compartment. It was the generator that was broken, with all the reduction gears. Kem doubted that his father would ever be able to fix it. Dirt blew up around the wheels, and the wagon began to look suspiciously like a permanent feature of the landscape. The little girls, Kem's sisters, came in the evenings to play among the olive trees, pausing now and then to gaze with the solemnity of scryers into the fountain. He thought to ask them what they saw there, in those green waters, but it was too late: the Oasis moved south, continuing its slow progress through the heart of the desert, and Kem supposed he would never see his family again. For him, they may as well have died in that empty place.

Life in the Oasis was no more difficult than life in the

wagon had been. Kem was assigned to the galley, as were most of the new boys, and saw little of the countryside they passed. He guessed it was like all the other country he had known—dry and motionless—though he could feel through the rising and falling of the deckplates that it was at least not quite so flat as the wagon routes. He tried to imagine the land wrinkled up like a blanket, forming bulges and swails, and thought of the way the light would fall there at the first and the last hours of day. But his imagination took him only so far, and by the time he got off duty after supper it was always dark, with just a smudge of brown at the edge of the earth, no different from other sunsets.

The most amazing things were the luxury of abundant water and the number of people that ate and slept and chattered and sobbed quietly in the night, from loneliness he guessed, all around him.

Kem had thought the Oasis might be different; a more alien place. From outside—as often he had seen it, during those windy months when the wagon crossed the Grind—its profile was intricate and asymmetrical, like a walled village. He had glimpsed formal gardens and game courts, groves of shadow-gray trees, alleys, market stalls, fountains and sun decks, wooden fences and metal bulkheads, and rising among them the struts and propellers of windmills, a navigation tower, armored gun emplacements, lookout platforms, and banks of spotlights.

Only up close did one perceive that the Oasis was not a village at all but a single welded artifice, a landship; it was wrapped in a curving metal hull the lead-gray color of thunderclouds, its great bulk suspended a stride or two off the ground, raised on treads. It moved by dragging itself across the earth. Realizing this, each time, made Kem's stomach twist, as though he had picked up what he took to be a rock or a shard of pottery and had found himself holding a piece of ancient, sun-whitened bone. Like all wagon-boys he had longed to go to the Oasis, to climb aboard and ride it across the Grind. Like all fathers Kem's had kept him away, hidden among the wagons, until the recruitment gangs were well gone and the trading stalls winched up to storage bays, traders and soldiers and passengers at their stations, hatches slammed, sun wings retracted, warning bells struck, steam vented from blowholes, deckhands sent scurrying up ratlines to rig wind-blades and wave good-bye to the dust-grimed impoverished folks they had entertained and terrified and defrauded for a week or two, and the great landship was once more underway.

The Oasis was a marvel. And a monstrosity.

People were always ready to talk about it, among the wagons, around the evening fires—the more so when it was safely gone and another year would pass before they saw it again. Wagon drivers with swollen joints, tired and envious, held forth about how the Oasis crawled on tens of thousands of cleated toes. It drew its power, they said, from the air and from the sun, stored it in giant flywheels or drew it like water into a cistern of capacitors. Though restricted by its bulk to level ground, it was not much troubled by blast fissures, small-to-medium-gauge rubble (such as one found in the crumbled cities), or even bodies of water, up to a certain depth. So it passed in its annual transit as far south as the Bright Land and north all the way to the Carbon Bank Forest. Slower than a wagon, it could still do maybe forty kills a day, under good conditions, and was seldom without a train of lesser craft as it rumbled across the Grind. Collecting the stuff thrown over its side, sifting this for things odd or usable, was sometimes worthwhile; but in any case, as people believed, one could count on being safe from attack. The sight of the Oasis seemed to discourage both pirates and wargangs.

Or so they had said among the wagons, around the fire.

But from the inside—seeing the Oasis so to speak from the pit of its own belly—Kem found the legend transcribed to a set of small, irreducible facts. Its grandeur was diminished by drudgery. Its vast scale was broken down to a series of compartments and passageways, some of which were barely large enough to stand straight up in. And in contrast to the prodigies Kem had expected to meet, the people who lived here were no more splendid or heroic—and certainly no more hygienic—than himself. After a week or two, with the wagons and his family somewhere behind, in that unseen direction which the logic of inertia informed him at every lurch must be the past, Kem could not remember very well

how the Oasis had once looked to his boyish eyes, or even
how boyhood itself had been. His life seemed to have crossed
an unmarked frontier. He supposed that now he was a man.

He was just getting used to things, to his new life, when he
awoke one night amidst the clanging of bells, ringing to
summon the deck crew to take its positions at the guardrails.

Kem did not believe, afterward, that it had been the bells
that woke him (though he remembered them, like part of a
dream), but thought instead that he had felt in some deeper
way a quickening of the pulse of the Oasis. As in a desert
storm, everything happened all at once, without warning—
bodies moving beside his bunk, flashlights picking out steel
beams and bulkheads, the distant thud of something soft
falling against a metal plate, sliding off, falling again. There
was a smell of urine and rancid beer. From farther back in the
shadows he heard someone say *It's the border*. But that
meant nothing and just made him wish he had gotten to know
someone here, anyone, that he could talk to. And only then,
coming fully awake with irritation, Kem understood that the
Oasis was groaning to a halt.

He rose from his bunk, twisting himself free of sheets that
were damp with sweat, and joined the shuffle of boys and
young men up the passageway, toward the hatch. He could
feel the swirling energy of the great flywheels, which he
imagined to be something like free-spinning millstones, as
they absorbed the kinetic energy of the slowing craft, losing a
tiny part of it in the vibrations that passed into Kem's feet.
He could feel the tension in the bellies of his crewmates. He
knew that some drama was going on outside, in the warmth
and clutter of the night, and that he himself had no part in it.
Still he pressed forward.

By the time Kem reached the main promenade from the
sleeping quarters beneath the galley, most of the several
hundred residents of the Oasis were up and about. Search-
lights from the observation deck played across a stretch of dry
dirt he could just make out by leaning over the taffrail. The
beams caught clouds of dust a couple hundred strides away,
against the blackness, but what had stirred the dust—not

wind—wasn't at all clear. Fear stroked the ridge of Kem's spine, making him twitch his shoulder blades. The sweat on his back felt cool in the dry desert air.

It was not the best possible vantage. The terrace behind the galley was no more than a wide curving ledge. There were no olive or palm trees here; only tanks that stood belly high, filled with cattails and sedge and swamp iris, where the waste water was filtered down for recycling. A stagnant sweetness filled the air. Kem's view of the rest of the Oasis was cut off by a partition that rose beside him, covered with vines, the first of several inner circles that messboys were forbidden to cross. About all he could see, by standing against the rail and looking back over the wall, was the tower itself: the spiraling minaret with its tiny windows, a medusa's-head of antennae, a gunmount. Just below the gun, circling the tower, was a narrow catwalk, and at its railing now and then a tiny figure could be seen to raise field glasses or point into the darkness, in a direction Kem could not follow. Something was out there, clearly. Yet just as clearly the fascination of the moment lay not *out there* but with the tower itself.

"Is it him?" said a voice from the level of his shoulders.

Kem looked down to see a boy no older than thirteen, though the face and bearing suggested something of the jaded veteran. "Who?" he said—"Is it who?"

The boy scowled and looked away. It was the first time Kem had spoken to anyone outside the normal conduct of his duties, and this was how far it got him.

From up ahead, out in the desert, there came a popping sound, a sudden pressing-outward of air, which Kem recognized as rifle shots. He had expected something like this. He thought of his father, his father's exasperated sigh, the reflexive gesture with which he had reached for his bow at the first sign of trouble. Kem expected these people to react the same way—to dig into their breeches and caftans and pull out carbines, shotguns, throwing-blades. But the sound of gunfire seemed only to amuse them. Many of the boys were grinning, and slowly, beginning on the other side of the garden wall, spreading like ripples, there grew a general shout, a cheer.

A thought presented itself in Kem's mind. *The border*, it

said. He frowned, for it had come with such suddenness and clarity: an echo of something he had heard a few minutes ago. *It's the border.*

So, he thought. We're crossing a border. A border to what?

Because his own thoughts had distracted him, while around him the galley boys joined in the bellows and cheers, Kem seemed to be the only one staring up in that particular moment toward the minaret. More lights had blinked on there, glaring down, so it was difficult to see anything at all. But for a moment, one of the lights was blocked out by a head that jutted like a hawk's out of the blackness. The face was invisible, but Kem could make out a halo of thick pale hair, and something just beneath it, bright and warm like gold, gleaming on someone's shoulders. Then the head was gone, and the spotlight scored his eyes.

Another thought had appeared, though, in the instant before the gleaming vanished. This thought too, Kem decided, was almost certainly an echo. Only in this case it was a distant one, for he could not remember where he had heard the words, the name, before.

Thinking about the halo, the head blocking out the light, Kem heard it again.

It's him, said the echo. *It's Captain Hand.*

The attention of the younger boy at his side fell on Kem with a certain detectable pressure. He looked down into the boy's sharp eyes; he felt himself being weighed, *admeasured*, classified. "You're the one," the boy said, "that Delan's got his eye on."

But he may as well have been talking to himself. He gave a slight private smile. Then his bearing changed and he stepped closer, nearly touching Kem and looking beyond him: conspiratorial.

"Come on," he whispered. "While they're all out here. I'll show you something."

Kem found the lack of explanation or formality strange, but not in a disagreeable way. The boy edged past him through the milling, gawking cluster of their crewmates, toward a black gap in the shadows. Kem hurried after him and they went through a hatch. He did not recognize the tight little hall they came into, but that didn't mean much; the boy moved fast ahead of him on well-acclimated feet. The only light came at wide intervals from bulbs that glowed red and gave an odd sense of depth to things, as though nothing were really solid at all. The hall curved leftward.

"Um, my name's Kem," he ventured.

"I've heard"—not looking back.

Kem frowned; it seemed to him that he ought to have more control here. (The other boy was at least three years younger, for one thing.) He said, "Who are *you?*"

The boy stopped, but only because he had reached another hatch, barely a crawlway. He drew himself up and declared:

"I'm Sander."

—giving each syllable its own deliberate weight, as though to fend off the indignity of a nickname.

Kem started to put a hand out, but withheld it. "Well . . . hi."

The boy Sander made his slight, agile frame a degree more compact and vanished through the door.

Kem had to duck to follow. He found himself inside a cramped, but to his way of thinking luxurious, little stateroom. Besides the usual narrow bunk there were shelves screwed into the bulkhead bearing dozens of books, a bedside lamp, a washbasin, and most amazing of all—just below the ceiling—a tiny porthole, hooked open now to admit noise and light and the torpid desert breeze. Kem drew breath in appreciation.

Sander seemed to enjoy this effect. With a glance around, betraying for the first time a quantum of hesitation, he plunged an arm underneath the grimy mattress on the bunk. The arm groped, then emerged with a flat wooden container, about as large as one of the books. This he opened with care, less for dramatic effect, Kem thought, than out of respect for whatever were its contents. By the yellowish light of the porthole, Sander held up something that looked like a flavoring herb: crushed dull green leaves you could sprinkle on your soup.

"Diviner's sage," announced Sander, grandly. (It told Kem nothing.) "Here, smell it."

He took a pinch of the stuff between two skinny fingertips

and pressed it into Kem's palm. It smelled stale, faintly acrid, unremarkable. Kem held his hand out for Sander to take it back.

Behind them, like dull mallets, boot heels struck the metal plates of the hall. Sander's eyes narrowed. As the steps got louder, the boy became a blur of purposeful activity: snapped shut the wood box, slipped it back under the mattress, adjusted the artless rumple of the sheets, spun at last to face the hatch but only obliquely so, his stance favoring Kem as though to implicate him in their trespass. Only when the steps reached the hatch did he notice the pinch of leaves still in Kem's open palm.

"Stupid," he hissed, "swallow it!"

Kem raised his hand to his mouth without thinking as the hatch swung open and Sander turned to face it with a child's large, guileless eyes. The leaves were gritty and sour.

A shadow filled the doorway. Kem tried to swallow, but his mouth only filled with saliva and he fought the reflex to gag. The shadow grew like a magic seed to become a head, a bearded face, wide bare shoulders. Halfway through—catching sight of the two of them already there—the man stopped and gave a quick, startled snort. It was all Kem needed to flesh out the half-formed image of a buffalo. Terrified, he choked down the stuff in his mouth. Immediately he feared he was going to throw it back up again. An awful moment went by.

"Ah, Sander," the man said then. He straightened up, pressed himself into the now distinctly crowded little chamber. He did not exactly smile, but there was something like pleasure in his dark eyes. His voice though rough-edged was stately, and he went on after a moment, "You've brought a friend."

Kem relaxed a little. The urge to vomit passed. Sander—once more master of the moment—gestured with one of those small, efficient arms.

"I've been telling Kem here," he said, "about your books and all. And how you know the Residents. Kem's new down in the galley. Just signed on back at the last trade stop."

Signed on, thought Kem unhappily. Just signed on. A polite term, he supposed, for the untidy business of buying lives. He attempted an ironic smile, but probably got it wrong; it was not an expression he was used to, having come into the fullness of manhood so abruptly, and such a short time ago.

However his expression may have looked, it was evidently acceptable to the big man, who brought a finger up to scratch his heavy white-on-black beard and thoughtfully nodded. He was old enough for creases to have spread from the corners of his eyes, though not so old that any strength had left his broad and hirsute chest. His skin was the brown of moist earth. He asked Kem, "How are you getting along, then?"

Kem thought about this—not about an answer to the question so much as the question having been asked in the first place. How was he getting along. As though more than one answer were possible. As though to live as a messboy in the guts of the Oasis, seven years of his life reduced to black scrawls in a ledger, was a thing he might have chosen for himself, a thing he might conceivably enjoy. He looked at the bearded man in genuine curiosity, and the bearded man looked back. Those black, studious eyes really seemed to be waiting for an answer.

"Oh, I'm doing okay I guess," he allowed finally. "I haven't gotten sick. People leave me alone, pretty much." He couldn't think of a whole lot else you could ask for.

The man nodded kindly, a little sadly even, which made Kem think maybe he *did* understand. He held a large dark-skinned hand out. "My name is Delan," he said. He spoke slowly and very precisely, like a teacher at one of the winter camps.

Kem took the hand and did not shake it so much as allow it to hold his own. The grasp was warm. He nodded.

Sander watched the two of them like a broker overseeing an exchange. He told Kem, with a quick tightening-up of the eye muscles that stopped just short of being a wink, "Delan is a squirrel."

Oasis patois: a language Kem did not speak. He nodded uncertainly. Delan released his hand and looked at Sander, maybe in annoyance. Outside, there were clanging noises and sometimes shouts—not of alarm, more like someone yelling orders or relaying messages to somebody else, far away. Kem had begun to feel an odd twitching someplace inside, his stomach maybe, which he took to be a symptom of nervousness, a sign that he ought to go.

He was just opening his mouth to say something to this effect when Sander, taking charge, told Delan:

"I'm going to take Kem to watch the stuff they're doing on deck. He's new, you know."

"Yes, of course." The man met Kem's eyes and smiled indulgently, and now you could tell that the look was a signal between the two of them, that the indulgence was meant for Sander, precocious calculating Sander, and not for Kem, who being older must understand. Kem didn't know how he could tell this, or what he was supposed to understand. But that's what the look meant. He felt very strange all of a sudden, callow and awkward. He thought maybe he needed air.

"Come back and visit me again," Delan was telling him. "Come on a rest day. I'll show you where I work—the tower, the communication gear. Perhaps you'll find it interesting. A change from the galley, in any case, I venture to say."

Kem nodded, murmured something polite. Mainly he got out of there, out of Delan's cramped and sweltering stateroom. The red lights of the corridor lined up before him like so many flowers, swollen blossoms the color of blood, with the sun shining through them. The fabled Black Sun that shines at midnight.

Sander's hand was on his elbow. Guiding him. Small fingers like clamps, gripping him hard. The boy spoke from below Kem's shoulder: "Go back to bed and stay there." Kem murmured a faint protest. The flowers, something about them. Sander shook his head, squeezed harder at Kem's elbow.

It doesn't last long, Kem remembered him saying. (This was later; it was very far away.) *You'll be all right,* he remembered the boy telling him. *Just go to bed.*

He did not go to bed. He stood at the juncture of two corridors where Sander left him—the boy growing smaller as he vanished up one of them, having directed Kem down the other—and after a while he understood that he was in a familiar place, a passage near the galley. One of the reasons it

looked strange to him now, he guessed, was that except for
Kem it was empty. He was not accustomed to seeing the
Oasis this way. Plus, it was probably very late at night, the
midwatch, and things always looked different then. Kem
remembered the first night he had woken up at some hour
like this, in an unfamiliar bunk, deep in the belly of the craft.
It was dark except for the dull red glow of a bulb over the
hatch, and although Kem had wanted very badly to go to the
head, he had been afraid to get out of the tiny bunk that was
his only haven—and even that, for only a few hours at a time.
He had lain until his bladder was about to let go on its own.
At last he had gotten up and walked silently naked over bare
metal deckplates, bracing himself on the bunks of other boys.
Damp breathing came from all around him. By the time he
reached the head he had gotten used to the darkness—or
rather that queer half light—and the experience did not seem
so frightening or extraordinary after all.

He supposed it would probably be like that now.

He supposed that once he got used to standing alone in
the passageway with Sander gone and something wrong with
his vision, the noise of people doing things on deck in one
direction and the abnormally subdued throbbing of the generators in the other, fingers white and damp where they
squeezed a handrail, body swaying as though the craft were
still in motion—once he got used to *that*, there would be
nothing frightening or extraordinary about this moment, either. In the meantime he was covered with sweat that grew
chilly but would not evaporate; it rolled down his temples
into his eyes like acid tears.

He understood that if he went *that* way, the way Sander
had pointed him, he would come in twenty strides or so to
the boys' berthing space, and he could climb back into his
bunk. The thought of his bunk did not attract him. He
understood too that if he went *this* way, the way he was
looking now, where a faint warm light seeped down from an
unglimpsed opening, he would find himself back on the deck
where all the boys had stood before and where he had hooked
up with Sander in the first place. The thought of joining his
crewmates did not attract him either, but something tugged
him in that direction; maybe it was the light. Maybe in the

course of weeks lived belowdecks with nothing but dim bulbs and the greasy daylight that came through badly smudged windows he had developed a craving for brightness. Anyway, he began moving like a brainless insect toward the light and clamor that came from the wrong direction, where Sander had told him not to go. *You'll be all right*. He supposed he would probably be all right anyway. At least he had no particular fear. He had, in fact, the peculiar feeling that he was seeing everything quite clearly, that for maybe the first time ever the actual state of things was being made clear to him. Diviner's sage, he thought. He emerged from the hatch onto the narrow deck with its tanks of cattails.

It was all but empty now. The galley boys must have been rounded up, as they were routinely in daytime, for some tedious job that involved a lot of hoisting or tugging or holding-down. Only a couple of them were left—younger than Sander, crusty little savants who huddled behind the sedges of a gray-water tank talking in low tones and passing something back and forth which each raised to his lips. They gave Kem one glance and paid him no further attention. It must be a skill you acquired, that instant parsing of humanity into clear groups: your allies; those in a position to do you harm; and the most numerous category, to which Kem clearly belonged—those who made no difference at all. As he watched them, the boys laughed at some no doubt vulgar and puerile joke. They didn't give a shit. Kem envied the little bastards.

Out of the shadows of the upper decks, floodlights pointed like weapons into the night. Here and there they found some target—the post of an ancient road sign, paradise trees, a pillar of weathered rock—and each thing they struck became luminous as though filled with a light of its own and seemed to float in the blackness. There was no way to judge the size or distance of things. The glowing objects looked large and very near; the backdrop seemed limitless.

There was noise, too. The shouting had ended, but there was still the throb of unseen engines, bells echoing off bulkheads, the grind of winches. As he listened, Kem was sure (then he disbelieved, then he was sure again) that he heard the snorting of a beast. The dust blowing up off the floor of the Grind—stirred more by the cooling fans of the

Oasis than by any midnight breeze—was redolent of something sourly organic, like rancid meal. Kem's stomach turned, his head filled with tiny screams like cicadas', and at last he was afraid.

Just go to bed, Sander had told him. Now he could hear, as he hadn't before, the dark undertone in the boy's words. Overhead, from a deck used by lookouts, a voice called:

"They're coming down now! They're coming—"

The voice seemed to lose itself in an unguessable excitement. Floodlights swung around, rearranging the landscape. Kem gripped the rail hard. With a metal sigh, restraining bolts eased back and a bay door around the curve of the hull fell open with a thud. The snorting of large animals came again, louder. Kem's heart quickened; then onto the stage of the night leapt a great-legged stallion as pale as the moon. It raced ahead for a dozen strides or so and then stopped, rearing, the muscles of its flanks rippling in the flat light, ghostlike, exultant. Kem shivered, as though winds of pure energy made him cold.

On the back of the giant horse, a rider dressed in night-colored clothing hung on with no apparent effort. It was a man, Kem thought, with long pale hair. In one hand, away from the horse's flank, he carried a weapon, maybe a long-barreled gun; or on second glance Kem thought it might be only a staff. The man gave the stallion its moment of freedom, allowed it to buck and rebel and try to dislodge him; then he gave a short tug at the rein and the two of them, man and beast, seemed to fuse together like a single composite being, its motion arrested, its mass of power held in check. After a long moment, the man raised his staff over his head, pointing it straight up at the sky, and tossed his head back toward the Oasis. From both sides of Kem, and over his head too, came a rowdy cheer.

Kem was fairly certain he was imagining some of this; at least some. At least the part where the stallion turned its own great head to look back, like the man, toward the Oasis— turned to look in particular toward that dim-lit lower deck where Kem huddled cold and nauseous against the rail—and stared through its black animal eyes with an expression as hard and cunning as any man's: a perfect counterpoint, in

fact, to the look of pride and arrogance on the face of its
master. Except the look in the stallion's eye was a different
one. Its meaning was inhuman and dire. It shot through Kem
like the final terrifying line of a story told past midnight
around the fires; but perhaps he was slipping, at last, into the
dream that for some time now had threatened to engulf him.
Perhaps his grip on the rail had already gone slack before he
saw or dreamed that awful eye; perhaps the smaller boys had
already come up beside him and taken his arms and struggled
under his weight. *Hey, what's the matter,* they might have
asked him, *are you okay,* even as a hundred other hooves
beat down the dust of the Grind and the knights of the Oasis
plunged bellowing into the darkness; *Let's get him back to his
bunk,* they might have said, even as the stallion in its awful
beast's mind told him the black thing that was all he could
hear and all he could dream about. In the end Kem could
only lie in his own vomit on his bunk, not quite asleep, afraid
that if he closed his eyes he would never wake again. For the
stallion, in his vision or his dream, had spoken a prophecy to
him, not in words Kem knew but in the secret language of its
bleak inhuman eye; and the prophecy was
     Death.

In the mornings they woke the galley boys early, before
dawn. Now in autumn, as the days contracted, there was only
a dull glow from the glass prism set into the deck above
them, where an hour from now the sun would smash into a
hundred bright refractions. On a perfect morning, in summer, the light from the prism would have been strong enough
to read by.
     There were no perfect mornings at the Oasis. The galley
boss came through long before sunup banging a soup pot with
a wooden spoon, stumbling indifferently against bunks in the
darkness, brushing the limbs of boys now starting to wake
and cursing in slurred breaths the day ahead, the galley boss,
the Oasis, the world at large, and especially that terrible
turning of the Wheel, some forgotten time ago, which had
consigned them to this work and this life. The galley boss
would curse back or maintain a hung-over dignity, silently
sweating into his collar. Then he would be gone and the boys

would stir sullenly and begin to rise. In the crowded berthing space, they would shove and climb and twist around one another like clumsy ballerinas, putting their bunks in order, making their way to the head, tugging their clothes on.

When Kem woke up that morning he remembered nothing for a moment about what had happened the night before, what he had seen, how he had gotten to bed. He sat up carefully, as always, keeping low and swinging his feet into the aisle so as not to knock his head on the bunk above him. The first thing wrong was that he still had his galley smock on. Then he realized that his face and chest were sticky with vomit. He thought too that his whole body stank, but it was hard to sort out his own smells from the smells of the unwashed, overwarm young bodies around him. At last, frame by frame, as his brain engaged, Kem remembered.

Whatever had really happened last night—whether or not it had been some kind of dream, induced by the fingerful of leaves Sander had pinched from the man's stateroom—Kem was certain he had never seen or felt anything like it before. He had no desire to repeat the experience. Yet even now, trying to stand up without becoming nauseous again, trying to organize his thoughts, especially about what to do with his ruined clothing, he felt a certain fascination, an inclination to run the thing again and again through his mind, right up until that final moment with the stallion. . . .

"You better get moving—" (just as Kem was staring once more into that black eye; his body jerked and his head scraped the bunk above him) "—or they'll *really* kill you."

Kem rubbed his head and looked ruefully at Sander. The boy stood a few inches away, studying Kem with no particular expression. He was quite composed, completely naked. Kem nodded.

"Okay," he said. His breath tasted like a bad memory.

"Probably you should have just gone to bed," said Sander— omitting, however, to point out that he had told Kem this the night before.

Kem shrugged. It seemed to him that Sander was rather too all-of-a-piece. The colors of the boy's hair and eyes and body were virtually the same, and that color was exactly what the word *sand*, perhaps the root of his name, implied.

Moreover his bearing and his attitude partook of the same
neutrality. Nothing about him stood out or contrasted with
anything else. Even his skin (the boy's stomach was at a level
with Kem's eyes) was flat and featureless, its surface neither
broken with muscle nor shadowed by hair. Kem gave a
moment's thought to all this—to the mysterious wholeness or
completeness of things.

"What *was* that?" he said then. "Why did you tell me to
swallow it?"

Finally, a very slight expression slipped over Sander's
face. He seemed to regard Kem with a private but not
unkind amusement. Then with typical swiftness he raised
a thin arm with its index finger sticking into Kem's chest,
drawing attention to his filthy smock. The pale eyes grew
stern.

"Take that off," he said. "I'll wash it while you get cleaned
up. You can hang it here to dry." Reaching down, he plucked
one of the springs of Kem's bunk like a rusty harp. "Don't
worry—nobody'll want to steal it."

Kem thought this made a good deal of sense. He stood up
at last; it felt no worse than he might have expected and even
perhaps a trifle better. Other boys pushed around him so that
it was difficult to undress. The effort made him dizzy; he
bumped his elbows and almost knocked Sander onto the
soiled coverlet of his bed.

"Hey," the boy said sternly, bracing himself. He grabbed
Kem by the arm. In that instant—looking into Sander's grave
little eyes, seeing the impatience that was being held in
check there—Kem understood that here in this harsh and
alien place he had found a friend. He had not wanted a friend
especially, and could not remember ever having one before.
But now he had Sander and he was glad.

The instant of knowing this passed. Boys shuffled past
them, headed for the galley, and Kem hurried to sponge
himself partway clean and put on his only other set of
clothing. The unhappy business of life at the Oasis went on,
and nothing that had happened last night or this morning
made any difference, really, at all.

• • •

They were talking while they worked about the crying and about what would happen now that the Oasis had stopped. These two things had something to do with one another but Kem could not tell what. He was scrubbing the deck today, the hard-grimed tile beneath the grease vats and the great steam cookers, so all he could do was listen while the other boys talked, catching some phrases and losing others. Not that he would have spoken anyway, probably; but down under the grease vats you surely couldn't talk and if you could manage it you'd be smart not even to breathe.

The crying was a sickness people got who rode the wagons, out on the Grind. Kem didn't know if people in other places got it too. They did, probably. What the crying did at first was get inside your head somewhere, in the delicate flesh around your eyes, and it burned like pepper. This made your eyes water up and tears run down your face, hot tears that turned your skin pink. They weren't like normal tears, really; it was just your body trying to wash the sickness out. You could see people who had the crying with their cheeks rubbed red from wiping tears away, and you didn't know if it was just a symptom of the disease or if they really *were* crying, because by now they knew they were going to die. After a while the sickness crept deeper into your head and you got angry. People became violent quite often as the crying went through them. But again, you couldn't tell really why. Maybe it was a symptom; maybe the disease changed something in their brains. Or maybe they were just mad at the people who were going to outlive them. Maybe they were mad at the world, the hospital camps, the hot sun. The crying made you confused after a while, and it was a confusing thing to watch from the outside. Growing up on the Grind, Kem had seen the whole thing many times in all its stages. At the end it left you weak and insane and if no one helped you you died after a week or so, because your tears flowed so fast that your body dried up. He had seen people sometimes the wagons had left behind, lying in the hot dirt of the Grind with tears running down their cheeks, not understanding anymore what had happened to them, unable to dry their eyes. Kem's father always stopped and said a little rhyme (*Sister Moon come soothe me / with your cool soft*

hand, / *Brother Comet laughing / lead me home again*. . . .)
like a prayer over those poor souls. Then he took out his bow
and shot them.

There in the galley, Kem tried from underneath the grease
vat to understand what the other boys were saying, but all he
could catch was that somebody somewhere had the crying,
and the Oasis had stopped. He couldn't tell whether there
was some cause-and-effect involved. Once or twice he thought
he heard the name again, the one that seemed always in the
air yet seldom was spoken straight-out. Captain Hand. Could
he be the person who was sick? Kem set down his scrub
brush and cocked his head to hear better.

From behind, someone kicked him. A heavy shoe struck
the skinny part of his rump where the bone is and knocked
him forward so that his head banged into a pipe. Both ends
throbbing with pain, Kem twisted back to see the galley boss
glaring down.

"Quit fucking around there," the man said.

His voice was dispassionate. The cloudy eyes were too
worn-out to harbor much vehemence; they only stared at
Kem with an impersonal disdain for all things—first among
which, probably, was the man's own station as Lord of the
Messboys. "Quit stretching your ears out," he said, "and get
the cleaning done."

Kem was by now so accustomed to harassment (though he
didn't think he would ever get used to being kicked in the
ass) that he might have ignored it altogether. But the pain in
his head made the dizziness come back, and this in turn
brought a certain daring.

"Hey," he called after the galley boss, who was already
shambling off.

The man turned, slowly, like a dim creature trained to talk
but not to listen.

"What are they talking about?" Kem rose to his knees; he
gestured past the wall of shiny equipment that separated him
from the rest of the boys. "Why have we stopped? Is it
something about the crying?"

The galley boss regarded Kem for a long moment without
any change in his demeanor. Then a sneer formed at his
mouth. He raised a hand to wipe the sweat that had collected

there, in the stubble of a mustache. He said, "That's no fucking business of yours, boy. You just stick to your job and leave the rest to people that know what's what."

Kem doubted that the galley boss himself was one of the people he was talking about. He said more boldly, having given some thought to it, "That was Captain Hand last night, wasn't it? On that white horse."

The man's facial muscles became still as though their power had been diverted. It was not as though he were startled; it was more like Kem's words had given rise to some other process that required all of his attention. After a second or two he shook his head.

"You're the kind of boy," he said, "that takes too much notice of things. That'll get you in trouble, one of these days."

Kem was left with his pail and his scrub brush and a vague sense of having learned something, though upon reflection he could not think what.

The days in the galley went by without rest or interruption, except for a short break in late morning and another in midafternoon, during which the scraps of breakfast and lunch, respectively, were made available to be picked through. It was during the second of these breaks that Kem found himself standing over a warming tray next to Sander. The tray was full of some kind of stew that nobody had eaten much of, owing probably to the large globs of uncooked fat that made up a good part of it. Kem felt as though he were covered with oily sweat from top to bottom. He kept his eyes off the food and hoped there would be something palatable left over from dinner. Sander on the other hand looked dry-skinned and cool, as though he had passed the day inside the reefer. His white galley smock was immaculate. He surveyed Kem critically but without comment while gulping a considerable bowl of fat. At last, licking his fingers clean, he said, "You'll feel better by tonight."

Kem scowled. It seemed to him that Sander might be just the person to ask about the conversation he had half heard that morning—or for that matter about anything else—but something restrained him from doing so. Something in the unspoken terms of their friendship recommended a greater caution or reserve. Instead he asked, "Is it this bad down in the engine flats?"

One of the things you were threatened with, if you showed signs of laziness or talking back, was being sent down to work on the terrifying machinery that drove the Oasis. Kem imagined the engine flats as being dark and loud and even hotter than the galley. But you never knew.

Sander said quite seriously, "I could get you out of here, if you want. I know somebody."

This told Kem both more and less than he had asked for: a pattern, he supposed. He stored the comment for later reflection. "I was just thinking," he said.

They stood in silence. The afternoon break should have ended by now, but the galley boss was nowhere to be seen, and Kem savored the sense of found time.

"As a matter of fact," said Sander, after a while, "*you* know somebody, too."

"What?"

Sander watched him carefully, like someone making a study. He said, "You know somebody who can get you out of here."

Kem was unsettled—not by the boy's words, but by his tone of voice, his cunning expression.

"Don't you remember Delan?" Sander said.

Kem might well have pointed out that because of Delan, and the little box under his bunk, he had gotten sick last night and was having a truly horrible day. He merely nodded. "So?"

"So," said Sander, glancing around them, "if you really want to get a better job, Delan's the guy that can help you. He knows *everybody*. I'm not kidding."

Kem wondered if the boy's air of furtiveness was part of the act, a way of making an impression. He guessed not. He asked Sander, "Then how come you're still working here? Why don't you ask Delan to get you out?"

Sander stuck his nose up, as though his dignity had been affronted. "It's not that bad," he said, with a slight air of pouting. "The boss likes me. I bring him stuff. Anyway, I'm too young. For Delan, that is."

Kem frowned. "What do you mean?"

"*You* know." Sander gave Kem that sly, worldly look that seemed to be his favorite expression. "Delan likes you to do things with him. If you want him to help you. A trade, kind of. You know?"

Kem didn't know, but Sander's tone of voice gave him an idea. He said, "Is that what a squirrel is?"

"What?"

Kem thought he might actually have taken the younger boy by surprise. "A squirrel. You said last night that Delan is a squirrel, remember? Does that mean—"

To his great chagrin, Sander opened his mouth wide and laughed, showing the perfect white teeth Kem would have bet were inside there.

"No, stupid," said the boy, quite pleased now. "A squirrel is somebody who works in the tree. You know, the tree, the navigation tower? That's Delan's job, to go up there where they take fixes and draw maps and so forth. So he's called a squirrel. Get it?"

Kem clenched his own (slightly crowded and discolored) teeth. He didn't like being laughed at, especially by a little kid. "So how come you two are such good friends?" he demanded. "What do you do with him?"

Sander shrugged. "I take people to meet him. People I think he might . . . you know, want to help." He looked meaningfully at Kem.

Kem felt hot again, dizzy, mildly confused. He said, "Well, I don't need to be helped."

"Yeah, well." Sander turned to stare impassively at the door of the galley. "Me neither, right now. But anyway, it's something to remember, is all."

He gave a very slight nod, and Kem—following the boy's cool gaze—saw the hulking silhouette of the galley boss at the door. The man was talking to somebody in the passageway, just out of sight. Slowly he turned to stare into his domain. His motions were unsteady; he must have been drinking, or worse, during the break. He called out:

"I need a volunteer. Somebody who isn't afraid of a little real work."

Kem felt a wave of collective dread pass through the messboys all around him. With practiced, fluid motions, they

slid behind counters or turned their faces down or otherwise
rendered themselves invisible. The blurred eyes of the galley
boss slid across them, struggling to focus. Then they fell upon
Kem and grew sharp. The man gave his weakly, sneering
smile.

"You," he said. He looked almost serene. "You, Big Ears.
Come with me."

For the first time Kem was led down passageways that took
him far from the galley. Ahead of him strode a tall man in fine
clothing who was said to be a Resident, whatever that meant.
Kem had been instructed not to speak to the man nor
attempt to deal with him in any way, unless ordered to do so
by the Resident himself. So far the man had steadfastly
ignored him.

The passage widened as they hurried along. Sunshine fell
onto Kem's shoulders through skylights—the first time since
coming to live in the Oasis that he had been in the sun. Even
through battered polyglass it felt hard and hot. The Resident
wore a palm hat with a neck shield: a sign of much time spent
on deck, out of the protection of trees and awnings. Kem
marveled at such freedom of movement. The guards who
stood at hatchways and strolled down the halls stepped aside
in a show of deference as the Resident bustled by. (For Kem,
however, they resumed their usual air of contempt.) Kem
supposed that Residents must be privileged passengers, un-
touched by the web of rivalries and hierarchies that bound
the crew.

In due course they reached a large door that stood open to
reveal a cargo bay. The interior was dark, but at the opposite
side, fifty or sixty strides off, a great hatch was propped open
to admit the full glaring light of afternoon. Kem squinted; his
eyes were accustomed to the gloom of the galley.

"Well, come on there," the Resident snapped.

Kem hurried after the man, who led him into the bay and
past a jumble of crates stacked up like things some giant had
discarded. Markings scrawled on them said COTTON, and
CAREFUL: GLASS, and SPARE PARTS, ELEC.—a wealth
of material goods beyond Kem's comprehension. In the wag-

ons, all commodities had been treasured and guarded and passed along until the last trace of utility was gone, then they were gotten rid of. The ruthless economy of migratory life required it. Yet here in a single bay of the Oasis were crates piled higher than the wagons themselves, filled with things of which no use was being made whatever.

The Resident pointed irritably at a particular box and told Kem: "Open this, now. And mind you don't touch anything inside."

The box was made of wood and secured with rope and staples. Kem glanced about for some tool that might serve to open it, but saw nothing.

"What are you waiting for?" the Resident said, almost frantic with impatience.

Kem supposed that in this man's eyes he was little more than a beast, a creature who could rend the packing twine and prize his way into the crate without pain or difficulty. Far from making him angry, the thought only saddened him. A real beast, at any rate, would have possessed a certain degree of power. Kem looked down at his humble messboy's hands, at the powerless creature that he was, and feared that the tall man was going to strike him.

"Oh, good heavens."

Kem looked up to find that the Resident, for the first time, had turned all the way around in his direction. The man's face was angular and rather sharp, but his expression was not the cruel one Kem had expected; he regarded Kem with a certain tendency to shy away, as though he—the wretched galley boy—were the one to be afraid of.

"Look at this," the man said more quietly, and even forced an awkward smile. "They've sent you off without so much as a screwdriver."

Kem nodded; he shrugged. He wasn't sure whether it was permissible to return the smile, and reckoned it safer not to.

"Well," the man said, drawing the syllable out, "I suppose it *could* wait. —Or no, look."

He pointed to the open cargo doors. Kem squinted and tried to see what the man was looking at; he could make out only a blur of motion against the blinding desert sun. At his side the Resident stepped forward, striding toward the door and calling out:

"Hello there! Look, can you come here for a moment? We need a bit of help."

Kem hung back. Gradually his eyes were able to focus on a pair of figures who had entered the bay from outside. One was dressed in the full regalia of the deck watch, complete with rifle and shoulder belt; the other was shorter and slighter. Behind them, out in the sun, Kem was surprised to see a horse saunter into view. It was smaller than the great stallion, and seemingly more docile; as he watched, it lowered its head to graze. The two figures from outside stepped closer, meeting the Resident halfway. Something passed among the three of them out of earshot. The Resident raised his arm, gestured toward Kem or the crate or, more loosely, *back there*, at the careless powers who had dispatched Kem without the proper tools. Across the bay came a faint, high sound that might have been laughter. Something about the sound made Kem feel very tired, as though he were drifting into a daydream of someplace far away. He might even have closed his eyes for a moment, trying to hear it again. In the very next instant, or what seemed like it, he felt his arm being given a shove, and cringed reflexively. The blow that he half expected did not fall. Fully alert now, Kem was startled to find himself staring into a pair of dark bright eyes at the same height as his own.

He was even more startled to find that the eyes belonged to a girl.

He must have done something stupid, shown his surprise in an obvious way, because the girl laughed again: the same sound he had heard more faintly a few moments ago.

"You must have had quite a night," she said.

Kem gave a feeble nod. He felt very foolish. The blood rushing into his head made his ears pound.

"Here," said the girl. From a sheath at her waist she drew a very large knife, more a weapon than a tool. She held it out to him. Looking at the long shining blade, the fingers that lightly held it, the slender wrist and arm and the waist where the sheath hung, Kem realized that the girl was very beautiful, the most beautiful girl he had ever seen. He forgot everything, even his own foolishness and his blushing face and the knife she was holding out to him. Then he remembered them again all at once, and remembered the Resident too who was standing only a stride away and the crate and the baling twine. He remembered too who he was and how he was supposed to behave and what kind of life he was condemned to. All of this and everything else, in an instant, Kem remembered. He looked away from the girl and shook his head slightly, rallying. He accepted the knife.

With as much single-mindedness as he could muster, channeling his shame and his anger down through that sharp edge, he slashed his way through the rope that bound the packing crate. Then, judging the blade to be thick enough, he forced it into a seam and pried the lid open. He stepped back, mindful of the man's order not to touch anything. He could feel the girl's presence at his side, only inches away from him, but he did not turn to look at her. Probably this was what was expected of him, just as he was expected to have no dealing with the Resident.

Lightly, a pressure came upon his arm. So deft and unexpected was the girl's touch that Kem turned involuntarily. She was watching him. Her brown eyes sparkled with good humor.

"Could I have my knife back?" she said.

Her voice was comradely and just loud enough for Kem to hear—not the Resident, who was busy digging in his box, nor the guard who stood behind them in the shadows. Something about the voice and the way the girl had touched him made Kem bold enough to look at her more closely as he held out the knife to her. In this second and longer look, he saw the things he had not seen before, the missing clues. She was dressed in simple clothes, maybe even a uniform of sorts: plain shirt, trousers tied with string below the knee, ankle-high shoes that looked sturdy enough to work in. Indeed, there was dirt on them. The hand that took the knife back and returned it to its sheath was pale but hardly delicate—not a pampered hand, Kem thought. And the girl's face (at last, Kem found the courage to meet her gaze straight-on), though it was more beautiful than anything Kem could think of, was also, in its way, rather plain. She wore no makeup over the fading freckles of childhood, and her leaf-brown hair was braided in a no-nonsense manner behind her head, with strands hanging loose. She was, Kem judged, not a Resident nor even a high-ranking member of the crew. Probably she had some job not much more august than his own. She might even (this was just a hypothesis, though it fit the evidence at hand)—she might even be a stable girl.

"Thanks," she told him.

With no more ceremony than that she turned around and walked toward the door. Her stride was quick and straightforward, on long legs and slender haunches. Kem had an irrational urge, for several moments, watching her go, to call out after her, to say something . . . at least to ask her name. He didn't, of course. He just stood there watching until she was gone, back into the desert sun. Now the Resident was telling him what to do, giving him things to carry.

He had thought for a time, for weeks, that he was a man. Now he knew with a considerable sense of anguish that he was only a boy again.

The Resident pointed upward: up a narrow stair that passed through an opening in the deck above and ended in sunlight, its two topmost balusters tasseled with bright fringe. Kem hesitated. It was another world up there. A world where they decorate stair rails. The Resident made a little noise in his throat that signified haste though not impatience; the man's opinion of Kem seemed to have attenuated now that he had what he wanted.

"Can you manage it?" he asked.

Kem nodded and adjusted his load: clothing mostly and nothing heavy, though made a good deal more awkward than was strictly necessary by having been stuffed into a large and badly proportioned oilskin bag. Kem supposed that from a Resident's point of view such a creature as a messboy ought not to be allowed to soil one's clothes. Well, at least his headache was almost gone; Sander had been right. Kem started to climb. As soon as both boy and bag were safely up, the Resident sprang (with real agility, for a man of fifty or so) up the ladder, joining Kem on the level above.

The level above. It was not even a metaphor; the air really was cleaner and the light more sparkling and everything brightly painted and clean. In place of metal bulkheads were walls made of wooden boards nailed neatly over the structural members of the craft and washed white. There were chairs with cushions grouped under awnings where you could sit at leisure safe from the sun. Signs were posted in a large round-hand script that Kem could read only with difficulty (though he knew how to read quite well by the standards of wagon people). One said MUSIC ROOM and another with an arrow said INFIRMARY and another on a door said RESIDENTS AND GUESTS ONLY PLEASE BEYOND THIS POINT. Toward the latter the tall man was steering Kem, and it struck Kem as odd that at this important divide no sentry was posted, no guardian of the sanctuary. Only this door and it swung open with a push.

Now they were in a hallway without signs or antecedents in Kem's mind. The deck was covered with a matting of sweetgrass that smelled sharp and clean when your feet brushed across it. The air that fell lightly into his lungs was as chilly as the updraft he had felt once standing in the mouth of a cave; only that air had been damp and smelled mildly of the chemicals they had dumped inside the cave long ago; whereas the air in the hallway was very sharp and dry, it was desert air, but it was like the desert at night in winter. Sun came through skylights, softened by muslin screens. The walls were painted a color Kem had never seen before, unless maybe jumbled among the hundred colors of sunset: a kind of warm pink flushed with orange, very pale. He was so taken with this color and the light and the air that he kept walking after the Resident had stopped.

"Young man."

Kem turned, surprised at first then embarrassed. The Resident was opening a big brass lock with an old-fashioned key. Most of the locks Kem had seen at the Oasis were the cheap electronic kind. Tumblers fell with a satisfying click and the Resident held the door wide—a very large door of black locust wood—for Kem to enter with his bag.

"Just set it down anywhere," the man told him.

Kem heard this but for the moment just stood there in the doorway holding the sack of clothes.

Before him spread a space too large to fit the notion of *stateroom* or even *cabin*. It was the largest interior space that Kem had ever seen that was only meant to be lived in. Twenty or thirty galley boys could have slept in rows along its walls. Kem had expected, to be honest, a degree of luxury, but the luxury he had in mind was a material sort: rich braided rugs and tapestries and candleholders and old books on shelves of polished wood. (In fact, the room was furnished for the most part plainly with matting and chairs like those on the deck outside.) He had not expected the greater and rarer luxury of abundant space. As he looked around, he felt as though the muscles around his eyes were unwinding, releasing the ordinary tension with which they focused on small rooms and narrow hallways and another boy's bunk closer than your outstretched arm overhead.

The Resident said, "Thank you for helping me. Would you like anything—something to drink?"

Kem found this sudden show of courtesy at least as alarming as the size of the room. He stared at the Resident, trying to judge whether the man was sincere in his offer. On second thought he decided that he didn't care: he was actually quite thirsty. He nodded.

The Resident, for unknowable reasons, gave a wistful-sounding sigh. He turned and crossed the room (would you call it an *apartment*?) to a kind of tiny personal galley, a column of shelves and a cooking tile built into the wall. He gestured for Kem to follow him.

"Here," he said. "You'll have to get it yourself."

He opened a small reefer and showed Kem a selection of pale liquids that looked like watered-down juice or tea. Some of them bore labels inscribed in a tidy hand: Carbo Veg 4X, Dandelion. Kem enjoyed the sensation of cool air from the reefer moving across his hands. With an effort not to seem overeager he took a tall smoked glass bottle, unlabeled and stopped with a real cork, and held it while he looked around for a cup.

"Oh, just keep it," the Resident told him. "Take the whole bottle. That way there will be nothing to clean up."

He made a gesture of something like impatience, as though to shoo away the thought of drinking after a galley boy. Kem felt wounded by this, but only slightly. He had no illusions about his status, and the man was after all, on the whole, being kind to him. He held the bottle close, taking pleasure from its coldness. He figured he ought to go before the Resident changed his mind.

"You seem," said the Resident—following Kem to the door but keeping a couple of paces back—"you seem like a good boy. If I need help again, I shall ask for you."

Kem nodded, not at all sure what to make of this or what the Resident might mean by a good boy. Thoughts of Sander and of Delan passed through his mind. He reached for the door handle.

"What name," said the Resident, "should I ask for?"

There was no way out of it now. "Kem," he said.

"Kem," repeated the Resident. "Kem. I will remember."

The door closed, and the good boy whose name the Resident would remember raised the bottle to his lips and drank greedily the chilled, honey-tasting liquid it contained. He had the peculiar feeling that some pact or promise had just been made. He breathed the clean dry air of the hallway and ran his feet over the fragrant sweetgrass mat, and for several moments he thought *I don't care, I really don't care*.

He dreamed about the girl. He woke up sometime past the middle of the night, an awful hour to lie in a hot, ill-ventilated berthing space feeling your heart pound, far from morning. It had been a sexual dream. Kem couldn't remember much except for the girl's pale skin and eyes that laughed as he pressed himself against her. Only then he had woken up, as he always did, short of climax—a kind of bodily remembrance of having shared the back of a wagon with two little sisters—and now lay sweaty and miserable with his penis swollen against his bunk.

He sat up. He supposed he could go somewhere and masturbate. Maybe the bathroom or maybe out on deck. He wasn't sure. He was still afraid of the Oasis, afraid of getting caught and getting in trouble (though there were boys who did such things openly to themselves and even to each other, making a joke of it). In the end, his state of suddenly urgent longing overrode the fear and he rose from his bunk in the darkness. The top sheet clung to him, and for the purposes of speed and economy he just wrapped it around his waist. His erection made it awkward to walk.

He had gotten almost to the door and was passing Sander's bunk—an upper one, near a porthole—when Sander opened his eyes and saw Kem and propped his head up.

"Hey," the boy whispered.

Somehow Kem got the feeling that Sander slept in the same way a cat sleeps, perfectly restful yet always alert. He imagined the boy lying here in a nightlong, dreamless doze, waiting for something interesting to happen.

"Hey," whispered Sander again. He leaned over the edge of his bunk to survey the situation. He gave the matter of Kem and the sheet and the airless night a few moments of thought. Then he said, "You were going somewhere to pull yourself off, weren't you?"

Kem turned away in embarrassment.

"Wait," said Sander, sitting up. "I'll come with you."

Kem wanted nothing less than this in all the world. He wanted now only to go back to his bunk and lie miserably in private. But Sander was climbing out of bed, taking over.

"Where were you going?" he asked. "The head? The deck?"

"The deck," Kem allowed helplessly.

Sander nodded. "Come on." He prodded Kem lightly, moving him along. He had changed from a cat to an irksome little terrier. He did not bother with clothes. Out on deck, standing among the tanks of sedge and cattails, the light of a three-quarter moon glistened from his smooth childish body.

"You know," said Kem, "you really know how to fuck things up."

Sander shook his head. "No, come on," he urged. "Go ahead and do it. I like to watch."

"Yeah, I bet," said Kem. He stared out into the invisible desert, into the breeze. The air smelled of galley soap and of water hyacinths, perpetually blooming in their tanks. He was glad he had come out, anyway, he supposed. In a way he was even glad he had woken up Sander.

"Do they have girls here," he asked, "who take care of the horses?"

Sander opened his eyes wide at this, perhaps looking for reasons or motives behind the sudden question. "Yes," he said after a while. "I think so. Why?"

With Sander, Kem decided, you had to trade. You had to have something to offer. The boy had come out here to be entertained by Kem bringing himself to orgasm, but now he shifted easily into a different medium of exchange. He would answer Kem's question (or so the bargain went, if Kem correctly understood it) but he wanted something in return. So Kem told him the story of his encounter with the girl. Then he told him about the dream, what was left of it. He hoped that was enough.

Sander perched on the edge of one of the tanks, where he could look at Kem from eye level. He nodded reflectively. "I guess she was a stable girl. Usually stable girls are older, though. How old do you think she was?"

"A year or so more than me, I guess. Seventeen, maybe."

"Mm." Sander took his small dick between his fingers. "So, what was her body like? In your dream. Was she totally naked?"

"Stop it." Kem walked the couple of paces to the edge of the deck. He pulled the sheet over his shoulders; the night air though warm was drying his sweat and cooling him. He found that for some reason Sander's talking about the girl in this way, in this context, disturbed him. He thought that sex in its entirety was rather disturbing and very strange.

"Where do they work?" he asked, not turning from the rail. "The stable girls. Where do they stay?"

"It depends." Sander had made his penis stiff and now sat on the edge of the tank, contemplating it. "They *work* in the stables, of course. And outside, but not too far away. Usually under guard. Most of them sleep in Girls' Berthing. That's near the big fountain. *They* get to take showers whenever they want. Or sometimes"—he waited for Kem's full attention— "*sometimes* they sleep with their boyfriends. You know, older guys on the crew. It's easy, if you've got your own room."

Kem found the boy's sly and prurient smile to be annoying and suspected, moreover, that Sander might possibly not know what he was talking about.

"Oh yeah?" he said. "So who's got their own room—besides the Residents, and people like that?"

Sander seemed to be ignoring him, to be following some private drama in which stable girls were constant and easy targets of lust. Still he was cool about it—twiddling with his penis as though it were a detached object of only transient interest.

"You can get a room," he said unexpectedly, "if you play it right. Anybody can. You just have to work on it. If you've got a girl, she can work on it for you."

"What do you mean?" said Kem. He was fairly certain that Sander was just talking big, but with Sander he could never tell for sure. "And how do you get a girlfriend in the first place?"

"You just . . ." Sander seemed to catch his breath. Kem had a moment of fear, thinking someone was approaching. But then Sander gave a short sigh, and tiny drops of semen splattered his legs dangling over the tank. He looked up at Kem, his eyes narrow, catlike once more. "You just do *that*," he said, softly, "inside them."

Kem was astonished and repelled. "You're unbelievable," he told Sander. "You're really unbelievable."

"Yes," the boy agreed. "I think I am." With deft motions, using a shock of sedge he had plucked from the tank, he began cleaning himself off. "But so is this whole place," he went on, half-attentively. "The whole Oasis is unbelievable. I mean, *you* wouldn't have believed it if you hadn't seen it, right? So don't worry so much. Do whatever you want to. You can get away with anything here."

Kem guessed he had just been given the benefit of Sander's entire philosophy of life, together with a practical demonstration. Do whatever you want to, he thought. You can get away with anything. The words gave him a chilly feeling, a sense of being up too late and unrooted. He yearned for something without focus; some connection maybe, some grounding. He drew the sheet tighter but still felt the chill.

He told Sander, "I'm going back to bed."

The boy watched him sleepily through cat's eyes. As Kem stepped past he said, "There's always some way to have what you want. You just need somebody to help you."

"No I don't," said Kem.

Sander said, "You'll see."

The Oasis moved on. It was late autumn, Fly South Moon, and night crept in early now and stayed late, and the messboys so seldom glimpsed the sun that they became like night creatures, their movements quick and furtive, with long stillnesses between. The air did not grow much colder, but the sky drew nearer to the land and there were skeins of geese on a southerly heading. The Oasis seemed at times to be following them, though it tended slightly eastward. From the deck behind the galley you could see the north star hanging low off the stern. Kem wondered if that was what the Oasis steered by, as the wagons did, or whether the great craft used a surer and more occult form of navigation, born of its intimacy with the earth. Sometimes you could sense a scuttling of night creatures below—kit foxes, burrowing owls— though there was too little light to see them and the tiny sounds they made were scarcely audible; you could imagine their panic and their stupefaction as the Oasis rumbled by, its treads pulverizing their burrows. On some evenings at sunset dark forms separated themselves from the ripple of blue mountains at the western horizon, and later in the night there would be rain. It came down hard in great sheets, crashing against the metal hull like something more substantial than water. These storms were mostly quite brief, and the more stalwart of the galley boys liked to stay on deck for their duration. Kem did not join them. He had heard (and believed) that the autumn rains could knock you down and kill you.

He never learned why the Oasis had stopped, what dealings had occurred there, what border it was they had crossed. The land itself was as changeless as the routine in the galley. The only difference Kem could see was within himself—a kind of bitterness had gripped him, though he did not know why. He thought he despised Sander, yet they remained friends, at least within the peculiar terms they had estab-

lished. Sander managed to get his hands now and then on
something good to eat (Kem did not ask how) and sometimes
a mug of beer, which the two of them shared on deck after
hours. Kem wondered what his own contribution to these
little feasts might be, and suspected that it was his ignorance,
his naïveté. The younger boy seemed to view Kem as an
interesting challenge; a project.

Their regular topic was the stable girl. Her image grew at
times, on certain nights, to fill Kem's mind. He knew it was
impossible, and that Sander must think him quite foolish. He
didn't care; he trained himself to disregard Sander's opinion.
(The boy was firm in his beliefs, even where small matters
were concerned. Once Kem had brought out the smoked
glass bottle he had gotten from the Resident—his only possession of note—and Sander had reacted as though it might
be charmed or possibly cursed. He urged Kem to throw it
over the deckrail. "You shouldn't take things from Residents,"
he said. Kem pointed out that he hadn't stolen the bottle, the
Resident had given it to him. Sander shook his head. Kem
used the bottle to decant his share of beer. There was a kind
of uneasy truce between them.)

Together those nights they discussed stratagems whereby
Kem might meet the girl, learn her name, discover where
she worked and slept. Most of their plans were foolish and
some dangerous and probably all of them foredoomed. In the
end they came down to one thing, and on that they foundered:
Kem must find a way out of the galley. But that was hopeless.
Promotions were infrequent and hotly competed for. Kem
was hardly a favorite of the galley boss. He refused to make
an effort, through the sort of small personal favors Sander
recommended, to improve his relations with that odious man.

"Fine," Sander told him. "Then you'll have to serve out
your whole two years before they move you to the deck
gang."

To his credit, the boy only once reminded him of Delan,
the squirrel, always ready to help the boys who befriended
him.

Kem wondered about the stable girl, though. He wondered
who she was and what it had been about her that in the space
of a minute or two had driven her image so deep in his mind.

He thought sometimes that it was not so much the girl herself as the idea of escape, of freeing himself from obligations and intrigues, that truly impelled him—more, that is, than a girl whom he had never actually met, and about whom he knew nothing at all. Or it might have been a different order of thing altogether: a wish for his life to be whole again. Kem trained himself to disregard this, too. He wondered if everyone's true motivations were as mysterious as his own—if even Sander, for instance, was driven by anything more than *do whatever you want to*.

He stood many nights by the rail on deck, though, wondering what he really did want to do, assuming for the purpose of contemplation that in this single instance Sander might be right.

One day before the afternoon break a messenger came down to the galley bearing a piece of paper with Kem's name on it.

The galley boss looked up from the paper with eyes still squinty from the effort of reading and peered around the room. Kem thought he saw a flicker of something, maybe disdain, as the boss's eyes brushed over him. He tightened his lips and returned to the hobart, where hundreds of dishes remained to be washed and the heat of the water had already turned his arms red up to the elbows. The sound of his name spoken aloud above the background din of machinery was so unexpected that in a way he did not quite hear it. In another way he did; he had expected such a downward turn of events. He looked up just as the galley boss was puffing out his chest to expel that single syllable again.

—Kem.

But by the time he heard it a second time his heart was already going fast and his hands were dripping hot dirty water onto the deck.

"Come on, then," the galley boss said crossly. "This fellow's got a job for you."

The fellow in question stood just outside the galley door, sensibly declining to enter. He was a youth just a year or two older than Kem and not quite as tall. His expression was sympathetic; he may well have served his time in the galley, too, not so long ago.

"I don't know if this is good news or not," the young man said, already heading up the passageway. "One of the Residents asked for you by name." He glanced at Kem across his shoulder, making a genial sort of appraisal. "What'd you do, steal something?"

"I did *not*—" The moment of panic was long enough for Kem to construct the bare outlines of a terrible and pointless plot against him, a frame-up.

The young man laughed. He went on cheerfully: "Or is it some old lady who thinks you're cute? Well take it from me—get them to give you money. That'll last longer than *they* will."

Kem smiled; he tried to make himself companionable. The young man seemed quite at home in this part of the Oasis—indeed, in this part of Life itself. He turned from one corridor to another with the ease of long familiarity, and the couple of guards they encountered seemed to know him, for they nodded as he passed. Kem wondered if his own life here would ever be so easy or so lighthearted. He wondered what the young man had done to arrange things this way.

They stopped at a hand-lettered sign, RESIDENTS AND GUESTS ONLY, identical to the one Kem had seen on the deck above, but this time screwed onto a doorway far from sunlight.

"You're on your own," the young man told him. He smiled, still with a faintly curious expression, and went back the way they had come.

Kem pressed lightly at the door, which swung on rusty hinges inward.

He was again, disconcertingly, alone. Before him was a dim chamber whose dimensions Kem could not judge (though they seemed immense) crammed as tightly as could be with rows of books. Some of the books were arranged on shelves and some in stacks and some more carelessly in piles. Many of the aisles were blocked with cartons that had simply been left in the middle of them, not even unpacked. The only light in the place came from prisms set in the high ceiling. It was absorbed quickly by the shelves and their dark-spined contents; very little made it so far as the bare, rusty metal of the deck. The air smelled strongly of mold, which must find a luxurious nest in these millions of rotting pages.

This was by far the most appealing place that Kem had been in the Oasis. There was a sense of quiet, despite the ever-present throb of machinery, and a feeling that however long you lingered here, you would be safe from interruption.

Even when interruption—inevitably—arrived, it did not startle him. A soft and oddly damp sound, like someone tidying up after a meal, came from one side, muffled by books. Kem turned without alarm to see the tall man, the Resident, settled on a low stool with only his head and shoulders visible. He was wearing (rather absurdly, it seemed to Kem) his palm hat. He looked around, not quite in Kem's direction, as though he were having trouble seeing in this light.

"Hello?" he said. "Is that Kem? Did I get the name right?"

Kem nodded, but the man still did not seem quite to be looking in his direction. He said, "Yes, sir. It's Kem."

"Ah, good."

Kem waited for the Resident to give him some explanation, some instruction at least. Instead the man sat absolutely still for several moments, more than long enough to make Kem fidget. Then he raised a hand to his face, dabbing with a napkin or rag. Kem supposed he had caught a cold, up there in the chill air of the Residents' quarters. At last he motioned for Kem to come nearer. He lifted a book from the table beside him and held it out, wordlessly. Kem took it.

Sun Tales and Moon Songs, in stark old-age graphics, said the cover.

"They say I can have you for an hour," the Resident told him. "I have been having trouble with my eyes."

A partial explanation, anyway; though for a few moments longer the man offered nothing beyond it. Then he looked up, blinked once or twice, and seemed at last to focus on Kem without difficulty.

"I neglected to tell you last time," he said in a tone of courteous, even quaint, formality, "my name is Tallheron."

It sounded that way, one word and not two. Kem thought

about this—the name itself, and the fact that the man had
seen fit to reveal it to a galley boy. He supposed some sort of
response was called for, but his background was short on
social nicety.

He ventured: "How do you do?"—which seemed like the
sort of thing a character in a story might have said. The man,
Tallheron, nodded slowly, which Kem took as a sign that the
old-fashioned words were acceptable.

"Well, Kem," Tallheron said, "I sent for you because I
believe you can read. I believe I saw you reading the signs in
the hallway, and the cover of that book. Is that right?"

With some reluctance Kem said, "A little. I can only read a
little." This sounded funny to him, less than a full answer, so
he added, "You know, from the winter camps."

Tallheron frowned. "The winter camps," he repeated, as
though the term were not familiar to him. Then he went on:
"I had been hoping, since you *can* read, that you would read
aloud to me from there."

Kem looked at the book again, doubtfully. He opened it at
random, to a page filled with small print and wide margins. It
did not seem too complicated, though he had to strain
somewhat to make out the print in the dim light.

"Sure," he said. "If you want me to."

Tallheron said, "Good." He settled back into his chair a
bit. "Good. I would appreciate that very much. I would do it
myself, you know, except for my eyes. I had quite a time
even finding it."

Kem could imagine so. He hefted the volume in his hand,
flipped a few more pages.

"The story I'd like to hear," said Tallheron, "is called
'Death in the Backyard.' Oh, but . . ." He gestured as though
in impatience. "But sit down," he told Kem. "Don't stand
there and tire yourself."

Kem sat on the deck. The metal was warm beneath him,
and alive with the jolting and shuddering of the great landcraft.
Kem negotiated the Table of Contents with some difficulty
(Tallheron had gotten the title wrong) and, though very
self-conscious, began to read in a loud voice:

DEATH IN THE ROSE GARDEN
A native folktale, as narrated by Rowan Free

In the land that was once known as Fields of Wheat
there lived a girl named Julia. She was an ordinary
girl except for her eyes, which were very bright,
and her hands, which were always warm even on
cold nights. This was when winters were cold and
the snow began to fall during Fly South Moon and
kept falling for a long time thereafter.

Julia lived in a village where there were very
few other children because the water was supposed
to be bad. There were large houses on the hillsides
around the village but not many of them had people
living in them. Their big windows looked down
through the tall grass and the trees and the bushes
that the people had once planted, and Julia liked
to imagine what the people who had left would think
now if they came home after all these years and
saw their houses this way. Sometimes the people
who had stayed behind went into the big houses
and took things away to the smaller houses where
they lived. Sometimes they cut the trees down to
make their cooking fires, but not very often, because
the people in Fields of Wheat believed that trees
were very holy and that it was bad luck to cut them.
So mostly they burned other old things that had
no spirit in them. There were many such things and
there were not many people to burn them.

Julia liked to play among the houses that people
had gone away from. She did not go into the
houses themselves, for she was afraid they might
be haunted, or unsafe for children. But she liked
to go into the yards where sometimes she found
wild beds of flowers blooming and rosebushes as
large as trees. In a book she had there were
pictures of roses, and Julia knew all their names.
She knew the stories, too, that the roses had—
where they had come from, what kind of plants their

ancestors had been. In a way Julia felt that through
the names and the stories of these flowers she
knew something about the people who once lived
in the large houses, the women and men who
had planted them here. Sometimes she pretended
to be pruning and spraying the flowers as her
book told her she must do, or the roses would die.
At such times, she imagined in her childish way
that she was tending not the roses but the old
gardeners, who must be dead now.

One day she was playing like this, pretending
to spray a strong poison onto a fine, ivory-
blossomed plant named Bishop Darlington, when a
very old man approached her.

"You know—" (Kem started as Tallheron spoke from the
shadows) "—you really don't have to read so quickly." His
voice was kind, as Kem imagined a grandfather's might be.
"The story will wait for you to finish it, you know. It has
already waited a very long time."

Kem nodded. He went on, making an effort to go more
slowly.

"Good morning," said the old man to Julia.

"Good morning," she said, smiling at him with
her very bright eyes. She did not run away from
the old man because she was not afraid of him, even
though she knew he was not one of the people
from the village. His skin was pale and a little bit
yellow, like the sheets of metal on the side of
the old house. He stood only a few steps away and
watched her with a funny expression on his face.
Julia thought that he was probably a ghost, though
he might be an old doctor from some other
village gathering herbs, or he might be a crazy man
dying of the plague who would try to kill her.
She held up her hand to shield her eyes from the
sun, so she could see him better.

"You ought not to come any closer," she said. "I
am spraying this flower with a horrible fungicide

which can make you vomit and give cancer to your children."

She reflected as soon as she said this that the old man's grandchildren and maybe his great-grandchildren, if he had any, were probably older than she. But she felt it was important to let him know.

She was very pleased when the old man nodded gravely.

"I see," he said. He stayed where he was and did not come any closer.

Julia smiled again at the old man and put down her imaginary spraying can. "I think that's enough," she said. "Now Bishop Darlington will live through the summer."

She was glad that the old man did not point out to her that Bishop Darlington had lived through very many summers without need of the poisons in her spraying can. He just looked at the rosebush for a long time as if he were admiring what a good job she had done and what a very good gardener she was. Indeed, when he did speak again, he said, "Well, thank you for taking care of my roses."

Julia looked at him to see what he meant. Her bright eyes shone in curiosity.

"You see," said the old man, "this was my house when I was a little boy—when I was a boy younger than you and not nearly so wise about flowers."

"Ah," said Julia. "So you *are* a ghost."

She was awfully much excited. She turned all the way around to face the old man and she held her hands out with the palms facing him. She did this in order to protect herself, though in truth she was not really very much afraid.

The man surprised her by getting a big smile across his face. "I suppose I *am* a ghost," he said to her. "At any rate, I feel that way."

He looked away from Julia and he stood there

for a long time just staring across the grasses
that had grown up as high as his waist in the old
backyard. As Julia watched him she thought that
this was not the way a ghost was supposed to behave.
Then she thought that since he was a very *old*
ghost, he might have forgotten some of the important
points of his profession. She cleared her throat.

"Aren't you," she said very carefully, when the
man had turned to look at her, "aren't you
supposed to tell me about how you became a ghost?
You know, the awful way you died, and all? So
that I'll feel sorry for you and not be afraid?"

The old man's smile had left his face and now
he looked very unhappy, which Julia felt was
much more appropriate. Like all little girls, she had
a great respect for the manner in which things
ought to be done. She waited patiently while the
man recollected the sad and fateful details of
his past life in order to begin his story.

"Well," he said at last, "I guess the truth of the
matter is that I died many, many years ago, of
a broken heart. Or at any rate the best part of me
did. It was back in the early days of the age
we're now living in, when this place still had another
name besides Fields of Wheat. There were more
folks like me living around here, in those days."

By *folks like me* Julia understood the old man
to mean the people who had lived in these very
large houses. In her mind she had certain vague
notions about those people, but few definite or
historical facts. It did not appear, however, that the
ghost was going to educate her just then.

"I was in love," he said. "The girl I loved lived
right up the street there, in the Tudor house.
We had known each other since I was a little boy
and she was a little girl. We were engaged to
be married. Of course we had heard about the
troubles everywhere. But somehow I guess we
believed our little village here was immune, that
nothing terrible would ever happen here."

He gave a sigh and looked away, into the rosebush
that Julia had been spraying, as though
something might be hidden there.

"Well, they came and they killed her. They were
rather polite about it, in their way. They
explained that they needed a girl about her age for
their sacrifice, in order to make their medicines.
I don't suppose you know anything about that, do
you? I'm sure nobody believes in such things
anymore. But those were awful times then, and
people were desperate and they were willing
to believe anything. So . . ."

The old man looked more than ever like a ghost
now. He was staring blankly out of his dim
cloudy eyes, and his voice sounded like something
coming from a machine. In this way he went
on:

"So they took her away and they split her skull
open and took something out, a little gland,
which they needed to make their famous Remedy.
They stayed out there all night, with electrical
fires burning in their lamps, and tapes of some kind
of ritual music, and their protectors standing
there pointing guns at the people standing around.
No one was going to stop them, of course. The
town folk were afraid, and I think many of them
were secretly glad, relieved that it had not been
their own daughters who had been taken."

The old man paused to look at Julia, and Julia
looked back with approval. This was a *wonderful*
ghost story, she thought. It was certainly the most
horrible thing she had ever heard from a grown-up.
She held her very bright eyes on the old man,
unblinking, in order to encourage him to go on.

"So," he said, "they stayed there all night, and
they made their Remedy. Then they sold it, in
the morning, for a very high price to anyone who
could pay. And there were people willing to pay,
believe me. In a way you couldn't blame them. As
I said, they were desperate. The sick and the

dying were everywhere. Doctors could offer nothing
but consolation, if that, and pills to relieve the
pain, in the final stages. The pain was quite horrible,
we were told.

"It was then, I suppose," the old man said, "that
the best part of me died. It was then that my
first life, my innocent life, ended—and my new,
longer, and unhappier life began."

Julia frowned. She had not counted on a new,
unhappier life. She was expecting Death, for
Death is the proper end of a story. She held
up to the man one of her small, very warm
hands, signaling him to stop.

"Because," the man said, ignoring her hand, "do
you know what they did? Do you know what
they did, after they held her down and broke her
head apart without even knocking her out first
and left her body there still warm and oozing blood
out?"

Julia felt odd and a little dizzy listening to the
man talk this way, even though she thought he
had gotten the story back on its proper track. Her
very bright eyes may have blinked a time or
two. Still she shook her head at the man's question,
so that he would answer it himself.

In a much quieter voice he said, "They gave me
a vial of their Remedy—the thing they made
out of her. They did this, you know, as a gesture
to us, the town folk. Someone must have told
them the girl they murdered had a sweetheart, a
fiancé. So they gave me a vial of it. They called
it the *Caput Mortuum*. Death's Head. They gave
me that so I might live to remember her, who
had died."

Julia thought that the very old man had finished
talking, that his story was over, until he added
in a matter-of-fact voice, a voice without any feeling
left in it, "That is why I became a doctor.
Because I believed there had to be another way. I
believed there must be other medicines, *true*

medicines, that are not based upon superstition or hysteria. And I resolved that day that I would find them."

So, thought Julia, the very old man was simply a man and not a ghost after all. Well even so, she told herself, she had been right about him all along. For she had thought as soon as she saw him that he might be a doctor from another village, gathering herbs. This was something of a disappointment, but Julia thought she must make the best of things. She asked him, "Are you here to gather wild berries and flowers to use in your medicines?"

"Not exactly," the man said to her, smiling kindly. "I am here to experiment with a different kind of treatment—something that I have seen used now and then with great success, though I have never tried it myself."

Julia nodded, thinking this might be informative to watch. She put away her imaginary garden tools and stood up, smoothing her skirt. "Do you need any help?" she asked the man. "I know all about the things that grow in this village. I am very observant, and I have lived here all my life."

The old man only smiled at her, and in his smile Julia thought she could see something else, something that very old people often feel that makes them stare at things absentmindedly and sometimes sigh, which Julia thought must come from knowing how close to dying they are. After a while of looking at her this way, the man said, "Yes, Julia. I think I can use your help."

Kem paused in his reading. The story had made him uncomfortable. Tallheron was leaning forward on his stool and blinking his eyes again. He did not seem to be paying attention. Kem felt a bit annoyed; his throat was dry from all this reading. He said in a louder voice, "Sir, do you want me to keep going?"

Tallheron looked up. He did not seem sleepy or distracted, as Kem had supposed. Quite the contrary, his expression was alert and even agitated somewhat.

"You may rest if you like," he said. "In fact, perhaps we should leave off there and pick it up next time. That has given me enough to think about for the time being."

Kem nodded. He wondered when "next time" would be. Was this going to be a regular occurrence? He memorized the page number (one thirty-three), closed the book, and held it out for Tallheron to take back.

"No, no," said Tallheron, waving the book away, "you keep it"—exactly as he had done with the smoked glass bottle. "It will be simpler that way."

Since he said nothing else, and in fact did not seem quite to be meeting Kem's eye, Kem supposed that today's session was over and that he must go back to the galley. The volume of *Sun Tales and Moon Songs* felt suddenly heavy in his hands, an encumbrance, a thing that needed attention. Among other things, he was not sure how well it would fit into the tiny drawer under his bunk, or whether one of the other boys might steal it. Still he accepted the fact of the book being his to care for without complaint, because it meant a change, a subtle alteration in the terms of his life. He left without saying good-bye to Tallheron, who did not seem to notice or to care. Tallheron was an odd man, Kem decided, though perhaps that was the way with Residents.

As he stepped from the library, a guard eyed him suspiciously, glancing down at the book in his hand. Kem felt the accustomed twinge of paranoia, expecting the guard to demand proof of something—ownership of the book, the right to be walking down this hall. The guard just looked away, giving Kem as wide a berth as the passageway permitted. His contempt was reassuring. Kem was not a criminal, after all; only an untouchable.

In the galley, alone once more in the privacy of his own unhappiness, Kem thought about the peculiar little story for a while. He wondered why Tallheron had wanted to hear it—to hear that story in particular, out of a book that contained dozens of others, in a room that must have held millions. Something to think about, he had said. Or no, *enough* to think about. There might be a difference. Kem thought there was. He had trouble concentrating on the hobart, and scalded his hands. The galley boss inspected the blisters with obvious satisfaction.

"Have to put you on the cutting line tomorrow," he said. The cutting line was where vegetables were chopped, and there was a substantial risk of losing a finger. The galley boss smiled.

That night Kem stole some candles. It was a minor theft, at worst: the candles were tiny things that had been set out in glass holders on dinner trays that were carried to the upper decks, the wardrooms where senior members of the crew dined (as Kem imagined) in ease and splendor. They were half-burned and would have to be melted and recast before they could be used again. Kem figured that two or three of them would burn long enough to get him through the story.

It was a good secret, having the book. Kem lay in the dark bunk for a long while as the other boys grew tired of their nightly rude games and bantering and fell asleep. The Oasis was never really quiet, but with your eyes closed and only the growl of the engines below the deckplates you got a certain feeling of calmness, of things settling down. Kem spent some time savoring this and the knowledge of his plan before he allowed himself to take the trivial but thrilling risk of lighting a candle. The flame seemed to float in the glass of the holder. Kem watched it, thinking that in the dark room, the little fire in the glass seemed almost to have its own soft noise, a breathy sound like the wind, maybe the sound of the chemical transmutation inside the flame.

For a time the candle held his attention. Kem stared at it and though he did not forget about the book, the comforting weight of it on his stomach, he did not feel just now the desire to read. It was peaceful, lying there. The Oasis lurched and rumbled yet Kem felt very still.

After a couple of minutes he decided that what had seemed to be a faint sound made by the candle flame was really no sound at all: it was silence, or the closest thing to silence that he had known since coming to live here. What

made it seem like noise was the ceaseless movement in
Kem's mind, the current of his thoughts, which at other
times he was too distracted to hear. They surged into the
little circle of candlelight, roaring through his ears; and then,
as the candle burned down and the silence deepened around
him, they faded away.

The book of *Sun Tales and Moon Songs* lay open at Kem's
stomach the next morning when the galley boss came through,
shoving his way past the tangle of wayward limbs and the
piles of discarded clothing that cluttered the narrow aisles of
the berthing area. The man banged his wooden spoon on his
soup pot desultorily, as though he held out little hope for the
coming day. When he approached Kem's bunk, though, his
mood seemed to change. He stopped his spoon-banging.
When Kem raised his head, the galley boss stood abreast of
him, his small oily eyes alight with a kind of menacing
curiosity.

"So," the man said. "Taken to reading ourself to sleep,
have we?"

Kem had the feeling of struggling upward through layers
of semiconsciousness. Despite the unseemly fact of the galley
boss glowering inches away, part of his mind was still caught
on the shards of the night's last dream, and part of it on the
dream before that, which may not have been a dream after
all. A secret: a candle: and then, this mind-gate having
opened, he felt the weight of the book still there where he
had laid it. He had not meant to fall asleep. He had meant to
finish the story and then put the book back in his drawer,
hidden and safe.

It was too late now. The galley boss lowered his head into
the confined space of Kem's bunk, investigating. You could
smell last night's mescal on his breath.

"Ah," he said, lifting a glass candleholder. "Just borrowing
this, I imagine?"

Kem struggled up, onto his elbows. He bumped his head;
the book slid sideways off his stomach. Kem made a grab for
it, reflexively, but the galley boss caught it first.

"*Sun Tales*," the man read slowly, squinting at the spine.

"*Moon Songs*. What the hell is this? Who'd you steal it from?"

"No," Kem said, feeling confused and somewhat panicky. He always had a feeling, when talking to the galley boss, that he was guilty of something, that he had committed some serious mistake. But this time he hadn't. "No," he said, "I . . ."

Behind the galley boss, a few paces up the aisle, Sander had materialized, drawn as always to the momentary source of entertainment. He seemed to be signaling to Kem, shaking his head, forming words with his small mouth. Kem got the general sense of a warning, but he could make nothing more of it than that. The galley boss was riffling the pages of the book with his greasy thumb.

"Stop that," said Kem.

The galley boss did stop, but only to look at Kem in amazement. This changed to a look of something like evil glee.

"No," struggling to explain himself, Kem stammered, "it's not . . . look, it's not even mine, it was—"

"A *present?*" the galley boss said sneeringly. "From one of your many *admirers?*"

Kem felt himself growing warm. More quietly, struggling for control, he said, "It was just given to me. To keep. Until later."

The galley boss glared up and down the aisle as though warning the other boys to be about their business. (Sander, presciently, had already vanished.) Then he looked back at Kem. "Lying is a serious thing, boy. Who'd you take this from? What do you want with a book, anyway?"

Kem wasn't so afraid of the galley boss as not to feel affronted. He straightened up as best he could in the cramped space of his bunk.

"You can ask him yourself," he said. "His name is Tallheron." And he added, having saved the clinching point for last: "He's a Resident."

The galley boss stood still and without expression for a second or so, absorbing this. Then he dropped the book. It landed in Kem's lap, heavily. The man took a step back.

"A Resident," he repeated, each syllable falling cleanly

from his mouth, as though the word had shaken his dull mind
to alertness. "You got that from a Resident," he said slowly,
"and you brought it here?"

"He gave it to me," Kem said—feeling now that he, not
the galley boss, was having trouble grasping the point.

"I'm sure he did," the man said. "I'm sure he did give it to
you."

He hardly seemed angry at all now. He acted as though
the conversation were over, or all but. He turned up the
aisle, addressing Kem as a judge might address a criminal
already convicted, the question of his guilt settled beyond
doubt.

"Pack your things," he said. "You're moving to the engine
flats." He turned away, symbolically and physically putting
Kem behind him. To the other boys, the room at large, he
muttered, "They don't pay me to train idiots here."

The last thing Kem saw as he was led by a pair of guards
down a badly lit passageway was Sander standing behind him,
watching, shaking his head with an expression that might
possibly have contained a hint of sadness, though it also
implied another thing, maybe that he had tried to tell Kem
something, to make life easier for him, but now Kem was
going to have to learn the hard way, he was going to have to
discover things for himself.

Then Sander was lost from sight, and
Kem followed the guards around a corner and
toward a dark stairway,
leading down.

LONG NIGHTS

The darkness rose from its hiding place under the hatches and deckplates and behind the closed doors and down all the shadowed passages of the Oasis and came to surround Kem and fill him, like the air.

He awoke some time in Long Nights Moon to find himself strapped to a thin mattress in a chamber with no head space, where the dark was almost absolute. The pounding of treads on alkali hardpan a couple of arm-lengths below him was like the driving of spikes by the hundreds and thousands with mighty hammers. There was no surcease. Cold air and a tiny bit of light migrated upward through cracks in the hull where rivets had come apart. They were more than balanced by the heat of black engines throbbing close above. A couple of I beams saved Kem from being mashed between the two of them, darkness and light.

For a while he lay with his eyes closed. He was not quite still: one at a time he moved his limbs, recalling which muscles were sore, which tendons strained, which patches of skin bruised or scraped or blistered. Nothing hurt too badly.

Kem expanded his chest and tried to draw some strength from
the vast power plant above him into his lungs and from there
into his heart and his muscles. He tried to gather the energy
to roll off his mattress and go out into another day. It was not
physical strength he needed but some other kind, the power
that fills the air before a thunderstorm, the power of the hard
raw land. If he concentrated, if he filled his chest with air in
just a certain way, maybe the power would enter him. This
idea was not his own (he had gotten it from the Bell Dog),
but it seemed reasonable enough to Kem and on that basis he
had accepted it, provisionally, as he had learned to do. There
was so little you knew for sure down in the engine flats—
where you were going or why or what would happen there,
all matters of conjecture—so you learned to pick up ideas and
save them, believing them if you cared to but holding on to
them just the same. We are all in the dark, the Bell Dog said.
Like the blind bat, in the dark but with our ears open.

Kem smiled, invisibly. He let the air out of his chest,
feeling as tired and powerless as ever, and bent to loosen the
straps that had held him safely through the night.

The first thing he saw outside his compartment, as always,
was the ground. He stepped out onto a catwalk made of metal
crosshatching. Through this, five or six arm-lengths down, he
saw the earth stream by: dark brown, like spilled coffee,
where the shadow of the Oasis lay over it, pitted and striated
with burnt-sienna ridges where it was grazed by the morning
sun. He couldn't decide whether the earth had changed in
some way as the Oasis traveled south, but it seemed to him
that it had. It seemed to him that the earth was in some way
even more desiccated and even more harsh than it had been
on the wagon routes. Wherever they were now, hardly anything seemed to live. Nothing moved but the Oasis and after
a time you could forget even that. Only now and again some
object would slide into view—a ball of russian thistle, a bone,
a rock—and it was mostly by watching these things fall
behind that you could get some sense of actual velocity, of
yourself going ahead and the earth standing still.

Going ahead, Kem thought. Going ahead meant you were
leaving things behind you, things you would never see again.
He spat through the catwalk and watched the spittle strike

the dry ground with complete futility, just as if it had fallen on the unliving metal of the deck.

Kem thought as he stood there, bracing himself against a strut with one hand, leaning over the edge of the catwalk rather daringly, of his two little sisters. It was them and not his father, so much, nor his mother who had died years ago, whom he missed. Their long brown hair; their smells of things green and new; their laughter. The laughter had been often at Kem, at stupid things he did, idiocies of adolescence, but whatever anger and chagrin that had caused him were gone now, gone with the little girls and with the wagon. Kem wondered how that had all worked out: the broken generator, the new tools. Not well, he imagined. He remembered the way the late-summer sun had slammed down onto the wagon roof and onto his father's legs sticking out from under the engine housing, the rest of his body lost in dry shadow. He remembered the dirt blowing up. Below the Oasis the ground was hot in the morning sun and the smell of it—steel treads scraping the rock-hard caliche, dry shale dust, pulverized greasewood and sage—came up to fill his nostrils. It was not a good idea to brood, he realized. He realized that he had not had much of a life and therefore had nothing much to remember. It was just that he was alone here, at the bottom of the Oasis, only three months into his contract, six years and nine months yet to go, with the sun carving messages onto the ancient ground that no one could ever read, at the start of another day.

In the narrow bay that served the engineering gang—snipes, they called themselves—as a mess hall, Kem took a seat and stared down at a bowl of pasty-looking gruel. He had worked long enough in the galley to be suspicious of anything whose ingredients he did not immediately recognize. Around him boys and men ate hungrily, spilling food onto their coveralls and talking among themselves. Their mouths seemed to be full of blackened teeth. On the whole, they stank worse than galley boys. Nonetheless there was something engagingly carefree in their manner, an amiable slovenliness. If they resented their lot in life, if they felt as Kem did the oppressive weight of the great machinery around them, they did not much let it show. Maybe their previous lives had been worse. Maybe they had come from over the western mountains, out of the salt barrens. Or maybe they had been born right here—that was a thought—born and raised beneath the decks of the Oasis; maybe this was all the world they knew. A loud world of metal and rubber and oil, its sky painted primer gray, its horizons as close as the nearest bulkhead.

Well . . . or maybe Kem didn't really know the guys. After Sander, whom he had not seen in many weeks, he had made no friends, nor scarcely spoken to anyone except the Bell Dog.

Pushing his bowl away, Kem leaned back in the chair and waited for the day's work assignments to be read out.

In a short while, a young man in a pressed gray uniform entered the room. His hair was combed and damp. Careful to avoid touching anything, he stood with his feet widely planted, swaying with the motion of the craft, and flipped through a sheaf of papers. This was a junior mate, one of the assistant engineers: a different breed altogether than the snipes who fell silent now before him, listening as the mate began reading off a series of numbers and phrases like some elaborate code. Twelve-two, compressor room. Twelve-thirteen and seven-four, wait here for the Oil King. Eleven-five, eleven-seven, thirteen-two, bleed the starboard tubes. The list went on and Kem waited for his own number to be read out, for that is what the snipes were, numbers. Each snipe was identified by his work billet according to a system that tracked both specialization and experience (hence the numbers sometimes changed), and in that sense they were all, if not interchangeable, at least quantifiable. Much of the business of engineering, Kem had learned, consisted in quantifying things.

"Five-zero," the young mate was saying, and Kem registered his number without looking up, "steering box."

There it was, then. Kem stretched and wondered momentarily why his number was the only one assigned to this job. But of course his number, Kem himself for that matter, was only a small piece of a great whole, a human piece in the vast machine that was the Oasis; and besides, down here there was almost nothing you could know for sure. For instance: it stood to reason that the young mate was also just a piece of the machine, a larger piece than Kem but not so large as the

chief engineer himself, who in turn was not so large as the
Captain. But the chief engineer never showed himself, he
only sent these assistants; and the Captain of course was all
but invisible, a distant guiding presence in whom you simply
had to believe, the way some people believed in a god and
others in a government and still others, their numbers diminishing, in a fanciful scheme called science. Maybe someday
Kem would understand more; maybe he would know how the
great machine really worked and for what purpose (he assumed
it had a purpose, but that could be wrong) and how all the
pieces fit in. But he doubted it. Meantime he guessed that if
he made his way to the steering box someone else would
show up to direct him or anyhow, in some fashion, the next
piece would fall into place. And he guessed that that was fine.

A funny name, steering box. Perhaps it was some quiet engineer's irony. For the place was gigantic: five or more heads high
and as wide as the Oasis itself, a dimension Kem could hardly
guess, for you couldn't quite make out the distant hull in the
gloom. The only light came down from a kind of hollow column
or tower that pierced the ceiling and kept going upward,
narrowing as it went, and finally opened up to daylight, a tiny
round piece of blue sky which you could see if you stood (as
Kem was standing) straight under it. Only you couldn't tell how
high up it went because of the distortion of perspective. Maybe
it was twenty heads or maybe fifty or maybe a lot more. By the
time the light bounced off the gray metal of the shaft and then
spread out into the cavern of the steering box, it didn't make a
whole lot of difference. Kem thought he was alone here, in all
this open space, but he couldn't see well enough to be sure.

Steering at least made sense. A dozen cables as thick as your
wrist were stretched taut between blocks and winches across
the chamber, shoulder height off the deck. The cables moved
frequently, jerking an arm-length or two then stopping again, as
the winches groaned and their clutches engaged, and the cables
in turn transferred the motion to a set of immense gears which
made the treads of the Oasis turn at slightly different speeds. The
tension in the cables, the amount of energy that passed through
them from one gearbox to another, was terrifying. Obviously if a

cable broke while you were standing nearby it would kill you, it would break you like a damp twig. Kem found, though, that it was interesting and even enjoyable to stand here calmly in the midst of such awful power—knowing that he could be destroyed in an instant, that only a parlous balance of forces kept him alive, the work of the engineers who had built this machine a long time ago, and deciding that he was going to trust it, trust those old engineers who were probably dead by now, because he was an engineer himself, he was at home among inhuman forces and the dangerous works of humankind. It was not faith after all but measurement, quantification, that held chaos at bay.

"Standing like a lizard."

Kem nearly jumped from the surprise of hearing another voice. He turned to see the Bell Dog, who had come upon him silently out of the shadows and stood now only a couple of paces away.

"Lizard doesn't close his eyes when he stands, doesn't rest. Just keeps his eye open so he doesn't miss nothing." The Bell Dog smiled. His dark eyes, almost black, glowed like clean glass.

"I was just . . ." Kem stopped because he didn't know what he was just doing—nothing much, waiting, thinking.

The Bell Dog seemed to examine him, looking up into his face because the squat little man stood a head shorter than Kem, who was by no means tall. "You not eat breakfast?" he finally asked.

Kem frowned and shook his head. The Bell Dog went on:

"Not much energy this morning. Too bad. Big job up there, need some good help."

It had taken Kem a while to understand that the Bell Dog was not simpleminded, was in fact a smart and even an educated man, at least when it came to understanding machines and why they worked or didn't work and how to fix them. He was perhaps a shade less good at explaining such things to others. Kem was often assigned to work with him—whether or not at the Bell Dog's behest he did not know—and the two of them got along rather well, he thought, and he was glad now to find that they were to be together.

"Up where?" he asked. "Big job up where?"

The Bell Dog only nodded. "Very big," he said. "Very

delicate. Needs a fine hand." He looked down critically at Kem's hands, as though to see if they qualified. There was no way to tell if he was being deliberately comical. Kem guessed he was, but he wasn't sure enough to laugh. The Bell Dog had not answered his question; but then he had a way of not answering questions, or of answering them in his own time and fashion.

"Hurry, then," the Bell Dog said, shooing him. "Up, up. Hurry."

Kem bent his head back. The tiny piece of hot blue sky at the top of the shaft burned afterimages onto his retina. "Up there?" he said.

The Bell Dog did not answer and Kem saw that he was looking up as well, just staring like Kem at that single bright spot high above them. There was a moment in which Kem felt himself very close to knowing, somehow, what the Bell Dog was thinking or feeling as he stood there in darkness, watching the light, but the moment passed and Kem figured after all it was not difficult to imagine the feelings one would have at a time like that—envy, wonder, wistfulness—though it had not seemed quite like any of those things. Then the Bell Dog turned away, as he did most things, all of a sudden, and he said, "Yes, yes. Up."

It was not apparent how to get there, up to the mouth of the shaft, though Kem could see a small ladder that clung to its inner surface. *Up* of course was the difficult matter, in the Oasis—*down* being the direction that would take care of itself if you blinked at the wrong instant. It had not been hard at all to go down from the galley to the engine flats. Getting back up again was going to be the tricky part, and in this respect the structure of the Oasis neatly meshed with its organizational scheme. Hatches were battened from the top down and right now Kem was at a loss to find a way up to the hole in the ceiling.

The Bell Dog, not always a patient man, waited patiently. Kem supposed it was some sort of lesson, part of his apprenticeship. He strained his eyes through the great hollow of the chamber but saw nothing that would be of help: no pull-down ladder or ratlines or scalable pieces of machinery. As near as he could tell you would need to levitate those first five heads or so and not even in the Bell Dog's stranger stories (and there were strange ones) could anyone do that.

Yet it seemed possible, it must be possible; the distance involved was not—as many things in the Oasis were—so far removed from the human scale as to be incommensurable. It was an interesting problem, was all. A question of engineering. You just needed time to think it through.

Kem's time ran out. The Bell Dog reached into the open neck of his coveralls and pulled out something that dangled from the end of a· chain. It was a shiny rod about as long as your hand, hollow at the center, that seemed to be made of silver or at least of something silvery and bright. Squatting down, the Bell Dog tapped the rod against the metal of the deck. A resonant, penetrating chime seemed to grow louder as the Bell Dog raised the rod over his head, pointing it toward the hole in the ceiling like a little wizard aiming his wand. The chime slowly faded. Within a few moments, it was answered faintly by the hum of machinery. Kem looked up to see a shadow growing larger in the hollow of the light-shaft. The shadow descended. It was a basket, woven of tough fiber, lowered on a wire. The basket looked small while it was coming down, but when it reached the deck you could see it was big enough to hold two people easily, and the Bell Dog motioned for Kem to climb in with him.

"Those people expecting us," the Bell Dog said, which Kem figured was the answer to the riddle of how to get up, the day's first lesson. He nodded; the Bell Dog sounded his chime again; and with a clunk of gears engaging, the basket was hoisted off the deck.

Yet somehow (Kem reflected, as the steering box receded into darkness and the walls of the tower grew lighter around them, a paler and paler gray) this answer was not a satisfying one. "Those people expecting us"—it was not an engineer's solution; it implied that the problem was rigged to begin with, or that it could be solved only by the inclusion of some outside agency. Perhaps the Bell Dog thought so too: perhaps that explained the scowl that creased his coppery skin.

Kem wondered, though—just before the basket came to a stop, adjacent to an open hatchway—why his mind held on with such tenacity to the image of that little ladder, five heads high, leading out of the darkness.

Whoever were the people expecting them, they were not in sight when Kem and the Bell Dog climbed through the hatchway and stood at the end of a wide corridor that ran for several paces and then reached a T intersection. The Bell Dog slammed the hatch, then came to stand beside him. He did not look as puzzled as Kem, but he did seem to be waiting for something.

Nothing came. The corridor branched into two curving arms; it was a characteristic of the Oasis that lines tended to curve into circles or spirals, probably so as to follow the contour of the hull, though Kem often felt that the arcs were folding in upon themselves, bringing you back where you started. The Bell Dog signaled Kem to proceed down one of the hallways, the one curving leftward, moonwise. The Bell Dog set off in the other direction.

"You find them," he said over his shoulder, "you call."

—Find who, Kem started to ask, but did not. He was suddenly alone in an unfamiliar part of the Oasis. The throb of machinery, never still, was muted by distance and by the intervening bulk of deckplates so that he had a persuasive and unaccustomed sense of silence. He kept his footsteps as quiet as possible—though he knew that this was purposeless, that he should probably try to make his presence known. But he felt awkward and out of place in his oil-blotched coveralls, and after all he had no idea of whom he was looking for or what would be expected of him. The Bell Dog was vexatious that way.

The corridor branched again. Kem reckoned that the best thing to do would be to continue bearing left, so that he would be sure to remember the way back. On this new stretch of hallway there were a number of doors, all closed, and Kem wondered if he should knock on any of them. He did not. The new sensation of walking freely down an unfamiliar hall was too rare to give up so soon. He began to relax somewhat, to breathe more easily; but by then he realized that he had almost certainly come too far and that he ought to turn back again.

It was then, however, that he heard the voices. They were indistinct, just a ripple in the distance and not much louder than the steady background rumble that rose through the deck. There were five or six or seven, a couple of them louder and more distinct than the rest, and they were accompanied by occasional outbursts of laughter—not the uproarious sort, but simple momentary chuckles or giggles of the kind that happen when companions are together in relaxed circumstances. It was the sort of thing you heard now and then down in the engine flats, during slack times of the day. Only this was different, and Kem took a few more steps until he was standing close outside the door that the voices were coming from. What kept him standing there was that the voices were female; they belonged to young women or even to girls younger than Kem. And what made his heart pump fast and hard was that among them there was one voice in particular—one laugh—that he thought he recognized.

He waited and listened but that voice did not come again. He might have arrived just at the end of something, a gathering in the process of breaking up, because the sounds on the other side of the door sounded less merry and more purposeful. Someone seemed to be giving instructions (he thought he heard the word *important* more than once) and there were footsteps.

The footsteps should have been enough of a signal. But Kem was still hanging on, hoping for one more word or bubble of laughter from that voice that he thought he knew, which is what he was doing—just standing there, ear cocked toward the door like a spy—when suddenly there was no door, only an open space where the door had been, and in the open space a little girl of maybe eleven or twelve, looking surprised to see Kem but not as surprised as Kem and surely not embarrassed and even panicky as he was to find himself discovered. The little girl's expression became one of (Kem feared) wry amusement. She slipped past him as though he were merely the first of many inconsequential obstacles she expected to encounter that day. Kem recovered so far as to step aside to let her go. Then, still blocking the doorway, he looked back to find himself staring into the palely freckled face, the sharp brown eyes, of the girl he had met once in passing many weeks ago, down in the cargo bay.

She watched him for a moment with what seemed to be mild curiosity, no more. It did not appear that she recognized him, nor that she was unduly surprised to find him standing there. Those eyes that Kem especially remembered swept over his coveralls, the hand tools hanging from his belt.

"I guess you're here," she finally said, "about the wiring."

Kem guessed he was. As he listened to her voice, he heard again that offhand, musical quality that had lingered in his thoughts, foolishly, through much of the autumn. He was pretty sure that if he tried to speak, the words would get caught somewhere around his epiglottis and come out damp and indistinct. He looked down at the deck, just to the side of where the girl's legs were covered with undyed cotton, bound above the ankles with violet kerchiefs.

"Well," she said, which brought his eyes back up. The girl was smiling. It was an easy smile to look at. Kem had a vague sense of half a dozen other girls standing behind her, watching them. She said, "So you're a snipe these days."

Something in her tone or her choice of words—comradely, inviting confidence—made Kem respond without thinking about it: "Yeah. They kicked me out of the galley because they thought I had stolen a book." It came out fine.

The girl nodded, faintly sympathetic. "They took me away from the horses," she said, and it seemed to Kem that they had this in common, at least: the same *they*. The two of them stood there in silence long enough for it to begin to feel awkward, then she said, "So how do you like it?"

Kem said, "It's okay. It's really not bad." Which until now he had never thought, even to himself—that life in the engine flats was any better than endurable. "I like it pretty well, actually," he said, and he realized that it was true.

The girl smiled as though she were glad to hear this, glad to hear of someone enjoying himself here, where so many people were unhappy. Kem thought of what he ought to say next, maybe ask her what she was doing now that they had taken her away from the horses, maybe even tell her his name. But while he was standing there trying to get the knack of this conversation thing, footsteps clomped loudly around the bend in the hall and there was the Bell Dog, hands on his hips looking irritated and a trifle out of breath.

"There you are," he said to Kem. He looked at the girl and, as though this might need some amplification, he added, "There he is."

The girl laughed—a thing that she did easily, Kem thought, and not always at times when he felt like laughing himself. She said, "Well, I've got to be going. They're waiting for you, anyway."

She was pointing at another door, not the one she had just come out of, but only the Bell Dog was paying attention. Kem felt something like misery and something like desperation growing in him as he understood that the girl was about to turn away and walk down the hall and that would be it, that would be the end of it, just like before. And indeed, she started to turn, she even had taken a step down the hall but then she turned back, and with a grace that made it seem quite natural, she held out her hand to Kem. He took it and felt her slender figures and the warmth of her palm.

"My name's Davina," she told him.

For some reason her smile was gone and the moment had a funny feeling, a sense of intimation, which Kem felt and which he thought the girl felt too.

"Davina," he repeated, making sure he had it right. He said it again simply because it felt good to do so, and then he remembered to say, "My name is Kem."

She nodded. She said nothing more. And then she was gone.

There was a problem with wiring as the girl had said, and Kem knew very little about wiring. Therefore the Bell Dog did most of the work and Kem should have watched him carefully so as to pick things up, but his mind, of course, was elsewhere.

His mind was elsewhere. That was an expression which Kem had heard and he knew it was just a way of talking, but in this case it seemed to him that the expression was true in some deeper, perhaps even literal, way. His mind was elsewhere. Where was his mind?

It seemed to Kem that there was something odd about this girl, Davina. It seemed to him very odd that the two brief meetings he had had with her should affect him in such a strong way. It was almost like he knew this girl, not in the sense that he had just met her but like he had known her already; or perhaps it was the opposite or the converse of that, perhaps what he felt was that the girl Davina already knew him.

Kem wondered it if was possible that this was a perfectly ordinary feeling, that other boys felt this way about other girls, but it was hard to imagine so. It was hard to imagine that when one of the older snipes boasted about some girl he knew or some girl he had fucked, what it felt like to him was anything like the way this felt to Kem. Though Kem of course had just learned this girl's name not an hour ago, and in no sense could he really claim that he knew her, except that it felt that way. It was a strong and ineffable feeling and Kem had a hard time disregarding it.

The Bell Dog seemed angry at him, at his inattentiveness, but despite the possible consequences Kem found it easy to disregard *that*. Which, of course, put the situation in a strange sort of perspective, because he could disregard the one thing that was actual and immediate and not the other which may have been imaginary.

Kem tried to remember if he had ever felt anything like this before but he couldn't think so.

Kem tried to remember if he had ever known any girl, really known her, other than his little sisters. Naturally he had known many girls in a certain way, to a certain extent, by the nature of life among the wagons. But by the nature of life among the wagons he had not known any of them for very long or very well. Certainly he had not known any girl so well that she got stuck in his mind and lingered there for no clear reason, her image and the sound of her voice and the way he had felt in her presence remaining bizarrely intact for a long time afterward. And yet there had been many girls whom he had known longer and better, in an objective way, than he knew this girl, Davina.

Kem wondered about these things and about other things, about the feeling for example of intimation, as though some important future happening or consequence were strongly implied, that he had felt when he had taken Davina's hand. He wondered about that and he remembered the warmth of her hand and even, it seemed to Kem (though he might have been mistaken), the way she smelled, standing close to him:

warm and somehow yeasty, like new bread. But chiefly he wondered what this all could mean—whether conceivably it might mean that on the strength of two fleeting encounters, nothing more, he had fallen in love.

Anything was possible. The Bell Dog continued to seem angry at Kem while they yanked wires out of bulkheads and lifted deckplates and lowered ceiling panels, looking for faulty connections, for much of the day. But when the job was done and they were back in the lift-basket, on their way back down, his mood brightened and he seemed to relax. He let his head fall back and watched the spot of sky receding from them. Afternoon light fell from a distance onto his broad and somehow exaggerated features. Kem followed his gaze, looking up the hollow shaft toward the sky.

"What's up there?" he said. "I mean, in the tower. Where does that ladder go?"

The ladder hung beside them and marked their descent, rung by rung. It would be a frightening thing to climb, Kem thought: narrow, tilted slightly backward from the vertical, so you would have to struggle just to hang on.

"Other world up there," said the Bell Dog. "They do other work than us. Whole different kind of thing." He pointed down, toward the engine flats or possibly the ground underneath, unseen but perceptible through the steady shuddering of the landcraft. "We do our little work. They do their great work."

He waved a thick hand. The gesture was one a conjurer might make, summoning things into existence out of the air. Kem thought that the gesture and the Bell Dog's tone of voice did not match up with his words—that when he said *great work*, for example, there was nothing like respect or admiration in his voice; there was even a hint of disapproval. Kem wondered if the Bell Dog was trying to warn him about something, steer him safely away, but he couldn't tell for sure.

Of course, there was very little you could tell for sure about the Bell Dog, including exactly where he stood in the baffling hierarchy of the Oasis. When Kem had been assigned to work with him, he had taken it all for granted as part of the ordinary course of events, the newest snipe being apprenticed to the clownish lifer, little better it seemed than a half-wit. But Kem had liked the Bell Dog anyway, and the Bell Dog had appeared after a while to like Kem also, and gradually Kem had come to notice certain things—for example that the Bell Dog, alone among the snipes, never appeared at the morning duty-call, and that the most interesting or difficult jobs often seemed to be reserved for him.

Looking back on things, on the way things had worked out, Kem thought perhaps his own version of events might need revision; he thought that, for starters, the Bell Dog may have picked him out right at the beginning, chosen him not as an apprentice but as an audience. He recalled that when he was dragged down to the engine flats, clutching the book that had gotten him into so much trouble, the Bell Dog had been standing there and had taken the book, hefted it solemnly, stared at the title page, then handed it back again.

"This yours?" he had asked.

Kem thought at the time that the little man might never have seen a book before. "It's a collection of folktales," Kem had explained. "Native legends and so forth. They come from, um ..." (trying to say it in a way the Bell Dog would understand) "... from the old people, the people who were here to begin with."

The Bell Dog had only looked at him. Then after a moment he had said, "You like these stories? You believe them?"

"I like stories," Kem had said. Perhaps he had shrugged. "We used to hear stories about the old people, back in the wagons. They used to live all around here."

The Bell Dog had turned and walked away and the next morning he and Kem worked together for the first time. Now they sat in the basket side by side, with the winter sunlight trickling down the shaft and bringing out the burnt-clay features of the Bell Dog's face, and Kem wondered whether very much had really changed or only his perceptions of things, the things themselves remaining more or less immutable: the sky above, the earth below, the Oasis filling the space between them, the Bell Dog tending his machines.

The basket came down with a thump and the Bell Dog climbed out, moving with an alacrity that suggested quitting time. Unlike other snipes—this was another thing—he measured the working day by the sun. There was no need for that; the engine flats were lit round the clock by artificial means; but the Bell Dog's sense of time was rigid and certainly Kem did not demur from laying down his tools in midafternoon.

"Long night ahead," the Bell Dog told him, moving away, passing into shadow. "Long Nights, long sleeps."

It sounded good to Kem. In fact he thought he might like a nap right now, before the evening meal. He made his way aftward through the engine flats and across the metal webbing to his compartment. And there, waiting placidly, as though expecting him at just this minute, was Sander.

Something about Sander struck Kem as different from the friend he remembered and the difference was not one Kem liked. The boy stood propped against a metal strut, watching Kem through cool tawny eyes. He was wearing clothes that could not have come from the galley: loose-fitting trousers and a billowy shirt made out of clean, unbleached linen. Some kind of insignia had been sewn onto the front of the shirt, in a place that would have covered his left breast if Sander had been big enough to fill it but instead fell around the bottom of his rib cage. The shirt belonged to somebody else, Kem figured. Sander looked to him overly preened, you might say even pretty. Neither of them said anything for a while but it felt comfortable enough to stand there studying one another from a couple of paces apart.

At last Sander said, "Hi, Kem," and when he smiled he looked much less like somebody's pampered kitten and more like an ordinarily troublesome fourteen-year-old boy. Kem liked him again and they shook hands. He had missed Sander and it was truly good to see him. He removed his tool belt and sat down on a beam that ran above the deck like a low bench. Sander remained standing, perhaps in consideration of his new clothes.

"So," he said to Kem. "Have you had enough of this place yet?"

The boy's eyes assumed that narrow, appraising set that Kem remembered. Kem remembered also why he had so often found Sander hard to bear. "Actually," he said, "I kind of like it here. Better than the galley, anyway, I guess."

"Hm." Sander looked around. There was not much to see, and perhaps that was his point. "You like being a snipe, huh?"

"It's all right. How are things in the galley?"

"I'm not in the galley anymore." Sander shifted his weight from one foot to another and appeared to strike an attitude. "I've been promoted a year early. I'm a messenger now."

Kem considered briefly what an early promotion probably meant and how it connected with Sander wearing somebody else's linen shirt. He said only, "You're a messenger."

Sander nodded. "I carry messages everywhere. I've been all the way up to the Captain's quarters. I'm really learning my way around."

Clearly he expected Kem to be impressed, and actually, to a degree, Kem was. Sander went on talking, telling stories of his new job, boasting of the people he had met and the goings-on he had witnessed. There was something winning in his manner, a light of genuine enthusiasm in his eye as he rattled happily onward, and Kem thought that after all it was hard to begrudge Sander his minor triumph over the hardships of life in the Oasis. And there was no denying that the role of messenger suited him. Kem found it easy to imagine the boy passing smoothly from one circle of the Oasis to another, furthering intrigues in which he personally had no role.

"So," he said, when Sander stopped talking, "what are you doing now? Are you finished working for the day?"

Sander gave him a slight, calculating sort of smile. "Almost," he said. "I've got one last message." He reached into a deep pocket of his trousers and pulled out an envelope, thick and expensive-looking paper, bearing a single name in red ink. Kem twisted his head, trying to make it out, and Sander extended the envelope as though to make it easier. Then Kem saw what the name was and about that time Sander said:

"Here. It's for you."

Kem stared dumbly at the envelope, held lightly and with

deceptive casualness between two skinny fingers. There was
nothing casual at all, really, about Sander's expression or
about his tone of voice as he said, "Do you want it, or do you
just want me to tell you what it says?"

Kem snatched the envelope away, somewhat angered, but
Sander evidently did not intend to give up his advantage. He
waited for Kem to examine the seam of the envelope, which
was sealed with wax and showed no sign of having been
tampered with; then, as Kem cracked the seal, Sander pressed
on:

"It says, 'Please come, or if that presents difficulty please
send the book back. I need to know how the story ends.' It's
signed 'Tallheron.'"

Kem unfolded the letter anyway and it was exactly as
Sander had said. He folded it again, returned it to the
envelope, and had an odd sense of the past having caught up
with him. He supposed the past had a way of doing that. He
had not thought of that gaunt old man for some time and he
had never gotten to the end of the little story, the story of the
young girl and the mysterious stranger, because of the bitter
taste that whole business had left in his mouth. Now he
supposed that out of courtesy if nothing else he must at least
return the book.

Sander was watching him carefully, but in his fashion he
kept his thoughts to himself. He only betrayed his curiosity
so far as to say, "I guess he's talking about that book you got
in deep shit over. The one you got from the Resident."

"Tallheron *is* the Resident," Kem said, bemused that
Sander should not have known this. "And look, you can see
from this note that he knows I didn't steal it from him."

Sander frowned. "But nobody thought you did."

"Oh yeah? Then why'd I get kicked out of the galley like
that? Not that I'm sorry," he added, mostly to himself—"not
that I'm sorry it happened."

Sander seemed to forget himself. He came to sit down on
the beam next to Kem, staring as though his friend had said
something remarkable, or perhaps merely inane. "You don't
get it, do you?" he said. "You still haven't figured it out."

"Figured out what?"

"Figured out," said Sander, "about the Residents."

Kem shrugged. "All I know is that at first the guy treated me like I was some sort of animal or something, like I was carrying the plague—wouldn't let me touch any of his stuff and made me carry his clothes in a bag and then he just gave me a bottle and told me to keep it so he wouldn't have to clean up after me. Then after a while he got more friendly and wanted me to read to him from this book. So I did, and we got about halfway through the story and then I brought it back to the berthing area and fell asleep holding it and then the whole thing went to hell. I tried to tell everyone that Tallheron *let* me take it, he wasn't afraid to let me touch things anymore, but—"

Sander was shaking his head. "You don't get it at all. It's not the Residents that are afraid of *us*. It's us that are afraid of the Residents. Or anyway" (curling his lip at Kem) "we ought to be. That's why the boss got so pissed off at you—because you'd taken something from a Resident, and brought it down to the galley. That's a major violation."

But why, Kem started to say, only Sander gestured him into silence.

"It's the crying," the boy said. "Get it? The Residents have all got the crying and they're all paying a shitload of money to be here at the Oasis because otherwise they'd be out in the desert and they'd be dead. It wasn't *you* that wasn't supposed to touch that old guy's stuff. It was that old guy and all his germy stuff that wasn't supposed to touch *you*."

Kem had a very peculiar feeling as though his entrails had detached themselves and were drifting around loose inside his gut. He thought back hard over his encounters with Tallheron, his visit to the man's stateroom and the various minor contacts they had had. It made him shiver.

Sander nodded, as though in approval now that Kem seemed to have grasped the true nature of the situation.

"But why," said Kem, "why are they here? In the Oasis, I mean. I mean, what good does it do, really, if they're all just going to die anyway?"

Sander slid closer along the beam. He fairly purred into Kem's ear: "Are they? Are they going to die? Is your friend Tallheron dead?"

"But . . . he's got the crying."

"Sure. But he's had it for a long time. And he's still alive." Sander pointed. "He wrote you that note."

Kem felt himself shrink from it, from the piece of paper in his hand. But that was senseless; he knew the crying was not so easy to contract as all that. Still he moved the envelope a safe distance away.

"They say," Sander was telling him, "that there's some kind of treatment, but it's this big secret, and the Oasis is the only place you can get it."

"What kind of treatment?" said Kem.

Sander shrugged. "Like I said, it's a big secret. Maybe the Captain knows. Maybe there's a secret formula or something." He fixed Kem in a hard-eyed glaze and said, "Maybe that's what your Resident friend is trying to find out."

Kem thought about this for a moment and thought about the curt little message scrawled on expensive paper.

With an imperfect attempt at ingenuousness, Sander said, "So what's in this story, anyway? The one he needs to know the end of. Do you know what he's talking about?"

Kem nodded; then he shook his head. "I don't know how the story ends, no. I haven't finished it."

Sander appeared to be restraining himself. His age and his impetuousness betrayed him: his legs began twitching, and presently he gave up all pretense of casualness. "God," he said, his voice barely above a whisper, "suppose it's in there. Suppose the secret is right there in the story!" He glanced at Kem, suddenly worried. "You've still got the book, haven't you? You didn't throw it away or anything?"

Kem nodded. "I've got it"—and then he perceived that for very likely the first time, he possessed something that Sander badly wanted. There were certain possibilities here and Kem's mind ran quickly through them.

"Well?" said Sander. "Aren't you going to read it? I mean, don't you want to see?"

"I guess so," said Kem. He spoke cautiously. He remembered the Bell Dog's remark about the bat: in the dark, but with his ears open. "But really I guess I ought to get Tallheron's book back to him. I mean, it's his, and all."

"I'll take it," said Sander readily. "I'll take it right up to him. I know where he lives, there in the Residents' wing."

Kem nodded. "That's a good idea," he said. "You promise?"

Sander nodded with all the gravity he could muster, given his obvious fixation on the object at hand.

Kem waited a bit, giving his friend a good taste of victory, and then he said, "And you've got to promise something else, too."

Sander tilted his head a bit. He seemed to sense that Kem was up to something.

"Just one thing," said Kem. "I know you can do it. I want you to help me. I want you to help me find somebody—find out where somebody lives, and help me figure out how to get there."

Sander looked uncertain but only for an instant. He nodded. "Sure. Who?"

Kem stood up. "Let me get the book," he said. "I want to see how the story ends, too. Then we can talk about the other thing."

He ducked into his sleeping compartment, crawling over the mattress to where his small store of personal possessions stood arrayed on a shelf. He laid his hands on the book but then paused, remaining there on his knees for several seconds, thinking it over. He had the feeling that after months of screwing things up he may finally have done one thing right. He crawled back out and opened the book to the page he had marked months ago. He offered the book to Sander.

"You read it," said Sander, affecting an offhand air. "I don't know how."

Kem was surprised, but then he considered that Sander must have been very young when he was brought aboard the Oasis, that his schooling must have ended a long time ago; and that, besides, in Sander's scheme of things the ability to read must count as a relatively minor talent. A party trick, like.

Sander said, "And you can skip the beginning. All I want to hear is the important stuff. Whatever your Resident friend is looking for."

Kem nodded. He skimmed the story to refresh his memory and then, about halfway through, he began reading aloud.

    . . . Julia thought she must make the best of
things. She asked him, "Are you here to gather

wild berries and flowers to use in your medicines?"

"Not exactly," the man said to her, smiling kindly.
"I am here to experiment with a different kind
of medicine—something that I have seen used now
and then with great success, though I have never
tried it myself."

Julia nodded, thinking this might be informative
to watch. She put away her imaginary garden
tools and stood up, smoothing her skirt. "Do you
need any help?" she asked the man. "I know
all about the things that grow in this village. I am
very observant, and I have lived here all my
life."

The old man only smiled at her, and in his smile
Julia thought she could see something else,
something that very old people often feel that makes
them stare at things absentmindedly and sigh,
which Julia thought must come from knowing how
close to dying they are. After a while of looking
at her this way, the man said, "Yes, Julia. I think I
can use your help."

Julia watched while the very old man (whom now
she thought she must call the Doctor) walked
through the tall grass toward the large, tumbledown
house. She followed him but let him stay a little
bit ahead, so she could keep her very bright eye
on him. He did not seem to mind. He stood
where the back stoop had been (people had taken
it apart and burned it many years ago) and gazed
across the mound of honeysuckle that covered the
bones of a dead azalea. He was looking at
something, Julia could tell, some definite place, but
what he was seeing there existed only in his
memory. There was nothing where his eyes were
pointed but the tall grass and yarrow and Queen
Anne's lace of the old backyard. After a little while
the Doctor glanced at Julia, who was still behind
him, and began taking very careful steps into the
yard.

"One," he counted. "Two. Three."

It was like following a secret treasure map. Julia grew excited and hurried after him along the narrow path he made through the weeds. That way she kept the burrs and hitchhikers off her dress.

"Four," the Doctor counted. "Five. Six. Seven."

Julia hoped he would stop there, because seven was a very important number where treasure maps were concerned, and there were other things mysterious about it. But the Doctor kept counting up to ten. Then he stopped. Julia felt that ten was not at all a magical number. In fact it reminded her of arithmetic, but she guessed that doctors didn't believe in magic anyway. The Doctor bent down and looked carefully at the ground for several seconds.

"What you need now," she told him, "is something to dig it up."

The Doctor looked up at Julia quickly as though he were surprised. "Dig what up?" he asked her.

"The treasure," she told him.

The Doctor still looked a bit uncertain, but he said, "Ah." He gave Julia the sort of smile one gives to little girls. This did not annoy her much because, having been a little girl for many years, she was used to it.

"What you need," she said, "is a good trowel."

She reached into the imaginary tool bag where she kept many of the indispensable implements of her hobby, excepting those that were large or hazardous. She pulled out the nice trowel with the comfortable handgrip she had broken in earlier that summer in this very yard.

"Here," she said. "This is very strong. The head was drop-forged from a single piece of steel by a company called Bulldog."

The Doctor seemed very pleased with this information, though Julia felt that his pleasure did not derive from a proper regard for quality hand tools. Nonetheless he did extend his hand to take the trowel. Julia gave it to him and for a moment their fingers touched.

The Doctor drew his hand back fast. He almost dropped the imaginary trowel. Julia thought he must have been surprised, as most people were, by how very warm her hands were. Perhaps, being a Doctor, he was more than other people attentive to such things. He said nothing, however. He took the trowel and pretended to pass it from hand to hand. Actually what he was doing was reaching into his pocket to get a knife. It was an unusual-looking knife made all of shiny metal. Julia guessed that he was not used to working with the soil, as she was, or he would have equipped himself with something more suitable.

Using the odd knife and the imaginary trowel, the Doctor began to dig. He went about it incorrectly, in Julia's view, taking a little gouge out of the dirt and then moving a couple of inches over and taking another. It was like someone preparing a seedling bed, making small, evenly spaced holes for the tiny plants to go in. Julia supervised this operation without comment. It was best, she felt, to let a new gardener find his own way. Sure enough, after a few minutes of fumbling about in the soil, the Doctor gave a happy cry.

"I think I've found it," he exclaimed.

Julia came closer to look across his shoulder. The Doctor began to dig very carefully, forcing the blade on his knife into the soil with a gentle pressure, then scraping the dirt back with his fingers so that a larger and larger hole was left in the ground. After a while of this he had exposed something dark and flat which Julia took to be the lid of the treasure box. It was not very big, but after all, this was only a backyard and not a pirate's cove. Julia believed that at all costs one had to be realistic.

The Doctor's old, bony fingers were trembling as they pulled the box from the soil. It was made out of wood and it was rotten, and as he tried to lift it, the bottom fell cleanly away. Something very little came out and rolled onto the ground. The Doctor gasped. His fingers scrabbled in the dirt where the thing had fallen. At last he found it.

It was a tiny bottle of dark green glass. Its mouth was covered with a black plug of some old-fashioned material like plastic. Julia wrinkled her nose. She knew all about plastic. She foresaw the worst.

The Doctor held the little bottle very close in front of his face. He tapped it once or twice to get the flecks of dirt off. He clutched it so hard that Julia was afraid he might shatter the glass and cut himself.

"Do you know what this is?" he asked Julia.

She knew perfectly well what it was. The Doctor's question, however, was the kind of question that you don't really want an answer to. She knew this also. She kept quiet, and the Doctor kept talking.

"Do you know what this *is?*" he said again, probably for effect. He raised and lowered the bottle as though it were a thing of great weight or immeasurable significance. "This," said the Doctor, "is *her.*"

Even though Julia knew this—even though she knew that the tiny bottle was where they had put the Remedy they made from the girl who was going to marry the Doctor, after they killed her— hearing the Doctor's words caused an icy feeling to pass along her spine. She arched her back like a cat.

"She died," the Doctor was saying, his voice a windy whisper, "so that I might live."

As he said this, he took the tiny bottle between the finger and thumb of one shaking hand. With the other hand he clutched the plastic stopper. It

had been sealed, those long years ago, with
some kind of tape. The tape gave way with a crinkly
sound as soon as the Doctor twisted it. That
in itself, Julia thought, let alone the plastic, should
have told him. But the Doctor, she had begun
to understand, was a poor sick old man who needed
desperately to believe. He started to twist the
cap off, then he stopped. He rested on his knees
in the dirt.

"I believe the seal may have broken," he said.
His voice was quiet, steady, the way you expect
a doctor's voice to be. It was the kind of voice you
would use to tell a mother, for example, that
her little girl had the plague and was going to die.

Julia felt very sad for him. She said, "But what
about the other medicines? What about the real
medicines you were going to find, when you left
to become a doctor?"

He looked at her at first angrily, but the anger
faded right away. Then his look was only tired.
"There are no other medicines," he said. "There is
only the Remedy. I cannot explain it. I suppose
no one can. No one wants to believe it. But it is
only the Remedy that is effective."

With no hope left he twisted the cap. It was so
brittle with age it broke off in his hand. He
peered into the bottle and if he saw anything there
at all it did not encourage him.

"It's gone," he said. "It must have leaked out.
There's nothing left."

Julia had her hand up and would have touched
the old man, out of pity, but he surprised her
by tossing the bottle lightly to one side. The great
weight and significance the thing had possessed
a minute ago were gone, and the Doctor seemed
already to have forgotten all that. He looked at
Julia with a different kind of face than she had seen
before—different eyes, different meanings.

"I am sorry," he said, in that quiet and steady
voice. "I am very sorry, Julia," a genuine doctor's

voice, calm, full of regret, "but now I'm afraid there is no other way."

Julia would not have tried to run, but the Doctor could not know that. His old, bony fingers closed around one of her elbows, crushing the pretty lace trim of her dress. It caused her pain, too, but Julia bore this stalwartly, being an ordinary girl in most respects.

"There is no other medicine," said the Doctor with his steady voice. In his other hand, the hand that was not clutching Julia, he held the shiny medical knife, now dirtied quite a bit, which seemed a much more appropriate tool than it had a few moments ago. The Doctor hefted it as a gardener might heft a well-made trowel, admiring the suitability of its design. "It is only the Remedy," he said, "that is effective."

But even this, you see, this third possibility, Julia had foreseen. In the first moment she had looked at the Doctor she had thought of this. She had thought he was a ghost and he *was* a ghost, having lived another life in another time. She had thought he was a doctor and he was a doctor, too, though the power to heal had left him. Now Julia knew that she had been right about the third thing as well. He was a crazy man dying of the plague, and he was going to try to kill her.

That was the power of her very bright eyes: to see things.

The Doctor rose from his knees, and you could tell how much pain that caused him. In the final stages, every sensation is painful, even the light coming through your eyes is a cause of agony. The Doctor was not that far along, but even so Julia felt great pity for him. As he rose to his feet he looked down at Julia with a calm, professional eye. He was examining the shape of her head, she thought, and trying to decide where to open it. It was the way you looked at a lump of quartz, say, before you broke it open to make a

crystal. Perhaps it was the way a sculptor looked
at a stone. It was a special power, a gift, to see the
spirit inside things, the art, the beauty. With
her very bright eyes Julia saw the great healer the
Doctor had been and was very sorry.

"This will not take long," he said. "Unfortunately
I am afraid it will hurt very intensely, for just
a moment. I cannot make you unconscious, you see.
It will not work that way. Your consciousness
is a part of the Remedy. I do not understand it,
though I have studied it very carefully. I *am*
sorry, Julia. It is the only way."

Julia shook her head, "No," she started to tell
him, but the Doctor did not pay attention. He
was possessed now by the vision he had, the
sculpture in the stone, the crystal in the lump
of quartz. He had that gift, to see such things, even
though he did not have Julia's very bright eyes.
He led her easily and even gently to a smooth place
of lawn and he said, "Lie down now please,
Julia. It will not take long, I promise you."

Around them in the old backyard there were tiny
field orchids blooming in shades of ocher and
brown. These were hard to find even on a sunny
day, for they were such an unremarkable color.
When you saw one, you marveled at how lovely it
was, how unusual. And yet in old backyards like
this they were quite common, actually, nowadays.
There was one in easy reach of Julia, where
the Doctor laid her down among the grasses, just
coming into bloom. Julia reached out and
snapped the blossom from its stem. It had no scent,
but its coil of blooms was speckled lightly like
the egg of some ground-nesting bird. The Doctor
watched her, a young girl picking a flower, with
eyes that grew shiny with regret. His knife was dirty
with the rich brown earth. Shaking awfully, his
arm rose into the air and the medical knife, a good
and well-made tool, shiny despite the dirt, came
whickering down.

Julia raised her arm. The blade of the knife sliced through the tendons above her wrist but was deflected by one of the two thin bones of her forearm. As she had suspected, the Doctor did not have the strength to crack her skull, though he could certainly have killed her. In the middle stages you begin to lose your powers of judgment. You miscalculate such things.

"It is in you, too," Julia told the Doctor. "I can see it."

The Doctor cried out. Perhaps he was horrified by the sight of the young girl's blood, the flesh sliced away from the bone and dangling. Perhaps her words, spoken so quietly, so steadily, as a doctor might have spoken, frightened him. His old, bony fingers seemed to shrivel around the knife.

With her good hand, the hand that had plucked the orchid, Julia took the knife away from him. The Doctor gasped. He clutched his fingers where Julia had touched him with her very warm hand. The hand was warmer than ever, quite hot in fact. It held the knife lightly, as one might hold a small snake one had plucked out of a garden.

The knife began to melt. It glowed white and became soft and then gooey, like syrup. Julia shook her hand and it ran off, dripping onto the ground and spattering among the grass. When they fell, the drops became cool and shiny again.

The Doctor drew back. He was very afraid. Perhaps he thought the disease had gone quite far, further than he thought, and that he was having hallucinations.

Julia said, "There is no need to take it from someone else when you've got it inside yourself."

With the alacrity of a young girl she took the Doctor by the hand. She did not use her good arm now, the orchid arm, but the other, the arm whose tendons were sliced and whose flesh dangled loose. Blood flowed from it onto the Doctor, wetting his sleeve, soaking through. He cried

out, a great loud bellow, perhaps in horror or perhaps
because Julia's blood was very warm, indeed
quite hot, and scorched his flesh where it ran.

As she had tried to tell him before, Julia said,
"There is more than one Remedy."

Before, the Doctor hadn't listened. Now he
listened with a cringing, terrified attentiveness.
Julia's grip on his hand was very feeble, since she
had lost most of the tendons she would have
needed to tighten her fingers. But the Doctor winced
from the pressure of it. His old eyes, once weak
and dull, were honed to the sharpness of pain.

"There are other ways," Julia told him. "Other
sacrifices."

Her damaged hand grew hotter and hotter. The
Doctor's skin began to singe and then to scorch
and blacken. He cried out as though she were killing
him.

She was, in fact. For that was the power of her
very warm hands: to destroy things.

After a few moments, the Doctor fell down to
the smooth place of lawn and was consumed
by fire among the flowers and the grasses. The stench
of his disease rose into the summer air and was
lost among sweeter smells, more innocent breezes.

Julia said very gravely, as she mended her arm,
"Now you are like us. You were one of the
people who went away, but now you are different.
You are one of the people who stayed behind."

The young boy beside her in the old backyard
was very excited. His eyes grew bright, glowing
with the light of understanding.

"I'm still alive!" he exclaimed. "You didn't kill
me!"

"No," she said. "How could I?"

When her arm was mended and the boy had had
a chance to rest, they stood and ran off together
through the tall grass, each holding the other's very
warm hand. There are people who claim to have
seen them there, playing in that field together, and

there are people who claim to have spoken to
them. Throughout the dry lands, miraculous cures
are attributed to the People Who Stayed Behind
to this very day.

"The End," said Kem. "I guess."

"That's it?" said Sander. "That's all? Nothing more about
the medicine, or how they make it or anything? She just fries
him, and then he's this kid and they live happily ever after?"

Kem closed the book. "It's just a folktale," he said. "They're
a little odd, sometimes."

"Shit." Sander stood and stretched himself out, his slender
body unfolding inside the loose-fitting clothes. "Well that's
not much. But maybe it's some kind of code or something. I'll
have to think about it. Or maybe I'll show it to somebody."

"You promised to take it back to Tallheron."

"Oh, sure. I'll take it back. But I mean, he doesn't have to
have it today, does he? I'll just hang onto it for the night and
deliver it tomorrow morning. Afternoon, at the latest."

Kem gave him a hard stare, trying to get the idea across
that this was a serious thing, that he was holding Sander to
his word. "You promised something else, too," he said.

"Ah." Sander pivoted. "So I did. I promised to help you
find somebody." He smiled, as though the recollection pleased
him. "All right, then: what's her name?"

Kem waited until the beginning of the next quarter (the latter
half of the wane) which the Bell Dog observed as a rest day.
Then he took the map that Sander had drawn for him and he
pulled on a set of clean linen clothes identical to those the
younger boy had worn on the day of his visit and again a
couple of days later when he had come back, all necessary
plans having been laid. Kem supposed these loose-fitting
cream-colored pants and shirt were what messengers wore, as
galley boys wore white smocks and snipes wore blue coveralls. Sander seemed to take pleasure in fulfilling his part of
their deal: the map was meticulously drawn in four sections,
one for each of the decks involved, and the recommended
route inscribed in red. There was even a small arrow pointing

at (if Kem read the symbols correctly) an emergency stair, with a small label that said Wagging Dick Route.

"What's this?" Kem asked.

Sander smirked. "That's for if you get caught fucking her and her boyfriend comes after you with a knife and you have to go running off down the hallway with your dick wagging."

Kem scowled; but not much could dampen his excitement about this, and he recalled the night when Sander had revealed to him what appeared to be his guiding philosophy of life. *Do whatever you want to,* the boy had told him. It was like something a mother might have said. Only of course the way Sander meant it was different from the way a mother would; twisted ninety degrees, like. Anyway, there were no mothers in the Oasis. Not as far as Kem knew. It was not that kind of place. *You can get away with anything here.*

Well, Kem hoped so. He hoped that Sander was right and that for once a little bit of that wonder he used to feel, catching sight of the Oasis across the Grind—a gleaming magical place, he had imagined—would turn out not to be just a kid's foolish daydream. He hoped that there *was* something wonderful about the Oasis, at least one thing, and that Sander's map would help him find it.

In this state of mind he set out from his compartment to a hatchway leading up—the same hatchway through which he had been led in the opposite direction three months ago. To his surprise (though Sander had told him it would be like this) the hatch was not locked, and there were no sentries there.

"You don't think," Sander had said, "they've got enough goons to post one at every stupid door, do you? Don't you know how many doors there are in this place?"

Kem did not; but now he knew at least that there was nothing at all about this particular door to keep him from lifting its dogging lever and pushing it back on its well-greased hinges and stepping through.

Suddenly he was not in the engine flats anymore, and to all appearances he was not a snipe. He was not dressed like a snipe, and except for the persistent grit in his pores and beneath his nails, he did not particularly feel like one. What he felt like was a prisoner making an escape.

Two young men walked past him down the corridor, wearing clothes somewhat like Kem's but with different breast insignia. Kem smiled at them and nodded, and although he was certain that his smile was horribly unconvincing and his nod was more like the abrupt sort of jerk a puppet makes, one of the two young men smiled and nodded back and the other one ignored him. They kept on walking. Kem—though he felt like doing something else, laughing or jumping—kept on walking too.

It's true, he thought. You can get away with anything here.

But if this part was easier than he expected (step through the hatch; stroll blithely down the passageway) then the next part turned out to be harder: follow Sander's map through the maze. It was not that the map was inaccurate. Everything so far had been just where it ought to have been. But following a map was something Kem had never done—there had been no need for maps on the Grind; there were landmarks and steering directions and certain tricks to do with stars, but nothing drawn out on paper—and it was a hard thing to get used to. It seemed easy enough when you looked at the clean lines and symbols, but another thing altogether when you were in the midst of pipes and ducts and partitions, certain things painted one color and other things another, signs everywhere directing you someplace or warning you away, hallways branching off invitingly in directions Kem was not (he hoped) supposed to follow, and it always seemed that the proper route, when he found it, did not look at all the way he had envisioned it, sitting on his mattress studying the map by a reading light.

The place where he had met Davina was marked GIRLS' BERTHING, and Sander had embellished that with a crude line drawing. When Kem approached it, however, he found that the layout of the deck did not correspond to the markings on Sander's map—nor for that matter to his own memory of the long, curving hallways where he had come that morning with the Bell Dog. The hallways here were short and they ended in large doors bearing signs that said REC DEPT PERSONNEL ONLY. There were two obvious possibilities, either that Sander had made an honest mistake—a deck or flight of stairs having been accidentally omitted, for example—or else that he had deliberately drawn a misleading map for reasons Kem could not guess. The boy was not given to joking. If anything, he was more serious than you would expect of someone his age. Too serious. Therefore if this was a deliberate thing then some further thing, some plan or trap, was involved.

Kem didn't have much time to hang around and figure out what to do. Up the hall behind him came half a dozen older guys, carrying large trays loaded with food. Kem recognized those trays. They were the kind of thing you busted your ass getting together on short notice if you worked down in the galley, assortments of dried meat and cheeses, pitchers of wine and fruits that somebody picked and sent down on dumbwaiters from bushes that grew in hydroponic gardens on some deck far above, in the sunlight. The galley boys were never told whom the trays were for or where they were being sent; the only thing you knew was that a few hours later the trays would come back, sometimes picked clean and other times barely touched. If there was any wine left the bigger boys would drink themselves into a sloppy state and occasionally meet with some accident, the galley not being a very safe place under such circumstances. Now Kem stood watching these older guys hustling up the hall with these trays and what he felt was not so much alarm as curiosity.

"Hey," one of the older guys said. "Get that door there, would you?"

Kem was at first not sure that the guy was speaking to him, but as they came closer and he could see the impatient looks on their faces, he hurried to beat them to the door. It opened wide with a light shove, then the half-dozen guys got there and basically blew past him without saying thanks or excuse me or have a grape, asshole.

Kem hardly noticed. What he noticed instead was the white hot sun that flared into the hall when the door was opened, and only in retrospect, as the door swung back on its springs, did he have any attention left over for the amazing sight that had lain beyond it.

It was a courtyard. Kem retained an impression of high walls washed in some pale color, light green or blue, with trellises covered with blooming vines, jasmine and passion fruit and bougainvillea, and between them an open space maybe thirty strides wide. The courtyard was square, it looked like, and there were chairs and tables scattered around it, and in the center was a pool or possibly a fountain. Of all the things he had seen in those couple of seconds, the one that stayed with him most vividly was the diamond flash of sunlight on the ripples of dark water. The sky was hidden by the high walls but a piece of it seemed to have been caught in that little pool, turning the water a cool and bottomless blue.

Kem drew his breath. He was torn between confusion over what he should do next and excitement over what he had seen. So great was his agitation that it came as a surprise to him to realize that for the last couple of minutes the Oasis had begun slowing down, braking to a halt. In another minute it had stopped completely. He felt once more, now with an engineer's sensitivity, the transfer of titanic energies from the drive shafts into the flywheels. He heard the pneumatic shocks being bled off like exhausted giants exhaling; in his mind he could see catclaw and cholla cactus and anything else not fastened securely to the earth being blown like bits of trash away from the air vents. With a tremor so vast that it seemed to rise from the earth itself, the Oasis settled down.

Kem figured there were two ways to go from here: he could step through that door, into that shining courtyard, or he could go back the way he came from. He thought about the way the older guys had ignored him as they blew past, as though he were unworthy of their interest or notice, except by way of kicking a door open, and that made the choice easier. If he were of no interest to anyone then he had nothing to worry about, did he?

The courtyard was empty except for the tables and chairs, half a dozen trays piled high with food, and the central fountain. The sun beat down from the oblique angle of late morning, throwing about half the deck area of the courtyard, including the place where Kem stood, into a shadow that was dark only by contrast with the almost unbelievable brightness of the other side. Around the fountain, fine sprays of water danced in an unpredictable rhythm that was close to randomness. Smells of jasmine, hot metal, and chlorinated water crowded the air. It had been a long time, weeks or months, since Kem had been out in the sun, and the Oasis had been moving south, or southeast, all that time, and confronted with the result of those two things in tandem he could barely hold his eyes open. Wherever this was, this piece of earth the Oasis had come to, it was much brighter and hotter here than on the Grind, especially considering that it was Long Nights Moon, the season still quaintly known by some people as winter. To protect the trays of food, the guys had draped little white cloths over them. The chairs and tables were white, too. All the surfaces where the sun fell were so intensely alight that they seemed to float insubstantially.

Kem felt himself starting to sweat, perhaps as much from nervousness and a kind of giddy, vertiginous feeling as from the heat itself. It was awfully hot, though. In his hand, the map drooped, soggy from his sweat.

After a little while Kem realized that he was no longer alone, that people were entering the courtyard on the opposite side, the sunny side, through a pair of doors that had opened on silent hinges. They seemed to be speaking among themselves, six or seven of them, some still hanging back in the shadow of the door; there was enough ambient noise here—as there always was in the Oasis, everywhere—that he couldn't hear what they were saying, only a susurration of voices. He watched them react as he had done to the startling brightness and the heat. They blinked, they adjusted their hats and collars so that their faces were nearly invisible. Because of these distractions, probably, the newcomers did not notice Kem right away, and he had a brief opportunity to study them.

He took them to be crew members of a low-ranking sort. They wore pale uniforms of a pastel shade washed nearly white by the sun, with broad-brimmed hats and gleaming epaulets that might have been silver or gold. Though he had only the most general impression of their build and facial features under all that protective clothing, Kem got the feeling that these crew members weren't very big or very old. He wondered if, with their epaulets and all, they might be some sort of cadets, privileged kids who got to hand out nibbling iced fruit in the sunshine while the likes of Kem sweated in the oily confines of the engine flats. On the other hand it was conceivable that they had just wandered in here the same way that Kem had: there was something reserved or tentative about the way they hung back near the doorway, seeming to confer among themselves, and for all Kem knew they might be looking over at him wondering what kind of big shot he was, standing there as if he owned the place.

They had noticed him now. One or two, then suddenly all of them, turned to look in his direction. Some turned back away as soon as they caught his eye, but a couple kept staring. Kem wondered what the hell he was doing, hanging around here like this, a stupid snipe, badly out of place amid this sunny splendor. Then one of the newcomers broke away from the rest and began walking across the courtyard, not exactly in Kem's direction but coming closer, moving among the tables around the fountain. This person paused to lift one of the trays of food and to hoist it like a bundle of clothes or something onto a shoulder, then proceeded with it now distinctly right toward where Kem was standing. He didn't even have time to get scared. The distance across the courtyard seemed to contract as the figure, bent slightly under the tray, came closer in long no-nonsense strides. Then the other person paused, looking straight at Kem, and it was Davina.

"Hello," she said. Her features blurred into focus from the shadow of her hat; her expression was quizzical. "I thought it might be you." She brought the tray down from her shoulder and set it on a table in front of him. "They shouldn't leave this stuff out in the sun like that. Are you supposed to be here?"

The question came unexpectedly, as Davina herself had, out of context. And yet it was an obvious question, maybe the only question that really made sense, just as Davina was herself the only person that Kem had really expected to see and now he was face-to-face with her and only the circumstances made it odd or surprising. He folded the map over once, as an afterthought.

"I don't know," he said. "Probably not I guess. But it was a rest day and I wanted . . ." The words were right there, in his mouth practically, before he realized it. *I wanted to see you.*

What if he had said them, right then, right out loud? What if he had told her, *I've been thinking about you ever since we met, not just the other day but that first time, way back in the fall?*

He wasn't going to find out. Not now, at least. Through the door behind him, the door through which he himself had entered, a group of people emerged, talking loudly, then another group, three or four in each, and the people began spreading themselves out across the courtyard. The door was still open and there were still more people coming through, and all of a sudden the courtyard, which had seemed so large a couple of minutes ago when it was empty, now seemed very small and densely crowded as though the walls were drawing tight and forcing everyone together. There was a slight tug on Kem's sleeve and Davina had moved around beside him, was motioning him toward the vine-covered wall.

"If you just kind of keep back," she murmured, "nobody will pay attention to you. I've got to go to work but I'll come over in a while and maybe we can talk or something later."

She spoke in a rapid and expressionless blur of words which Kem understood was probably intended to prevent anyone from overhearing but which also had the effect of making it impossible to place any significance on those two sentences. Nothing else was needed to amplify his sense of dislocation. Davina slid smoothly away from him, into the crowd, and her place was taken by people mostly about the age of Kem's father, showily dressed in clothes that were in varying degrees impractical, given the singular remorselessness of the sun: fabrics too heavy and colors too saturated, right through the spectrum from a deep, purplish blue to a bloody crimson all the way around to a yellow that was filled with as much orange as it could hold without melting and flowing like saffron in ghee. Many of them—mostly but not exclusively the women—wore necklaces and headbands and earrings and other ornaments in such profusion that it gave you a weighted-down feeling just to look at them. They all seemed to talk loudly at the same time to everyone else at once, as though they all knew each other too well (which was not unlikely, Kem thought, given the closed or circular nature of the Oasis) to be really interested in what anyone else was saying; but it seemed to Kem also that they were looking past one another, directing their comments to a point just beyond the next person's shoulder, as if there were someone else they were hoping to see or planning to meet here, and perhaps that was a feature of this life, too: the constant search for the next source of entertainment.

What Davina had said was true—if you just stood back in the shadows, nobody would pay much attention to you. Kem had backed himself up until his shoulders were buried in bougainvillea, and he felt well concealed there. Now and then someone's gaze fell upon him—those roaming eyes, weirdly dispassionate, always searching or wondering—but the eyes never stayed for very long and when they turned away, especially if they had met for an instant with Kem's own, it seemed to him that they bore a very slight trace of disappointment or even disdain. It was as though those eyes were detached from the bodies they belonged to—from the shoulders that were squarely, confidently set and the mouths that animatedly spoke and the hands that demonstrated, pointed, waved. The eyes were like wanderers out of some fable, ever moving, asking the same question again and again.

Beside him someone had come to stand wearing a wide-brimmed hat and a pastel uniform. At first Kem thought it was Davina, and in relief he turned to speak to her before he realized it was somebody else, another girl. She did not look at Kem right away but just stood next to him scanning the crowd.

"You're Kem, right?" she asked suddenly, tilting her head. She was about his age and his height, and he thought she was pretty in a way that was hard to be precise about. Not as pretty as Davina. Her hair was blond and her face was slightly pink from the sun. He must have been looking at her in a funny way, because the girl smiled and said, "I saw you that other day, in the hall? You were there to work on the wiring."

"Oh. Hi," Kem said weakly. He did not remember this girl at all, which meant probably nothing except that his mind had been on Davina. But this made it easier to feel relaxed with her and easier to talk. He said, "Is this your job? I mean, are you all here to serve food or something?"

The girl smiled at him again and Kem supposed he was not being terrifically articulate. She didn't seem to mind, though. "We do a lot of stuff," she said. "They send us all over the place. Mostly I think we're just here to make them feel at home. You know—most of these people were pretty rich, where they came from, and they're used to having servants and things like that. Really we don't do much but stand around and smile at them."

Kem nodded. "So, um, is this a party or something?"

"A reception," the girl said. She spoke the word with precision, as though she were not answering his question but correcting him, informing him of something. Kem did not understand this; but then the girl grew quiet and nodded in a way that directed his attention toward the middle of the courtyard, as though this too were part of what she was informing him of.

There was a general movement and a murmur spreading among the crowd. A new group of guests was making its way toward the fountain and it seemed to Kem that everyone else was pretty anxious to let them through, if only in order to get a better look at them. He shifted this way and that, rising up on his toes and trying to find a good vantage, but he couldn't see much. He caught sight of someone that he thought was Davina, way on the other side of the courtyard, and as he looked at her he thought that she was looking back. He smiled. Davina—if it was she—did not respond, as far as he could tell. Kem started to raise his hand, to wave at her.

Suddenly the man was between them: a tall man, dressed in pure white, his hair thick and long and golden like a leonine crown. It was the same one who had ridden out that night on the huge stallion. The crowd fell silent, all at the same instant; it was as though in one moment the man had not been among them and the next moment, magically, he was, and now there was nothing else anybody wanted to look at. Perhaps this man was what those restless eyes had been searching for.

For a number of months now, since Kem had first seen him, there had been a name that he had linked with this man in his mind, but he still did not know for sure that this was Captain Hand. Now perhaps it was time to find out. He

turned to the girl beside him. Something about her expression—
fascinated, even rapt—made him hesitate to speak, and anyway the silence in the courtyard had become so brittle that a
single whisper would have shattered it.

The man—the Captain, or whoever he was—did not need
to say anything or do anything, in particular, to hold these
people's attention. Indeed, he did nothing much at all; just
stood fairly still, only looking around and smiling now and
then, but even the smile was a quiet one, and Kem got the
idea that the Captain (he decided to think of him as that,
provisionally) was himself waiting for someone or something.

It was a bit of an anticlimax, when it happened. The
climax had been the appearance of the Captain, and now
there was nothing but a slender and nicely attired but
otherwise unremarkable man who joined the Captain beside
the fountain. The Captain laid a hand upon this man's shoulder: a hale-fellow-well-met kind of gesture, as though assuring
him of his place among the circle of guests. Then, drawing
the newcomer close to him, he spoke to the crowd at large:

"Friends, I would like you all to meet Mr Newcastle, who
has been so good as to join us."

There was an immediate and hearty response from the
crowd, a clapping of hands and a disorganized mumble that
Kem took to be the sound of everybody saying "Welcome" or
something of that sort all at once.

The Captain went on: "Now please go right back to what
you were doing, and I hope all of you will have an opportunity to welcome Mr Newcastle in person before you go."

Then, with one last quiet smile, the Captain plunged back
into the crowd, not vanishing suddenly this time but gradually
blending into the people around him, who seemed to press
inward and absorb him. The feeling of the reception changed
then: that sense of anticipation was gone, and the richly
dressed men and women broke into smaller groups, found
seats around the tables, and began devouring the food and
drink laid out for them. The sounds of their talking were
subdued; once again Kem could hear the throb and grind of
machinery, the whirring of fans, the rumble—so deep as to
be mostly visceral—of the energy-storing flywheels.

The girl who had stood beside him was gone. Kem looked

around for Davina, and after a moment he spotted her, standing across the courtyard with a pitcher of wine in one hand and a cobalt goblet in the other. He admired the grace and the efficiency of her movements. Even her smile, as she held out the newly filled goblet to a waiting hand, was a miracle of easeful economy. She let go of the goblet and turned with the pitcher toward Kem, meeting his eyes across the distance as though she had been perfectly aware of him, of his attention, all along. She made a very slight motion with her arm, gesturing to one of the doors. Then she turned away, receiving another goblet, dispensing more wine, and Kem thought—or more precisely hoped—that what she had meant was that he should go to that door and wait for her there.

His path across the courtyard brought him within a couple of strides of the table at which the Captain—it must have been the Captain, truly—had seated himself. Kem was practically on top of the man before he recognized him.

There was something odd: the Captain was not nearly such a distinctive or arresting figure now, though he was demonstrably the same man who had caused the assembled crowd to catch its breath only minutes ago. It was as though he had somehow turned himself down, as one might crank down the valve that fed fuel to an engine.

And then there was a second surprise, which came just as Kem was recovering his balance. His eyes slid past the Captain and along the table and what interrupted them was a funny sort of detail—a part of someone's arm, barely more than a patch of earth-brown skin, that in some way looked familiar. It was odd to think that you could recognize someone's skin, but Kem did not have much time to reflect upon that before he heard a voice speaking his name, saying hello to him. His eyes followed the forearm up and all the pieces fell into place; it was Sander's friend, Delan.

Delan was sitting next to the Captain at the table, and the newcomer, Mr Newcastle, was sitting across from them. With Delan's greeting they had all turned to look up at Kem, and now they were sitting there waiting for Kem to say something back and it felt as though the earth itself had stopped.

Delan spoke again, merrily, dispelling the unease of the moment.

"Kem," he said, "perhaps you have not met Captain Hand."

"No," said the Captain. But he did not extend his arm or turn all the way around, only settled his eyes into Kem's own, long enough and hard enough to be uncomfortable. Then he looked away, and Kem felt as though the breath had been kicked out of him. He moved past the table feeling dizzy and not looking back. Davina was waiting for him at the door, saying something that he did not respond to. He felt her take his hand.

"This way," she said; he heard that. Then they were in a hallway, leaving the courtyard. The light was dim and the hallway curved leftward, moonwise. "This way," Davina said again. Her voice seemed to reverberate in his awareness, though it may have been the acoustics of the hall. *This way. This . . .*

Kem felt as though he were waking from a dream or falling into one, and in both places—the dream and the place he was waking to—there was a girl beside him holding his hand

he was being drawn

inexorably

inward.

TALL SKIES

"Because you looked so innocent," the naked girl told him. "And because you were cute. And because you were kind of sweet, that day. You know, down in the cargo hold."

This was the answer to a question, Kem's question, but now that he heard it he was not glad to have asked. Probably many questions, probably most questions or all questions were exactly like that. It was better not to know, probably. It was better to live like a snipe, guessing and reasoning but not knowing for sure. Because when you knew something for sure it diminished the thing somehow, as though the mystery that had once surrounded it was like a shadow and without the shadow the thing seemed flat.

Now he knew why Davina had been interested in him and why she had brought him back here to her room, a cubicle that she shared with a girl named (she said) Blueberry, who Kem guessed might be that pale girl he had talked with in the courtyard.

Now he knew why she had taken him into her room and

run her fingers down his neck and kissed him and slipped easily, as though it were only an afterthought, out of her clothes. It was because he looked so innocent, and he was cute, and he had been kind of sweet, one day.

Well, what had he thought? What had made him think that the weird feeling he had when he was around her—an intimation of something hugely important, which made him think of her as somehow unique and of the two of them as separate from the world around them—would be exactly how she felt about him? That had been stupid, and it had been even stupider to ask.

But because he had asked, he now understood that as far as Davina was concerned, he was something like an interesting diversion. His innocence must strike her as a pleasant change in routine.

"Don't worry," she had told him, when she had slipped out of her clothes and then had begun to unbutton Kem's shirt, pressing herself down against his thigh so that he could feel the heat of her crotch through the thin fabric; and Kem had looked around toward the door because they were just standing in the small empty space in the middle of the room, next to the bunk bed. They had barely come through that door and he wasn't even sure which bed was Davina's.

"Don't worry," she had said. "Blueberry and I have a deal worked out. We never interrupt each other when one of us is in here with a boy."

She ran her hands along his bare, skinny chest. Her fingers kept moving far down enough to get tangled in his pubic hair; then she unclasped his pants without looking and with considerably less effort than it had taken Kem himself to do so, the first time he had tried them on. He supposed she must have dealt with this kind of clothing more often than he had.

How he had felt, standing there with all these new sensations piling up on top of him—unfamiliar room, naked girl, pants caught down around his knees—how he had felt then was immeasurably embarrassed. He looked away, his eyes passing across a tiny desk and onto the bed and down the smooth cotton sheets, and he was ashamed. He knew he could not do what he thought he wanted to do more than anything. Davina's hand was stroking his back and she moved it casually around to touch his penis, which was shriveled up as though in chagrin.

"Aw," she said.

But she said this not in disappointment but with a playful tone in her voice, like make-believe sympathy. The poor little thing. She pressed Kem lightly so that he sat down on the lower bunk. Then she pulled his pants the rest of the way off, tugged the sheet down, and slid in tightly against him. She drew the sheet up to their necks.

"I'm sorry," she said. "Don't you want to, I mean . . . be here?"

Kem said, "Yes," and then "Yes, I did," and then he propped his head up on his elbow and looked her in the face and said, "Why did you want me to come here, anyway?"

That had been the question.

Later as he walked down murky corridors glancing almost indifferently at Sander's map (though he found that he remembered the route pretty well) he thought that maybe *innocent* had not been exactly the right word for what he had been, or that maybe that had been putting it rather kindly. Maybe what he had been was ignorant, nothing more. Surely it had been ignorant of him to think that some kind of fairy-tale, boy-meets-girl romance was going to happen someplace like the Oasis, with someone like Davina. But more than that, it had been ignorant even to want such a thing. It had been a serious misunderstanding. He saw that now.

He saw now that the whole idea of sex that he had had all his life was a little bit off; it was twisted by ninety degrees or so, like so many other ideas he had had, from the real situation. It was like that saying of Sander's—*do whatever you want to*—and how your mother might have said that but you would not have understood it correctly when you were a child. Sex was like that. You thought it was going to be a certain way—thrilling, profound, satisfying, whatever—and it *was* those things, but not in exactly the way you had thought. There were no flowers or music or flashing lights or whatever you expected. There were sounds and smells and other sensations, however, and they seemed to cling still to Kem as he walked down the hallway. The memory of all that, the sense of carrying it away with him, lightened his step and made him feel tough and wise and invulnerable.

What had happened was this. What had happened, after Kem asked his question and Davina gave her answer, was that he had gotten somewhat angry. It might have been the word *cute.* But whatever it was, he had felt different all of a sudden; he had understood in some new way that here he was, cute or not, in bed with all his clothes off beside a girl he thought was beautiful, with all her clothes off too, and he was not just going to lie here and be talked about like he was some little kid. He was going to fuck this girl and then even if he hadn't done it very well or very expertly what the hell, he would have done it anyway and then he could walk away and maybe next time, with the next girl, he would know what he was doing.

So he reached over and he had put his arm around Davina, around her arm and her shoulder and her bare smooth back, and he had become aware for the first time of how really great it felt to have her breasts pressed against him, her legs twined with his like fingers, boy-girl-boy-girl. And he had rubbed his hand between her thighs, having no idea really what he was doing, but this had not seemed to matter because when the moment came Davina had brought him into position and with the first blind thrust he was into her, and before he had time to think about it any further—as though a train had come up behind him and by the time he heard it roaring down on him it had knocked him flat—he started coming from somewhere deep inside, and when he was finished he felt like he had exploded. The orgasm had left him inside out. It was as though he were living inside a new skin, and the new skin was his own stretched-out heart.

Now he was walking down the hall feeling like neither a boy nor a man nor anything in between but something different, a new type of being. His clothes were disarranged and he wore them that way happily, like a badge. He had just done what more than anything he had wanted to do, he had gotten away with something big, and he felt sure that he was only getting started, that there was a lot more to come, and that it was going to be incredible.

That night he slept badly. The Oasis was moving again but its rhythm had changed. Something about the way the great engines strained at their task, as though the power were being sucked from them as fast as it came shuttling down from the generators, suggested that something was different, the terrain below irregular or a hard blow coming broadside-on. Something. From down here, as always, it was difficult to tell. Still, Kem lay flat on his mattress with his limbs spread out, enjoying the feel of those limbs more than he usually did, not minding too much his inability to sleep and just listening to those engines, feeling the throb they made.

It may have been his imagination, but it seemed to him after a while that the Oasis might be descending, making its ponderous way down a grade in the terrain. You could not feel the grade directly—a couple of degrees were hard to discern—but the way things felt, the way they sounded, metal joints creaking and couplings straining and steering cables snapping more frequently than before, all made Kem guess and after a while believe that they were edging down some gradual, inconceivably long slope. The strain he sensed in the sinews of the craft was not from pushing extra hard but from trying to hold things together, to keep the great machine intact and all its systems meshing normally despite the fact that the force-equations had changed. The stress on the structural members was coming from different directions; the parts of the huge machine now existed in an altered relationship to one another as the craft in its entirety had altered its relation with the earth.

The more Kem thought about this the more excited he became, not exactly at the change itself but at the way he was able to perceive it, the way he felt what was happening right through his spine and understood it the way he understood his own bones. He was looking forward to talking to the Bell Dog, telling him how he felt and seeing what (if anything) the Bell Dog had to say. He had an idea that the Bell Dog felt and thought in very much the same way: directly, bodily, rather than through measurement or calculation.

But when he finally got to sleep—what with the great happenings of the day—he slept soundly right through breakfast and through morning assignments. He would not be seeing the Bell Dog after all.

Oversleeping was not the end of the world. What happened when you overslept was that a mark was entered beside your name in the billet roster and you were automatically rolled over into the night crew. You would have to work the whole shift (which might go on till daybreak or might not, depending) then be back at morning assignments and if you weren't, you found yourself on the night crew on a permanent basis. Somebody had to be. If you screwed up on the night crew Kem had no idea what happened, since it seemed from there, there was noplace lower you could go. The guys who got rolled out of day work more or less disappeared, as far as the other snipes were concerned. Sometimes you would see them around and sometimes not.

Aside from the fact that it lasted about twice as long as the day shift, working at night was not without its advantages. For one thing, you often got to go abovedecks, where snipes were barred during the day, out into the moonlight and the desert breezes. There were always little maintenance chores to perform—parted seams to weld back together, lights to replace, waterlines to unclog—and generally once you were assigned to one of these tasks you were pretty much on your own. The chief of the night crew was a wiry middle-aged guy with the name of Mole. Kem supposed it was a nickname. Mole was somewhat feared and generally avoided around the mess deck, though the worst that Kem could really see in him was that he was irritable. He was also extraordinarily jumpy, which seemed like it might be an occupational hazard, considering the large number of ways you could get killed without putting yourself out about it in the dark. He walked around with a mug of yerba buena tea which he mistakenly understood to be a calmative. When he caught you doing anything out of line, he beat some sense into you, and if this was not effective then your case slid into that dark region beyond Kem's knowledge. So all in all, a shift with the night crew was not the end of the world.

The problem was, how to kill the time before the shift started. Kem felt what he supposed was a common masculine desire to boast about his adventure with Davina, but he couldn't think of anyone to boast to. He thought about this while getting himself together—changing into the same shirt and pants he had worn yesterday—when he looked up to see Sander. The boy seemed to have materialized at the entrance to his compart-

ment. He did not speak but leaned in the doorway as he had
leaned that other day—lightly, careful not to soil his uniform.
Kem wasn't sure exactly how long he had been there, but it was
that way with Sander: you looked up and there he was.

"So," Sander said. His amber eyes were cool. "Got thrown
onto the night shift, eh?"

Kem shook his head at the boy's bizarre omniscience.

Sander gave him a narrow smile. "I deliver the duty rosters,"
he explained, "to the chief engineer. I saw your name."

"Ah." Kem was relieved. "So you've seen the chief engineer? I mean, personally?"

"All the time."

Kem did not ask more. He supposed that you had to allow
Sander his little advantages.

"So." —This must have been Sander's way of inviting Kem
to talk; though now that he had an audience, Kem found
perversely that he was no longer so eager to tell his story, or
maybe it was just hard to know how to get started.

"Your map was screwed up," he said. "I got lost there for a
while and wandered into some kind of reception."

Sander cocked an eye. It was hard to tell—no, it was
impossible—whether the map being screwed up was news to
him. Something seemed to be.

"You were there?" he said. "The whole time?"

"At the reception, you mean?" Kem shrugged. "I guess. It
was just this bunch of people in fancy clothes and there was
this new guy, Newcastle. I mean new to the Oasis, apparently.
Captain Hand was there, he introduced him." Kem paused,
but Sander did not react. "And I saw your friend Delan."

Sander narrowed his eyes. "Delan told me he went," he
said. "He didn't tell me he saw you, though."

"Well, he saw me."

Sander pressed his lips together. "You must have left," he
said, as though he were sounding Kem out about something,
"by the time it happened." He looked into Kem's eyes before
going on. "One of the ladies there kind of had too much to
drink, I guess. She was just leaning around the fountain and
then all of a sudden she keeled over and by the time Hand
got to her, she was dead."

"Dead?" Kem blinked. It was hard to conceive.

"Hey," said Sander, shrugging in what Kem supposed was meant to be a worldly manner. "It happens."

"It does?"

"Sure. With the Residents. They're pretty unstable, you know. I mean it's just a treatment, right? They're still sick. They can pretty much just—*phht*, anytime."

"You mean those people," Kem said, trying to get this straight, "all those people at the party, they were Residents? They all had the crying?"

"Not all of them. Delan was there. The Captain. And usually some of the mates show up. I mean, hey—it's a party."

Kem was uncomfortable, almost queasy. He remembered the way he had felt in the midst of that odd throng of people, and he remembered the way their eyes had not seemed quite right, not quite connected to the rest of them, and he thought that maybe that made more sense now. He thought too about the day he had met with Tallheron in the cluttered library, the way the old man had not been able to read for himself, had scarcely been able to see.

"Wait a minute," said Kem. "What about Tallheron, where was he? I mean, if all the Residents were there. I would have noticed him."

"I didn't say they were all there. Anyway..." Sander shrugged lightly, tossing his head, and Kem was pretty sure what that gesture was supposed to mean.

"You were supposed to give him his book back," he said tersely. "Didn't you see him then? You promised you would."

Sander sniffed. "I promised that I'd *take* it back. Not that I'd put it in his hands." He stuck his nose up. "I left it outside his door."

Kem stared back angrily. Then he thought of Tallheron and grew sad. This was not, none of it, what he had imagined he and Sander were going to talk about. But there you had it. It was part of the Oasis and there was no escape, no haven.

"So," said Sander, "anyway, how'd the other thing go? Did you get your pole greased, or what?"

Kem was surprised to feel himself growing hot, possibly blushing. He supposed that Sander would want to hear all the details. And although a short time ago he had been very much in the mood for relating them, now he was not. He felt

at this moment that the whole thing was between himself and
Davina and it ought to stay that way.

But that was just his ignorance again, right? That was a
kid-idea, the kind of thinking he had left behind him—back in
the place where he had left the idea of Davina that he had once
had. Who she was, what there might be between the two of
them. He nodded thoughtfully and he looked at Sander and he
said, "Yeah. Yeah, I did." And he added, "It was great."

He was prepared to say more, to elaborate at any length and
to exaggerate or even flat-out lie, as the occasion called for. But
Sander's reaction was not what he was expecting and he stopped.

The boy was looking down at the deck. He seemed to be
thinking about something, musing, reflecting; Kem had even
less idea than usual what could be going on in his friend's
mind. He changed tack so far as to say:

"It worked out just like you said it would. You really *can*
get away with anything here." Which although perfectly
sincere came out sounding idiotic and hollow.

Sander spoke without looking up. "Yeah, well that's cool,"
he said. "It's cool."

He did look up then and Kem was surprised at the change
in his friend's expression. Kem had supposed that Sander
would take at least an ordinary prurient interest in what had
happened yesterday with Davina, but what he saw instead in
Sander's face was something like indifference but not exactly
that. There might have been a bit of envy there or a bit of
resentment. Kem would have to think about that later; in the
meantime he tried to think of something to say, but Sander
thought of something first.

"Just remember, though," the boy told him, "it isn't going
to be the way you think. It never is. Nothing is the way you
think it's going to be here, so you might as well get used to it."

And with that—as though he intended his actions to bear
out his words—Sander turned away from Kem and pushed
himself off the bulkhead. For several seconds, as the boy
made his way over the metal crosshatching, Kem could see
his back, the loose-fitting uniform, the fair hair that was
growing long and bounced off the boy's narrow shoulders.
Then Sander was gone and Kem felt—as he had felt all along,
but in a new way now—alone.

• • •

Up on the trading deck where market stalls stood empty and shuttered, and olive trees gathered in loose formation around a central wading pool, Kem knelt beside an irrigation runnel watching the melted face of Long Nights Moon, near the end of its wane, bobbing in the water. He reflected, not for the first time, that there was a certain circularity here. For this was where his sisters had come on those first few mornings, after he had been signed on to the galley crew, traded by his father for a scavenged motor and a set of tools. He tried to remember how he had felt then. Not about the trade, his sudden turn of fate—it had simply seemed to him as though his life were about to end. But about the other things. The Oasis, mostly. This deck, the bustling market, where wagon people came to barter with the agents and procurers and storekeepers of the craft—people whom now Kem had come to regard simply as fellow members of the crew, people like himself who had one day as the euphemism went "signed on" and who had been trained in one or another specialty. The haggling tended to be surprisingly well balanced, for though the wagon people were desperate they were also poor, there was little they could offer beyond the few treasures they kept for times of need, for example, their children. And the traders of the Oasis, though skilled, were for the most part indifferent. They knew their place in life and they knew that no minor triumph over a family of vagabonds was going to advance it. Kem supposed that an engine and a set of tools had not been a bad deal for an elder son who would have left the wagon in a year or two anyway. Kem was not very tall and had no particular talents, and the tools had been of a very high grade.

He still winced, though, at the memory of the little girls, the gravity with which they stared into the pool, where every day at sunset a pump would be turned on (Kem knew the snipe whose job it was to do this) and a cool- and clear-looking column of water would play three heads or so above the deck, splashing people nearby and making the children squeal. You could see what an illusion that was, clear and cool, for the water in the runnel was pumped up from the gray-water tanks behind the galley, and although it had lost most of its unpleasant smell it would still be unsafe to drink and very warm besides, having trickled from tank to tank in the sunshine.

His sisters, of course, had loved this water and had taken their places here every evening by the fountain. There had been other wagon children too, a little pack of them, but no children from the Oasis. Children lived here, though. Kem had seen them since that day, kids as young as five or six who had been traded by families even more desperate than his own. Kem wondered where they lived and what would become of them. They could be traded away again, of course. There were places in the desert where children were scarce and fetched a high price, almost any price you could name. But perhaps the children remained here—at least some of them, the brightest or strongest or most beautiful—to be raised as true citizens of the Oasis. After a while, he supposed, for a kid especially, the Oasis would come to seem perfectly normal; the world that moved would come to be the real world, and the world that did not move, that only lay and suffered and endured, torn by the treads of the landcraft, would be strange and hard to believe in.

Kem wondered if Sander had been one of those kids. A child of the Oasis. No family, none of the usual strictures or urgings or aspirations of family life. *Nothing is the way you think it's going to be here*. That was what Sander had said—another of those sweeping remarks he was so full of. Kem thought that like the others, this statement could be applied to a number of things. To the reception, for instance, where most of the celebrants had been victims of the crying. To Sander himself, who looked like such a kid, like someone's younger brother, but who was really this worldly-wise and unscrupulous little philosopher. And to Davina, of course. But Kem did not just now want to think about Davina.

He thought instead—and the thought was not unconnected— of the two little girls, his sisters, as he had seen them last, or at least the final image of them which he had chosen to preserve. They were there at the pool, laughing and scrinching their faces up as the water blew over them, bending down to splash their hands in it. The water itself fit Sander's principle to a *T*, but that is not what Kem found most striking about this memory. What it was, was something that he had not even noticed at the time. But he saw it now—it was a sight so familiar that you got used to it and quit seeing it after a while; but now Kem was seeing it again.

Behind the girls, across the trading deck and beneath the shadows of the olive trees, a small group of men used to gather. They would show up about the same time Kem did, the hour when the fountain was turned on and the kids would come from the wagons. There they stood, among the trees, smoking clove cigarettes, talking quietly among themselves. Their talk did not, however, seem to be the main attraction; nor did the fountain nor the sounds of the market nor the faint breeze that sometimes stirred the evening air.

As Kem remembered them now, he remembered these men staring out into the brighter space in the center of the deck, where penumbral sun caught the tiny flecks of water that rose in the air and filled them with orange light, as though for an instant once again something was not the way it seemed to be, and these droplets of water appeared to be on fire. That was the light, that fiery orange, cooled and diffused by the spray, that filled the faces of the children playing there, lit up their smiles, made their delicate cheeks and their necks and their naked arms, wet from the pool, seem to glow, to radiate a pure inner light.

But the light in the eyes of those men had not been the same. And as he thought about that now and heard once more the sounds of the trading deck, the occasional cry of some poor wagon driver that he had been cheated, he had been robbed, Kem was glad his sisters were far away, away from the Oasis, and he hoped that if he ever saw them again it would not be here.

Toward dawn the chief of night crew came around to see what Kem was up to and found him poking around in the fountain. He must have taken this for a good sign—cleaning out the intake filters or some such thing—because he came over and stood next to Kem and pulled out a jay. Mole, Kem thought; he watched how the man squinted his eyes in the light of the match. Mole seemed to be in the mood for talk. "Got that sucker all reamed out, huh?" he said, indicating the fountain,

which he presumed Kem to have cleaned. "Guess they'll be
firing that thing up soon."

"Oh yeah?"

Mole offered him a hit on the jay, which Kem waved away.
Then for no reason Kem changed his mind and said, "Okay,
thanks." The jay was laced with something spicy and something cool, and it made the back of his throat tingle.

"Yeah," Mole said. He spoke in such a way as to hold the
smoke in. "Be stopping soon. Do some trading then. Wheel
and deal." He exhaled. "Big shit, too—not just your puny
little wagon crap."

Kem was mildly curious about this and decided he would
not take exception to the remark about wagon crap, a category to which he supposed he himself once belonged. No
longer, though. "So what's up?" he said, trying to sound cool
about it. "Where's this big stuff coming from?"

Mole had just taken another lungful and he choked something out that sounded like right hands or white bands or god
knows what. Kem started to say pardon me but Mole turned
to him bleary-eyed and just handed the remains of the jay
over to him. Then he exhaled, blasting smoke into Kem's face
that smelled of sour wet breath.

"I ought to quit smoking that shit," allowed Mole, "but I
can't think straight without it. The Bright Land," he added,
with enough emphasis to make sure it came out loud and
clear this time.

"Ah," said Kem. He took a hit on the jay, so saturated now
with resins that it practically choked him. The earlier hit
must have been having its effect, because Mole's words
seemed to reverberate in his mind; in fact he could see them
there, written out, with a kind of incandescent brilliance and
smoke all around them, like something spelled in fireworks.
The Bright Land.

It was one of those places you heard about. You heard of
the crumbled cities and the Carbon Bank Forest and the salt
barrens and you heard about the Bright Land in the same
loose, uninformed kind of way. You didn't hear anything
detailed or wholly believable; you never, for example, heard
anyone claim to have been there or to have seen the various
wonders ascribed to such places; but you were always meet-

ing people, out on the Grind, who had *known* somebody who had been there, and the tales you heard—towns of people with monstrous deformities, great trees as tall as the Oasis, hideous apparitions, miraculous cures—were always told as things that had happened to this other person, always just one person removed from you. The legends attached to the Bright Land were neither the most terrible nor the most difficult to believe among these, but they were of the same general sort.

"So," said Kem, "the Bright Land, eh?" And he added, though he sensed it was a bit uncool, "No kidding?"

Mole had grown sullen. He merely nodded and he began to squint again. His angular face jutted out, pointing across the fountain and beyond, into the desert and the night.

It's a funny thing, Kem thought. You only really notice the stuff you've learned to see. Kem had learned to see bulkheads and decks and mechanical fittings. His duties as a snipe had trained him to perceive the world as an arrangement of objects connected in a certain way, a certain relationship one to the other, and always at the center of things, in this way of perceiving, was the notion that the whole arrangement had a purpose, there was a definite job or function that these interconnected objects were meant to perform and if they were performing it correctly then all was well, all was harmonious. If not then you studied the objects and their relationships and determined what was wrong. And because he had learned to see the world in this way, he had spent his time on the trading deck more or less as follows: he had first run his eyes around the boarded-up stalls, the olive trees, the open space between them and the fountain; then he had begun patiently but not without a certain inner satisfaction to trace out the series of mechanical connections that enabled the place to operate, the irrigation runnels and the pump that fed them and all its parts, the electric lines, the switches, the clamps, the emergency backup systems, the protective sheathing, and the metal deckplates that kept most of these things out of sight.

What he had not done, because it was not something that a snipe would do, was to raise his head as Mole's head was raised; to squint with bleary eyes at the horizon. But he did so now, and he noticed the light that was gathering there, in a direction that Kem supposed must be east, more or less.

The light was pinkish but no, not exactly that. It was yellowish but not yellow like the sun. All you could see of it was a sort of wedge, a piece of sky delimited by the superstructure of the craft on the right-hand side and by a cluster of olive branches on the left. The light was brightest down near the place where the sky disappeared beneath the deckrailing; as you craned your neck to look higher, the peculiar colors faded into the general deep blue of the night and by the time you got to the moon, about four points up, it was imperceptible.

Well, maybe it was nothing. Maybe if you worked up in the navigation tower—if you were a squirrel and not a snipe—you saw such things all the time and never gave them a moment's thought; only Kem didn't believe that. Something to do with his idea that all things were part of some bigger thing, and that the bigger thing had a purpose, made him think of this patch of oddly colored and unnaturally bright sky as a kind of question, to which there was somewhere an answer. Kem looked toward Mole, and he found Mole looking back, smiling, as though he had anticipated Kem's reaction and in fact had been waiting for it.

"Amazing shit, huh?" he said, and Kem wondered if he was talking about the light or the jay.

"I guess," he said, with caution.

"Yeah." Mole turned back to regard the light in the sky and he shook his head. "Amazing." And when he turned away again, he gave Kem a clip on the arm that almost made him cry out; maybe because he had felt a need to reassert himself as chief after all this familiarity, or maybe because they had both kind of drifted out there and he had figured it was time to reel them in. He looked at Kem for a moment—Kem was rubbing his upper arm which Mole had hit—and then he said, "But you've never been there, have you?"

Without waiting for an answer he gave a little laugh and a companionable smile, then he turned and started walking. On his way he said more gruffly, without turning around, "Shift's over"—leaving Kem to wonder what *there* meant, where he had never been, which was another question but at least one that had a very probable answer.

The Bell Dog took one look at him—a long look—then shook his head like he had seen everything he needed to. He did not look again as he handed Kem a sanding-board and nodded toward the small craft, something like a tiny sailwagon but without the wheels, that was propped upside down on sawhorses before them. They stood alone on a narrow upper deck. From the edge of the deck dangled the jacob's ladder they had used to climb up. The only other way out appeared to be a narrow door with no handle. "You do a good job on this one now," the Bell Dog said. "No dozing off. You hear?"

Kem did not think he was in danger of dozing off despite having just come off the night crew. He felt something—in the air, like—that gave him a feeling of expectancy. Maybe it had to do with the little jay he and Mole had smoked. Or maybe he was still riding the high he had gotten from Davina. He wanted to talk to the Bell Dog—not about anything in particular but about the way he had been feeling lately, the way he had felt when he lay on his back and sensed the change in the Oasis, and then last night as he watched the light above the desert, and maybe the way he was feeling now. For some reason he thought the Bell Dog might understand such things.

But this morning the Bell Dog did not seem inclined to talk or even to listen. After handing Kem the sanding-board he took up a scraper of his own and walked around to the other side of the small craft so that the round-bottomed hull rose between them. Kem could hear him working over there, a meticulous scratching, but could not see. He rubbed a bit at the hull, which did not seem much in need of repainting.

"What is this?" he wondered out loud. "Is this some kind of boat or something?" Kem had heard about boats but had never been anyplace where there was enough water to actually use one.

"Captain's gig," said the Bell Dog; nothing more.

Kem wondered if he had done or said anything wrong, anything to make the Bell Dog displeased. He could not

think of anything—other than oversleeping yesterday, of course—
and besides, the Bell Dog had not been this way all morning,
only since they got up here into the bright light and he gave
Kem a good looking-over.

Kem settled down to work in silence. Time passed slowly
and he had a bit of trouble keeping his mind on the task.
Perhaps it was that the work did not seem necessary, or that
he did not understand exactly what this thing was, this
captain's gig, that he was working on. Or perhaps—probably—
this is what you had to expect when you'd been awake all
night. After a while the Bell Dog came around to see how
Kem was doing. He was doing poorly: there were spots he
had missed and spots where he had rubbed too hard, marring
the wooden hull.

"Gosh," said Kem, "I'm sorry. Hey, I mean really. I'll try
to do a better job. Really, I'll—"

The Bell Dog grimaced and waved his hand, as though
Kem's words were more upsetting than his shoddy workman-
ship had been. He said, "You not a snipe today."

Kem started to speak but the Bell Dog shook his head and
Kem kept his mouth shut. The Bell Dog went on:

"You a good snipe when you want to be but today you
want to be something else. So you tell me"—he looked at
Kem, his dark eyes peering up with a curious, almost childlike expression—"what you want to be now."

Kem was ready to argue, but in that moment he realized
that what the Bell Dog said was true: for some reason today
he did want something else, to be something or to do
something other than this. He looked aside, breaking off
contact with those dark, sapient eyes, and thought it over. He
thought about the way he had felt the other day, away from
the engine flats, wearing the clothes Sander had given him,
strolling jauntily down the hall, smiling and nodding at the
older guys he had passed. He remembered how one of the
guys had smiled and nodded back, and he thought, *I want
that.* He didn't know exactly what those guys were, but he
wanted to be one of them. He wanted to wear clean clothes
and stroll out on deck in the sunshine and know a little more
about what was happening in this place.

So quickly that he surprised himself, he turned back to the

Bell Dog and said, "What's the Bright Land? Why are we going there?"

The Bell Dog did not seem to find this question out of order. He only nodded. "Thought so," he said. And after a moment, he added, "You all right—you done a good job, but I think you finished now. I think you need to do something else."

Kem felt very odd, hearing this. He wanted to say that it was all right, being a snipe was fine, he did not want to leave the Bell Dog and go work with anybody else—but the words did not come for him. He just stood there holding the sanding-board awkwardly, like it had been stuck in his hand and he had no idea what to do with it. After half a minute the Bell Dog turned away, walked back to the other side of the captain's gig.

"You finish the job anyway," he called over the hull. "You do what Bell Dog tell you and you do it good."

Kem bent down and he began to work again and this time he did so more carefully and with his concentration much improved. He stared hard at every grain of wood and every fleck of paint. He did not speak again all morning, and he tried not to think about what the Bell Dog had said or how he had felt or what, in his heart, he had already decided.

It had been Kem's idea that he would resume his talk with Bell Dog later that day, after the work was done, or perhaps first thing in the morning. He would ask for the Bell Dog's help in being transferred out of the engine flats, into some job or some apprenticeship that would get him up there in that clean and well-lit world he had glimpsed the other day. The world where Davina lived. It was not Davina herself, so much. At least Kem didn't want to think so. It was something else. Maybe it was just that he kept thinking about that light, hanging in the sky above the deck in the hour before dawn. Down in the engine spaces, you would not have known the light was there. Kem would not have even seen it except for Mole, he would never even have looked up—that's how accustomed he had grown to being a snipe. At least when he had been a wagon-boy, he had been able to look up and see the sky.

But at lunchtime the Bell Dog bustled away too fast for him to speak to, and he did not return at all during the afternoon. The next morning Kem was assigned to a new work team that was tearing down a backup compressor and cleaning the turbine blades and putting it back together again. It was a long project and Kem was kept on it all day and the day after. He did not see the Bell Dog during this time, and he lost all sense of what was going on in the world beyond the engine flats. The Oasis was still heading slightly downhill, from what he could tell, but by now he had gotten used to that. After a while you got used to anything, he supposed.

He supposed that this was what he should have expected. He should have known all along that he was helpless, that he was stuck being a snipe for the rest of his time aboard and that he might as well get to like it. The most he could hope for was to work his way up to being a team boss, a supervisor, and carry around a clipboard and sip tea from a mug with his name on it and generally act like an asshole. Or maybe he could get himself transferred to the night crew and smoke spiked jays with Mole every night. Why had he ever expected anything else?

On the eighth or ninth day, however, he woke up earlier than usual with the strong idea that big things were going on. He could not have said where that idea had come from, but it seemed to him that there must have been something that woke him up—some disturbance, maybe an unusual noise. Then he was wide awake and he realized that the Oasis had stopped.

It must have stopped just a little while ago, for Kem could still hear the throb of the main generators, which had not yet been taken off-line. He got up and felt around for his clothes. It was not as dark as it would have been a couple of weeks ago. The moon was now Tall Skies, a quarter full; and besides, this far south the nights never got as long as on the Grind.

On the breakfast deck there was only one other snipe around, probably a night-shift guy hanging out waiting to be let off and sent to bed. Kem started to go over to him, ask him what was going on and how long ago the craft had stopped, things like that. But then the guy turned to look at him—looked straight at him, as though he had known Kem was coming—and it was the Bell Dog.

Kem stopped walking. He stared back, somehow afraid to get any closer. It was odd to see the Bell Dog around the mess deck and odd to see him, as he was now doing, drinking strong morning tea. The Bell Dog seldom appeared outside of normal working hours and from what Kem had seen he never drank much of anything.

The Bell Dog smiled at him and Kem relaxed somewhat, though he was still puzzled.

"Big day," the Bell Dog said. "Big day at the Bright Land."

Kem felt a peculiar and somehow familiar sense of excitement churn in his stomach. It was the same excitement, he understood, that had been growing there since that night he had stood on deck with Mole. Now the excitement seemed to rise from his stomach and fill the rest of him, right up to his eyes, which were wide open staring back at the Bell Dog and probably making him look very much the crazy kid. He could see some of that played back to him in the amusement that crossed the Bell Dog's face, Kem walked the rest of the way over and the two of them stood looking at one another.

"So you ready to go?" the Bell Dog said. "You want to eat anything?" He held out his mug. "Want some tea?"

Kem shook his head. His excitement seemed the sort of thing that could nourish itself. "Go where?" he said. "Ready to go where?"

The Bell Dog ignored him and indeed Kem had almost been hoping he would, he had been hoping that the question had already been answered practically with the first words out of the Bell Dog's mouth. He followed as the Bell Dog led the way out of the mess deck and down a narrow corridor that cut aftward between the main engine blocks, where the noise was finally loud enough to overcome the electric buzz of Kem's thoughts, and at last through a little hatch and down a ladder. Kem found himself on a tiny platform scarcely capable of holding himself and the Bell Dog at the same time. As

though the Bell Dog noticed this too and was disturbed by it,
he made shooing gestures at Kem, seeming to suggest that
Kem should jump over the side.

"What?" said Kem. He almost shouted, not because it was
noisy but because their passage between the engine blocks
had battered his hearing.

"Down," said the Bell Dog, almost shouting too. "Down,
down," he chanted, just as once a while ago he had chanted
Up, up.

Kem looked down and he was surprised to find that they
were practically, already, standing on the ground. It lay only a
step or two beneath the platform. Some kind of fog rolled
over it, maybe steam from the boiler vents though it did not
feel hot like that. It felt cool and it smelled funny,, sour or
dank somehow like it had risen from someplace very old.
Kem hesitated for a moment and then he stepped down into
the fog, his feet striking the ground and his legs nearly
buckling, the sensation was so unfamiliar.

How long had it been since Kem's feet had touched the
earth? It was last fall, Fly South Moon, when he had gone
aboard the Oasis and since then he had never left. He was
surprised at how the ground felt soft—even this ground, flat
and dry and almost white. He looked up to see the Bell Dog
standing beside him, also looking downward. As he watched,
the Bell Dog grubbed at the earth with his heel. It broke into
chunks like damp chalk.

"Salt," said the Bell Dog, distastefully. "Ruined land.
Nothing grow here."

He shook his head as though he did not wish to dwell on
this. With a glance sideways at Kem he began walking—
heading nowhere in particular that Kem could see but just
out into the fog, away from the looming bulk of the Oasis.
Kem stepped after him, and as he did so he heard from
somewhere off to one side the piercing hiss of a valve being
opened, air being released. The Bell Dog did not slow down
but Kem could not help glancing now and then across his
shoulder as they hurried along. The Oasis seemed to grow
and to swell as they walked away from it, rising everywhere,
filling the predawn sky. The upper parts of it were invisible,
and it curved away toward the horizon to the right and the

left as though concealing its true dimensions. The hissing
sound began to fade, and the last thing Kem could see,
before the whole thing vanished in the swirl of fog behind
them, was the way the craft seemed to kneel like a monstrous
black beast as the air was squeezed from its shocks and it
settled onto its ground-struts. But the Bell Dog was hurrying
him along, and Kem found that so great was his curiosity
about where they were going, what lay ahead of them in the
gray dawn, that he was able to turn away from the Oasis and
for the time being to forget about it. Imagine: to forget about
even that.

"You like stories," the Bell Dog said. He said it a little bit like
a question and a little bit like a challenge. "This is where
stories come from."

They were standing at the edge of what seemed to Kem a
sort of ruin. His limited field of vision filled with walls and
roofs and pilings, the remains of buildings of some kind. They
were all broken up but in what seemed a haphazard or
accidental way—some were smashed to pieces while others
nearby were more or less intact; most of the debris had
accumulated in piles but a few things, a section of wall, a
door panel, lay apart, near where Kem and the Bell Dog
stood. In between the ruined buildings were smaller things,
flotsam from the lives people once had lived there. Kem saw
remnants of furniture, small machines, boxes, even a wagon
or two. The wagons were what he found most unsettling, in
that they suggested that whatever had happened here had
happened quickly, before the people could get away.

The fog was beginning to lift; a steady breeze blew out of
the east, into their faces, carrying the fog back toward the
Oasis in long wisps like shreds of cloth. From what Kem
could tell staring ahead he did not think that the wreckage
went on very far; it was more like a narrow band stretching
from north to south or possibly a crescent, the distant ends
just starting to bend off eastward, into the wind and the
morning light, before he lost sight of them. What it looked
like more than anything—you could see it this way if you
squinted your eyes—was a collection of playthings, a toy

village, that once had been spread out over a large area but then the giant who had set it up had grown tired of the game, bent down, and with the back of one forearm swept the whole thing off to one side.

"The Bright Land," Kem said, out loud but softly. You could see why this place would be called that. The ground was almost white. Behind the last shreds of fog the sun was coming up, and the white ground that stretched out eastward must have acted like a mirror, doubling the sun's apparent brightness, because it was hard to look in that direction. Nonetheless they stood there, the two of them, staring east and just hanging around. Kem figured they were waiting for something but except for the sunrise itself he couldn't figure out what.

Then out of nowhere the fog was gone and Kem drew his breath and the whole adventure leapt on him all at once.

In front of him, past the narrow stretch of ruined houses, the ground sloped down a little bit then flattened out again. But when it flattened out, it was not ground anymore. It was something alive, shifting and seething, its surface on fire with the morning sun, and it spread out forever, and it looked to Kem like some precious molten metal, platinum or gold. He did not understand for a minute that what he was looking at was not fire but water—water in incredible, limitless volume, covering the earth. It was as though the broken houses on the edge of it had stood at the contested border between two worlds. No wonder the houses had been smashed.

Yet all seemed peaceful this morning. The water moved up and down a little, its nearer edge washing up the slope to splash among the broken pilings then retreating again. The pattern repeated, part of an ancient cycle.

This is where stories come from. Kem looked out at the part of the world that was covered by water and he recognized it from stories he had heard. In those stories, it was called the Sea. Kem supposed thinking back that he must have dismissed the Sea as just wishful thinking on the part of wagon people. Imagine: a place as broad and flat as the Grind but covered everywhere with water. The idea had seemed preposterous. So Kem had disbelieved such tales even when they were told by someone who swore it was true, it had really happened to someone, a friend. . . .

"Not the Bright Land," the Bell Dog said. He said it quickly, as though mildly irritated, and Kem realized it was a reply, though one long in coming. He swept one hand in an arc, right to left, indicating the ruins. "This place is something else, another place." He paused, regarding Kem, perhaps gauging his attention. "Used to be called," he said, "Body of God."

Kem frowned. Without thinking (for example, of whether this might offend the Bell Dog's quirky sensitivities) he said, "Body of which god?"

To his relief the Bell Dog laughed, and for a moment Kem thought this was going to be his only answer. Then the Bell Dog said, "Big god. Jealous god. God that wanted to tame the water."

Kem nodded; he knew the one. "So they called it that," he guessed, "after the water wrecked the town? They figured the god had been killed after that?"

The Bell Dog shook his head, impatient. "Before that," he said. "Long time ago. Other story."

This was one of those moments when Kem could not help finding something comical about the Bell Dog's manner: the little man gravely full of his own thoughts, meaning to be stern but coming across as merely grumpy. "Well then," Kem said, "if this place here is Body of God, then what about the Bright Land?"

The Bell Dog started walking, not bothering to answer. Kem followed, having gotten used to this by now. As he did, obeying some fleeting impulse, he glanced quickly over his shoulder. He quickly regretted it. Behind him, a surprisingly short distance across the flat white ground—or maybe it only seemed that way, an illusion of size and perspective—the Oasis hulked like a gray-black citadel. Its armor had been lowered into place and you could see, here and there, the barrels of its guns sticking out like whiskers. Kem thought that near the very top, on the catwalk that ran around the navigation tower, he could see people moving, at least one, a tiny figure dressed in white. That might have been anything, though. A bird, a tatter of fog, a glint of metal in the sun.

Only somehow Kem didn't think it was any of those things and he had a very unpleasant feeling as he hurried after the Bell Dog—a sense of eyes falling upon him, eyes that he did not want to meet.

The ruins came to life. The first thing Kem noticed was a bird—his attention drawn first by its cry and then by the graceful downward swoop of its flight. It was mostly white with a long beak and steel-gray markings on its belly and its wings. Twice it circled some pilings just at the edge of the water and finally it chose a spot and landed, taking what seemed to Kem a precarious perch but which the bird evidently found satisfactory. It preened itself a bit and utterly ignored them.

That was the beginning and it was remarkable enough (the only birds Kem had ever seen were the predators and scavengers of the desert, with occasional glimpses of migratory flocks far overhead, imponderable) but the rest was more remarkable than that. There was a cat, a tawny-haired hungry-looking animal, that skulked about the wreckage as though hunting for its breakfast, and after a while Kem began to see that there were plants too. There were slender reed-grasses at the edge of the water, here and there intermingled with tiny white flowers at the ends of long wandlike stalks. Farther back from the water some kind of shrub, spined and rangy, bore pink blossoms and tiny orange fruits. In places where debris had collected there were trees-of-heaven (Kem supposed there were trees-of-heaven in the Underworld) but they seemed little more than saplings, the largest perhaps four or five years old, and their leaves were yellow, chlorotic.

From this jumble of plant and animal life it might have seemed a long leap to humankind, but Kem was accustomed to the notion that people could endure in the most hostile environments—which this was not, by a stretch—so he was not wholly surprised when a piece of cloth fluttered at the corner of one of the broken dwelling places and the piece of cloth turned out to be a dress and the occupant of the dress turned out to be a little girl. She had hair as black as the creosoted timbers and her eyes flashed darkly, like the Bell Dog's.

The girl ran when she saw them and made a sound like *aiyee*, a cry an animal might make. She fled behind a pile of broken lumber. Kem could see her hiding there, peeking over the top.

He felt a pressure on his arm. The Bell Dog's hand lay on him. "Here," he said, meaning *this* way, northward along the crescent of the ruined village. He waved to the little girl and strode off.

A village. Kem supposed that if there were people here you had to think of it as that. He thought he saw more eyes, more crowns of black hair bobbing up behind the walls and the junk piles, and he was led to change his appraisal of the place, the true extent of its ruin.

Body of God. When you looked at it, you saw that not everything had been destroyed after all, in the struggle between land and Sea. Kem began to notice that among the old houses there would appear now and then one whose pole foundation was still intact, more or less, though the house itself might be reduced to nothing but a platform, a subfloor with a couple of broken wall sections at best. And it was on these naked platforms that the people seemed to have made their new homes. He saw pieces of cloth stitched end to end and strung up on lines and poles to form crude but, he supposed, quite serviceable tents. He saw salvaged timber knocked together to make windbreaks (the wind blew steady and easterly, off the water) and here and there someone had even thrown up a sort of rough wooden hovel, built from scratch; though from what he had seen Kem was inclined to think that this might be tempting fate. In the way of ornamentation, taking the harsh edge off things, there were universal and rather touching tokens of domesticity—handmade toys, names carved on clapboards, scarlet geraniums in pots.

What Kem really wanted to see of course were the people who grew those flowers and built those toys. But the people stayed just out of sight and the Bell Dog hurried him along as if in a gesture of reassurance: we will not be staying long, we will not bother you. Kem was caught off guard, then, when the Bell Dog stopped abruptly before a platform that was

bare on top except for a sort of lean-to of faded orange
sailcloth. A rickety ladder with a dozen broadly spaced rungs
led up to the edge of it, and without ceremony the Bell Dog
started to climb.

"Me too?" called Kem, when the Bell Dog was nearly at
the top.

The little man looked down at him. He was smiling. His
brown skin was covered lightly with sweat, but for once he
did not look like a man who has been working hard; he
looked like someone just ending a bit of pleasurable exertion.
He said, "If you want breakfast."

The woman who lived at the top of the ladder greeted the
Bell Dog as Hózh'q (Kem would make him spell it out later)
and he introduced her as Sitiké. He added—though already
Kem had begun to suspect something like this: "Sitiké is my
sister." Kem was bewildered, but at the same time in another
way he was entirely at ease. He felt neither awkward nor
intrusive here. In this respect as well as in more obvious
physical ways, the woman Sitiké bore a marked resemblance
to the Bell Dog. Being around them made you want occasionally to smile. Kem guessed Sitiké to be the older of the two,
by a couple of years, but that was only a guess. She was
already nearly done making plenty of food for the three of
them—a mystery that she dispelled by saying, "We heard you
coming far off, last night."

Kem supposed so. In fact the thing he found striking about
this modest living place, not much more than a campsite
made on pilings, was the feeling of silence that attended it.
There was the wash of waves breaking below and the plaint of
gull cries and the steady whir of wind, but with all that there
was a sense of quiet that was almost a perceptible thing, a
presence rather than an absence. Kem sat down without
being invited to, near the seaward edge of the platform, and
listened to it.

Across from him, on the side relatively sheltered by the
sailcloth, there was a row of deep wooden boxes, out of which
grew a peculiar assortment of flowers and herbs and grains,
including a plant with reddish leaves that looked like some

sort of dwarf, bushy maize. The Bell Dog seemed to find this interesting too, for he went over to examine the plants at close hand. Sitiké looked glad to be left alone in what passed for a kitchen: a black pot rigged with a grill in which she burned driftwood, a large plastic washtub, several jars of dried and ground provisions (few of which Kem recognized), and an unmatched assortment of pots and tools, no doubt a triumph of scavenging, displayed on shelves made of woven reed boxes that looked like they had once been traps of some kind. Sitiké spoke over her shoulder while she put the finishing touches on griddle cakes.

"We took some wagons up last fall," she said, "and brought that dirt down from the mountains."

Kem looked around but saw no mountains or, indeed, any change in the featureless topography; which perhaps underscored what she was saying, the magnitude of their journey.

Sitiké turned around and looked at Kem across her shoulder. Her face was strikingly like the Bell Dog's—skin the same dark color, features wide and somehow flattened, hair thick and dark. But despite what he took to be her seniority in the family and despite the rough conditions in which she lived, there was a gentle quality about this woman, an air of serenity or maybe even happiness that was not what Kem would have expected. Next to her, the Bell Dog looked careworn and tired.

"Many years ago," Sitiké told Kem, "people went into those mountains to bring back the timbers to build this town. Now we have to go there just to bring dirt!"

She smiled as though this were an amusing turn of destiny, but Kem did not think that Sitiké really found it funny in any way. The smile turned more wistful as she shifted her gaze around to her brother.

"The tide is higher this year," she said. "Even higher than before the storms. At the neap, you can spear fish right off the side there."

She nodded over to where Kem was sitting. He had let his feet down over the edge of the platform, dangling his legs. He didn't know much about tides except that they figured in stories he had read, often as metaphors: tides of change, et cetera. He believed the moon was somehow involved.

The Bell Dog did not seem to care about tides right now. Between his finger and thumb he held one of the reddish leaves of the maize plant.

"This new?" he said. It was the first thing he had said since greeting his sister, and his tone sounded disagreeable. "This some new strain you bred?"

Sitiké turned back to her cooking and Kem felt a charge building up in the silence between the two of them. After a while in a nonchalant voice the woman said, "It's from them out there."

The Bell Dog seemed to be waiting for this yet at the same time he did not seem ready to hear it. He tore at the leaf where his fingers held it; it broke with an audible snap. The Bell Dog let go of the leaf and it fluttered down toward the deck. Then the wind caught it and threw it aside, out of the Bell Dog's reach and over the edge of the platform and then it was gone. The Bell Dog's anger seemed to go with it. He sighed. He looked at his sister, shoulders slightly stooped as though in contrition.

"Guess you have to eat," he said.

"Yes, we do," Sitiké said. She spoke with her back turned, scooping food onto three plates.

"And I guess you can't do without your masa." The Bell Dog sounded friendly enough, bantering, but you could tell there was something here, some issue, that he didn't want to let go of. Kem recognized this peculiar family dynamic.

"Well, why?" Sitiké turned and carried the plates, balanced expertly, to a little table made by setting a wide plank on two of the woven reed traps. You had to sit cross-legged with your knees tucked under, and Kem found this to be a friendly sort of arrangement, the three of them sitting there with their knees bumping. "Why should I?" Sitiké resumed after they had gotten settled. "It's just food, for heaven's sake. They've put some amaranth genes in it so the protein is better. And carotene. And here—see how nice it tastes."

The Bell Dog looked down balefully at the hot and crisp and (Kem found) very tasty griddle cakes before him. He poked one with his fork as though expecting the mutant thing to protest or rise up and counterattack. But of course it behaved perfectly well and the Bell Dog had little recourse in the end but to eat it and express some grudging appreciation.

They went ahead with their simple meal principally in silence. Kem thought for a little while about how this was by some margin the best food he had eaten in months, owing he supposed to the care that had gone into preparing it, but after that his mind went back to the thing he had been wondering about since he had heard the phrase, spoken tersely by Sitiké, *them out there*. That had been the thing that upset the Bell Dog, which was intriguing, but the words were intriguing also in their own right, and Kem tried to recall whether Sitiké had indeed, as he now thought, made some gesture with her arm, a signal to accompany the words *out there*. Kem could not imagine what this meant since it seemed there was not much out there that you could point to. There was the desert on one side and the Sea on the other and that was about all.

So he said, "What did you mean, 'them out there'? When you said . . ."

He shut up because of the way the Bell Dog looked quickly around, not at Kem but at Sitiké, and Sitiké looked back as though surprised not by the question but by the fact that her brother hadn't told Kem already. Then the Bell Dog, in the same grudging way he had tasted the griddle cakes, cocked his head out toward the water, wind blowing his hair back across his face, and he said:

"Out there. The Bright Land."

Kem looked. The sun had climbed a couple of points higher in the sky, veering off southward, and now although it was brighter than before it was not so hard to see if you kept your eyes down along the surface of the water, where the Sea ran out to meet the sky. The horizon itself was lost in a shining haze, but somewhere between here and there, Kem could make out something darker, more substantial. It was first nothing much more than a color and a vague shape, a squiggle, as though somebody had smeared black ink across a silvery background. But little by little the thing took on certain rather distinct attributes: mass, form, dimensionality. It looked like a complicated series of structures, or a single structure with a number of modular parts, and it seemed to thrust itself right out of the water, for there was not any sign of an opposite shoreline, a counterpart of the shore on which they sat; but chiefly it was huge, as big at least as the Oasis, filling an arc of the horizon perhaps half a point in width, despite the fact that it was so far away that it was hard to focus your eyes on.

"That's the Bright Land," Kem said. It started out being a question but did not end so, because now that he saw it, now that he sat here dangling his feet above the white salt flats, straining his eyes over iridescent water whose wave-tops the sun brushed with fire, he figured he understood. He figured he knew now why there were stories here, why this was where the stories came from. There were many things, a million stories, he still did not know. But at least he knew that.

The water rose until they were trapped on the platform, surrounded by little choppy waves. Kem sat till about mid-morning watching the tide come in. With the rise in the water level, Body of God underwent a transformation. Up and down the shoreline, as far as Kem could see, people began lowering rowboats into the water, or climbing down ladders onto things that Kem had taken for scrap lumber, wall sections and the like, but which now could be recognized as rafts, some of them complete with masts and makeshift cabins. Sitiké did not bother with a boat but simply lowered a piece of rough hemp netting from the side of her home, jiggling it until it arranged itself to her satisfaction, its lateral ends snapped on the seaward pilings and its middle slumping inward, distended like an animal's belly, to trap whatever booty might be carried on the tide. From the decks of the modest fleet other nets were cast out, along with a varied collection of lines and rods and traps; much of the stuff looked like it was old salvaged equipment but some things, the traps notably, must have been newly made. Body of God was not just a village, then, but a fishing village at that, and Kem was amazed and somehow pleased to watch this bit of languorous local industry. He was also interested to note that the people here all seemed to be of a similar physical type, which is to say the short and muscular type represented in Kem's experience before now only by the Bell Dog. Their skin tended toward sunbaked, rust-toned brown, a color like that of desert clay.

With Sitiké's net in the water there was nothing much to do but wait for the tide to turn. Kem would have enjoyed going out in one of the little boats, but Sitiké did not seem to own one. So while the Bell Dog—restless, as always—undertook some repairs to the sailcloth tarp, Sitiké supervising, Kem found his eyes straying now and then toward that enigmatic place across the water. The Bright Land.

At one point he thought it might be a row of towers and at another point, as the light changed over the water, it looked more like an island, complete with buildings and trees. Then the light changed again—it kept doing that—and the place dissolved to its blurry, primordial form, a shadow upon the Sea, without shape or substance.

An odd thing, though, was that while Kem sat there staring across the water he became aware of a sort of weight or pressure that was growing at his back, like a thunderhead building up over the desert. The sky seemed to darken and the air to grow heavier, and Kem turned around expecting to see gray clouds gathering in the west, climbing out of the hot ground, but what he saw was the Oasis.

Of course it had been there all along. It had never left nor ever been farther away than a few hundred paces, but somehow—what with the Sea before him and the fishing boats and the Bright Land and the glitter of sunlight—Kem had not looked back at it for quite a while. Now he looked and he wondered how he had ever thought of the Oasis as a thing of wonder, of magnificence or even its own form of ominous beauty. At this moment, with the image of the Sea still shimmering in his mind, it looked simply huge, dark, overpowering. Water lapped at the base of its hull, the tide having risen and the shoreline receded so that the Oasis stood now with its connection to land all but severed, a looming promontory. You could have paddled in one of these fishing boats right up to its flank, if you wanted to. But nobody wanted to, it seemed. The boats kept well to seaward, and when a wave or the slow drift of the tide carried

one of them too far inshore, close to the Oasis, the fisherman
or -woman wasted no time paddling back out again.

With its armor lowered into place, covering most of the
portholes, the Oasis looked not so much like a movable craft
as like a gray, forbidding fortress. You expected to see armed
warriors prowling its parapets. What you saw instead was a
rather indolent-looking crowd of hangers-on, visible from
about waist up over the deckrails. Some of the little figures
wore simple light-colored shirts or tunics and Kem figured
these were members of the crew. Others, congregated chiefly
amidships, were dressed more colorfully, and Kem thought
with an uncomfortable tightness in the stomach that these
must be the Residents. At the upper levels of the craft, on
little balconies, were smaller groups of people and sometimes
solitary figures and Kem had no idea who these could be or
what they could be doing. Kem had once asked the Bell Dog
what went on up in the tower, and the Bell Dog had said
something about *great work*. He had not sounded very happy
about it. Maybe these were the people who performed the
great work, whatever it was.

At last Kem's attention was caught by something happening on a platform between two high gunmounts. Half a dozen
people in uniform appeared to struggle with a large piece of
cloth. Kem thought he heard a sharp metallic noise like a
coupling being broken and then the fainter grind of machinery. The platform began to move. It seemed to telescope
forward, away from the superstructure, until you could have
dropped something off the end of it and the thing would have
fallen straight down into the water. Which was, Kem gathered,
more or less the idea. From the sides of the platform two
thick metal arms were cranked up, each of them trailing a
wire that led down to the object with the cloth or tarp on it,
and pretty quickly Kem got the idea that he was looking at a
system of davits and winches that was about to lower something into the Sea.

The Bell Dog came to stand beside him. They watched as
the davit-arms flexed outward and the wires drew taut. The
object they were attached to rose from the platform and
swung into open air beyond the superstructure. It was a boat.

In fact it was the captain's gig—the little craft he and the Bell Dog had sanded and painted a week ago.

As he looked on, the motion of the davits stopped and the captain's gig was steadied at about the level of the platform. The half-dozen crew members who had been fussing with it seemed to steady themselves as well, and Kem noticed that elsewhere around the Oasis, on lower and more public decks, people were craning their necks, peering up as well as they could—not very well—to see what was going on. On the whole, Kem and the Bell Dog had the best seats.

Then the figure of Captain Hand, all in white, strode out onto the platform and stepped without delay, shunning the hands that were extended to help him, into the boat that swung lightly on two wires.

It was funny: a little while ago, even though he had known more or less what the man looked like, Kem would surely not have been able to recognize Captain Hand at such a distance. But there was something about him, an air or an aura more than any physical attribute. Kem had seen it that day in the courtyard, the reception for a new Resident, and now he saw the same quality again.

Hand appeared to give some signal and the gig was lowered in a smooth and surprisingly rapid movement down the flank of the Oasis until it struck the water and the wires went slack. The Captain bent quickly fore and aft, releasing the wires and setting himself adrift on the light waves. For a second or two it appeared that the steady forces of the wind and the tide were going to slap him against the hull that rose like a sheer gray cliff beside him; but the Captain sat down and the rattle of a small engine came over the water and the gig nosed out eastward, away from the Oasis and toward the open Sea.

Kem felt a surge of utterly irrational fear. He felt sure for a long, insane moment that Hand was coming after him, coming to drag him off the platform back to the Oasis. Kem understood that this was absurd, that as far as someone like the Captain was concerned Kem might as well not even be alive. He understood that. Nonetheless it was only by forcing himself to look away, to catch his breath and glance aside at the Bell Dog (who still sat watching, motionless, his expres-

sion gone sour) that Kem managed to break free of his
delusion.

When he looked back again, the gig had picked up speed.
Its bow nosed up out of the water, and it was making very
swiftly for a gap between the structures and pilings and
miscellaneous debris of the village. In less than a minute it
shot through, clear of the village and out into the open Sea.
Hand was now standing at the wheel; he was not wearing a
hat, and you could see the wind pushing his hair back.

There could be no doubt now, either, about where the
Captain was headed. Kem took his eyes off the gig for a
moment and looked beyond it, eastward. The dark shape on
the horizon appeared to have grown closer, though this must
have been a trick of the haze on the water, a mirage. The
border between Sea and sky was a contested one; it seemed
to shift now and then as though some skirmish were being
fought there, a dispute over territory. Like Kem's heart and
his mind, the horizon had grown indeterminate.

"What is he doing out there?"

The Bell Dog did not reply. He had not answered any of
Kem's questions all morning and he did not seem inclined to
start now.

"Well," said Kem, "then how long is he going to stay? I
mean, is he just going out for a visit, or what?"

The Bell Dog was tying strands of rope together, making a
net. Kem might have asked what the net was for but that
would have been fruitless too, he guessed. "And how come,"
he said, pressing it, "he's gone out there by himself? Doesn't
he usually take some, um, bodyguards or something?"

The Bell Dog looked around at Kem as though to see if he
were quite through. Kem was not. He said, "And what about
the Oasis? I mean, is it just going to sit there waiting till he
gets back, or are they going to let the crew come down here
to the village, or what?"

This was not entirely a disinterested question. Kem was
beginning to wonder how long the Bell Dog was planning to
hang around his sister's place, and these two matters might
likely, he figured, be intertwined.

To Kem's surprise, Sitiké said, "The people don't like them coming to the village. They're afraid...."

Kem thought she was going to say something else, what the people were afraid of, but maybe that was the end of the sentence. They're afraid. Well, Kem could understand that.

Sitiké went on: "When the tide is low, they'll walk up there. Some people wait all year, they grow special plants that the traders will pay a high price for. But most people stay away."

Kem nodded slowly. He wondered what kind of plants would fetch a high price at the Oasis and the image that came to him was of a tiny box filled with dried leaves, hidden under a mattress. He shot an eye over at the row of plants that grew in boxes at the west edge of Sitiké's platform, and it seemed to him that any plant would be worth a lot if you had to go to a distant mountain just to get the dirt to grow it in.

"Why do they stay away?" he said. He was thinking of how the wagon people, who also waited all year for the Oasis, would scramble to get on board as soon as the hatches were down.

Sitiké smiled and her brother scowled at his rope tying. She shook her head. "I guess they feel," she said, "that the Oasis represents something that is . . . that has gone wrong."

She spoke softly and slowly as though to make it clear that she had no wish to offend. And yet the Bell Dog looked offended. Without looking up he said, "Not wrong. Not right either. Can't be." He did look up then, right at Kem, and he added, "Machines can't do wrong. Machines do what they're built for. Only people can do wrong or right. Only people can decide."

Kem was quite surprised, actually speechless. After maintaining an irritable silence for most of the morning, the Bell Dog had now abruptly delivered himself of something like a short lecture, a lesson in ethics.

Sitiké said, "But it isn't just a machine, is it?" She waved a hand toward where the Oasis sat. The tide was coming down and the water was draining away from it. "It's a *place*, really, isn't it? A place that moves."

Kem thought that they were both correct; but he kept his mouth shut.

"That's what the people don't like, maybe," Sitiké went on. "It doesn't seem right—a place where people live that is not connected to the . . ."

Ground, Kem expected her to say, and would have been prepared to argue that the Oasis was certainly connected to that. After all, the ground was pretty much all that Kem had seen of the world for a couple of months now: the ground underneath the Oasis, the beaten caliche, so hard that the treads of the craft seemed to explode when they tore into it.

But Sitiké did not say *ground*. What she did instead was to sweep her hand, her whole arm, around in a kind of circle— beginning at the Oasis and moving downward, toward the earth, sweeping across the platform eastward, a little flourish at the opposite end of the arc to draw attention to the Sea and then the hand moved upward, skyward, brushing past the sun and a few cream-colored afternoon clouds and ending at the Oasis again. She said something that sounded like *sheemay*. She said it breathily, as though in imitation of the wind.

Kem looked quickly at the Bell Dog. The Bell Dog had stopped working at his rope and just sat there, his eyes following Sitiké's hand. The dark face was furrowed thoughtfully.

"And the people wonder," Sitiké said, "how you can live like that. How you can be someplace that is not a place at all, really, because it goes away. They wonder if that is safe. They think that it is dangerous to lose your contact with *sheemay*. If you do that you may become confused, you may not know anymore what is right and what is wrong. Like a machine doesn't know," she said, a sort of verbal prod to the Bell Dog. "A machine acts but it does not know. Just like that."

The Bell Dog shook his head. "You never lose contact with *sheemay*," he said. "You carry *sheemay* in your heart."

"Hearts can become confused, too," said Sitiké.

The Bell Dog exhaled sharply. His face took on a certain resoluteness. "May be true," he said, which surprised Kem a little. "But every person has to decide. Move or be still. Stay or go."

Something about the way he said this made Kem think that it was being said to him, that maybe this whole discussion was somehow for his benefit. He even wondered whether this conversation might in some manner be the reason for his visit here. And more faintly, in the back of his mind somewhere, he wondered about the Bell Dog's choice of words. *Move or be still.* The words struck a chord in him and he tried to figure out what they reminded him of. *Stay or go.*

Then he remembered the little story, the one from Tallheron's book, and he remembered the Bell Dog saying that here was where the stories came from. He looked up at Sitiké, and without quite meaning to he spoke his thoughts out loud.

"The people who stayed behind," he told her. "You're the People Who Stayed Behind."

She nodded. "That is the decision we made," she said, "a long time ago."

They remained in Body of God for a week. When the tide was down, as Sitiké had predicted, some of the people from the village ventured up to the Oasis, where they were received by the traders and sent back with the kind of oddments that you might expect people in a remote place to want: books and brightly colored clothes and exotic foods and bottles of liquor. Sitiké kept herself busy and affected not to notice. The Bell Dog took Kem out for walks along the shore, where the two of them—Kem especially—were the object of much quiet attention on the part of the townspeople. Small groups of people from the Oasis, mostly older crew members though occasionally Residents also, in twos and threes, ventured out; but these expeditions were mostly made on horseback, and Kem and the Bell Dog did not cross paths with them.

Kem suggested more than once that he and the Bell Dog might borrow one of the fishing boats for a brief outing. He had never been in a boat—he had never seen one until the day they painted the captain's gig—and in a way, too, he felt that since they had come to the Sea they might as well go out onto it, if only for a few minutes. The Bell Dog did not seem to feel this way. He had not talked much since the first day, except now and then when they came upon some object washed up on shore, which at Kem's insistence he would identify. After a while Kem began to develop a private theory of why the Bell Dog was averse to climbing into a boat, and the theory had nothing to do with being afraid of the water.

Evenings were the best time to look at the Bright Land. Sometimes, if the sun was hot and the air relatively still, there would be a haze over the water and not much to see. But on certain evenings the wind came briskly off the Sea and the air grew as clear and sharp as glass. Kem would sit for a long time very still on evenings like that, peering at the dark forms that thrust themselves out of the Sea, with the last rays of sun coming from practically right behind him. The sun made a difference; it made the place out there, the Bright Land, appear less monolithic, and not so dark. You could see that there were other colors, varied shapes, that only the distance and the refraction of light off the waves made it seem one vast gray thing, a mirror of the Oasis. Sometimes the sun fell at just the right angle and for a minute or two there would be a tiny glint, as if from glass or polished metal, and on still rarer occasions there would be a whole array of them, rows of infinitesimal glowing dots, as though the sun had found a wall and the wall was covered with windows.

Captain Hand was still out there. At least, he had not come back during daylight. Kem had no notion of what the Captain could be up to in the Bright Land; but of course he had no notion of what the Bright Land was—what sort of people lived there and why, what kind of work they did. He just had a snipe's dumb faith that there was a reason for things, that all the parts fit together. Other than that, he had only two clues: the red-leaved maize plant, and a cryptic comment that Mole had made on night shift. Mole had said something about wheeling and dealing—something about big stuff, not the sort of thing that went on with wagon people. But from what Kem had seen, the trade between the Oasis and the people of Body of God did not add up to much. Fancy clothes, bottles of booze: it was even below the standard of the Grind.

That left, Kem figured, only one place for the big trading, the real wheeling and dealing, to be going on. Only one place and only one trader.

The thought, the unasked question, nagged at him.

Kem spent a day and half a night thinking matters over

and considering in turn such factors as the strength of the wind, the duration and frequency of tides, and the relative quality of darkness between the middle of the night and that early hour when the citizens of Body of God began to stir.

At about the time when Tall Skies Moon, nearly full now, was straight overhead, Kem eased himself over the side of Sitiké's platform, descended the ladder, which creaked but not loudly, waded through waist-deep water forty or fifty paces until the shadow of a neighboring platform fell over him, and untied a small, manageable-looking fishing boat. It was all disarmingly easy until he tried to climb aboard. The little craft wiggled and slid away from him and almost capsized, and by the time Kem—having splashed around quite a lot and made much more commotion than he had planned to—rolled over the gunwale and landed like a big wet fish on the deck planks, which to his dismay held a good deal of standing water, he had gotten a pretty lively and thoroughly enriched understanding of the concept *afloat*. But thank the Goddess, whose great symbol hung fat and yellow above him, the noise of his crime did not seem to have awakened anybody and he had calculated the tide right. It was the beginning of the ebb, which proceeded with slowly increasing vigor as Kem sat in the boat inspecting the oars and the tightly furled little sail and tried to figure out what to do next. Somehow his planning had not gone much beyond the stealing-the-boat part.

The tide was with him, though, and the wind was light. Kem figured he had a couple of hours to get as close as he could get to the Bright Land and then a little more time, perhaps three hours or three and a half, to get back, working against the tide but with the breeze behind him. The way he figured it, he would paddle out and sail back. The fishermen did it. And dawn would find him lying on Sitiké's platform, feigning sleep, having seen the Bright Land up close, he hoped, and just possibly having learned something.

The problem he had had just getting aboard the little boat should have served as a warning. Well, it did; but Kem had gone too far to heed it. So he sat in the boat letting the tide carry him away until Body of God was well behind him, a vaguely defined irregularity along an invisible shore, and then he discovered that he did not understand how to row.

He got the oars into their bits all right. But however easy the rest had looked when he watched the village people doing it, that whole business of dipping the oars into the water, tugging on them in such a manner as to propel the boat, lifting them out without undoing what little good you had just done, then repeating the process in an orderly fashion proved complicated and unbelievably strenuous. His arms grew numb after just a few minutes, and when he paused to rest he found that he had succeeded primarily in getting the boat turned around, now roughly parallel to the shore so that the wind began to catch it and force him back.

Still, he kept at it. There was a peculiar sense of inevitability about this—as though Kem had known as soon as he saw the Bright Land, perhaps as soon as he heard the name, that he would go there—which he had taken to be an augur of destiny but which he saw might just as well be a foreshadowing of doom. He kept at it anyway. His rowing technique improved, and the tide was still with him. The moon rolled westward and across the Sea its beams struck someplace slick or shiny which glimmered faintly, and Kem urged himself on.

The first hour passed. Kem felt himself growing exhausted. He had not thought, either, that you could get thirsty in the middle of so much water. One sip of the Sea convinced him that you could get very thirsty indeed, though he managed not to vomit and come that much closer to dehydration. Fortunately the wind had dropped to almost nothing, and in the peculiar clarity of the night Kem felt sure that if he turned around he would find the Bright Land sharply outlined by the moon, bearing down upon him. He shipped his oars. For a few seconds he allowed himself to breathe deep and long of the rich Sea air. Then he turned around, and the Bright Land had vanished.

Kem felt his heart rest momentarily and then pound hard. He looked around wildly and for a moment he felt himself to be completely lost, far from shore with no referents, alone in the middle of the Sea. Then his reason or what passed for it reasserted itself. He reminded himself that the moon was still where it ought to be; the wind, though presently slack, must surely blow again before long; and if worst came to worst the tide would turn in the hour before dawn, and surely they did not kill people for stealing fishing boats. In this frame of mind he looked around more carefully for the Bright Land—and sure enough, with a bit of straining his eyes over the dark Sea he found it again.

And then he understood how badly things had gone wrong.

The Bright Land was not close at all; it was not where it ought to be. It was off to southward by a full point of arc, maybe more. Which meant that the fishing boat had gone too far northward. Kem looked repeatedly at the moon and back at the Bright Land and back at the moon again, and that's just the way it was. Something must have happened, some unforeseen factor must have come into play. Or perhaps Kem's ignorance was so great that it alone was enough.

However that may have been, Kem was off course very badly, and he figured that whatever had gotten him here might still be working against him. He even thought, as he stared at the jutting silhouette of the Bright Land, that he could sense his little boat drifting parallel to the shore and not away from it. It may have been his fear or his imagination or it may have been something else. But Kem had seen enough to decide that this whole venture was a botched job. He stuck his oars down in the water, then he thought better of it and decided to go for the sail.

Maybe this proved (as Kem would think later) that he was incapable of learning from experience. But despite his conspicuous lack of aptitude first as a boat thief and then as a navigator, Kem figured he'd go ahead and try his hand at being a sailor. The rigging of the little fishing boat was altogether different from that of the sails of his family's old wagon. So it should not have surprised him too much when he heard this godawful ripping noise and looked down to find that he had stuck most of his arm through much of the sailcloth, and things were now pretty clearly starting to turn against him.

Don't panic. Don't panic is the important thing, Kem told himself. He got what was left of the sail aloft and tied it with a vengeance. Then tried to guess where Body of God might be.

He figured it ought to be *there*. He grabbed the tiller and
spent a minute or so enjoying the challenge of steering a craft
before the wind. Then the boom came whizzing around to
thwack him on the shoulder. Kem felt weak and very frustrated. He tightened the lines until the ripped-out sail was
trimmed as well as he could manage. The torn edges of it
flapped, but somehow that was a hopeful sound, the sound of
the wind that was carrying him in a direction that he chose to
think of as homeward.

He had misjudged it again. He held the boat to its new
course for half an hour or so, then as the moon got lower and
land was still nowhere in sight he nudged the tiller over and
swung farther to southward. He figured that the longer he
was out, the more time the current running offshore would
have to push him north. He dreaded the sun coming up, but
at least in daylight he would be better able to figure out
where he was.

While he was thinking about this the wind was doing
something odd to the sail, wrenching it in a new direction
and working the running lines loose. Kem saw that there was
a lot to this sailing business that he hadn't counted on. The
tear in the sail seemed to be getting worse. Kem strapped the
tiller in place with his belt and stood up to tighten the lines.
The wind caught the sail nearly broadside, heeling the boat
over. Kem wobbled; he reached out for the mast to brace
himself, but the boat heeled farther. Black water lapped at
the starboard gunwale. Kem could not figure out how to
disengage himself from the mast without slipping and possibly falling overboard, and he did not attempt to do so. He
kept hanging on like an idiot, while in the slickest kind of
slow motion, the wind blew stronger and the boat heeled
more sharply and Kem's weight came down on exactly the
wrong place, and very easily, even gracefully, as though it
were something the boat was designed to do, it capsized.
Kem got a stomachful of water and a heartful of adrenaline
before he hit the surface gasping, still clutching whatever he
could hold on to of the boat, and he thought, Now what the
fuck can possibly happen next?

• • •

Nothing much happened in the couple of hours left till dawn. Kem did not, for instance, drown. He managed to hold on to the capsized boat, whose keel stuck like a fin out of the water. Once, for a couple of minutes, he made an effort to get the thing righted. He grabbed hold of the elevated gunwale and pressed with his feet against the keel and rose up out of the water, tugging backwards, and for a second or two the mast came up, quivered a few inches above the horizontal, then settled back down again. In a way, Kem was relieved. He had given it a shot and it was hopeless and now he could settle down to await his destiny.

His destiny arrived about dawn. Kem was lying flat on his stomach on the upturned hull. He had not exactly dozed off, but at a certain point he looked up and was surprised at how bright it had suddenly gotten. He realized of course that such things do not happen suddenly, nor altogether slowly either—they happen in their own time—but the bigger thing he realized then, the overbearing thing, was that somehow the Bright Land had moved up close, that they were very nearly on top of him.

He sat up; the boat creaked and swayed beneath him. He did not know whether to be terrified or fascinated—a little of both, he guessed. The Bright Land was straight ahead and the sun was agitating at one side, off to the left, so that Kem figured he was seeing the place from the northern end, a different aspect than the one you saw from the village.

The first thing that struck him, with some surprise, was the color of the place. It was blue. It was a deep, weathered greenish blue that was not like any color Kem had a name for. If anywhere, you might find this color among the many colors of the desert sky—Kem thought he had seen it there, just before sunrise—and he thought this fact might have something to do with how the Bright Land could seem to change size and shape, sometimes even to disappear, when you looked at it.

The next thing Kem saw, or tried to see—it was a hard thing to take in all at once—was the extraordinary form of the place. It was many times as large as the Oasis. It seemed to

consist of several sections, like a chain of barely separated
islands, and each of the sections was taller than the Oasis
though perhaps only half as wide. From a distance Kem had
gotten the impression of towers rising from the Sea, but that
was barely half it. Colossal cylinders thrust up from the waves
and rose a hundred heads or higher. *Towers* did not seem the
right name for them; each was an awesome, independent
monolith. Kem supposed they were made of metal, though
he could not tell for sure—they were painted that mysterious
desert blue—and they bristled with detail: spiraling ladders
and handrails and lateral struts, dozens of hatches, hundreds
of windows, jointed protrusions that might have been cranes,
flat or slightly concave appurtenances that Kem could not
even make a guess about. Starting about two-thirds of the
way up, a series of decks and superstructures spanned the
area between one cylinder and the next. It made Kem a little
dizzy to look at them. His head came down full of vaguely
formed images: pipes as wide as silos; great windmills and
pump-jacks and other machines he could not identify; entire
buildings set on decks with other buildings just as large on
decks above them; and on and on, up into the sky.

With his head still down Kem squinted at the rising sun.
He noticed something else now—it had been there all along
but it had not been conspicuous. Now, with the sun streaking
in, it seemed to gather Kem's attention.

It was earth: nothing more than that, nothing less astonishing.
Rising in mounds at the base of the towers, filling the space
between them, it was a real island, a piece of solid ground. If
you could forget about the gigantic structure that rose above
it, it was a beautiful, eerie place—dune grasses and wildflowers
covering its shores, windblown pine and maleleuca and live
oak, windblown and gnarled, massed behind them. Kem felt
an urge to paddle for the shore, to hurry there before the sun
got any higher. Equally he felt an urge to stay away.

Then, over the slap of waves around the Bright Land and
the wailing of shore birds and the sloshing of water in and out
of his foundered boat, Kem became aware of one other noise.
It had seemed like a natural sound, but only because he was a
snipe. What it was, was the sound of an engine. Kem figured
it must be coming from the Bright Land and he craned his

neck trying to trace it. Too late he understood that he was wrong; the noise was coming from a boat and the boat was advancing upon him, though not with any degree of haste.

Kem supposed it was just as well. He was ready to be rescued—or captured, as the case may be. The boat was coming out of the east, out of the sunrise, and for a while all he could see was an evanescent blur, the shadow of a small craft and the sunny aura of its lone occupant.

Oddly enough, it was the aura first of all and only then the boat that Kem recognized. By the time the captain's gig pulled alongside and its engine slipped into reverse and a muscular hand extended to help him aboard, Kem knew who his rescuer was. And he figured now for sure he was about to take it up the ass and he wasn't even going to get kissed when it was done with.

Captain Hand spoke exactly one sentence the entire way back to the Oasis. It was "I have met you, haven't I."

Kem muttered something, yes sir one day I believe so at that reception, some such blather, but the Captain's single sentence had not been a question and Kem's reply seemed to fall on wholly uninterested ears. After that Kem settled glumly back in the gig's tiny passenger seat to endure the ride. He entertained himself for a time by imagining the various forms that his impending doom might take, and later—for the Captain seemed in no hurry, or perhaps he was just killing time until the tide advanced a little farther—by trying to figure out how in the world he had managed to reach the Bright Land after all, despite his earnest and steadfast efforts to get lost, sink the boat, and drown.

The best he could figure was this. The offshore current had been northerly and strong, but that had not been the end of it. No. If that was all, then he would be far north of the Bright Land, scudding along some distant shoreline or maybe lost at Sea. Something else must have come into play. The flow of water must have somehow veered east; it must have borne him in a spiral, like a whirlpool at whose center lay that mysterious island. Kem tried to imagine what could give rise to a current like that. There might, he supposed, be some odd contour of the shoreline that deflected the water in an arc. Or there might be crosscurrent, as for example from the mouth of, a river. In either case, the Bright Land had been right there, if not his destiny then at least his destination. The end of the line.

As the gig puttered onward, the sun crawled up and the tide came in and without any show of effort—or impatience or anger or you name it, absolutely nothing—Captain Hand pointed the bow at the line of little bumps that began to swell along the horizon. He held it steady; the bumps grew bigger and more jaggedy and eventually metamorphosed into Body of God. The Captain held to his course. The Oasis loomed huge behind the ramshackle houses. As they got closer, Kem could see fishing boats putting to Sea. He imagined but could not make out the place where one boat would be found missing. Guilt stabbed at his chest. He closed his eyes.

When he opened them, the gig was flying toward a solid mass of wood, houses and boats and pilings. Then the Captain made one very slight motion of the hand on the wheel. The gig went into a sideward skid. It slipped past a row of broken pilings, hurling its wake against them, then the keel seemed to dig in and the little craft shot off in a different direction. Hand made another slight adjustment; a cry of gulls rose around them as the gig tore through a shallow patch of water that must have been their nesting ground.

Then they were past the village and nothing lay ahead but the Oasis. It loomed huge and monstrous. Two steel lines dangled just above the waterline, and without needing to be told to Kem went about the grim business of hooking them up.

"Well," said Mole. He drew the syllable out, making something reflective out of it. "Well. Well."

He walked around Kem regarding him from several angles. Kem got the feeling he was looking for the weak spot, the part that would break first.

"Let's get one thing straight," Mole said. He came to a halt directly in front of Kem and peered closely at him; you could smell the sour breath, the odor of a spiked cigarette, the stink of his clothing. "Let's just forget about that time we had a smoke together. Okay? Let's just pretend that didn't happen."

Kem nodded. He was surprised a little that Mole would even care about something like this. Surely Kem was not capable of getting anyone in trouble but himself. But maybe that wasn't what Mole was thinking of.

"The only reason I did that," Mole was saying, "is that I figured you were the Bell Dog's boy. I figured you were all right."

Kem nodded. He guessed he had thought something like this himself—that he was all right, that he was in some sense under the Bell Dog's protection. He didn't think so anymore.

"Well," Mole said again. "It looks like you're my boy now. Doesn't it?"

Kem wondered whether he should respond to this. He wondered if he should nod or lower his head in submission.

He did not have time to do either or even to wonder anymore. Mole leered for barely another second, then he hit him. Really socked him good: Kem fell backwards and his head filled with white light. Then it grew dark, then it grew light again. It was like he was having trouble deciding whether to fall down or not.

When his eyes came back into focus, Mole was still standing there, looking somewhat appeased. He inspected his knuckles, as though checking for damage. He looked up at Kem and gave him a weak sort of smile. No hard feelings, like.

"Now pick up your shit," he said. He pointed at the pile of Kem's possessions that lay on the deck. One of the things that happened when you got rolled onto the night crew was that you lost your sleeping compartment, your own little place in the world. There was a group berthing space, darker and more crowded than the galley boys'. Mole turned and took a few steps away. Kem could tell he was expected to pick up his stuff and meekly follow. Or else just to leave it. For a moment he couldn't decide.

His eyes fell upon the set of loose-fitting linen clothes that Sander had given him, heaped and tangled on the filthy deckplates. He thought of all the things those clothes had meant and how those things were lost now. And inside him a mute and helpless rage seemed to grow as each of the things ticked off in his mind. The sense of freedom he had once had, strolling along the deck. The shock and then the thrill of sunlight, that day in the courtyard. The smell of the fountain, white flecks of water burning orange at the tips where they fell through the sun. And Davina. Of course he thought of Davina. Her smile, the smell of her. Her long fingers on his arm. The way she had slipped those fingers beneath these very clothes, pulled them off and dropped them in a heap like this but not the same at all.

And in the middle of this, for no reason he could discern, Kem found himself thinking of Sander. He was thinking of a distinct moment—a moment in which Sander had made one of his terse little pronouncements, one of those things that came back to you later like a weird echo, with all its implications rearranged.

They had been standing in the galley, Sander and Kem. It was hot, and Kem was covered with greasy sweat, but Sander stood before him looking fresh and cool as though he had spent the day in the reefer. The boy had just said something along the lines of *I know somebody*. It was an explanation, Kem thought, but he could not remember what it was supposed to explain. He remembered what Sander said next, though. He had looked at Kem and he had said *As a matter of fact, you know somebody too*.

Kem had stood there feeling ignorant, as always, not having the slightest idea what Sander meant. So Sander had spelled it out for him.

You know somebody, he had said, *who can get you out of here*.

"Well what the fuck's the matter?" Mole called to him. His voice rattled along the bulkhead, distant and tinny. "You writing a note for your mom, or what?"

But Kem was not paying attention, instead, there in the pit of the Oasis, he was thinking of Sander's friend, the refined-looking man with narrow, smiling eyes.

And Sander's voice was saying
Don't you remember
Delan?

BIRDS CRY

Shimá: the raped earth. That
was the word Sitiké had used that Kem had not understood.
Now he knew how it was spelled and he knew what it meant
because he saw the meaning laid out below him. From a
height of eye twenty-seven heads above the scarred face of
the old planet, Kem stood on the navigation deck watching
the Oasis crawl slowly as though in pain northward, following
a river known to wagon people as the Gut. Body of God lay
two months behind him, and out of the East, off the flood-
plain on the other side of the river, a weary-looking spring
was sending up new green shoots that may have been rice or
may have been sterile loosestrife, a billion sprigs of the same
plant spread by stolons, or may simply have been hybrid
lawngrass that someone planted long ago, that had displaced
everything else, and that was good for nothing.

Kem had seen the Gut before and may possibly have come
with his family to this same bleeding ocher stretch of its
shore, because the river marked a kind of terminus of the
wagon routes, a resting place for the winter, though its water

was considered unsafe to drink owing to contamina upstream
and it was prone to mighty, unpredictable floods. East of the
Gut the land was still somewhat productive and there was
intermittent fighting to control it; people were pressed into
service by this or that local power to be killed over fields of
cotton—or so the wagon people heard. They kept to their
shore though the river looked easily fordable, especially in
dry weather. Somewhere along the Gut—farther north, Kem
supposed—were the winter camps where he had gotten what
little schooling he had, where he had learned to read and
write, to recognize birds and snakes and rocks, to manipulate
various systems of currency and measurement. There he had
learned, also, not to trust any form of authority, not to go near
the Oasis, and not to make friends. It is one thing to know
and another thing to act, but Kem had not learned that until
recently. Now he knew that and much else besides and of
course the knowledge, like all knowledge he supposed, had
come at a price, and most of that price was yet unpaid.

Across the deck from him—the deck was a good ten
strides wide but shallow, with windows along the forward
side—the mate of the watch stood sleepily before a shelf of
small electric machines whose purpose it was to display
scraps of information in the form of graphs and numbers and
lights. If the business of engineering consisted in quantifying
things, the business of navigation was nearly the opposite: it
consisted in taking hard facts and softening them, reshaping
them into a rough semblance of the physical world. The facts
themselves, the raw material, came in many forms—numbers
from these machines, the declination of stars at dawn, the
exact time the sun attained its zenith—and it was the mate's
job, often now delegated to Kem, to collate these facts and
interpret them and draw lines to represent them on a chart,
compare the result to what he saw outside the windows in
front of him, reconcile the discrepancy (for there was always a
discrepancy), and distill all of this at last to a set of discrete
recommendations. Turn right. Turn left. Increase speed. Maintain your heading. Stop. These recommendations were conveyed
by the mate through a voice tube up to the bridge itself, a
sanctum Kem had never penetrated, the place where all
decisions were finally made by a senior mate or possibly by the

Captain, if the Captain was there. But even that was not the end of it. The decisions once made must be relayed all the way down to the engine flats to be acted upon by the snipes, Kem's old comrades—motors throttled up or down, steering cables manipulated—so that even here on the navigation deck, as everywhere else, there was a certain roundness or circularity. That's the way the great machine was put together.

The mate of the watch was a young man of a type that by now Kem found pretty familiar. He was tall, taller than Kem, with pale hair brushed back from a face oddly lacking in particulars, the face of a statue, to fall on athletic-looking shoulders. His eyes were clear and studious. His manner was calm. Though he did not talk much he was not disagreeable, nor were any of his colleagues among the junior mates of the Oasis. They were a well-mannered and disciplined and generally silent lot, and Kem supposed that if they did not go out of their way to be friendly, it was because he was not one of them. He did not look like them, and he had not signed on to the Oasis as they had, voluntarily, and anyway they all must know how he came to be working in the tower. They must know, in the parlance of the Oasis, that he was Delan's boy.

Kem turned away from the young mate and looked back out at the Gut, the yellow gash of its bank, the empty steel-blue sky. Delan's boy, he thought. It was a funny way of speaking when you thought about it. It did not mean what he would once have thought. Or not necessarily. Or not only that. It meant that he was under Delan's sponsorship, Delan's protection, but not just that either. It was a two-edged thing; at once it made you larger than you would have been, and smaller. Larger, because you acquired some of the status, the immunity, of your sponsor; smaller because you were to that extent less an independent personage yourself. Once, not long ago, Kem had been the Bell Dog's boy, then briefly Mole's. And now he was Delan's.

Well, the work was better.

And he was where he had wanted to be—in the sunlight, up in the winds and the infrequent storms, with a view down into the lower decks of the Oasis, the olive groves and pleasure courts, the storage bays, the market square, and up (raising his eyes at last) across the desert, out to the horizon where other worlds and other lives seemed to swarm, up into the broad and flat and many-colored sky.

And he had free time now; time that was mostly his own. For the first couple of weeks, while he underwent a kind of probation, he had been obliged to return after work to Delan's crowded stateroom, far belowdecks. It was not something he enjoyed but on the other hand it was not as bad as he had feared. Delan stood his watches mostly at night, not on the navigation deck but in a place called the squirrel cage, where they practiced a dark art called communications. Communications with whom, and for what purpose, Kem did not know. Even when the two of them were in the stateroom together Delan displayed a talent that Kem supposed you picked up after years of living in a place like this—the ability to maintain a degree of privacy and distance under the most crowded of circumstances. He had talked a bit to Kem and offered some encouragement, and that was all there was to it, almost.

Almost. On two occasions, Delan had made advances toward Kem, and both times Kem had laid back resignedly to permit the inevitable violation. After all, it was what he had known was coming and it was not a high price to pay, he guessed. Delan had gone ahead with it the first time in a style that you might describe as painless: he did not speak nor make any unwarranted show of tenderness, for example kissing Kem during or after the ritual. The sexual act itself was courteous, tidy, and brief. Kem felt lousy afterward, hollow and unwholesome, but he had felt worse.

The second time had not gone so well. Delan, evidently frustrated by Kem's passivity, had broken away and sat on the edge of his bunk looking agitated but saying nothing. Kem almost felt obliged to give some comfort or even encouragement, but of course in the end he could not do that, and the whole miserable business ended with Delan walking out. When he returned a couple of hours later he said only, "I have found you a room," and at Kem's show of astonishment he gently and sadly smiled.

"I have never wanted," he said, "to make anyone unhappy. Some boys find that they enjoy it. Many do not."

He shrugged then and turned away, and Kem stammered something, words of thanks—at which Delan raised his hand, palm wide. His eyes were harder now.

"There will be a time to thank me," he said. "Don't worry. I will be thinking about it. I will let you know."

So that's how matters had come to rest: Kem moved into a tiny box of a cabin up near the main water tanks, and Delan remained amicable though somewhat distant when their watch schedules brought them together, and Kem could not meet the man's dark and calculating eyes without thinking about the payment that Delan wanted and deserved and that he would someday—with exquisite tact, Kem did not doubt—demand.

The watch on the navigation deck changed at about sundown. You had to be specially qualified to stand duty at night, when the world outside receded and flattened in the darkness and there was no horizon from which to measure the positions of stars. Kem thought he would enjoy the challenge, guiding the great landship through the dark, but he knew he was not ready for it. A new mate came on duty and a new apprentice, an older boy. Kem explained briefly to the apprentice what had happened during his watch and what course they were to follow—orders that had come down from the bridge an hour before. The apprentice nodded wearily, cast a glance over the shelf of blinking, unreliable equipment, and said, "Have fun."

The end of another watch.

Kem left the navigation deck and stepped onto a small platform cantilevered outward from the body of the craft. From both ends of the platform a frail-looking stair with treads of perforated metal wrapped itself around the tower. As did all stairways in the Oasis, this one followed the pattern of an eagle's flight: the right-hand or sunwise spiral carried you upward and slightly inward, as the tower grew narrower near the top. Kem stood looking that way though he knew it was forbidden to go there. Upward and inward: in that direction lay the squirrel cage, the bridge, the Captain's quarters, and who knew what else—the deepest of the many mysteries of the Oasis, the innermost of inner circles. There were no signs to warn you to keep out and no guards that Kem could see from the platform. None were needed, probably. Certain things in the Oasis were immediately clear; you may not know where all the pieces fit in the vast machine, but you knew where your own piece belonged and what a small piece it was.

With a dispirited shrug Kem turned, followed the stairway moonwise and down. Despite their frail appearance the treads had a sturdy feel, and Kem guessed they were made of some rare light metal, the kind of material that scavengers mined from ancient scrap heaps and sold to a very few high-paying markets, the Oasis being one of them. He found himself reflecting upon the vast wealth—incalculable really—that had gone into making this thing and that was needed still to maintain it, to keep it steady on its course through the heart of the desert. It made you wonder: where all this metal had come from, the machines, the skill to put them all together, the sheer human energy implied by the craft's existence. The Oasis was old, of course—it was hard to tell just how old— and once upon a time, the stories said, there were more people in the world than there are today. More people and more things in general, money and metal, water and food, for there was something about the world that Kem saw every day from the navigation deck that suggested not poverty but bankruptcy, a fall from riches.

But even apart from the problem of its origins there was something about the Oasis, some unasked question, that troubled Kem particularly though he could not quite fix his thoughts upon it. Maybe it had to do with the notion he had acquired as a snipe that every machine had a purpose. *Machines do what they're built for*—the Bell Dog had said that. So what was the Oasis built for? What—besides repeating its slow annual journey, inscribing again and again the same circle on the dead reckoning charts—what exactly did it do?

And there was another thing. There was the Bright Land. Kem had not gotten a chance to study that strange island in detail. But he had seen enough—soaring towers, vast superstructure, expanses of metal painted that indefinite shade of blue green, the color of the desert before sunrise—to recognize in them something of the Oasis. Not just the awesome scale of the two things, something more subtle than that. You might say they bore the same signature, that they were products of the same mind or at least of the same mind-set. But this did not answer any questions and in fact the more he considered it the more Kem felt troubled. For it had been one thing to live among the wagons and to regard the Oasis as a unique marvel, a thing apart from the rest of the world. But the existence of the Bright Land raised another possibility: that there was another world, an entirely alien realm of being to which the Oasis pertained, in which it was not unique but ordinary—the great craft itself only one part of an inconceivably large and terrifying whole.

Still somewhat troubled by these thoughts, Kem was not in the best or clearest frame of mind when he reached a lower landing and entered a hatch whose dogging lever hung slack from constant use and whose paint was chronically soiled by hands pressing against it. The hatch opened to a passageway that wound through the section of the craft where junior members of the crew were housed in a warren of small identical compartments. A narrow, transverse passage led to Girls' Berthing, the place where Davina lived with her roommate Blueberry. The route was familiar because Kem had followed it countless times now, sometimes several times in one day, and on many occasions he had made the return trip without having seen Davina. Often he had hung around her room, waiting for her to show up, feeling very much the stupid kid and presumably the object of amused discussion among the other girls who lived nearby, and on such evenings, more often than not, Davina had never come back at all or had done so very late and not been too happy about finding Kem there. More than once it had been even worse than that and those times he did not like to remember. Only the sounds that came through her door did not leave his head so easily; her voice had always lingered like that, it had always been easy to recognize and hard to quit thinking about.

Yet there had been good times too, good nights which sometimes turned into wonderful early mornings, and it looked for a while like this was going to be one of them.

"Hey," Davina said, opening the door briskly as soon as he knocked. "I was hoping you'd come."

Kem stepped into the room and she closed the door behind him. "I said I would," he reminded her.

Davina did not appear to hear him though Kem figured really she heard everything, every nuance, and forgot nothing, and he had had plenty of time to observe the process at work by now. She had just taken off her uniform and she stood before him in a T-shirt that stopped somewhere short of her navel and a pair of skimpy underpants, both washed the same soft red, a color produced by the oxides skimmed from mineral wells, the cheapest of dyes. Like everything about her it was perfect and unaffected and it made Kem's heart feel bruised just to look at her. She was turned about two-thirds away, laying her uniform out on the bunk and folding it carefully, bending over so that her long narrow back and taut buttocks stuck out at him. The skin of her thighs was olive-toned and you could just see tiny dark-brown pubic hairs caught between them and pink cotton. Kem could not tell whether he loved this girl or whether he was just trapped in an agony of sexual need. They had been together only a couple of nights ago but by this time, as far as Kem's body was concerned, it might have been a year. He longed to possess her in some conclusive way but of course he could not. He sighed. Davina turned and caught him trying to adjust his clothing so that his swollen dick was not scrunched up in his pants. She smiled.

Yeah, smile, he thought.

She stopped folding her clothes and came over and kissed him in a way that he did not think he liked: fondly, on the forehead, like he was her cute kid brother or something.

"You're kind of funny sometimes," she told him.

This statement he found very much in the category of the kiss. He raised his arm to stroke her ass and she allowed him to do so for several seconds; she even rocked along with it, back and forth on the balls of her feet, but there was still something light and playful about her movements, whereas there was nothing light at all anywhere about Kem except possibly his head, most of the blood having rushed down from there. Without warning Davina broke off and turned back to the bunk and finished what she was doing with her clothes. And just about the time Kem was weighing the consequences of going over and yanking her underpants down around her ankles, Davina said over her shoulder:

"There's a party tonight. I thought maybe we could go."

Kem went a little limp. He had been to a couple of these things Davina called parties and what they were was a bunch of snotty young crew people he didn't know sitting around somebody's room drinking stolen tequila. At best, you got bored and drunk and felt bad the next day. At worst—and Kem had learned that the worst was what you should expect, generally—you threw up and made a jerk of yourself and everyone got pissed at you.

"Well," said Davina, turning around now to smile at him, "what do you think?"

Kem looked at her standing there with her T-shirt twisted around and her hair pulled back casually, just to keep it out of the way, long brown strands flying in front of her suntanned face and everywhere, a little girl's expectant look in her eye, and despite everything—things known and things unknown, the great dark mysterious power that churned within him— he managed a weak sort of sporting smile and he said, "A party. Sure. Why not?"

"It's supposed to be this really big thing," Davina told him. This was in a low-pitched voice, by way of explanation for why they were walking down a hallway Kem had never seen before. The hall was wide and it turned frequently, each turn taking you sunwise and a few steps higher. Kem figured they were probably working their way up one of the bulkier parts of the superstructure, aft of the navigation tower. He had an image of something he had seen from above, looking down from the platform: a wide gray mound with terraced ridges, something like a low pyramid, with a little garden court on top. They turned another corner onto a farther stretch of empty hall. Kem marveled at the luxury of wasted space. Davina went on with her party talk: "A lot of the big shots are supposed to be there. You know, the officers and all? And they even said the Captain might show up—like just, you know, to put in an appearance."

Kem's heart filled with dread. He did not want to hobnob with big shots and least of all did he want to be seen by the Captain. Their last meeting had been pretty disastrous. But here was Davina, obviously excited and happy at his side, and he could not find it within him to disappoint her. Yet even this, he reflected sadly, even this act of a seemingly generous heart, probably came down in the end to simple horniness, a hope that if he survived the party he might be able at last to pull those pink underpants down. "It's got to be around here somewhere." Davina glanced, maybe nervously, at the numbers on doors. She had not brought a map or any written directions. Kem suspected, though, that she did not really need them; that as always, she knew exactly where she was going. Or at least that she would recognize it when she got there. They walked a while longer and Davina said, "It ought to be right in here someplace." They were standing before a doorway on which the following symbol had been painted, evidently with some care:

Kem pointed at the symbol and said, "Look at this"—not supposing that it would mean anything to Davina, but because it seemed an odd thing to find in a place like this. To his surprise Davina gave a short laugh.

"Ah," she said. "Gardner's place."

She made to open the door but Kem said, "What? Are you sure this is right?"

She gave him a disconcerting look. "Can't you read?" she said. She pointed at the symbol as though she were spelling something out for a child, and not even an especially bright one. "See? Place, of, gardener. Gardner's place." Then she smiled in a more companionable fashion, and Kem was amazed once more at how far that smile could get her. "That's like him," she said, "he's into all that kind of old stuff."

Kem did not have time to ask what kind of old stuff or who

this gardener or Gardner was. Davina opened the door and a funny kind of odor hit him right away and then all the rest of it: the lights, the boisterous chatter, the music. And Kem understood with a hopeless feeling that for once she had really done it. She had brought him to a real Oasis party, the kind he had been hearing about in a vague kind of way since the time he worked in the galley. And though the idea terrified him there was absolutely no way to get out of it. He followed Davina through the door.

Once when he had stood in the cabin of Tallheron, the old Resident, he had been impressed by the size of the room, and by extension the standing of Tallheron himself. Now he took about three steps into this place where the party was going on, which was about as far as you could get before the crowd thickened up, and compared to this Tallheron's room was nothing. This was not a room at all, for starters, but a cluster of rooms, an apartment—doorways led off to the right and the left and, most incredibly, straight ahead, right through the outer skin of the superstructure onto a sort of enclosed balcony. There Kem saw rows of tiny lights, strung on poles, and beyond them an intricate fretwork of silhouettes against the blue-black sky: spires and minerets, ladders and catwalks and balustrades, all the intricate webbing of the Oasis, which looked so purely functional by day but which now, seen as a kind of exotic backdrop, took on a decorative and even weirdly beautiful appearance, as though it were the work not of engineers but of sculptors. People drifted in and out of the doors, and somehow without concentrating on it Kem and Davina found themselves drifting among them.

The current took them past a table laid heavily with food and with glasses of something cool and sweet—it did not taste too dangerous to Kem—so they took some of that and kept drifting. Music came from more than one place, as though invisible players were standing here and there among the crowd; the notes were soft and mostly percussive, with breathy-sounding winds weaving in and out of the rhythmic line, stating themes and then forgetting them, picking up something else, falling silent.

The rooms were full of *things:* bowls and pillows and woven panels on the walls, trinkets on shelves, engravings, kachinas, statues, drums, pieces of ancient machines, decaying photographs, scraps of fabric woven into rugs. Everything looked very old. Some of it was discolored, warped out of shape—like these computer parts, strung up like a mobile, whose plastics and silicates had not aged at all well—and some of it was pretty well preserved. But everything, the mass of it taken together, gave off this air of antiquity that went way beyond quaintness, beyond nostalgia or even fascination with the past. It went all the way to obsession and it was truly bizarre.

Someone bumped into Kem. He looked absently down to find that his drink was empty, and then he realized that Davina was introducing him to somebody. It was their host.

"Gardner," she said, "this is Kem. Kem, this is Gardner."

She spoke the name loudly as though she suspected Kem might not remember it. Kem looked up into the tanned face and the meaningless, sociable smile of a guy maybe halfway through his thirties. Gardner was a little taller than Kem but his build was more muscular so that he looked much bigger. He held out a big strong hand.

"Hi, Kem," he said, and Kem said hello and shook the hand hard, thinking What an asshole. It was nothing in particular; there was just something about the guy. Then Gardner turned to smile more widely at Davina, like she might have missed a couple of teeth the first time around, and as he did he placed his hand lightly on her upper arm and he said, "Now you two have a nice time, all right? If you can stay around until later I've got something I'd like to show you. Out on the balcony. Something new." He winked, as though to say that the phrase *something new* was meant ironically, in this place where nothing looked less than a couple hundred years old. Then he stepped away, removing his hand from Davina's arm only when it would have distorted his posture to keep it there any longer. He merged with the sizable crowd.

Davina rolled her eyes. "He's so weird," she said. "I mean, he's pretty interesting too, but it can be pretty strange to listen to him. He just goes on and on about how things used to be, the way people lived. You'd think he'd been there. You should talk to him sometime, Kem."

"Yeah, sure," said Kem. The surliness of his own voice

surprised him. It must have surprised Davina, too, because she looked at him as though in confusion. The thing was, Kem had begun to figure out what it was about this Gardner that bothered him. It was the way Davina had acted when she introduced them. Like she thought the two of them ought to meet, they ought to be friends. Like they already had something in common. Kem didn't like Gardner, though, and he could only think of one thing they could possibly have in common.

He looked at Davina. He felt stupid and pathetic and small—and angry too, angry at himself for being so jealous and possessive. But he couldn't help it: was that a good enough excuse? He said, "I think I'm going to get another drink. You want one?"

Davina looked down into her glass and kept her head there for a second or two. Kem had the idea that she was not really checking to see if her drink needed refilling but was perhaps seeing something in there nonetheless, stirring in the waters. "No thanks," she said, looking up. Her expression was empty. "I'm all right for now. I'll just wait here."

Kem nodded and walked off feeling that he had blown something. He wandered into the next room where the refreshment table was, and there he ran into Sander.

The boy stood squarely in his path with his hands on his hips and his head tilted slightly to one side. He eyed Kem, and as though it were some form of challenge, he said, "Hello."

He was astonishingly changed. Kem hadn't seen him for a couple of months—he had been meaning to but what with one thing and another, one thing meaning Davina, he hadn't gotten around to looking for him and anyway he figured Sander would show up as he always did. Only he hadn't. And now he was standing in front of Kem and Kem could see right away that something remarkable had happened.

The boy had gotten noticeably taller. He must have been hit by one of those sudden hormonal tempests that makes kids grow an inch a month, stretching all their limbs out without really touching their heads or torsos, so that all of a sudden you find yourself looking at this childish face perched on a long neck a few inches higher than you think it ought to be. But in Sander's case there was more to it than that. His

hair had kept growing, too; now it fell thickly past his
shoulders onto his back. It had once been the same color as
his skin, a medium sand tone, but now it was almost white
where the sun had bleached it, and his skin had gotten
correspondingly darker. You could see this quite well because
Sander's attire no longer ran to loose-fitting linen. He was
wearing a sleeveless shirt that left his skinny arms and
shoulders exposed as well as a good bit of his narrow chest,
and pants that were tight around the hips and then grew
baggy as they went down. He was barefoot, which made his
new height even more impressive. The clothes were made of
something like silk, with a soft sheen that seemed to echo
the moon-white luster of his hair. All in all, Kem found it
discomfiting to see his friend looking this way and even for a
moment felt self-conscious standing here talking to him. He
brushed the feeling away.

"Aren't you going to say something?" Sander asked him.

"Oh—hi," said Kem. Once he said it, it seemed to open
him up and he said it again more warmly. He held his hand
out to take Sander's, and then he tossed that gesture away
and in the spirit of the party, the noise and the crowd and the
drink he had knocked off, he stepped forward and hugged his
friend. The hug lasted only a couple of seconds because
Sander did nothing, just stood there; Kem could feel the
boy's thin bones beneath his shoulders, and his skin felt dry
and cool. He stepped back and looked at Sander again, not at
his face but into it, trying to see behind the unblinking tawny
eyes. He could not. Something else had changed about
Sander, he thought, besides his clothing and his height.

"I guess," Kem said thoughtfully, "you're not a messenger
anymore."

Sander smiled. He said, "I am nothing."

Kem thought he heard another voice behind this remark,
a subtle overlay. You are something, he thought. Not a
messenger but something.

He told himself that it didn't matter. Whatever Sander did
and whatever he had become did not change the fact that he
was Sander, still beneath it all himself and still Kem's friend.
Kem couldn't decide whether he believed this or not. He
said, "I'm getting another drink. Want to come with me?"

Then he added—a separate thought—"You want to meet Davina?"

This idea seemed to please Sander or to amuse him: he smiled, which relieved Kem somewhat, and after gathering up a couple of drinks (the glass looked absurdly large in Sander's delicate fingers) the two of them pressed their way through the crowd. Davina wasn't where Kem had left her. He felt panicked for an instant but the feeling receded and he told himself that naturally the current of the party would have borne her away; so they set out looking for her and soon enough, without effort, they reverted to familiar roles—Kem the bumbling naïf, Sander the precociously worldly guide.

"Who *are* these people?" Kem asked in a whisper, motioning around at their fellow party-goers.

"Oh god," the boy groaned, "they're hideous, aren't they? Look at that one—she looks like one of your snipe friends inflated her with a hose. And that one *must* have bought his teeth at a jumble sale."

"No, I mean really." Kem glanced around. They were back in the main room, the one with doors leading out to the balcony, and it seemed if anything to have gotten more crowded than before. "Who are they?"

Sander had a way of pointing with his head—casting his eyes in a certain direction, seeming to tap people with an invisible extension of his nose. He indicated in this manner a portly man slouching against a wall.

"There's the new boss of Recruiting," he said, "and there's somebody from up in, I don't know, Records or something. That's all the staff types ever do, anyway—hide in a corner."

"Mm." Kem waved his hand broadly around the room. "But I mean . . . everybody. Who *are* they?"

Sander looked around and then back at Kem, frowning as though he had not yet gotten the point of the question. "Who are they? They're . . . I don't know, they're just the people you meet at parties, I guess."

This did not seem like a satisfactory answer yet it was telling in its quirky way. Kem said, "These aren't Residents, are they?"

Sander looked at him in surprise, maybe that Kem was such a bumpkin. "Some of them are. They don't lock them

up, you know. Don't worry, you can't get the crying just by
looking at them."

"I know—"

But Sander was not done with it. "You have to have
intimate contact," he went on, his lips caressing the syllables.
"That's how you get it. Like when you fuck them. Or they
fuck you. Either way works."

Kem thought that this was the old Sander, all right, the
one who was unrelenting when he had made up his mind to
shock you. He remembered the night the boy—so much
smaller and younger in memory—had sat on the edge of a
tank of cattails and jerked off. Kem supposed that this was
just Sander and you just had to not care, though he could not
help feeling that some of it was uncalled for. Surely after a
while he would have said everything and done everything
and there would be no one left to shock.

"What about this guy Gardner?" he said, backing up a bit.
"Do you know him? Is he a Resident?"

Sander laughed. Not loudly or rudely, but clearly amused
by the extent of this misperception. "Are you kidding? Gardner
is an Investor."

Kem thought he detected a capital *I* in the word but did
not have time to ask anything more because Sander said:

"Oh, look. There's Delan."

Kem turned and yes, there was Delan across the room,
looking very much as he always looked with a simple open-
necked shirt and his usual relaxed, genteel comportment. He
had adorned himself to the extent of wearing a string of
turquoise beads which made his skin look even richer and
browner, but in the context of the party this counted as a
show of restraint. He was talking to the man Sander had
identified as the boss of Recruiting. The man was speaking
animatedly. At a certain moment he looked across the room
and pointed, and for no apparent reason he seemed to be
pointing straight at Kem. Kem flinched slightly. Delan turned,
following the man's gesture, and when their eyes met he gave
Kem a pleasant and faintly amused smile.

Sander said, "He gives me the creeps."

Kem frowned at him. "I thought you two were friends. I
thought—" He shut up, because what he had thought was

that Sander was Delan's boy in a fuller sense of the term.

"I think he's *hideous*," Sander said, hideous apparently being a major concept with him tonight. "I haven't gone near him for months."

Kem did not know what to think about this. "I guess we ought to try and find Davina," he ventured. He led them across the room, in passing picking up two more drinks. What they did then—and Kem could not remember later whether it had been his idea or Sander's, or whether they had just sort of done it automatically, drifting on the inexorable and ever-strengthening current of the party—was to walk straight through the doors leading out onto the balcony.

The night swelled around them and winds off the desert blew in their faces. You could smell water, an unusual smell, blowing up in the easterly breeze off the Gut. You could smell the rotten stalks of last year's crops, whatever they were, and Kem thought also you could smell the earth itself, the still-living ground, a full and sweet smell that was a composite of all the things that grew and teemed and spawned down in the soil. Were smells naturally stronger at night or did you only notice them then? A string of tiny lights ran from a post at the edge of the balcony along the railing and from there up into the limbs of some kind of fruit tree, espaliered against the rail but overgrowing it, hanging over. The tree was flowering and you could smell that too, sweet in a different way from the soil. There were insects around it, eager, buzzing. The music from the party was soft, then loud, then soft again. The winds wove their melody, which Kem thought he recognized now, recognized as being a melody and not an intermittent or accidental falling of soft notes. There was a pattern. There was a pattern and it encompassed the night and the insects and the smell of soil. Earth music, Kem thought; and it seemed to him that the flute (it was a flute, a very old native flute, he unaccountably realized) as it dived among the pulsing waves of gongs and drums and finger bells, like a heron, plunging in then out again, breathed its syllables into the living night, the syllables forming a word that Kem knew but that he was not learning again, its meanings inexhaustible, and the word was

Shimá.

• • •

How the party had gone so long Kem could not have said. It must have done so without him, he thought, and yet here he was among the other people on the balcony where the night air had turned cool and there was an augury of dawn in the sky. Beneath him, the Oasis rumbled. The feeling of its restless and inevitable movement rose into his bones. "Hey," a voice murmured quietly, lazily, and for an instant Kem was startled that the voice was Davina's. But of course it was. They had been together for hours now, or anyway he guessed so. At some point he had taken his shirt off; he found it now lying beside him, on the cushion where he and Davina were half lying and half propped up against the rail of the balcony. Davina moved her legs against his, pressing herself into him. She seemed still caught in the languid, half-dozing state that Kem was emerging from. He guessed they had been lying like this for a while, oblivious of their surroundings, but he was not certain.

He raised his head and looked around for Sander, for anybody else he knew, and at first he saw no one. Then he realized that he was staring right at Sander and what he hadn't seen was only the visual detail he had been looking for, the silky fabric of his clothes. He hadn't seen them because Sander wasn't wearing them any longer; the boy stood willowy and naked against the opposite rail looking out, or Kem supposed so, across the empty bays of the Oasis. Wind blew his hair sideways, and Sander shook his head lightly, clearing his vision—an eerie, slow-motion gesture, like a figure in an old recording, an androgynous and beautiful youth cast in a tragic role, the colors of the tape aged out now to something less than black and something more than white. Muted tones of gray and green and blue, the colors of the approaching dawn.

Davina tried to draw him closer but Kem held back; he had the sense of coming onto something, maybe a memory or maybe a different sort of mind-thing altogether, a flashback, an epiphany. It had elements of the present in it and elements of the past. Across the balcony Sander raised his arms in a gesture that might have been stretching or might have been purely expressive, a farewell to the night. There were other people near him, near Kem and Davina too, and it seemed that nobody had quite a complete set of clothing on. Some were naked like Sander and the rest were partly clothed like Kem. And unlike the crowd he remembered from the early phase of the party, the people on the balcony were all pretty young—Kem's age being about the average or slightly lower—and they were all, it seemed to him, pretty ordinary. Just plain crew members or people's kids or something. Or nothing. That's what Sander had said he was and now Kem had some idea of exactly what he meant. *Just the people you meet at parties*.

Somewhere—in the old recording, Kem supposed—a selection had been made. Gardner had appeared on the balcony at some point and as Kem thought about it he saw it happening, he saw the supple movements of the man's shoulders as he made his way through the crowd and he saw that smile again, the perfectly neutral smile, a carrier with no message. Gardner came over to Kem and Sander who were just standing there, not even talking—but then the recording was flawed in that way, it had lost its audio track—and now he was putting a hand on each of their arms, one hand for Kem and one hand for Sander. It was the same way he had put his hand on Davina before and Kem had thought he knew what that meant; but *nothing is the way you think it's going to be here*. That was another of Sander's remarks and now it had come spiraling back again, like an eagle in flight, twisting sunwise and upward to a new level of meaning. Kem saw the new meaning unfold in Sander's eyes—for some reason that is what he saw, the expression there, the moment of surprise and then the slower and ever-so-graceful moment of surrender, before he became aware of the biting or pricking sensation that came from his own arm, as though an insect were stinging him.

The recording skipped forward. Davina was there and she was saying something. What time is it, where did you go, some question. It may have been Davina in the present or Davina in the past, if there was a difference, and one Kem or the other turned to kiss her, which seemed to answer many questions at once. The kiss went on and the recording picked

up speed. Scenes flickered by, their words and images
compressed to a chirping, flashing montage. Colors shifted,
sliding up the spectrum from cool to hot. The balcony
began to feel crowded, as though other people were pressing around him. Some of them seemed to be part of the
recording, like Kem, and others seemed to form a kind
of audience.

There was music but it was not the same as before. The
soft, earthy sound of the flute was gone and the music had
grown lively in an erratic sort of way. It made Kem feel out of
balance. There was an urge to move or to escape the confine-
ment of things—rooms, possessions, clothing—which Kem
felt but which he sensed was not his urge alone. He saw
Sander move across the balcony and someone was waiting
there, someone Kem did not know. He did not want to watch
this part again.

"Kem," said Davina, a voice among other voices. "Kem,
look."

This was a surprise—even the memory of it was surprising—
because the balcony was empty now. Well, almost empty.
Gardner was still there and a few people stood behind
him—back in the main room where they hovered indistinctly,
a swarm of eyes. Kem thought he knew or once had known
who these other people were. One of them was wearing a
turquoise necklace, which might be an important clue, and
another...

Next to Kem, all around him, the recording wavered and
it was as though the night were starting to melt. Davina ran
her fingers down his chest; it felt like a gentle movement, a
show of tenderness, but he could hear the rending of fabric
and he felt a series of little tugs as his buttons popped off. His
breath was coming hard and the world around him grew as
insubstantial as fog. It was as though the old tape had been
used and reused too many times; now and then you could see
a second scene imposed on this one, a distinct story line.

It was the dawn. The sky was turning yellow and pink and
the sun was rising. This distracted Kem enough that for a
moment his attention wavered—he knew that Davina was
pressing against him and his loins were throbbing and in a
certain way that was all that was clear to him. But also in

flashes he was aware of something else, the other scene superimposed on this one became clear at certain instants, and Kem saw or remembered these two eyes: clear hard eyes that touched you in a way that you could feel. He did not want to look into those eyes, he wanted to get on with the orgasmic surge that was rushing up on him, but something—maybe it was the brightening sky—compelled him to look anyhow. He looked and the eyes looked back and *please I've got to remember this, let me remember* he pulled himself back, shoved Davina away from him, and somehow he was moving across the balcony and he could almost see himself, a clownish figure, comic interlude of the recording.

You think you fucking own us, the clown was saying, hurling the words at the audience, the swarming eyes, which did not seem to hear them. *You figure you bought us and now you own us and now you can do whatever the fuck you want to, but you can't. You just fucking can't.*

The audience—whatever audience there was—did not respond in any way. The only stirring came from the insects, the ones who had been hovering watchfully about the overgrown, espaliered fruit tree. One of these insects buzzed over, and as the clown stood there, his costume all asunder, waiting for a cue, and the eyes of the silent audience continued to stare, the insect stung him on the neck.

And that, from what Kem could tell, was the end of the show.

It was hard to believe that you could go into certain experiences and later come out of them and find that things were in every way the same. It was hard to believe that the world outside did not quiver, at least, when the world inside you shattered and you had to build it up again piece by piece on a shaky new foundation. It was hardest of all to realize that when you stepped out into the world again, this strange new being that you had become with everything changed inside, your heart and guts and lungs in different places than they had been before, that everyone out there wouldn't recognize what had happened right away. And yet this seemed to be the case. Kem stepped onto the navigation deck two hours at

most after letting himself out of Gardner's apartment and
leading Davina, who must have been socked good, down the
trammeled and over-familiar hall to Girls' Berthing.

Everything Kem did that morning seemed to swell up
from the plane of simple action and take on this storybook-
style, 3-D shadowing. His new body was hungry just as his
old body had been. And so—though he didn't know why, had
no idea why he should bother with such things inasmuch as
he obviously had lost his mind—he ate breakfast. Tea and
bread and honey, no big deal. Then because he felt dirty
(and here is where the storybook symbolism gets labored and
obvious) he took a shower. He stepped into the shower
and he washed off a little and then he stepped out again. It
was not a ritual of purification nor did Kem emerge from it a
different person, cleansed of his sins, vouchsafed with a new
sense of purpose. He felt actually quite shitty and he did not
see the purpose in anything at all, neither the trivial things
he was doing now nor the supercharged, mind-twisting things
that had happened last night. Both seemed equally banal and
lacking in effect, though for a passing few moments he
thought he saw how you could get to prefer the one over the
other, the colors and shifting depths of the night over the flat
unchanging landscape of the day. The first of these at least
seemed more likely to penetrate the tough casing that had
grown like a shell, by slow accretion—though oddly he hadn't
noticed until now and of course by now it no longer mattered—
around his heart.

He was early for his watch and that gave him a chance to
stare out the window for a while, watching the featureless
land below and the dirt-brown, sluggishly flowing water of
the Gut.

He was surprised to notice the train of wagons they had
picked up. Twelve or fifteen of the tiny vehicles straggled
behind them. Kem guessed that they were not much different from the one in which he had spent most of his life. Only
something was missing from this idea. Maybe it was that the
wagons looked so small and mean from up here, twenty-
seven heads above the Grind. Or maybe it was that the part

of his life he was remembering—the time when he had been his father's son, the brother of two little girls—no longer seemed so real. It seemed to have no particular relation to the person he was now, the new person with everything rearranged. Kem figured that as far as this new person was concerned those things, the wagon and the pitiful little family inside it, could not quite be said to be true. It was not that he disbelieved them. He knew he had been that boy and he knew he had once had certain aspirations, certain half-developed plans as to the basic structure of his life. But it was like studying history, how you believed it and yet you never really got the idea that it actually had happened. You sat in the winter school and they told you These were all cornfields once, once there were farms here where now there is only the Grind, and you got the concept but at the same time you did not really grasp that it might be true. They told you Once there were great machines that flew through the sky, and Once people dreamed of conquering disease, of mining the deep Ocean, of mapping the secret places of the soul as clearly as we have drawn maps of the Grind. But even though you remembered these things and you wrote them down on the test, you never accepted them, you recognized them for what they were. They were stories. They were 3-D exaggerations of a flat and featureless past.

There had never really been machines that could fly. Why would you want to fly when there was nowhere to fly to?

No one had ever really thought you could conquer disease. But even if you could do it—well, what then? You lived to be a thousand? You kept getting older and more worn-out and more shriveled up?

And surely nobody had every really set out to map the soul. The soul did not even exist, probably. It was a way of speaking, a metaphor, nothing but that. Kem looked down at the storybook wagons, remembering a made-up past, and he felt quite certain that the soul was just another thing that you heard about, the same way you heard about bright and magical lands somewhere over the shining Sea: a source of hope, something to hang the future on. In other words, a bunch of crap.

• • •

Somehow the watch went by. Kem performed competently though by midday he was totally exhausted; he had gotten through the morning on something along the lines of spaced-out desperation, but there were limits to everything, even the frantic energy of despair.

Perhaps it was owing to his peculiar empty-headed state, but Kem didn't notice for a minute or more after it had happened that a new person had come onto the deck. Also perhaps he did not give the newcomer much thought because the way the man conducted himself suggested that he belonged there—staring at the shelf of machines, then out at the window, then back. The thing that got Kem's attention was his watch partner, the young mate. Kem was struck by how the guy—who looked a little like a statue to begin with—had frozen up even more than usual. He stood with his back jammed up against the bulkhead. Only then did Kem look at the newcomer and recognize Captain Hand.

For some reason he was not surprised. Maybe he was too tired for that. Maybe he was expecting the Captain to show up, as people who are old and sick must expect the Angel of Death to call on them.

The thing was, Kem had developed a certain theory. It had to do with what had happened last night, much of which he did not remember and most of which he did not understand. But from what he did remember he had constructed or reconstructed a certain chain of events. The beginning and the end were missing; but in the middle there had been an outburst before a dimly recognized audience. All he retained were pieces of that, but the pieces were something. They added up.

Maybe what they added up to was this unprecedented visit. Kem stood feeling curiously detached, all by himself before the dead reckoning table, watching Captain Hand.

Hand did not seem particularly mindful of Kem, however, as he looked back and forth between the window and the row of machines. He was wearing his white uniform, and if he had been awake at a late hour of the night there was no way to tell it from his composed, highly energetic presence. That energy was, in fact, the most striking part—you could almost feel it pulsing from him, slapping your spine like waves hitting an antenna. Despite his exhaustion, Kem found himself standing up straight and feeling quite alert.

He was not prepared, though, for the Captain's sudden glance in his direction. The leonine head turned and the eyes caught him like whips, grabbed him and pulled him. Then they let go just as suddenly and Kem's heart squeezed violently shut, shoving oxygen into his brain like a drug kicking in.

The Captain said, "Where do you think we are? Where does your last fix have us? Here, show me on the chart."

He was clearly speaking to Kem and not the mate. While Kem stood dumbfounded, trying to slow his heart down, the Captain walked over to the dead reckoning table, and slowly a certain normalcy began to assert itself. The mate loosened up from his rigid stance and moved to follow the Captain and Kem looked down at the chart, crisscrossed as tightly as a spiderweb with lines he had drawn in his periodic efforts to establish the craft's position. The Captain stood before the table, waiting.

Kem tried to speak: well the horizon wasn't very clear this morning, only a couple of stars and not really good ones, the numbers coming from the satellites weren't tracking well, ten digits off or something, we've been trying to spot this cairn to starboard, you can see it here on the chart—

"What does that mean?" Hand interrupted. "What do you mean, the numbers from the satellites? Can you tell me?"

Kem did not know where to start; it seemed incredible that the Captain should not know this so he assumed it must be a kind of test.

"Well," he said, "there's this machine—it's that one, the blue one on the end—and it's supposed to be getting . . . like, a signal or something, from these satellites. They're like stars. Only this morning the numbers were all wrong, I thought maybe we were picking up the wrong frequency. But then, see, if you chart the numbers that were coming through you can see they sort of follow, in a way, but they're off a little bit. But they're consistent, though, see? So I was thinking . . ."

Kem felt his voice falter as though it had run out of something. Hand was watching him with no expression whatsoever. Kem found it odd that all of this, this situation, was not more unnerving. Actually he felt rather comfortable, sure of himself, under the Captain's gaze, and when he glanced at the mate again—leaning anxiously forward, glaring at Kem in obvious irritation—he managed a fleeting smile.

"They are like moons."

Hand spoke so suddenly that Kem was not sure right away he had heard right. He had, though. His mouth twitched.

Over the Captain's shoulder the mate said, "The satellites, you mean, sir."

Hand moved his head around, the slightest of motions, and the mate fell silent. Looking at Kem again the Captain said, "They are like moons, not stars. Artificial moons. People built them, long ago, and other people put them up there, in the sky."

Kem nodded; he felt like a kid hearing a fairy tale, one that sounded old and familiar though you couldn't remember how it ended.

"There were many of them," the Captain went on. "I believe at one time there may have been hundreds. A dozen or so remain active, perhaps a few more we cannot locate." He paused; his eyes seemed to look beyond Kem, out at some distant place, the place where lost things go. "There was a paper written once, a brochure, about one of those satellites, among the last ones built. The brochure said, *It can be confidently predicted that HV-47—that is the name of the satellite—that HV-47 will have a useful life of 50 to 75 years.*" Hand smiled. The smile seemed to include Kem: there was some joke that they shared, some understanding. "That was a lie. The satellite had been engineered to last twenty-five years at the most, by which time it would have been technically obsolete in any case. So it was a lie, probably meant to justify the cost of the project. And yet—"

Hand turned and walked across the bridge. Kem followed because it was clear that he was intended to. They came to a halt in front of the blue machine, a more-or-less cubical device bearing the legend *StarGazer*. They looked at it together, Kem and Captain Hand, at the little numbers dancing across its face.

"And yet—" the Captain resumed "—and of course this is the greatest irony—the lie told by that unknown brochure writer has turned out to be prophetic. The satellite has survived for many times its design life. It is now . . . well, I would say it is about as old as our Oasis, more or less. Older than anyone knows. And still functioning, in a manner of speaking. Though of course," Hand waved loosely at the blue box, "all things are imperfect. The greatest failing of HV-47 may be that it has outlasted our ability to monitor its signal. But how could its designers have anticipated that? How could they have known" (waving broadly, indicating the world beyond the windows) "that *this* would happen?"

With a quick motion he spun and flipped the power switch of the blue box and the numbers faded to darkness. He asked Kem, "What does all that tell us, do you think? What is the lesson of the story?" He said it slightly smiling, as though to reassure Kem that it was only a question, nothing crucial. Not a test. And after a few seconds, as Kem had expected, Hand supplied the answer for himself. "Perhaps," he said, "it is warning against hubris. Perhaps it shows us that there is a limit to how much we can know by reason alone, by calculation. For even our own works are mysterious to us—their results cannot be predicted, or at any rate not known beforehand by any normal means. The engineers who designed and built that satellite truly expected it to fail after a generation."

He lifted a finger. "That is one lesson, a cautionary one. But there is another." The other hand came up, a second, apposite finger. "The other lesson is a hopeful one. It has to do with greatness. It has to do with the remarkable extent of human capability. Not our limitations, but our *lack* of them. The unboundedness of our minds. For ultimately, you see, it is the box that fails, not the idea emodied within it. The idea, a human creation, immaterial, endures. The box, a material object, is mortal. This is rather different from the usual line of thinking, is it not?"

Kem supposed that it was, though he was not at all clear what the usual line of thinking might be. The whole satellite business was news to him. He guessed he would have to think about it.

Hand was smiling at him, and for the first time Kem got

the idea that there was something detached or ironic about the
smile; a hint of something like amused tolerance. Then
the Captain turned and strode directly to the chart table. He
placed a finger on a certain spot without seeming to pause to
think or even look.

"I think you will find," he said, "that we are here."

He departed quickly after that and Kem spent a few
minutes reflecting on things, chief among them the peculiar
second wind he seemed to have caught. He felt wide awake
now, alert but also calm. He was calm enough, for example,
to just get out of the way while the young mate fussed about
with lines and coordinates, trying to improve upon Kem's last
fix. He did so finally by a little: that is, the mate's fix was
closer by a couple of kills of chart distance to the spot where
Hand's finger had briefly and decisively come down. Still it
was off by a good bit, a thumb-width or so on the chart.
There were two explanations for that and of course there was
no way objectively to judge between them.

But for his own part, Kem made a judgment—not a
rational judgment but one in which he had confidence nonetheless. He felt pretty sure that by just that thumb-width, the
mate and all his instruments and his calculations were wrong,
and that Captain Hand was right.

In the long run, the most amazing things are the ordinary
ones. Kem had come to think that. It is not so surprising, for
example, when some calamity occurs. You get sold by your
family. Your boat capsizes. A stranger with eyes that could kill
you shows up one day and starts telling you about artificial
moons. These and other, stranger things are the stuff of
everyday life and you see them all around you.

What is truly amazing is that each morning, despite knowing what you know, you climb out of your bunk anyway. You
go to work (if you are a snipe) among machines that could
explode at any minute and destroy you. You go looking for
your girlfriend. You hope for the future, for a better life. You
make plans.

You even think sometimes—this is amazing too—you even
think that you've got time on your hands. Time to kill. You

look for ways to kill it. As though time were something that exists without limit, with no end in sight, just the way that once upon a time (so they said at the winter school) you could have stood here and thought there was no end to the corn-fields. Only the end had come. And it had not been an end in geographical extent, a sudden drawing-in of the horizons; it had been an end in time. The old growers of corn thought they had time to kill so they had killed it. Now it was dead and dried up and gone.

Kem thought about this as he stood looking across the Grind, into the West where the sun had set a little while ago. It was Birds Cry Moon. The Oasis had climbed out of the desert and into the old exhausted grassland where corn had grown long ago and people had lived on farms and in prosper-ous villages. The villages were gone now—burned one piece at a time in camp fires, Kem guessed, or rusted into the ground. But perhaps the children of those farmers, several generations down, crossed the old fields in their wagons, blowing east and then west and then east again according to the season and the prevailing wind. In Birds Cry Moon the wind blew principally out of the southeast and the wagons were mostly gone; only a few hung back around the Gut, risking a flood for the sake of following the Oasis. Kem's father had not liked to do that; he had avoided the Oasis, generally, but now you could see how much good that had done him. The Oasis had been waiting for him finally, when the ordinary times ended, the times of dull journeys and family quarrels and long summer days with time to kill. Those times ended when the wagon broke down and Kem's father needed help. The Oasis had helped him, and he had paid for the help with his son.

Kem stood on a deck where there were chairs and tables, a few palm trees growing in large tubs, a net and balls and rackets with which you could play some game. There were other people on the deck but Kem stood alone at the rail looking outward and thinking about ordinary things, about the horizon where the sun had burned down, about the clouds still smeared with carmine and sulphur yellow on their undersides and about the land that was cooling off now, night creatures coming out, insects taking wind and long-nosed

bats devouring them, prairie dogs scooting among the stands
of buffalo grass, poison vetch in flower sending its deceptive
sweetness out on the air. These were everyday things that
Kem had known all his life. But tonight they seemed inde-
scribably valuable to him; their loss would amount to the loss
of part of himself. Without the sunset and the pale violet
luminescence that spread in its wake across the land, his life
would become narrower in some dimension, in breadth or in
depth. Whereas he could have done without any number of
nonordinary things—without the party in Gardner's apartment, without the view from the navigation deck, without the
Oasis itself, and he guessed even without Davina—and his
life would still be the same life. Lacking in drama, perhaps,
and other things, but still as broad and as deep and as long.

Overhead, a fall of woodcocks banked from the northeast
to the north, then off to the east again. Kem waited for them
to find a spot along the Gut to their liking but they kept
flying and soon they were gone in the twilight. At one point
he thought he could hear their squawking above the rumble
of engines and grind of treads but he wasn't sure.

It was late when he tried to explain some of what he had
been thinking to Davina. She had been expecting him and
when he hadn't shown up (she said) she had gotten worried.
So she came all the way down to his cabin, a place she had
only visited once or twice, it was so small, and that's where
she found him. She seemed very interested in what he had to
say in the immediate and uncritical way that girls are, but
when he stopped talking she made no comment, added no
thoughts of her own. That might have been because Kem
wasn't making sense—he suspected as much—or it might
have been that she was just interested in being with Kem and
that was the point of her visit, not talking, just being together.

Since that night at the party things had changed; there was
a hollow space between them as though something—all the
ordinary things that were there before—had been taken away.
Now there was a strange emptiness like the emptiness of the
Grind: a silence, a sense of loss. But this had an odd result,
because now that there seemed to be nothing in the space

between them it was like they were pulled together, sucked into that emptiness, and they kept coming closer and closer until they touched. Only then did everything seem all right, ordinary and comfortable, and now they were touching again, their legs overlapping while Kem talked and Davina listened, in the close atmosphere of his room.

They sat on the bunk side by side, there being nowhere else to sit. The bunk was narrow and it was barely long enough for Kem to stretch out on. That didn't bother him; and he supposed that if the cabin were any larger he wouldn't be in it, it would have been given to somebody more important and Kem would be up in Crew's Berthing sharing a room with someone else. He wouldn't have liked that. He liked having some privacy, a place to hide. He told Davina this and she said she understood. Nobody spoke for a while after that and Kem could hear the girl's slow, warm breathing. He lay back with his head propped against the bulkhead and he closed his eyes.

"You know," said Davina—the sound of her voice making him start, he had begun to drift off—"I ran into your friend Delan today."

"Mm." Kem waited to hear if there was going to be any more. Something in Davina's voice suggested there was.

"He asked how you were. He said he hadn't seen you for a while."

"Yeah, well."

In his mind Kem was seeing the turquoise necklace, the one Delan had worn to the party. The image had sour associations though Kem had not shared these with Davina.

She went on, "I told him I was going to your room to look for you. He said he was sorry he hadn't been able to get you anything better—a better room I mean—but it was the best thing that was available at the time. He said there might be something coming up, though."

Kem looked at her, as though he might if he looked closely enough catch some glimpse of Delan in her expression. He tried to imagine Delan speaking those words—*there might be something coming up*—and he tried to imagine how he had said them.

"Actually," said Davina, twisting around to look at him,

"what he said was, there's a good opportunity coming up and
he thought we might be able to take advantage of it. You and
I, he meant."

Kem thought about the things Sander has said, how Delan
gave him the creeps and so on. The memory seemed to tingle
along his spine. He sat up in the bulk and he said, "What
kind of opportunity? A better room, or what?"

"Well, there's a room, yes. I think so." Davina was acting
nervous, Kem thought; and he thought, Well here it comes.
"But it's not just a room, see—it's a job too. The work is
supposed to be pretty easy. Delan said something about
special projects. I guess there are these projects now and
then—you know, just things that come up?" She paused, as
though sensing that Kem was not reacting well. "And you'd
get a nice room," she added rather timidly. "We would, I
mean. Delan said it would be big enough for both of us."

Kem tried hard to think calmly and clearly. He did not
want to screw things up with Davina. But at the same time
he did not exactly like the sound of this mysterious job, nor
the funny way he was hearing about it, second- or thirdhand.

"Listen," he said, "if this job is such a great deal, why does
Delan want *me* to have it? What does he think I can do to pay
him back? That's how he operates, you know. He does you a
favor, then you do him one. You introduce him to some boy,
or whatever."

Davina was looking at him in a funny way, as though she
were curious about something but couldn't decide whether to
ask. "Actually, he did mention something about a favor. He
mentioned that you owe him one."

Kem felt an odd thing happen in his stomach; maybe it
was a discharge of bile. "Did he say anything else? I mean,
about what I owed him?"

Davina nodded but for a moment she did not say anything.
Kem guessed she had known all along how he was going to
take this. She had come down here not just to see him but
also to serve as Delan's messenger, and he didn't guess she
was particularly happy about that, either. Davina said, "He
just said, he knew you wanted to thank him. He didn't say for
what. But he said this would be thanks enough, if you took
this job."

Kem shook his head. There was something about this that didn't feel right, a piece that didn't fit in. He said, "Well, I guess I don't have a whole lot of choice. But listen—if Delan tries to talk to you again, just tell him to come straight to me, okay? I don't like you getting caught in the middle like this."

"Like I can't take care of myself?" Davina looked at him in a way that made him remember, as he usually tried not to, that she was older than he, that she had been at the Oasis longer, knew her way around better, et cetera. Kem looked away, feeling chastened and dumb. Her point made, Davina took his hand and drew it into her, holding it against her breast. "Anyway," she said, in a purring sort of voice, "I forgot to tell you the best part."

"Mm?" Kem was thinking about the warm place where his hand was and did not particularly care about the best part.

"Delan said to tell you," Davina went on, "that you must have made quite an impression on the Captain."

Reflexively, Kem drew his hand back. Then he tried to relax it, but could not. He waited.

"That's how Delan thought of you for this job," she said. Excitement was rising in her voice. "He said the Captain recommended you personally."

The big ramp came down with an enormous, muffled boom, and dust exploded from underneath it. Kem blinked as the air cleared and he noticed the new smell of big animals, of shit and straw. One of the horses gave a huge snort—it was amazing how loud that was, up close—and then the stable girls led them down the ramp. Brown and gray and sand-colored, just like the Grind; six then seven then eight. Eight horses. Kem was surprised there weren't more. There were only eight and all the people who would ride them, therefore, were already here. Kem had expected something; he wasn't sure quite what—knights mounted on armored steeds, he supposed, something more impressive than this; but here were the horses already saddled and looking fairly tame, and here were their riders looking like a bunch of ordinary crew members and one somewhat tired and puzzled kid. The kid of course being Kem.

The Oasis had made its approach to Riley County at night by a more or less ass-backwards route. Kem was on watch at the time; he had been standing watch at night for the past couple of weeks, the first and thus far only hint of the subtle elevation in his status. As against the engine flats, where the night shift was as low as you could go, nighttime duty in the navigation tower was considered a privilege, even an honor; for the senior mates were all asleep, and there was no one to keep an eye on you, and the fate of the Oasis was pretty much in your hands.

Kem found that he liked being up in the tower then. There were no lights except for a few small red bulbs, just enough to let you see where you were going without knocking out your night vision too much, and you were up there in the middle of the night sky, the smell of dirt and bruised sage rising in the cool dry air and owls and bats coming out of nowhere, fluttering by then vanishing, casing the empty decks for food. You could see where people were still awake, down in Crew's Berthing and other places, and you wondered what they were doing there, until one by one at last the lights would go off, except for a nearly undiscernible line of tiny specks that Kem believed might be the string of lights on the railing of Gardner's balcony. They burned every night, all night. For the most part though on the night watch your attention was consumed by the problems of navigating the Oasis in the dark, which were considerable, and in order to solve them you pooled your resources with those of the unseen bridge and the engine flats and now and again the squirrel cage (Kem recognized Delan's voice in the tube) and a kind of camaraderie developed among you, the watchstanders of the night. So it was that Kem had been up in the tower when the track-line crept up the chart toward the place labeled Riley County: an irregular shape outlined in red. The mate of the watch had taken the last couple of fixes himself and when one of them fell just short of the line he walked over to the voice tube and called up:

"I think it's time to wake the Captain."

And the watchstander on the bridge had called back down, "You think he doesn't know?" And the mate beside Kem had smiled before the other voice said, "Never mind, I'll tell him."

They had veered eastward then, pushing the craft down closer to the Gut, which was known at this time of year very often to flood, and then north again aiming at a gap between the river and a second body of water called Tuttle Creek. On the chart it did not look exactly like a creek; it looked much bigger than that. The Oasis had then—at an unexplained order from the bridge—cranked up its speed. It went booming through washes and swails in the slice of land between bodies of water, shaking hard and Kem figured probably rattling everybody awake, until just as the sky was starting to brighten the mate drew a circle with a dot inside it on the chart and said, "Well, I guess we're there," and the craft had stopped.

They came for Kem later, during breakfast. It was one of the mates and the little man who had once been pointed out to him as the boss of Recruiting. They didn't say much; only that a team was going out later, a trading party heading for Riley County, and that Kem was to go with them.

Well, he had known it was going to happen—not this, he had known they were going to choose him for this particular job. But some job, someday. *Special projects*, that's what he was supposed to be doing, and he had not yet discovered what that meant. Was this trading gang a special project? He guessed he would find out pretty soon.

They got up on their horses (the top of a horse is *much higher* than you think it is, Kem learned) and that's when the boss of Recruiting gave him the rundown. Kem decided after about twelve words that he didn't like the guy one bit. He was just a little runt—shorter than Kem and round in the middle, they had given him the smallest horse—but somehow that only served to make his air of distinct nastiness all the more disturbing. "They don't care much for us," the little man explained, "in Riley County."

Kem had already figured that out. On the far side of Tuttle Creek (which was very wide, as it looked on the chart: Kem would have called it a lake) you could see the outskirts of some kind of town, a bigger place than Kem had ever seen before. It looked many times larger than Body of God, and it did not look especially friendly. There were tall structures that had the look of fortifications, with things sticking out of them that Kem was quite ready to believe were large guns.

"They are distrustful of all outsiders," the little man went on, "but especially of us. The problem goes back many years."

Kem nodded as his horse loped along. They moved onto a trail that ran beside the water. Beside the trail grew taller grass than you saw out on the Grind: cordgrass and dropseed, already up to the bellies of the horses. The animal underneath him seemed to grow excited, and Kem wondered if that was because of the grass or the nearness of water or something else.

He asked the boss of Recruiting why they were going to Riley County, then, if the people did not like them. "I mean, isn't it dangerous or something?" he said. "Shouldn't there be more of us?"

The little man smiled and it was not a pleasant smile. Kem wondered if your smile looked as nasty as that why you would even bother to use it.

"We have," the man said, "an understanding. An arrangement, worked out between our Captain and the authorities of Riley County. We are allowed to bring no more than a certain number of people and to stay no more than a certain length of time. And the Oasis must remain there" (he pointed) "and must not move or disembark any additional personnel until we are back on board. Only then will the authorities deliver to us the commodities we have purchased—they will do so using their own vehicles and their own crews. Then we must leave."

The little man recited all this in a punctilious voice, with that same smile lingering behind his words. He seemed to derive pleasure from the existence of these terms and conditions— as though he were gratified to know that all forms of behavior were being carefully controlled.

"But what I don't get," Kem said, "is what we're doing this for. I mean, why go to all this trouble? Why let these guys tell us what to do? We don't do that anywhere else."

The little man shook his head. "We do it everywhere.

Everywhere we go, there are arrangements. There are certain powers who must be appeased, and we do our best to appease them, so that we may go about our business. The powers of Riley County are more ... *particular,* let us say, than most." He lowered his head and gave Kem a dark kind of look, a look that seemed to probe him. "But then, unlike most places Riley County has certain things that our Captain is willing to bargain for. And unlike other places it has the strength and the resolve to enforce its demands. There are not many places like that. There are not many places that can afford to quarrel with the Oasis."

They followed the trail for a while in silence, after half an hour or so coming to the place where Tuttle Creek reached its widest point, and there they found a dam. It was old and decrepit-looking but it managed to hold back the waters all right. The trader at the head of the procession turned his horse out toward the dam; there appeared to be a path or a narrow roadway there, with broken-down guardrails running along its sides. Kem wondered how the horses were going to take it—whether they would be spooked by the drop-off at the edge of the dam, the water churning out of the chutes way down in the creekbed—but these animals must have been specially chosen for their docility. The Recruiting boss nudged his horse out ahead of Kem's and that's how they were arranged, Kem staring at the little man's round back, as they rode across the water.

As they reached the other side, Kem said, "So what is this stuff they've got? I mean—is it the diamonds or what? The stuff that the Captain's willing to bargain for."

The Recruiting boss glanced back momentarily, then in a rapid motion he spun his horse around and grabbed hold of Kem's bridle. Kem was surprised—among other things, that the guy handled the horse with such authority. He held the two of them back until the rest of the party had gotten some distance ahead. Then he spoke to Kem quickly in a low voice.

"Now listen," he said. "The success of this entire visit depends on you, and you must do exactly what I tell you. Now."

He raised a hand to wipe off his brow; a line of sweat had collected there along a ridge just above the eyebrows. The man's eyes were small but they stabbed at Kem, they pinned him.

"When we reach Riley County we will be met by a party of armed police. They will verify that there are only eight of us and that we are carrying no weapons. We will then be allowed to enter the town, and there we will disperse. It is unlikely that any of us will be followed. In any case, you should leave the rest of us and blend into the crowd as best you can."

He took a breath and wiped his brow again but he kept talking. He told Kem that he was to pick up a new set of clothing, any type would do but ideally the clothes should be nondescript and they should not look new. Once out of his Oasis uniform, he was to get on with his task. There would be no time to spare. He had until tomorrow at dawn, at which time the trading gang was due to leave Riley County.

For a long moment Kem thought that the man was finished talking, that he was going to leave it at that—"get on with your task" with no clue as to what that task might be. Of course that was not the case. The little man was just saving this, the best part, for last.

"What we require," he said—and Kem would have sworn that he did, he really did, smack his lips now—"What we require is simply this. We need two young recruits. One boy and one girl. They must be of a certain age—I should say thirteen or so but the age is not crucial, what we are looking for is a boy and girl of a certain type."

He turned somewhat aside, as though checking to see that the others were out of earshot. Then he turned back and he said matter-of-factly:

"You have a friend. I believe his name is Sander. We are looking for a boy and girl who are of that type, more or less. Do you know what I am talking about?"

Kem shook his head though he had a feeling it was not true; he was afraid he knew what the man meant but he wanted to hear him say it.

"What I mean is, they should have a certain quality: seemingly innocent, and yet not entirely so—though by no means should they appear corrupted or spoiled. When I say they should be like your friend, perhaps I mean they should be like your friend *was*, a few months ago." The man blinked a couple of times; you could practically hear the points clicking off in his mind. "They should be young but not mere children, quite. The thing is, they should not be too physically mature. Pubescent but not much more than that. They should be attractive. I might say they should be beautiful, if you can manage that, but you must do the best you can. And listen to me, this is important. They must be quite willing to go with you. Do you understand me? To go with you and to cooperate fully. They must, in other words, be the sort of young people who are in the mood for adventure, for taking a few risks. I hope that is perfectly clear."

It was clear enough, and yet Kem could hardly believe he was hearing it. His mind felt crowded with questions, but the main problem was that the whole thing didn't make much sense. He tried to make this point to the Recruiting boss.

"I mean," he said, "if you just want a couple more kids on the crew, why don't you just buy some?" *The way you bought me*, he meant, but he didn't say that. "Why do it this way, with all this sneaking around? Everybody knows the Oasis buys kids, it's not like it's any big secret or anything. And besides, why send somebody like me to do it? I've never done anything like this before."

The man smiled at him. "We don't just want a couple more kids, as you say. We need two very special young people—the boy and girl I have just described. We cannot just go buy them because our agreement with Riley County does not allow that. We are permitted to arrive with eight people and we must depart with eight, no more and no fewer." He stopped as though to make sure Kem had gotten this—that he was being sent in to break the rules. "As to why we want you to do this—you in particular—that is not really your concern. But I will tell you this. It is very important that the boy and girl be willing to go with you, that they make no disturbance that would draw the attention of the authorities. Thus it is best if they like and trust the person with whom they are dealing. And Kem, the Captain finds you to be a likable young man. And he believes you can be trusted."

If ever there was an odd place and time to be given a

compliment, it was here and now. Kem shook his head,
unable to absorb it all.

"But what am I supposed to do?" he said. "I mean, do I
just go up to kids on the street and say Hey, want to run away
to the Oasis?"

The little man smiled. "You may do that if you like. You
may go about this in any way that seems appropriate. But let
me offer a suggestion." Kem was all for suggestions but he
had a feeling he wasn't going to like this one. "In Riley
County, Kem, you will find that there are a large number of
young people. Some have come here to escape the wagons,
and some have been left here on purpose by their parents, so
that they may receive proper schooling and have a chance to
lead a decent life."

Decent life. The words sounded bitter and cynical, coming
from this guy's mouth. But Kem had some idea of what he
meant. He remembered hearing about Riley County as a
kid—it was one of those places. It was not exactly a mythical
place, a source of legends, like the Bright Land, but you
heard about things: the diamond fields, the free hospitals, the
gardens. And Kem had known kids who had said they were
going there and he wondered if they had, if he might actually
run into them. He wondered how much they would have
changed, whether he would still recognize any of them; and
then it occurred to him to wonder how much he had changed
himself. Maybe it was he who would now be difficult to
recognize: once a scrawny wagon kid and now an agent of the
Oasis. A secret agent, at that. Chosen by the Captain himself,
because he could be trusted.

This thought startled Kem in that it gave him a surprising
and unfamiliar vision of himself. When the boss of Recruiting
spoke again—laying out a certain plan or approach which he
proposed that Kem might follow—Kem found himself listening in a whole new state of mind. And in this state of mind
the plan sounded reasonable enough; it sounded like it just
might work and that Kem might actually be able to pull it off.
For sure, he could go as the man suggested and look for
places where kids were hanging out. He could take it slow at
first, get the feel of the place, pick up the local vibes. And
then he could move in—select his target and strike up a

conversation. Start with the girl: that's what the man suggested. Start with the girl because young girls are easy to impress. Do whatever it takes to impress her. Once you have the girl it will not be hard to get the boy.

"Remember," the man said, raising a finger, "they do not have to be perfectly innocent. There are many young people in Riley County and not all of them have found a way to fit in. Some of them might be willing to do things—to have sex with you, for example—in exchange for your help. Feel free to avail yourself, if you care to. Do whatever you think best."

Kem felt almost dizzy with the strangeness of the thing. He thought it all through again, and while he was thinking the man set their horses in motion. They rode quickly to overtake the others, who were now a considerable distance ahead. It was only near the end, with the watch towers of Riley County looming over him, that Kem got clearheaded enough to wonder what he was supposed to do with these two kids after he got them. Assuming he really did. How was he supposed to get them out, if there were only eight people allowed in their party? Suddenly his mind was full of questions, now that the trading gang had stopped and a group of armed people, the police he guessed, were coming out to meet them. He wanted to talk more to the Recruiting boss, but the guy shot him a glance that seemed like a kind of warning. Then the police were ordering them to dismount, and the Recruiting guy muttered something which Kem barely heard.

It was, "The wharf." And he added, no more loudly, "Be there before sunrise."

That was the last Kem heard from him. He climbed off his horse and got frisked pretty roughly. Then he was turned loose on Riley County.

No one followed him, as far as Kem could tell. He walked for a while without wondering where he was going and without really bothering to look. His body felt charged with nervous energy and he was oblivious of everything else.

After a while he calmed down a little and he stopped walking and took a few deep breaths. Little by little he began to notice things, then suddenly he was noticing everything at once.

Riley County was not like any place he had ever been. There were buildings, solid structures made out of something like large bricks or blocks of pressed sod. You could guess at the nature of some of the buildings—those that were stores had brightly painted signs, and some of the others looked like they might contain offices. But many of the buildings were too small for that and Kem wondered if they might actually be people's homes. It was hard to imagine but then so was the fact that he was standing here. The buildings were set out in straight rows with wide lanes between them, and around some of them grew trees, bur oaks and black locusts, the largest living things Kem had ever seen, and low-cut grass and some kind of yellow flowers. Could these be daffodils? Kem thought he remembered his mother talking about daffodils: an almost mythic symbol of spring. He began walking again, paying more attention now to where he was going, and he saw that the town had a deliberate kind of organization about it: on some streets there would be a certain type of building and on other streets there would be another. This might be important to figure out at some point but for the moment Kem just kept moving. It might not be the greatest idea to be noticed hanging around and gawking at things, and he decided to get rid of his uniform.

He looked for a store selling clothes but he didn't see one. It seemed that he had wandered away from the part of town where stores were and he did not feel like going back. He thought about offering to trade clothes with someone but that would probably strike the other person as pretty weird. From here he could look way down the street ahead of him—all the streets were perfectly straight and the town seemed to go on and on—and up ahead he saw people milling around in the open, like maybe that was a market area or something. He headed toward that and meantime he began studying in a covert way the people of who lived in this place.

There were not so many of them in the part of town Kem was passing through, which made it awkward to watch them. He did not want to stare and his Oasis uniform (though it was a simple affair, shirt and pants of undyed linen) made him feel

self-conscious. The people of Riley County dressed different-
ly. They must have had access to an assortment of dyes,
because their clothing was variously colored. There were
even clothes of a pure blue shade that Kem had never seen
before; he had no idea what sort of substance produced a
color like that. The men wore trousers that looked thicker
and heavier than Kem's, and their shirts were more simply
cut. Where the women were concerned the pattern was less
clear; some of them dressed like the men while others wore
skirts that flowed loosely around them. In general the people
had an unadorned look that was not quite the same as the
look Kem associated with wagon people: the difference was
that between simplicity and deprivation. In Riley County
people's eyes were wider open and they did not look so
hard-pressed.

He walked for ten minutes or so. The only kids he saw
were a few very small ones with their mothers, playing in a
little field. Kem gave them a glance and was walking on by
but then he stopped, he looked longer at them. The playing
field was a simple thing, just an open space between buildings where a few trees had been planted. The trees were not
as old as others Kem had seen; they were arranged along one
side of the field in a row and seemed to represent some fairly
recent urge toward civic improvement. Rough grass grew
between them and there were dogtooth violets in bloom. The
little kids looked like kids anywhere, Kem supposed. The
mothers looked like mothers though for some reason Kem
thought they looked awfully young. One of them seemed
barely older than Davina. She looked at Kem and he started
to wave—the little scene had put him in a friendly mood—
but the expression on her face was wrong. She was looking at
him suspiciously, he thought, and at first he resented that.
Then he remembered why he had come to Riley County and
he turned and walked quickly away.

He felt odd; the encounter had upset him and he felt a loss
of momentum. Until now, he had not actually stopped to
reflect upon what he was doing. Things had happened pretty
fast—he had been awake on the bridge all night and they had
snatched him from the breakfast table and things hadn't
stopped moving since then. All at once he felt tired, and the

new idea he had had about himself (agent of the Oasis, trusted by the Captain, all that) collapsed in a heap of self-doubt. Persistent questions darted through his mind— like what do they want these kids for, why is this thing so important, why do the kids have to come from *here*, when the Grind is crawling with wagons full of them—and after a while it was too much to think about. Kem found a place to sit under a locust that had sprung up in what seemed like neutral territory. He figured there was no harm in catching his breath. Take it slow at first, get the feel of the place: that's what the man had said.

Around him, life in Riley County buzzed along in its easygoing way. People moved up and down the street and nobody seemed to pay Kem much mind, one way or the other. He thought about something the Recruiting boss had said, that in Riley County people were distrustful of outsiders, and he wondered if maybe that didn't apply so much to him, seeing as how he was only a kid. He stayed there a little longer, but after a while it felt like resting might be having the wrong effect: it was making him feel sleepier. Each time he closed his eyes they wanted to stay that way. So he got back up and stretched and tried to pull himself back together; and that's when he realized that someone was standing beside him.

A woman. She must have walked up while Kem was sitting there, nodding off. Now she stood right in front of him, a middle-aged smiling woman with her hair rolled up so there hardly seemed to be any of it. Her arms were folded around something, a sheaf of papers or a folder, and she bent forward a little bit. Her manner was solicitous.

"Good morning," she told Kem. "I venture to say that you are new to Riley County." Kem did not deny this (he was afraid to speak before he figured out what was going on) so the woman continued, "Well, let me welcome you to the town of Manhattan. Manhattan is the seat of Riley County and you are very fortunate to have come here."

Kem smiled and nodded. It seemed to him that the woman was making some kind of speech; her words sounded rehearsed and he figured the safest thing would be to let her finish.

"We welcome newcomers here in Manhattan," the woman said, "which as you may know is not always so in other places. But we do ask certain things of all our citizens. We are more than happy to receive anyone who wishes to live in our town but we do ask that everyone who comes here please observe those few laws that we have established to maintain order." She looked down at the sheaf of papers in her hand and then back up at Kem. Her next question caught him a bit by surprise.

"You're from that horrid thing, aren't you? That Oasis." Her smile was gone and she was staring at the insignia on Kem's breast. "You're wearing one of their uniforms."

He started to say no. He thought of a couple of crazy lies—he had just bought it somewhere, found it lying around—but that was stupid; and anyway he was curious as to what the woman was driving at.

"We are prepared to offer you sanctuary," she told him. "We will protect you if you wish to stay. We will simply refuse to let your ... your guards or keepers, whatever you call them, come and take you. There is nothing they can do, we are stronger than the Oasis and they understand that. So you may stay and if you are less than eighteen years old you may attend one of our free schools." She eyed Kem critically. "I don't expect you are, though, are you? Well, in any case we will help you find your way here. Let me give you some information. Can you read?"

Kem nodded that he could and the woman held out to him a sheet of paper covered with tiny handwriting. He glanced it over: numbers and words and short paragraphs arranged in columns. The woman was talking again.

"The first address there is a place you can go to get an initial allotment of things you may need. You will be asked to register there—one of the things we ask of all our citizens is that they register. The other addresses are places you may go to eat and for help in finding a place a live. Well." She looked down at her sheaf of papers again, maybe checking to see if she had forgotten anything. When she looked at Kem for the last time it seemed to him that there was something wistful about her expression.

"I must be honest with you," she said after a moment. "I

do not expect you will be happy here. Riley County has many things to offer, but it is not paradise. We expect people to work and we expect ... well, you see, we have a certain quality of life here. A kind of order that we are anxious to maintain. We have had many people come here from the Oasis, over the years, and as a rule they have not done well. They have had trouble fitting in. I imagine that living in such a place..."

Her voice trailed off and she looked away, across Kem's shoulder. It was so much like she was really seeing it, really looking at the Oasis, that Kem followed her gaze and for an instant he felt as though he were sharing her dread. But all he saw when he looked around was the row of buildings behind him—modest structures with little yards in front, here or there a tiny vegetable patch, clumps of those bright yellow flowers.

"I must go," the woman told him. "Good luck. I wish there was something more I could do, but we have people coming here every day."

Then she was gone, bustling away with her arms still folded in front of her. Kem watched her moving down the street, plying her good offices through the streets of the town of Manhattan, the seat of Riley County.

It was all too easy.

Kem studied the piece of paper that the woman had given him, a description of services available to runaways, migrants, and other newcomers to this remarkable place, and then he went up to a passerby and asked directions to the first address on the list. It was nearby and when he got there he found a large building like a warehouse. He hesitated; from the outside the place looked empty and it sat on a street with few trees, shabby and desolate. But he went in anyway and told a man inside why he had come. He didn't say much, only that he was new in town, but the man didn't seem to care; he nodded and gave Kem a form to fill out and a chewed-down pencil, then he disappeared up an aisle. The place was like one of the storage bays of the Oasis, high-ceilinged and cluttered, full of huge bales and crates. The man came back carrying a bundle of something secured with twine. He turned away and Kem figured that was the end of it.

Outside, the bundle turned out to be two sets of clothes. They were not new and they did not exactly fit him, but they were clean and in the middle of them, all wrapped up, was a package of dried fruit and jerky and a bit of paper money.

That's when Kem began to think it was all too easy. It was hard to believe that you could just come here and they would give you things like this. And yet that is what had happened. He wondered if they had known, back at the Oasis, that it was going to fall out like this. He tried to remember what the guy from Recruiting had said, or rather how he had said it. Had he said "Go buy some new clothes" or just "Go pick some new clothes up"? It seemed to Kem that it had been the latter, that the guy had known how Riley County operated and how easy it was going to be.

In that case, Kem thought, maybe the rest of it would be easy too. Maybe they did this—picked out somebody like Kem and gave him instructions and sent him into town— every year, every time the Oasis came to Riley County in its annual roll around the Grind. That was an odd thought, that this might have happened before, might have happened again and again for who knew how long. The Oasis was old and from the look of things the town of Manhattan had been here for a while itself. Kem began to get an eerie feeling, which he quelled by stepping behind a locust tree, barely hidden from the street but nobody seemed to be around, and took off his uniform.

For a moment, standing there in the shade of the tree with his clothes off, Kem felt as though he had been unshackled. He felt that he had gotten very far away from the Oasis and from everyplace else he had known, that he had removed all connections to his past and dropped them onto the ground among the stubbly weeds and the tree roots. Then he started to think of those connections again, remembering them one by one. He thought of his appointment at someplace called the wharf before dawn; he thought of the Oasis and his new room and the navigation deck; he thought about Davina. Then he chose a pair of pants and a faded blue shirt, that unusual color, from those they had given him, and he stepped

quickly into his disguise. I'm just a kid now, he thought. A
boy again.

He wondered if anybody was going to buy it.

Exactly how he spent the day Kem would have had trouble
telling, had anyone asked. It seemed to him that he was still
fairly early on in the process—still in the picking-up-the-
local-vibes part—when he noticed that the sun was caught in
the tops of trees across the road from him, heading down.
The trees waved strongly in a wind that had come up lately
from the Grind. It was a strange wind, out of the south
instead of the east as one would have expected at this time
of year. The sun had turned orange though it was still
rather high, a thing that sometimes presaged dust storms.
He wondered if the oncoming night would be cool as nights
sometimes were during Birds Cry Moon. The shirt he had
chosen was a thin one and the air seemed to move through it
easily.

He had seen a lot of Riley County—at least he could have
said that. He had walked all the way to the edge of town and
he had stood looking northward over what he supposed were
the famous diamond fields. There was not much to see, but in
places the earth had been piled up after having been scraped
off the bedrock, and in the distance some kind of machinery
was in operation: you could see a cloud that was either smoke
or dust hanging low in the sky. Kem was slightly disappointed—
but maybe that was the way with everything.

Later on he had walked back into town by a different route
and had spent some of his money on food. The food was
better than he expected it to be, perhaps because he was
used to the food at the Oasis. He had eaten all of it and then
bought more. Finally he had gotten so full that he had sat
down in an empty brush-lot and this time he really had
nodded off. It was when he awoke that he saw that the sun
had turned orange and the wind had changed. He got up
feeling groggy, full of a sense of urgency but unable to get a
handle on things.

There was no choice now but to do what he had been sent
here for. He had managed thus far not to worry about that by

keeping his thoughts on other things, on the food, the diamond fields, the quiet and welcoming town. There was no more time for that. He set out now with the idea of meeting some kids and striking up a conversation. He rehearsed in his mind the way he would do it. It felt odd and it made him nervous, and for some reason he found himself recalling that the woman who had talked to him had thought he was older than he was: she had thought he was eighteen or more, whereas Kem would not be seventeen for a month. He wondered if this meant anything with respect to what he was here for, whether kids as young as Sander would not trust him because he was too old. But Sander trusted him. Or he had once. Kem felt even more confused, and heaven knows what he would actually have done if he had run into any kids during the next half hour or so. He did not, though he walked faster and faster along the unfamiliar streets. Now and then he saw a group of people, their ages difficult to determine, walking some distance away, but a group was not what he wanted. Presently the sun touched the horizon, Kem was tired and his feet were sore, and he figured he needed to change his approach. He needed a plan.

The only thing that came to mind was the piece of paper the woman had given him. He pulled it out and he studied the addresses in the left-hand column. One of them had a street name he remembered seeing a little while ago. It was only a couple of blocks back, and when he got there he found that the address was not hard to find. The place was a big, nice-looking building with many windows and many lights burning inside. Kem stood out front for several minutes. He fidgeted and he wondered what the hell he was going to do next. It wasn't as though you could just walk in to someplace and grab a couple of kids and walk out.

He was still wondering when the door of the building opened and three boys emerged. It was dusk now and Kem couldn't tell their ages, but he felt pressed to do something so he set out down the street in the direction the boys were heading. He tried to work it out so that their paths would cross as if accidentally. As it turned out that didn't matter.

One of the boys turned and saw him. Then another: the first boy touched one of the others on the arm and they all stopped. Kem almost ran into them. They were, he saw, a bit too old for his purposes, fifteen maybe. Almost as old as Kem, although (and here maybe he got an idea of what the woman had seen in him, or rather failed to) they looked a lot younger.

The first boy must have thought Kem was someone he knew, because when he got a better look he seemed disappointed, maybe slightly embarrassed. He started to turn away; then he turned back and he said quietly to Kem, "Hey—you don't know where we can get anything ... you know, to drink or anything? Do you?" He added sheepishly, "We're new here."

That was it, then, Kem thought. The building must be some sort of shelter for new arrivals, something like that. He smiled in what he hoped was a knowing way and shook his head. He said, "I'm new, too."

"Where from?" said a second boy.

Kem jerked his head in the general direction of the Grind. "My family's got a wagon."

"Hey, me too." This was the first boy again. He indicated the other two and he said, "These guys are from up around the Lube."

Kem had no idea what this meant but he nodded. He supposed that as the eldest it was incumbent upon him to act cool. He asked them as coolly as he could where they were heading.

"Thought we'd head down to the water," the second boy said. "You know, just look around, like."

The first boy elaborated: "They say you can get stuff down there."

Kem nodded as though he had heard that too. He asked if he could go with them. They told him that would be fine. Then the four boys set off together, the pack easily growing to accommodate one more. Kem did not know if this was really getting him anywhere, but at least he had gotten back to a state of mind he had had somewhat earlier: that he could really do this. That it was really going to be pretty easy.

The water that the boys were talking about was, as Kem had surmised, Tuttle Creek. When they got there Kem found that you could get a good view of the Oasis by looking across it—you faced the craft broadside-on, its lights and its contrasting black silhouette reflected impressively in the water—and that the sight had become something of a local attraction. People were gathering along the waterfront to look at it. They were staring and pointing and Kem could hear their voices all around him—young voices, mostly. You could hear better than you could see now, because it was late in the cycle and the moon was not yet up; the only light came from several hundred strides away, the nearest buildings of the town, and more faintly from the stars.

He told the other boys that he'd see them later. They said all right and were talking quietly among themselves as he moved away from them.

The atmosphere of the waterfront reminded Kem of the way it was at the winter camps. There too you met kids of every age and type, all hanging around together late into the night because the novelty of being there, of having strangers to talk to, was so great that you couldn't sleep. Kem figured this was different in a way—most of the kids here probably were not wanderers as the wagon people had been—but in compensation for that you had the immense novelty of the Oasis. The huge craft sitting out there seemed to excite people, and Kem felt a bit of their excitement too. He almost felt the way he had when he was younger and he had seen the Oasis moving across the Grind. Almost but not quite. Some crucial bit of innocence— or maybe it was ignorance—was gone, and that was fine with him. He watched the people around him and he felt their excitement and he thought, Well, they're wrong, that's all. They think it's fantastic and they don't know what the hell they're talking about.

The ironic aspect of this line of thinking was not lost on him. He tried not to dwell upon it but looked instead over the crowd, and right away his eyes fell on this skinny girl. She was sitting at the edge of the water, on some kind of crate it looked like, and her feet were swinging in a manner Kem assumed to be the result of nervousness. This could be perfect, he thought. The girls looked about the right age, though there was only one way he knew to be sure of that.

He walked over before any second thoughts had a chance to form.

"Hey," he said to her.

The girl looked around at him in surprise. He had guessed the age right; if anything she might be older than he had thought. But she didn't look—what had the man said—spoiled. Corrupted. Not by a long shot. She had long hair of some pale color, thick and wavy down onto her back.

"Hello," she said.

Kem made some vapid remark, something about the Oasis. The girl looked at him like she didn't understand, and he pointed. "Pretty amazing, huh?"

"I think it's awful," the girl told him. "Did you see it in daylight? It's just . . . it's gray, it's just this awful big thing."

She looked up at Kem in a way that did not encourage him. The Recruiting guy had said that young girls were easily impressed and perhaps that was the problem: this one wasn't young enough. Kem muttered a few more things but he could see he had picked the wrong girl.

After that it got easier in one way but harder in others. Kem found that he was able to pick his targets, stroll up and start chatting—that was the easy part. The hard part now was that something like despair was building up in him, and each new kid he talked to made things worse.

It was not just that his efforts hadn't paid off yet. He hadn't expected that so soon; he thought of what he was doing now as warming up, and he figured that later on, when the kids with families had gone back to them, that's when something would break.

What it was that distressed him was the kids themselves. They just seemed so . . . *normal* was the word Kem was thinking but that was a funny concept. Kem had not known many kids that he would really have described as normal— wagon kids led lives that were too harsh for that and the kids at the Oasis were like a bunch of battle-scarred little veterans. Kem therefore had very little idea what "normal" might mean in the context of kids and he doubted that he was qualified to recognize it. But somehow, these kids around him—this seemed like it. The real thing. The dozen or so girls and the lesser number of boys whom he had spoken to

(Start with the girls, the man said) all had this quality that Kem saw and recognized and was calling, for lack of a better word, normal. They were unaffected and they were willing to talk to him and some of them, if they had any, offered him food or cigarettes or wine they had stolen from their parents. But if he started hinting around, like talking about the Oasis or anything beyond a certain point, they would go blank on him. They would seem to drift back into themselves and Kem would be moving again, looking for another one to try.

It was amazing; but so are all ordinary things. Ordinary kids are the truly surprising ones, whereas the other kind—kids who look older than they really are, who have no homes or families, who go sneaking around in the dark trying to find an angle, some scam to really take off with—totally screwed-up kids like Kem, in other words: those you can find everywhere and they are not especially worth wasting your time over.

All this naturally enough left Kem dispirited. He was normal at least in that respect, in that he wanted to feel good about himself and tonight, among the kids of Riley County, he did not. By the time the hour got late and the moon came out and you could tell by its flattened-out light that the crowd at the waterfront had thinned considerably, down to a manageable number of stragglers, Kem no longer felt so resolute about what he was doing. He tried to go back over the list of things that bound him to this task, that made it necessary for him to fulfill his assignment and return to the Oasis. He remembered them, only for some reason they no longer felt so compelling. The only one you could really call important was Davina. And even that, the thing that existed between him and Davina . . . when you got right down to it, it was so insubstantial that it did not even have a proper name. Kem's mind seemed to wobble, grasping for anything solid, anything to hang on to.

A decent life. That was the phrase the Recruiting guy had used. It had sounded hollow when he had said it, as though the guy had not believed in the concept. Truthfully Kem could not have said he believed in it either. A decent life. Kem figured he had seen too much by now, too many things had happened. Life did not seem like a particularly decent thing to him. And yet, he thought, and yet—

He looked around him. Maybe a concept was real whether you believed in it or not. Maybe somewhere people led decent lives; maybe they raised normal kids. Maybe this was the place. The woman had said something, they had a certain quality of life here. Maybe...

That was as far as Kem got. His line of thinking ended in a "maybe," a coin that has been tossed and has not come down.

While the coin was still up there, still twirling, the air of the waterfront was sliced apart by a voice so thin it seemed imaginary. The vice came from the north, somewhere up in the darker stretch of the shore farther away from town. At first Kem thought it was just a scream, but then he heard that there were words along with it. He listened to the words and a narrow smile came to his lips.

You fucker, the voice was saying. *Stop you fucker, you hurt him.*

Kem decided that the voice belonged to a girl and probably not to one of the normal, ordinary girls of Riley County. Without thinking about it he started to walk there, where the voice was coming from. Everyone else seemed to have frozen up. The moonlit scene was very still, almost motionless, except for Kem who was moving and the shrill voice of the girl whose screaming went on.

The fucker hurt my brother, the voice said. *Stop him, somebody stop—*

Now there was a new thing, a third element besides Kem and the voice. Somewhere ahead of Kem there was movement, something was moving up and down or side to side and then there was a noise. In a very short time, a matter of seconds, Kem saw that it was someone running. The person running was still half-concealed behind some tall grasses, but he seemed to be coming this way, back toward the town. All of a sudden there he was: a man, a young man, running furiously up the waterfront. His breath was loud as though running were not something he was accustomed to. He didn't seem to notice Kem or anybody else. You could see his eyes and they were not exactly wild; Kem thought what they were was frightened.

My brother's hurt, the girl's voice screamed, *somebody kill that fucker.*

Between the guy who was running and Kem there were maybe half a dozen people. The guy sort of stumbled into one of them and shoved him aside. Everybody else hustled out of his way—which, though Kem supposed it was normal enough, struck him as fairly chickenshit. He himself stopped moving altogether, waiting to see what the guy was going to do.

The guy veered off, away from the water. Kem waited until he was maybe five long strides away. Then he thrust himself forward; he came at the guy from the side and by the time the guy flashed onto what was happening it was over. Kem had him down and punched his face a couple of times, and that was the end of it. The guy was winded and looked like he was in shock.

"Kill him!" a voice yelled. "Kill that motherfucker!"

Kem looked up and there she was. She was running up the beach and when she saw Kem with the guy pinned underneath him she slowed to a walk.

"You got him," she said, the shrill voice all but spent.

"I got him," Kem agreed.

The girl came closer and Kem saw what he thought he had seen. She was skinny as a stick. She had brown hair cut off just below her ears, giving her something of a boyish look. And except for a pair of torn underpants, stained with something that might have been dirt or blood, she was totally naked.

"Here," said Kem. He stood up, keeping one eye on the guy down on the ground, and he peeled out of his shirt. He tossed the shirt to the girl, who put it on slowly, as though she were going numb. Other people were gathering around now—it figured, Kem thought—and one of them, a grown man, reached out to put an arm on the girl's shoulder.

She recoiled. "Don't touch me!" she yelled at him.

"Here," Kem said. He came forward, toward the man and the girl. "Just leave her alone, she'll be all right. If you want to do something, watch that guy. Or get the police or something."

Kem had reached the girl now and the grown man moved off, as though he were afraid of them.

The girl looked at Kem. Her eyes were big and she was shaking so badly she had trouble getting the shirt buttoned. Kem did a couple of buttons for her, enough to keep her small breasts covered. She mouthed something that Kem recognized as thanks though the exact syllable was unintelligible.

"Let's go," he murmured. "Show me where your brother is."

They walked up the beach and to Kem's relief the rest of the crowd hung back, leaving them alone. Little by little the girl seemed to be getting herself together. She held on to Kem's arm for a while and then she let go of it. She ran a hand up to her hair. Then she pointed. "Over here, I think."

They entered a little clearing amidst the tall grass. You would have had trouble finding it if you hadn't known it was there. In the middle of the clearing a boy lay stretched out flat, his limbs flung out and his head twisted around sideways. It did not look good, but when Kem bent to check he found that the boy was breathing normally. He actually seemed all right, just unconscious. He was about the same size as the girl, whose age Kem would have been hard put to guess at. She looked twelve but she acted more like twenty, especially as she began to recover.

"He hit him," she explained. "The fucker hit my brother just out of nowhere. Is he okay, do you think?"

Kem said that he was. He was going to ask what happened but he didn't need to. The girl kept talking, and Kem guessed that was her way of letting it out—as opposed to, say, crying.

"I know it was really stupid," she said, "but we'd been here a week, you know? And they kicked my brother out of that place, that stupid home. They said he was fighting but really everybody was picking on him. We didn't have any money. There are places you can go and they'll give you food, but if you don't have money it's really hard, we've been sleeping out here for a week now. All we wanted was a little money and we figured if one of us had to screw somebody to get it, at least maybe we'll be able to get a room somewhere so we can take a shower."

She paused for breath. Maybe she had become aware of what she was doing—talking to a stranger like this—but she looked at Kem and whatever she saw in his eyes must have made her feel that it was all right to continue.

"Either one of us would have done it," she said. "We agreed on that up front. Whichever one of us found somebody who wanted to go, that would be it. We were both ready. It just so happened we met *him*, that man you knocked down—that was pretty slick by the way. And he wanted me. So that was fine, my brother asked him for money and he paid us. And then we came out here. My brother sort of hung back, he hid back there in the grass in case anything happened. And it's a good thing he did. Or maybe it isn't. But see, the guy wanted to get rough, like. He wanted to hit me, and my brother didn't like that. It didn't really hurt much but it really upset my brother. So he came out and they got into it and—"

She stopped because it seemed that the boy, her brother, was coming around. She knelt down beside him and she stroked his head. The boy blinked a little, but Kem could tell he was having a hard time of it.

"Maybe you should just let him rest," he told her gently.

The girl made a kind of slow, quiet moan. "Oh, I just hate to see him hurt," she said. "I just hate it. I hate this whole fucking town."

"It's okay," said Kem. He reached over and took the girl's hand. "Your brother's going to be all right."

"No he won't," the girl said. She spoke quietly but the strength of her emotions was evident. "It will never be all right. We'll never be all right in this stupid place. I wish we had never come here."

"It's all right," said Kem. He held her hand tightly, feeling how delicate, how small and perfect the bones were. "It's going to be all right," he assured her.

And that's pretty much
all it took.

RIPE BERRIES

There never was a summer so hot. The days were long at the northern edge of the Grind, where the Oasis rumbled after leaving Riley County, and for every minute of most of those days sunlight soaked into the metal hull. Bulkheads near the surface became too hot to touch, and even deep in the craft, along passageways with no windows and little light, you could feel the heat seeping in. It was almost unbelievable and there was no relief from it. All night the heat that had built up in the vast body of the craft radiated back out, and by the time the metal cooled to a few degrees higher than skin temperature the sun came up and the whole thing started over.

The only place halfway comfortable was out on deck, if you could find a spot in the shade. There you had at least the sluggish current of air moving around the body of the craft. Actually of course it was the Oasis that moved while the air hung slack and lifeless, but from where you sat they were the same. The crew and mates and Residents alike stayed out as much of the time as they could. Kem wondered whether he would have survived this if he had still been a galley boy. He had heard that now and then one of the younger boys would succumb, the body's immature cooling system not being equal to the problem, and he believed it. He did not believe much of what he heard anymore, rather little in fact, but he believed that you could die from the heat of the galley. At least if you were a snipe you could unbolt hull plates or climb down onto the underframe; you could share in whatever coolness the earth had managed to retain through the months of summer. You could feel the air and smell damp things, probably small plants the craft had pulverized.

The Bell Dog had said that smelling a thing was enough, sometimes—that the essence of the thing was contained in the smell, and you could breathe it inside of you. The Bell Dog had spoken of such things, of essences, of secrets and tricks that would help you get by. Nowadays the people around Kem seemed to speak another language, a more sharp-edged and calculating one. You would hear about a certain place and what it had to offer, food or clean water or new recruits, and each of these in turn would be evaluated (the food for freshness and variety, the recruits for health— like that) and in the end the speculation would turn to whether or not the Captain would decide to stop here or stop there. Everyone assumed that such things were decided by the Captain alone, though for all Kem or anyone else knew it might have been otherwise, the Oasis might have moved and stopped and moved again according to principles that were graven on stone tablets somewhere, seared into the face of the earth, beamed down from the unseen artificial moons.

Kem resumed his practice of standing watches on the navigation deck, partly because of the fans that cooled the tower, protecting the equipment there from overheating, but mostly for the sense of forward motion, of progress, that he got from watching the track-line of the Oasis advancing slowly—a thumb-width or so per watch—across the chart.

For most of Frogs Return Moon, during the early weeks of summer, the craft made frequent trading stops in the empty brown patch of chart-space north of Riley County, where worn-out farms and wagon encampments sprawled on the bank of the Gut. Then the river split into two main tributar-

ies and the craft followed the left-branching one, changing
course to northwest. Ahead, the chart showed something
Kem did not understand: a field of green dots labeled Carbon
Bank. Kem asked the mate of the watch what this meant and
the mate gave a dry sort of laugh.

"Ah, the brave new woods," he said. "That's the Carbon
Bank Forest. Most people don't call it that, though, actually.
It's kind of a joke. Most people call it the Oak Barrens. But
you'll see."

Kem knew the mate was being sarcastic but he didn't get
the point of it until one morning about an hour before sunrise
when he was about to get off watch and there was just enough
light to see that the color of the world had changed during
the night. It had gone from plaster gray to something darker
and cooler, a dusty green. By the time the sun came up he
understood that more than just the color was different; the
Oasis seemed to float on a sea of stunted little trees, none of
them taller than two heads or so and most of them much
shorter than that. Tangled limbs bent and scraped against the
hull, trunks snapped under the treads, leaves were blown
high by the engine vents. There was something almost comical about this new terrain, something ludicrously out of scale.
The mighty oak from a tiny acorn grows . . . or something like
that, Kem remembered from childhood. Only here you had
these tiny little oaks with their branches sagging under the
weight of fat green acorns the size of testicles and still
growing. In the forepeak, some of the younger deckhands
made a game of leaning over the rail and snaring fistfuls of
them to hurl at one another. The acorns were soft; they
shattered easily where they struck, spilling their pale raw
fruit. Kem wondered if you could eat it. He wondered what
the Bell Dog would say.

By the time he got off watch and back to his room—the
comfortable new room he had earned by his exploits in Riley
County—Davina was already gone, out for her day's assignment. It was early morning and still relatively cool, and Kem
strolled out on the weather deck to contemplate the scenery.
He stared out over the billions of small trees and he reflected
on what it all meant—really meant, that is, to him personally.
And what it came down to, he decided, was that for the

second time in his life he had come to a place that he never could have gone in the family wagon. The first time had been at Body of God, when he had stolen a fishing boat and paddled out on the limitless Sea. And this second time was something like that, only when he looked around him now he saw not shimmering waves but something almost as strange: an endless expanse of tough little trees that grew so close together that they were like thick stubble on the world's scalp. To Kem, this pigmy forest was neither beautiful nor ugly, neither good nor bad. It was too large a thing and too extraordinary to be reduced to a single quality. Rather like the Oasis, in that respect.

Even before the Oasis stopped, there were rumors of a gathering at the Captain's place.

For another week the craft rolled deeper into the Barrens. It seemed to have no destination. Each day the Grind fell farther and farther behind, and each day brought some vague shift in the climate of the Oasis. First there were changes of a literal, physical sort: the temperature began to drop, the humidity to rise, the sound of bird cries to penetrate the thrash and grind of the craft's relentless passage. And there were subtler things: a sense of expectancy, a certain hushed or breathless quality as though everyone were waiting for a sound half-heard to repeat itself. Lastly came the rumors. A party. Or not just a party. An event. An annual rite. Gathering of the inner circle. Up in the Captain's quarters, the top of the tower. Invitation only. Some night very soon.

Like all rumors they seemed to originate from nowhere and to spread to all places at once. No one could remember how he or she had come to hear a certain thing, yet everyone attested that the thing must be true because everybody said so.

Kem was inclined to doubt it. He was inclined to think that the whole notion of a big to-do in the Captain's quarters was the product of a collective desire for some break in the monotony. The landscape of the Barrens was remarkably, even dauntingly the same, one day after another—its huge sameness was, in fact, far and away its most striking feature—

and after a while you came to feel yourself trembling on
the verge of something, panic or claustrophobia or simply
letting go.

Then, as quick as that, the Oasis came to a halt. The armor
was not lowered, the pneumatic shocks not bled off. The sun
wings were extended but not fastened in place, as though
they might at any moment be hauled back in. But the Oasis
did not move. Nothing happened at all. A day passed and
then another day passed and then another and still the Oasis
sat there. Kem wondered if there had been some kind of
mechanical failure, but his snipe's instincts did not lead him
to think so. Frogs Return Moon was near the end of its wane,
and by this time even Kem got the idea that there was
something odd going on.

Sander said, "So are you going or what?"

Neither Kem nor Davina saw any need to ask, going to
what? Kem just lifted the broad-headed racket he held in one
hand and tossed a ball up with the other. He smashed the ball
into the bulkhead in front of them. The effort of doing so
caused him to sweat. Davina stared at Kem and rather
pointedly (Kem thought) said nothing.

"Well I'm going." Sander smiled through narrow eyes and
took another sip of whatever it was, tall and blue and
garnished with pink stellate blossoms, that he was drinking.
His clothes were of almost startling whiteness, legless and
sleeveless so as to expose his long impeccably tanned limbs.
If you hadn't known him, Kem thought, you'd have taken him
to be the rotten kid of some Investor.

As though picking up on this thought, Sander went on:
"Gardner's taking me."

Davina looked surprised. "You know Gardner?" she said.
She squinted a moment, reflectively. "Oh, that's right, I
guess you . . ."

"So are you guys going or not?"

Sander was fairly shivering with pleasure. Davina began,
"Well we haven't," glancing at Kem, but Sander raised his
arms in impatience.

"Come *on*," he said, "you guys work up in the *tower*. If you can't get an invitation, who can?"

Kem did not like the precious tone that had infected Sander's speech. He scrounged up another ball and slammed it into the wall. From there it bounced back across the recreation deck, made a few erratic hops, and rolled under the safety rail, lost to the Barrens.

Davina was still watching him. "Is something the matter?"

The next ball ricocheted and almost hit another guy from the crew. The guy gave Kem a dirty glance. But then he looked away. Kem seemed to have become a known character, at least in certain circles. Known and avoided. Kem did not know what to think about this and it remained possible that the whole thing was his imagination. But the guy had looked away after the ball had almost hit him: that was a fact. As with other facts, however, the problem lay in how you interpreted it. Kem wondered if the word might possibly have gotten around that he was the Captain's boy.

"We don't have to go," said Davina. "Not if you don't want to."

"Sure you do," said Sander. "You *have* to. I mean, aren't you a little curious, even?"

"It's too muggy for a party," Kem said, though of course this was the least of it. "Anyway, what makes you think we can get in? I hear it's only for a few people. Investors, and people like that."

Sander said, "Maybe you guys can come with Gardner too. I'll ask him."

"Don't ask him," said Kem.

Davina kept quiet. She clearly was disappointed. Kem sympathized but did not intend to give in. He said, "Well, look, you go without me. Go with Sander and, what's his name."

He knew he had gotten the tone all wrong. He knew he was blowing it. Davina drew nearer to him and her eyes were understanding, but Kem could feel the determination behind them. He did not feel strong enough to fight that. She said, "Why don't you want to go? You're not afraid of the Captain, are you? Not anymore."

"That's ridiculous," said Sander. "What's the matter, Kem?"

Kem looked from one to the other of them, feeling helpless. What the matter was, was a certain argument he had
been having with himself; a one-sided argument, since the
other side didn't have a whole lot to say in its own defense.

It was about the two kids—the ones he had been sent to
bring back from Riley County. He had not seen them, either
of them, since that night. Or more precisely since that
morning: the twilight just before dawn, when he had stood
shivering with them in the chill breeze off Tuttle Creek. Kem
had not been sure they were in the right place, and as the
daylight increased he began to get anxious and finally outright scared. The kids had not acted scared at all. They
passed the time playing a game with wooden counters. Some
of the counters were light and some were dark and the
different colors seemed to war against each other. It was a
simple game and the kids had talked while they played it.
The boy was mainly worried about his jaw, which had been
socked pretty hard, and the girl was worried only about her
brother; beyond that, if they had anything on their minds, it
was impatience—they were eager to get out of Riley County
and on to this great place Kem had been telling them about,
this Oasis. They were ready, as the Recruiting guy had said,
for a bit of adventure. That, and a bit of food, a hot shower, a
good long sleep. Kem had told them they would have all that
at the Oasis, and they believed him.

In truth, of course, Kem had not known what to expect.
He did not know why he had been sent here to get these
kids. He did not know where in the Oasis they would be
assigned, where they would sleep, whom they would work
for. Sure, he could have made a few guesses: all that emphasis
on age, on physical appearance, implied certain things that
he did not really like to think about. *What we are looking for
is a boy and a girl of a certain type.* That was all the
Recruiting guy had told him and he never found out any
more.

Well, one thing, maybe. He had stood there shivering in
the twilight, wondering what was going to happen next—how
the kids would get to the Oasis and how he, Kem, would get
out of Riley County now that he had thrown his uniform
away. And at least he had learned the answer to that.

Just as the yellow-green, wavering glow of sunrise had begun to slide across Tuttle Creek, Kem heard the noise of an engine. The noise seemed to remain at about the same level for a while, not getting closer or louder. Then the boat popped into view: it had been moving along the shoreline, where the noise it made was muffled by tall grasses. Now it puttered right up to where Kem and the kids were waiting. It was the captain's gig. Captain Hand was in it, and he was alone.

The kids had looked at Kem—uncertain, but not yet afraid. Kem reckoned the fear would come; he was feeling it already.

"It's all right," he had told him. "This is ... a friend of mine. He's going to take you over there. Across the creek."

The captain's gig eased closer and Hand was standing behind the wheel. He tossed something, a little bundle, to Kem, and Kem saw that it was a uniform just like the one he had arrived in.

Kem explained to the kids that they should get into the boat and that he would see them back at the Oasis. The kids trusted Kem and they did what he told them to. Captain Hand said nothing: nothing to Kem and nothing to the two kids. Kem stood there watching the gig putter off across the water, and then he changed his clothes. He thought of hanging onto the blue shirt, a kind of souvenir, but then he decided he did not want that, he did not want the shirt or anything that would remind him of Riley County.

He thought about Riley County later, anyway, and he thought about the two kids. His thoughts assumed the form of this argument, which was still going on when Sander came down to ask him and Davina if they were going to this party.

The first side of the argument was that a party might be a good thing. It might dispel the peculiar restiveness that had come over him—and over Davina, he knew—while the Oasis sat dead still in the Barrens. And Kem *was* curious, like everybody else, about the Captain and his quarters and the things that went on up there. Besides which, he didn't want to blow things totally with Davina, and it looked like he was on the way to doing that.

But that was only one side of it. The other side, the silent

side, had to do with this final memory he had, an image of
Hand with his back turned, his little boat bearing the two
kids away. The kids had been waving at Kem and Kem had
waved back. That was the last he had seen of them. And
though he remembered them, remembered their faces and
their names, it was in an abstracted kind of way, as you might
remember characters from a story. And to a certain extent
Kem figured that that was just as well. He figured that if the
kids had been wrong to trust him—if he had been lying when
he squeezed the girl's small-boned hand and told her everything would be fine—then it was probably better not to know.
So he planned to stay clear of the Captain's quarters, at least
for the time being. Because he had an idea that up there, in
the innermost sanctum, he might find the answers that he
was no longer looking for; he might see those kids again, the
ones who had trusted him, under circumstances he would not
like. . . .

"What's the matter, Kem?" asked Sander.

"You're not afraid of the Captain, are you?" said Davina.
"Not anymore."

And Kem thought about this for a minute; he thought
about a number of things and then he said:

"Well, actually I guess I am. Yes."

It was Delan who saved him, as Delan had saved him
before—by providing, just in time, a way out. And as before,
Kem would wonder later whether *save* was exactly the word
for what Delan had done for him.

He was up on the navigation deck, leaning over the chart
table and calculating the distance from here to anyplace in
the world (his eyes kept edging glumly back to Riley County),
when someone tapped him on the shoulder and he looked
around without alarm or surprise, only a lethargic sort of
fatalism, to see Delan. As usual Delan was smiling; as usual
his dark eyes were narrow, seeming to harbor some private
intent.

"How are you doing, Kem?" asked Delan kindly.

Kem said he was doing all right. This was like their very
first encounter, that night in the crowded little stateroom:

Delan had asked how Kem was getting along and Kem had said he was doing as well as could be expected, or words to that effect. So many things had changed in the long months from then to now—Kem's age, now seventeen, among them—but the equivocal nature of his life remained the same. His life could be worse, a lot worse. Delan smiled at him as though he understood this and was glad to see that Kem understood it as well.

Actually the smile could have meant anything.

Delan took a few steps to the broad window and peered over the Barrens, the uncounted millions of stunted trees. "It's quite something, isn't it?" he said. "I find it quite amazing, still, even though I've seen it many times."

"You have?"

Delan nodded without looking around. "I suppose the trees must be growing, the old trees must be dying, but one hardly notices. Each year it looks very much the same."

This must mean, Kem figured, that this trip to the Barrens was a regular thing, that it was part of the annual circuit of the Oasis.

"Or perhaps it is just that I am aging along with the forest." Delan scratched his beard. "I do think of it as a forest, somehow. Not simply the Barrens, as people call it. It's hard not to, really, once you've gone out there. Once you've been down among those trees."

"You've been out there?"

Delan turned back to Kem and it was clear that he welcomed the question, welcomed Kem's evident curiosity. "I went out a few years ago. On horseback. A trip of a couple of days. I went out alone and escorted a new Resident back. It was most fascinating."

Kem was always unsettled by talk of the Residents. He walked over to where Delan stood and looked down into the treetops, trying to separate the individual plants in his mind. He could not. Delan continued:

"The place does possess a kind of ... strength. And a stillness, a feeling of quiet. A remarkable experience for someone like me, after so many years in the Oasis. You might find it remarkable, too, Kem. Even though you haven't lived apart from the world out there as long as I."

With part of his mind Kem listened to what Delan was saying, but with another part of his mind he remembered a remark Sander had made one night—about Delan giving him the creeps. There was something weirdly controlled about Delan's words and his mannerisms. Everything carried the weight of deliberation, and you had to wonder what was behind all that.

Kem said, "Yeah, I wouldn't mind taking a trip out there, I guess."

"Yes." That narrow smile again. "Yes. Well, as it happens, Kem, there is an opportunity for you to do that."

Ah, thought Kem. "There is?"

"The Resident I mentioned. The one whom I escorted to the Oasis, a few years ago. His home was rather close to here—a day or two by horse, at most. Not a difficult trip, by any means. And there would only be the two of you."

Kem had a familiar sense of the inevitable. "There would . . . ?"

"You and the Resident. You see, he has decided to leave the Oasis and go home again." Delan paused; his expression was entirely neutral. "He has decided to go home to die."

But even that—Kem's having been sent on such a grim outing—even that would not have been so bad or so disorienting, because there are certain things, as you learn when you live in the Oasis, learn pretty quickly in fact, certain things that you just buck yourself up and don't think too hard about and you get through. You get them over with. And this would have been a thing like that, a couple of days on horseback with a dying man, into the Barrens and out again, and that would have been that. Except that the Barrens, when he got away from the craft and into them, were really quite strange and very beautiful. And the dying man, sitting back-straight in his saddle a few yards ahead of Kem, leading the way, was Tallheron.

Though a little thinner than Kem remembered, Tallheron did not look awfully sick. In fact he did not look bad at all. His face was tan and his eyes were clear, and as the two of them worked their way through the trees—edging down a slope so gradual that Kem might not have noticed it, until they came to a gully carved out by a little stream, now in summer running almost dry, where the bones of the land were laid bare and the forest grew lush and deep green to a height of three heads or more along its course—Tallheron took off his palm hat so that Kem saw for the first time the pale brown hair that still grew thick and long on his narrow head, tied back with a strip of leather, and you would never have thought he was a dying man at all. He seemed almost happy.

Kem wondered how long it would take. He wondered if the crying would come on strong and fast and take Tallheron in only a week or two; or if the treatments they had given him at the Oasis would have some residual effect, prolonging his life; and if so for how long. A few months? A year? Would he live to see the oak leaves turn sunset red in the wane of Petals Fall Moon? Would he need firewood for the winter? Kem found it morbidly fascinating to contemplate such things; he felt as though he were walking out along the twilit boundary between death and life; trying to determine where the dividing line, exactly, lay. He had known death before (he was eight years old when a robber gang killed his mother) and of course he had known life, though not as thoroughly as he would have liked to. But he had never explored the netherland between them. Now he was here and he found it eerie and serene, dapple-shaded, sweet with leaf-rot, its silence punctuated by small animals that scurried out of their way, birds caroling for mates, a whir of wind and limbs that knocked together like jostling bones.

"None of this was here," Tallheron all of a sudden said, "not a single tree, when I was a boy. These were just fields then, ruined wheat fields. The land was dirt cheap, and we planted it in all the new grains. Leymus, jackson's gama, perennial sorghum. Illinois bundleflower for nitrogen gain. Maximilian sunflower in the triculture plots, but those we had to plow more often. Every three years at least, or the seed production wouldn't be enough to keep a family of mourning doves alive. The other fields could go for six, seven years, and then we'd burn them, sow a cover of winter vetch, disc it under in spring, resow the grain mix, and by Ripe

Berries the leymus would be too tall to see over and the bundleflower would be in full bloom. The gama often as not would take two seasons to give you a good fall crop. Well . . . But of course all that's gone now."

Kem wondered if it was a subtle symptom of the crying or just ordinary nostalgia—this rambling on. In his own briefer life he could not think of anything to get nostalgic over. Not the wagon, for sure. He called ahead: "So what's happened? To the fields, I mean? How did all these trees get here?"

Tallheron guided his horse around a hitch in the gully, up the slope a little. He seemed to know where he was going. For a minute or so he let Kem's question fade into the soft thumping of hooves on leaf-mold. Then he reined in.

"I suppose I brought them here, in a way." He stared at the ground. "But you see, we had lost so much soil. Even with the new grains we lost more every year. The winters were too warm, the roots rotted in the damp. In spring, when the rains came, the soil just washed out. We thought . . . it was my idea at first, though the rest were quick enough to go along, I must say . . . we thought perhaps if we could get some kind of tree in here, one of the bigeneric hybrids they were touting back then, we could check the bank erosion, at least, and keep our soil from washing down the Gut."

He waved his arm, up and down the gully, across the slopes. "And look how right we were. We've gained topsoil every year. Good black dirt you could grow old-fashioned wheat in. The problem is, we can't get rid of the trees now. We thought we'd seen every kind of weed there was. We never thought a damned *tree* would beat us. It was so . . . medieval."

Kem caught up with him. Since it seemed that for the moment at least they had reached a stopping place, he climbed down to relieve himself. Tallheron remained upright in his saddle, looking at the land around him but seeing something, Kem thought, other than what was really there. Who knows what a dying man thinks about, Kem thought. His whole life, probably; all the things he's done.

When Kem was finished he led his horse to the thin vein of water in the middle of the streambed. Here among the trees you could sense the heat of the sun falling hard just a couple of heads above you, but the broad tough leaves of the canopy blocked it out pretty well, and underneath the air was remarkably cool. He sat down, resting his back against a stout, deeply fissured trunk. He watched ants bustling purposefully among rocks coated with yellow fungus, withering ferns, the pale leaves of some forest creeper.

Tallheron said, *"Apios."* And when Kem said nothing, only looked up in mild curiosity, he pointed where Kem had been looking and repeated, *"Apios.* Ground nut. An old native species. You can eat the tubers. If you're hungry."

"You know their names?" Kem said. "All the plants?"

"I was a farmer. Most of us had studied a good bit, one way or another. It made the work more interesting. It also gave us some understanding of what was happening to us, when things began to get out of control. Not that they had ever been *in control,* truly, of course, though we did not fully appreciate that. But when the trees began to spread and it became clear to us that there was nothing we could do, that our farms were doomed and all the things we knew, the places we had lived, everything was destined to change in an irrevocable way ... well, at least we understood what was happening. We could follow the disruption in the ecosystem quite clearly, the decline of certain species, the sudden flourishing of others. It was as though we were doctors who had become hopelessly ill, but we were still capable of monitoring the progress of our disease. And one could only marvel at it, really. Such an ingenious feat of biological manipulation. A work of art, if you will."

He regarded one of the works of art in question: a young tree not quite as tall as he and his horse together. He plucked a leaf. "The unexpected fusion of traits," he said, holding it up to the sunlight, "the overwhelming redundancy of survival mechanisms. Suckering roots, prolific seeds, allogenic waste products pumped into the soil, volatile toxins in sacs under the bark—for the rabbits, you know. And such variability! The trees were tetraploids, though we didn't know that at the time. Not at first. Four sets of chromosomes instead of two, and each strand itself the product of extensive resequencing. We gave up even guessing at all the ancestors. There was simply no telling what would turn up among the progeny. Until finally we got to *this*."

His arm swept broadly, grandly, through the air, encompassing everything.

Kem closed his eyes. He guessed that Tallheron was not really talking to him but just talking, saying things he wanted to say, and anyway Kem was not able to follow very well. An insect buzzed somewhere near his left ear, and a bird cooed faintly in the distance. His horse lapped the water. He opened his eyes at last because he thought Tallheron might be watching him, but he was not; just staring off. Sunlight spattered the forest, making leaves shine like emeralds where it bounced off them.

"What's its name?" he asked. His voice was too quiet, as though it had lain in his throat and gotten soggy. He tried again. "I mean the tree—what's the name of that?"

Tallheron smiled, not a pleasant smile. "Our study name for it was *Metaquercus diabolii*. Devil's oak, or beyond-oak, more or less. I suppose nowadays it is called something else."

Devil's oak, Kem thought. It had a certain ring. The sun was still high, but it felt late in the day. Sitting here, propped against the tree, was making him sleepy. It entered his mind that Tallheron was pretty energetic for a dying man. Look at him: sitting so high and straight in his saddle, staring in sadness or in anger or in something else, who knows, at the land that had once been his home. And still staring, a minute or two later, when Kem—for the first time in a very long while, maybe for months, and without really intending to— fell into a quick and deep and untroubled doze.

He awoke trying hard to remember something. A dream, maybe. The sun was still up but it seemed that everything had changed. Tallheron sat on the ground a few strides away and the horses had wandered a little way off, browsing the forbs of the understory.

"What time is it?" he asked, struggling to prop himself up.

Tallheron had a way of disregarding you, at least sometimes, as though he were waiting for a question that really needed an answer, as this did not. Kem could see the sun as well as anyone. It was barely a point above the horizon, and a hint of evening coolness—such a rare thing, for summer— was already in the air.

"I thought we might just spend the night here," Tallheron said. "You seem tired, and I am tired, and there is no need to hurry. We should be at the farmhouse by noon tomorrow, with an early start."

Kem sat all the way up, and something (Tallheron's voice, speaking of his old lost home, or the imminence of sunset) made him think of what he had been trying to remember. He stood and brushed himself off.

"What ever happened," he said, "to that little book? The one with the stories in it? I mean, I hope you got it. I had to send it by messenger."

What he really meant was, had Tallheron found anything in it, finally? Were there any secret there?

Tallheron did not ignore him this time. He shook his head slowly. "That book. Yes, well. You know, Kem, in a way that is why I asked for you—asked that you be sent along as my escort."

Kem noted this—that Tallheron had asked for him, that it had not been Delan's idea, though Delan hadn't told him so.

"I did get it back, yes, thank you. Though I must say, I found it to be something of a disappointment. I suppose I was expecting too much. Too much from a simple volume of folktales. I must have been hoping for what used to be called a magic bullet. A sure-fire remedy. But of course if such a thing exists—which not even Captain Hand would claim, I believe—then one could not expect to find it in a storybook."

He stopped talking and turned his attention to a pile of sticks. Evidently he intended to light a fire. The notion was slightly remarkable—having wood to burn. Among the wagons they had used methane stills to fuel little cooking rings. But Kem wasn't really concentrating on that; he wanted to hear more about the crying but he wasn't sure exactly how to ask. He didn't want to be insensitive. After a moment he just said, "I'm sorry you didn't find anything. In the book."

"Oh, but I did. I did find something. It was not the magic bullet, the secret I was looking for. But it was something."

Kem came closer to where Tallheron was adjusting and readjusting the sticks for the fire.

"Imperfect knowledge, you see," Tallheron went on, "seems to me better than no knowledge at all. They used to say that a little knowledge is dangerous, but I'm not so sure. It seems to me that a little knowledge can be useful. At least it must be worth passing along." He left off fiddling with the wood for a moment and looked at Kem. "Which is why I wanted to talk to you. So that there would be someone to pass my little knowledge along to."

Kem was surprised and flattered and puzzled by this, all at once. He waited for Tallheron to continue. Instead Tallheron looked at him with those eyes that seemed only partly connected to the rest of him, eyes that seemed to look and look for something they could not find.

"My first mistake," he said finally, "lay in what I was looking for. You only find what you're looking for, you know. You only perceive what you are equipped to see. We do not see a path to our homes laid out in the stars because we are not birds and have no need for that. Nor do birds look at a hole in a cedar box and notice the signature of a jigsaw. All I mean to say is that we bring certain capabilities and certain basic expectations to everything we do—reading books as much as anything else—and these things tend to limit or define what we discover there. In my own case, I was looking desperately for any hint of a cure for my own private malady. I had examined perhaps a thousand books before I opened that one. And there it was—a story that referred to a disease, a plague, that very well might have been the crying. It was never called that, you know, but I assumed..."

Kem nodded. He had assumed too.

Tallheron shrugged. "Well, perhaps it was. Or maybe not. The stories in that book are very old—hundreds of years, most of them. Diseases come and go. Maybe it was something else. That is not the point."

Kem thought it was very much the point but he just sat there, waiting.

"The point is," Tallheron continued, "that when I got through with those stories, and after I spent a bit of time feeling frustrated, thwarted, I picked up the book again and I began rereading it more or less at random—a few pages here and there. And this time . . . I don't know, perhaps I no longer cared so very much. Perhaps I had given up, resigned myself to living the rest of my life among those poor wretches, those Residents, what a foolish word, there at the Oasis. In any case, when I looked again I began to notice something new. The book seemed entirely different to me. The stories seemed to have changed. Have you ever had that experience?"

Kem thought that maybe he had; it seemed to him that he had heard certain stories again and again, yet the endings always took him by surprise. He said, "I think I know what you mean."

"Yes." Tallheron nodded. "Well you see. What I noticed—the first thing I noticed—was that the stories are not so much about *people* as I had thought. Not real people, as you and I know them. Many of the characters do not even have names, or if they do then the names seem irrelevant—arbitrary—as one might name a character Julia because at one time long ago that was a common name, or simply refer to a character as 'the old man' or 'the Doctor.' Do you see? So that what the stories are really about is not any particular people, but *people*, do you follow? *All* people. Humanity at large."

Kem nodded doubtfully.

"And so," Tallheron spoke vigorously now, "so it is, that when a story speaks of a character being ill, it is not really a particular illness that is under discussion. You must see, don't you? It is *illness,* illness in general, that the story is about. But in a broader sense the story is not about illness at all. It is about *health.* Or perhaps what I should say is, it is about wholeness, balance, things of that sort. Order. A harmony of parts. How can I explain this?"

Tallheron looked up into the trees—straight up—where the sky had turned a glaucous shade, the color of rue. There are constant references," he said, "to a previous order of the world, an order that has been disrupted. A world that has been lost. There once was a land known as Fields of Wheat. There were people who lived in large houses. There were gardens, filled with roses. There were little boys and little girls. There was innocence. There was love. But what is there now?"

Kem thought maybe he did understand what Tallheron

was saying, at least in part. Still he did not know how to answer him. "The plague?" he ventured. "Now there's this plague going around?"

"Well, yes, but. There is a plague, there is this unnamed illness. But that is just one thing, one manifestation. If you stand back—if you just read without focusing so much on one single thing, let your vision remain rather general—then you think, Aha! This plague is not *all* of the illness. That is, it is one disease, yes, but it is not *disease*, it is not the whole of what is wrong. If you look around, you see immediately that in all its aspects, the world of the story is out of balance. No single part is in harmony with another. There is a little girl, you see, but there is no little boy. There is an old man but no old woman, no children. There are houses but no occupants. There are flowers, but instead of being watered or sniffed or worn in someone's hair, they are sprayed with poison. Of course there is disease, disease is what the story is about. But what is the nature of this disease? Is it some particular illness, a single contagion? I think it is not. I think that the disease with which the story is concerned is the *illness of the world*. The lost state of completeness. The old man, one half of an ideal whole, mourning his lost half. Seeking her, what little bit is left of her. Her essence. Failing to find it. Dying on account of it."

"But he doesn't die." Kem shook his head; Tallheron frowned, his chain of thought broken. Kem said: "The old man doesn't die, does he? He lives at the end. Doesn't the little girl, sort of . . ."

Tallheron cocked his head sideways, considering this. "Yes and no," he allowed, finally. "The old man does die, I think. He is consumed. In the end it is a little boy who is alive—the essence of the man, perhaps, the seed of the man, but not the man himself. A kind of wholeness is restored, but it is not simply a repair of the imperfect world. It is not a patch-up job. It is a return to an earlier order. A more perfect state. The ending actually is quite impossible. But that means nothing. Folktales are full of impossible things. All this tells us—I have thought for some while about this—is that we must look for the *real* meaning of the story on some other level. What is cured in this story? I believe it is not really the old man's illness. It is *illness*, the fundamental cause—disharmony, lack of wholeness, however we wish to express it—and it is remedied in a purely transcendent or mystical way. A new wholeness is emanated by the girl, and this wholeness somehow restores the balance of the story, at least to a limited extent. Anyway, that is how I read it."

The gaunt old man stopped talking. He sat quietly as though waiting for some definitive response, some judgment on Kem's part. Kem thought he would need some time to come up with one. He hedged: "So that's what you learned? From the story?"

Tallheron frowned. "That is much of it. Most of it. I'm sorry if it seems lacking in specifics."

"No, I . . . I mean, there's no need to be sorry. It's just—"

"It is only a pattern, of course." Tallheron seemed to grow cross. "But in a way, that very point is the important one. That there *is* a pattern. There is a pattern to illness, there is a pattern to health. I think these stories exist, if they exist for any reason at all—I take it as a matter of faith that they do—in order to help us recognize those patterns around us. So that we can avoid not just a particular disease but the very essence of disease, the pattern of lost connection."

"So there isn't really a cure? I mean, for the crying? Or anything?"

Tallheron smiled, not happily, but with a certain wry satisfaction, the look of a canny survivor. "The stories do not say that. They do not say there isn't a cure. They are not *about* a cure, that's all. Healers deal in cures, and storytellers deal in patterns."

"So, you think there is a cure, then? I mean, at the Oasis, what they do there . . ."

"Captain Hand is not a fraud, if that is what you are asking. I am not sure he is a healer, either. They do have *something*, something to offer there. But that is no more than is to be expected."

It isn't? Kem asked with his eyes alone.

"No," said Tallheron. "After all, the Oasis—or whoever is behind it—is very much part of the pattern of the disease. It is only right to expect that they should at least offer some kind of . . . of palliative."

"What do you mean?"

Tallheron seemed mildly annoyed by this, that Kem hadn't figured it out. "There was no crying before the Oasis came," he said. "Just as there were no trees. That's where I bought the first seedlings, you know. Rode down to trade at the Oasis, more then two decades ago. Before you were born. The crying was unheard of then. I traded our best stock seeds for a cartload of one-year oaks—or at least oaks were what I thought I was getting. Blackjack oaks. A new strain, thicker bark, tougher leaves, deeper taproot, that sort of thing. What I got, ultimately, was this."

He gestured around him, into the gathering dark. Shadows lay on everything now, creeping in around them.

"This," he said, without rancor, without bitterness. Only regret darkened his voice. "Devil's oak. Beyond-oak. And I got something else, too, I believe. On that trip to the Oasis.

"I believe I got the crying."

They rode in the morning through woods shot with yellow sunlight where the air smelled mysteriously of water. It was a strange smell to Kem, sweet and cool, and it seemed to come from nowhere, for there was no water around except the paltry trickle in the streambed, and there had been no rain for weeks. Kem's thoughts kept edging back to this as he and Tallheron rode for the most part in silence, having talked themselves out last night. After a while it occurred to him that the water he smelled must be coming from the trees, or rather through them—drawn by their roots out of the depths of the ground and lifted into their trunks and branches by subtle capillary pressure and finally dispensed through a webwork of veins into these innumerable leaves where it evaporated in the warming sun. And now Kem was breathing it, stuffing his lungs with the sweet-smelling water of life.

It was only a little past midmorning, earlier even than Tallheron had predicted, when they came to a place where the trees grew more sparsely, the unmarked trail they were following widened into a real roadway, its dirt packed in twin ruts and overgrown with multiflora roses down the middle, and in the distance straight ahead—for the road ran like an arrow—Kem could see the silhouettes of windmills, a row of silos, the sagging roof of a barn. Tallheron kept his horse to a steady pace, neither hurrying now that his home was in sight nor pausing to reflect on how far he had come, how strange and tortuous the journey had been. Kem guessed your feelings would be mixed, to say the least, in Tallheron's situation. For his own part he felt a rising excitement, a sense of adventure and expectancy. The roses along the track grew in sprays that were covered with thorns, but he hardly noticed when they snagged his pants. Perhaps it was that he had never, himself, had a home to return to.

The farm had been a big one. A scattering of small buildings stood like outposts half a kill before they reached the main compound, a rough square of hard gray dirt with the farmhouse on one side and the huge barn on the other. Old trees opened like giant vases overhead—elms, Kem thought—and you could tell where a vegetable plot had been, for the square of softer dirt there was now filled with devil's oaks.

The really amazing thing, though, was the machinery. Great, rusting hulks, the farm's machines and vehicles and ancillary equipment stood in daunting array across one side of the compound. More than anything else—more than the broken windows of the farmhouse, the collapsing barn, the overgrown kitchen plot—these abandoned, disintegrating machines seemed to Kem to convey the full sadness of all Tallheron had lost. In a way, his illness was not even the worst of it. It was just the finishing touch, a cruel afterthought. Kem could see why Tallheron acted the way he did: subdued, his voice flattened out, his eyes weary, as though the heart had gone out of him. Just looking around, you could see that the end of his life had been coming for a long time. The sickness—not just the crying—had been slowly, relentlessly coming on.

Tallheron climbed down from the saddle and left his horse to wander off. The animal seemed confused at first in these strange surroundings. Eventually it sauntered over to the side of the barn where a pipe ran down to a water-butt. Kem dismounted also and untied his pack.

"I guess we should go check out the house," he said. He

sensed that Tallheron was succumbing to some private darkness. "Come on, I'll bring your stuff in later."

Tallheron allowed Kem to lead him across the compound. Their feet stirred pale, powdery dust that Kem guessed must have blown up from the Grind, as the farm's own dust must once have blown farther east, before this young forest grew and its roots anchored the dirt where it lay. Up close, the abandoned farmhouse looked oddly hospitable; curtains moved lightly as a faint breeze—entering on the far side, blowing through—carried smells of something stale, like old clothes, through the broken panes. Head-tall hollyhocks bloomed among the weeds near the foundation. Together, Kem and Tallheron crossed the porch.

Tallheron seemed to hesitate. Then, abruptly, he turned and said, "Perhaps I should check the pump. If the pump is working there will be water for a bath." And only then, as Tallheron strode purposefully off the porch, making for the corner of the house, did it occur to Kem that the poor man had wanted to enter his house by himself, to have a bit of time alone to get his bearings. Kem hung back for a minute and then ambled around to the backyard of the farmhouse.

He found Tallheron standing at the base of a windmill. The windmill was smaller than the ones Kem had seen on the Grind; maybe the water table was higher here and you didn't need so much drawing power. Nonetheless from where he stood it was an imposing sight, its three long blades held higher than the elms and its main struts resting on concrete islands a half-dozen strides apart. There was a cistern about a third of the way up with pipes running in and out of it, and at its base, where Tallheron stood, was the black metal pump housing. Kem joined Tallheron in the mute ritual of staring down at the nonfunctional components.

"I don't understand," Tallheron said after a little while. "I've released the brake but the blades don't spin. And look: this wire had just snapped right off. What could have caused that?"

Kem gazed with a certain fondness at this piece of archaic machinery. All in all, it didn't seem in such bad shape. It was rusty, of course, and its gaskets had probably rotted, but those were minor problems. He traced the workings with his eyes, deducing how the thing was supposed to work. The pumps at the Oasis were different, but you could see that the same general principles applied.

"I think I can fix it," he declared, perhaps a bit rashly.

"You can?"

"Sure. I used to be a snipe. This doesn't look all that complicated. Have you got any tools?"

"There's a shed . . ." Tallheron gestured vaguely. Kem guessed that when the farm was still in operation there must have been a pretty good-sized work force—all those machines to operate, all that land to sow and harvest. The farms he'd seen on the Grind were small, hardscrabble affairs, run by a few families at most. He had never seen an operation like this. He guessed that Tallheron himself must have been somewhat removed from the actual hands-on workings of the place— less a farmer than a manager, an administrator. Or a captain. Something like that.

"That's okay," he said. "I can take care of this. You go on inside."

He felt himself slipping comfortably into a more familiar role—no longer an escort, whatever that was; something more like an assistant, a worker, a snipe, one of the more-or-less invisible positions he had held at the Oasis before Delan saved him from the night shift in the engine flats, and he had gone to work in the navigation tower, and things had started moving a little fast for him. He looked up at Tallheron and he gave him a smile, an honest smile.

"Don't worry," he said. "Even if this one doesn't work, you've got other pumps, right? Out in the fields? We can rig something up, for sure. Go on inside, get settled—I'll come in later and let you know how it's going."

Tallheron muttered a bit—the toolshed, hoping it wasn't locked, something—but when Kem rolled back his sleeves and settled down to poking in earnest inside the metal housing, the old man edged away, off to confront his own past and his own future; and Kem was glad to have no part in that.

The toolshed was locked. The lock was weathered but still strong. Kem's predecessor must have been a punctilious sort, dutiful to the end. Kem had to bring a crowbar around from the barn and pry the door off its hinges before he could get inside. When he did so he discovered right away what the lock was all about. The place was half toolshed and half armory: a dozen powerful-looking rifles and numerous lesser weapons were hung neatly from clips on a pegboard that covered one wall. Kem wondered if such a massing of fire-power could possibly have been intended for hunting, and he decided it could not. There was even a crossbow much like his father's, complete with a quiver of gleaming metal bolts. The shed smelled of linseed oil and powder and steel.

There were other tools of a more useful sort, however, and Kem picked out the ones he would probably need. The feel of the well-used and impeccably cared-for tools in his hand gave Kem a sense of assurance, of having gotten for once a step ahead of events instead of lagging behind them. He would fix the pump and then he would take a look at the wiring—wiring always needed work—and maybe later, this evening, while Tallheron read by lamplight in some favorite chair, he would check out the plumbing, look for glass to fill in the broken windows, really get the place in order before he left the old man alone. It did not amount to much, he guessed, but at least it was something he could do, something that was simple and good.

Kem gathered up his tools and strolled back to the wind-mill, where he set to work with a certain purity of purpose, a sense of the usefulness of his efforts, even a modest, worka-day pride. There was not much he had done lately that made him feel this way—almost nothing, really, since he had quit working for the Bell Dog. He had not missed this feeling until now when he found it again.

The sun fell heavily on his shoulders and the old farmyard seemed to come back to life, filling with the sounds of horses and tools striking metal and a young man breathing deeply from exertion, and that was a scene, a little miniature life, that Kem would have liked to hang onto. He wouldn't have minded a lot if time had just stopped for him there, in that old backyard.

Time did not stop, it did not slow down, and if Kem had imagined for an instant (out of those that continued to pass) that the Goddess responsible for such things as the twirling of cosmic bodies might be inclined to favor him in this way then he shortly had some sense kicked back into him.

The first sign that time was blundering onward took the form of a papery flutter, a gentle sound multiplied hundreds of times so that the air itself seemed to stir with it. Kem looked up to see a flight of swallows arise from shady perches under the eaves of the old barn, circle for a few moments above the courtyard, and then sweep sideways, skimming the tops of the elms and disappearing into the dark surrounding woods.

Kem wiped the moisture from his forehead and went back to his work. The problem seemed to be in the control circuitry, a little board that coordinated the workings of the mill. It was a purely electrical problem, in other words, not a mechanical one, and it seemed to be caused by a missing section of wire that should have run from the generator, which was connected by a belt to the blade assembly, down to the pump. Only that made no sense, that a single length of wire should be missing. If someone had been out to salvage abandoned equipment—as people always were, Kem guessed—then why would they have taken the wire and nothing else? It seemed more like vandalism than salvaging, and even so it was vandalism of an oddly selective sort. Kem supposed he would just have to find a ladder and restring the wire and not think too hard about it.

He was doing that, looking for a ladder, prowling around the musty old barn, when time made another lurch and this one left him gasping. Beneath his feet the decking of the barn shifted slightly as though the earth had been out of alignment and a massive hand had nudged it back into position. Everything was motionless again by the time Kem had time to react. He was wobbling, his knees had gone shaky from alarm, and only then, in the aftermath, did he hear the deep percussive sound—THOOMB, like a mallet thudding against the biggest drum in the world—that followed the jolt by half a second.

His heart slammed like a door, opened, slammed again. Then he was down on his knees, either because he had fallen or because he was crouching in terror. Anyway it came to the

same thing. He heard shattering noises, the sound of things
being blown apart.

For a few seconds his mind was empty and then it was
spinning frantically, wobbling like a top off center. He stood
up and moved to the door. *I've got to do something*—but he
did not understand what had happened or what was required
of him. At the open door he stopped.

The farmhouse was on fire. Smoke spewed through the
upper windows, black and oily looking, and Kem could see
flames leaping down below. The fire seemed to have no
center; it ran from one end of the house to the other, as
though it had started at once everywhere. Kem's first impulse
was to run across the compound but some force of will or
instinct or cowardice—pick one—held him back, and what he
did instead was step quickly out the door and circle around
the barn, keeping close, until he was at the entrance to the
toolshed.

I don't know why I'm doing this, Kem thought as he
slipped inside.

But yes he did. He didn't have time to think it through,
but he had a pretty strong idea of why he was snatching the
crossbow off its pegs and sliding a metal bolt into the slot,
drawing the cord back, flipping the safety on. He flipped the
safety off again, checking the latch, but what he was thinking
about was the broken pump. If there had been a pump then
there would have been water to fight the fire. But there was
no pump because a piece of wire had been cut. Kem grabbed
some extra bolts and ran out of the shed.

The flames were so hot that he could barely approach the
house. He managed to get close by coming in at an angle,
partly sheltered by an elm tree whose overhanging limbs had
started to smolder. The air rushing in toward the fire whipped
at his legs and the compound was filled with a weird, un-
earthly roar, as though some great half-living creature were
crying out in agony. The old dry timbers of the house were
breaking apart with loud cracks, like a series of gun blasts.

There was no way to get in. Even if there had been some
chance of finding Tallheron in there, still alive, Kem could
never have gotten inside and gotten out again. The knowledge of this coursed through him in a paroxysm of horror and

relief. He stood watching the house burn less than a dozen strides away, so close that the heat flared painfully, in waves, against his skin. He felt as though his clothing were about to ignite. He barely heard the sounds of panicked horses.

The sounds got louder. Kem blinked, he strained his ears, but he still could barely distinguish the frantic neighing and the clattering of hooves from the hundred other noises of the fire. Then a movement caught his eye—there, to the right, flicking at the corner of his vision—and Kem turned to see the horses coming at a full gallop around the side of the barn, bellowing, tossing their heads, manes madly flying, as though they were being drawn despite themselves into the maelstrom, driven to their own destruction.

They veered away. They laid their heads down low and turned so suddenly that Kem thought they were going to tumble, to roll on top of him. His reflexes kicked in and he leapt to the side, and the act of doing so set his mind back in motion. He saw that there were three horses in the courtyard and not the two there should have been. They made their turn and now were beating furiously, single file, toward the roadway leading out—the way Tallheron had led Kem only an hour ago. And astride the third horse, the last horse in line, pounding and pounding its flanks, whipping the poor beast onward and the other two before it, rode a thick-bodied man. Kem had never seen the man before, yet something about the look of him, whipping the horse, he thought he recognized. In the moment of recognition—the very moment, without thinking—he raised the crossbow and tightened his finger on the release. He felt the bolt fly as a subtle change in pressure against his shoulder.

The man's horse bellowed. Its stride faltered, and the big animal collapsed into its forelegs. The man was thrown from the saddle and tumbled across the ground, half a dozen strides, lay there still as Kem's fingers and arms and whole body began to tremble.

The other horses kept galloping. They were onto the road by the time Kem moved again; he stepped away from the burning house, feeling once more the pain and the immediacy of the fire. He began walking slowly at first then faster across the compound. The fallen man seemed to grow before him, becoming at every step more real.

With a groan, the man stirred.

Kem froze. Then he raised the crossbow and laid another bolt in. The man was lifting himself on his elbows, sitting up. He looked first at his horse—the horse lay very still, either it had died in the fall or Kem had killed it outright—and then, grasping the situation, jerked his head around to stare at Kem.

Kem stared back. The man's eyes were tiny holes, unreadable, a dozen strides away. There was a certain implicit logic in this situation—the man dazed and sitting on the ground, Kem hefting a loaded weapon—but for several seconds time ticked along in defiance of this logic, unable perhaps to change course so abruptly.

The man rose carefully to his feet. He was tall, big-muscled, wide-shouldered. He took a step closer to his horse, then another step, his eyes never leaving Kem's. Kem noticed that the man's clothes were gray, an almost colorless color. They had the look of a uniform, though they bore no insignia. On the ground in front of him, flung from the fallen horse, lay a leather satchel. The man advanced to within a stride of it, then he stopped.

"You've got nothing to worry about," he told Kem. "You're in the clear. There's a horse for each of us, if we can catch them."

Kem blinked. His arms, holding the crossbow, felt rubbery. He had no idea what the man was talking about.

The man continued to stare at Kem, as though evaluating him, silently asking some question. Kem knew what the question was but he did not know the answer.

"Come on," said the man. "The longer we wait, the farther off they get."

Kem felt dizzy but he struggled to keep still; he felt the crossbow waver somewhat, back and forth, up and down, as though the connection between his hands and his brain was shorting out.

The man raised his eyebrows, very slowly
—very, very slowly
—and then, as though the question had been answered,

the evaluation completed, he began to kneel, keeping his eyes locked on Kem throughout the smooth, steady, unbroken motion, knees bending degree by degree, almost imperceptible, arm reaching out toward the satchel, fingers opening the flap, the slightest trace of a smile creeping in from the edges of his lips while still and ever, imperturbable, the eyes looked on. And there was a moment there—one immeasurable moment—when time really did seem to have stopped. And Kem thought he could actually tell what the man was thinking, what thoughts and intentions and recent memories flitted through his mind as his fingers slid so deftly, so expertly, under the leather flap, tightened around the smooth worn plastic handgrip, and lifted the handgun from its pouch.

Kem's eyelids fluttered briefly, as happens sometimes when you're dreaming. Only Kem didn't think this was a dream he was having, a dream of death and fire; he thought that it was real, that he could really feel the gun in the thick muscular hand, wince at the pain from the shoulder where the man had broken it, and recall with perfect clarity the look in Tallheron's eye, the sound of that hopeless and weary voice, almost relieved now to know how the story would end, the end was coming quickly, quick as a bullet, sanctified by fire.

It might have gone further—Kem might have learned more—but he disengaged himself, tugged himself free, and time staggered forward again.

He lowered his crossbow. The muscles of his arms seemed to shriek as the tension went out of them. The heat of the burning house bore down so intensely that he began walking away, toward the road where the horses had gone. He walked without looking back at the house, or the windmill, or the sagging barn, or the man lying dead, his face contorted in pain, his fingers clutching the metal bolt running through him, grazing his heart.

He was lost.

The world was huge, the Barrens were endless, and Kem was wandering alone. The horses were gone. The Oasis was far away in an unknown direction.

But Kem was lost more thoroughly than that. He felt like

one of the satellites, the artificial moons, that had drifted out
of its place in the sky, floated off in the blackness where no
one could find it.

Tallheron was dead. He had been dying anyway, Kem
knew that, but now he was dead. A man had come and
burned his house and killed him.

Who, though? Where had he come from? No, that wasn't
the question—that was a question with only one answer—the
question was, Who had sent him? Why had he been sent to
Tallheron's farm, and what had he been sent to do?

To kill Tallheron? To kill Tallheron because he had chosen
to leave the Oasis? Or because he might have figured out
something about the crying, where the crying came from?

Or had the man been sent to kill Tallheron ... and Kem?
To wipe out the contagion of forbidden knowledge, killing
everyone who had been exposed to it? Maybe a little knowledge *was* dangerous. Tallheron had wanted to pass his knowledge along to Kem; maybe the man had been sent to kill both
of them. Or maybe ...

Could Kem himself have been the target? Had he seen or
done or heard too much? Was he a danger to anyone? It did
not seem possible. And yet—if it weren't true, if Kem had
not been the target, why had he been chosen as Tallheron's
escort?

Why *had* Delan offered him this job? He had known in
advance that Kem would like it, going out into the Barrens,
getting away from the Oasis. Avoiding the Captain's party.
Kem had avoided the Captain's party, all right. And almost
died for it. Had Delan known what was going to happen? Was
this some twisted form of emotional revenge—Kem had
spurned Delan, months ago, and now Delan had sent Kem
out to his death?

And if not Delan, who? Who had dispatched Death here,
into the stunted woodland? Why had Death tracked a poor
sick man and an ignorant kid to an abandoned farm?

But Death: that was just a way of speaking. It had not
been Death but just an ordinary man, some guy in a gray
uniform, who set fire to Tallheron's farmhouse.

And it had been Kem who killed him.

Kem was lost, more profoundly lost than he had ever

been, as he thrashed deeper and deeper into the Barrens, leaving something he could not name—maybe it was his own past—maybe it was everything he had ever thought about himself—forever behind him.

That night was the first of Ripe Berries Moon. The new moon sliced down through the treetops in the west even before daylight was finished, as thin and cool as an assassin's blade.

Kem had chosen a rocky outcrop to spend the night on, a high place with a bit of a view. He had walked several kills through unmarked woodland, but still he wanted to keep an eye on his own trail. It was crazy to think anyone was tracking him. But it was crazy to think anything at all, really, he supposed. It was crazy even to sit here, alone and lost in the Barrens, with no food, no extra clothing, no map, no supplies. All he had was the crossbow he had killed the stranger with and a handful of bolts. And a wrench—that was crazy too, but he had had this wrench stuck in his pocket when he went to the barn to get a ladder, and the wrench was still there. An idiotic tool, once functional and now purposeless. Kem supposed you could find a meaning here if you wanted to, an obvious sort of comparison, but he had never been inclined to read life that way, as full of symbols and portents. As having a pattern. It had just seemed pretty much accidental, the things that happened to you, the way it all worked out. Now he supposed that you could read life another way, if you wanted to.

You could look back (for example) over Kem's life at the Oasis, from the time he signed aboard until now, and you could see a certain order or pattern there, if you looked for one. For example: that night in Delan's stateroom, when Kem swallowed the diviner's sage, when he first met Sander. Then the afternoon with Tallheron, down in the library, reading a story from a book. The book had gotten him thrown out of the galley but also it had formed a sort of bridge between Kem and Tallheron, a connection that had lasted until just a few hours ago. The connection with Delan had lasted too, and the one with Sander had grown into a friendship. He saw these things now as a kind of web, an

intricate crossing and recrossing of threads. A web, or a
hunter's snare. The lines of connection extended to the Bell
Dog, Mole, the mates on the navigation deck, right up to
Captain Hand. And that's where they seemed to stop. At the
top of the tower, where all the threads were tied up.

There was one thing, though, that didn't fit this pattern at
all, and it was Davina. Kem could not figure out how Davina
could be part of the web of connections that held him like a
trapped animal, that bound him to everyone else. It seemed
to him that she was a separate thing, not part of the pattern;
that her only connection to any of this was her connection to
Kem. He thought of her now and what came to him was a
memory of softness, of warmth that accepted him, enfolded
him, held him safe. He thought of her face, her gentle and
accepting smile. The memory of Davina brought him a kind
of comfort, but also it made him feel unsettled, worried for
her. Afraid that she was in danger, that the net in which Kem
was caught would ensnare Davina too, inevitably. The more
Kem thought about it the more troubled he became. He
thought of the Oasis now as a very dangerous place, and he
doubted whether anyone—Davina or Sander or the Bell Dog,
any single one of his friends—was really safe there.

The new moon went down and Kem still sat, watching the
black woods he had passed through, the bright stars whirling
through the emptiness above, and wondering where, in all
that darkness, the Oasis lay waiting.

Sometime, probably not late, he lost the struggle with his
own exhaustion. He fell asleep with his back wedged
uncomfortably between two big rocks. That's the position he
found himself in when he woke up next morning, the sun
already warm on the back of his neck. His body gave a little
jerk, involuntary, in discomfort and surprise. An ache that
began at his coccyx throbbed up along his spine and into the
back of his head.

He rose to his feet. He was thirsty and groggy and he had
to pee, and in stepping across the rocks where he had spent
the night his foot struck the crossbow. He had left it propped
butt-up, the way you're supposed to, with a bolt still resting

in the groove. Dislodged, the crossbow fell sideways, struck the rocks in an improbable way; the cord let go with a plucking sound; the bolt flew sideways, whickering into the trees. Just like that, Kem thought. I could have gotten killed just like that, from being so stupid.

He gave the bow another kick. He felt something deep inside let go, burst open, like a valve failing under terrific pressure. He picked up the crossbow and he hurled it as hard as he could into the Barrens. It flew end over end maybe a dozen strides, struck a tall branch, and seemed to hang there. But slowly the branch arched downward, and in the end the crossbow fell out of sight and landed with a soft crack. Kem thought probably its stock was broken, and he was glad.

It was about a minute later, standing at the edge of the outcrop, pissing over the side, that he saw something that made him wish he had the crossbow back again.

It was not a definite thing that he saw, only a sort of small flicker or movement. It did not even happen in the direction he was looking—he was looking down, basically—but off to one side and a good distance away. By the time Kem registered the impression of motion in the treetops, leaves stirring with a papery sound and then becoming still, it was over. He fastened his pants and stood there with a rapidly growing sense of vulnerability. It had not occurred to him that this high place among the rocks, which enabled him to see a long way through the forest, would naturally make him visible from a long way off, too. He looked around him quickly, but there was only the fistful of extra bolts. He snatched one up—the barbed, sharpened head would make a serviceable dagger, he guessed—and scrambled down to the floor of the woods.

Oddly, he felt little fear, nothing like the panic that had filled him yesterday. Perhaps he was simply exhausted. Perhaps the logical part of his mind, for once, was overriding his emotions, telling him that probably it was nothing, probably the thing he had half glimpsed in the trees had nothing to do with him. A squirrel, maybe. A nesting bird.

Or perhaps he was so crazed—from desolation, from hunger—that he couldn't think straight anymore.

However that may have been, Kem felt calm and full of

purpose as he crouched at the base of a twisted, gnomish
little tree and formulated a strategy for his own survival. To
begin with, he figured he should get away from the rocks.
But not in the obvious direction, diametrically away from
where he had seen the movement in the treetop. That was
too predictable. He set off instead at an oblique angle,
placing his feet with care in spots where the ground was
padded with moss, or on exposed tree roots, spots where the
shifting of his weight would make no noise. He found that
with a little practice he could move pretty quickly this way,
proceeding by long zigzagging strides through the forest.

It was almost pleasurable. The sun was still low and there
was the same unusual sense of coolness and the smell of
water he had noticed before. Kem nearly forgot that he was
fleeing, possibly for his life, as he skipped from one soft spot
to the next. It seemed to him that he was in tune with
something—that through his having left everything else behind him, the Oasis and Davina and poor Tallheron and
everything that connected him with the past—he had entered
into a state of transcendent unity with those things immediately around him. With no past and no imaginable future, no
safe haven anywhere, Kem belonged only to the shimmering
present, the golden light slanting through the trees, the
waxing of Ripe Berries Moon.

For several minutes, maybe half an hour, that's exactly
what it felt like.

But the present is an illusion, as Kem should have known.
It is only a skin, like the surface tension on water, stretched
over the depths of the past, and the future does not exist at
all. You can skate on that flimsy surface for brief periods of
time, but when you lose your balance, as you must—when
you even stop to look around—you plunge right through it.
The past is all around you then. You drown in it.

Kem's present ended in a laurel-hell, a patch of glossy-
leaved shrubs whose pinkish blossoms were almost spent,
limbs intertwined in such a way that, although the shrubs
were quite leggy and sparse, Kem had to lift and duck and
squeeze his way through them. And when he got to the other
side he lost his footing, tripped over a root or stump or
something, or no . . .

It was a foot. Someone had tripped him. Kem fell face-first, barely managed not to impale himself on the crossbow bolt by getting an arm out, landed hard on the arm with an awful stab of pain, a crack that seemed louder to him than lightning though it was only a small bone giving way. Tears filled his eyes but he did not cry out; it was all happening too fast; a mighty grasp on his shoulder and his neck rolled him over and held him down, immobilized.

It took a couple of seconds for his vision to clear, and when it did he let out a slow groan, an expression of many things, a kind of surrender.

He squinted up through the harsh yellow sun at the dark eyes staring back down at him. Eyes he well knew.

"Got big problems now," said the Bell Dog. "Bigger problems all the time."

The Bell Dog splinted Kem's forearm with a rowan sapling, having snapped the little tree with offhand brutality into pieces of the proper size. He tied it in place with a length of trumpet vine. There were orange flowers where the vine had grown up into the sunlight and the Bell Dog just left them there, mangled by the lashing and tying, releasing their vague sweet scent in the morning air now that it was too late to do them any good.

Kem saw that once you started looking for these pregnant little details—helpless blossoms, snatched for some higher purpose in the moment of their flowering—you saw the damned things everywhere.

Resolutely, the Bell Dog did not say what he was doing here, how he had tracked Kem down, what his intentions were. Kem only asked once. He realized it was a lost cause, and he could tell the Bell Dog was angry—at him, he supposed, though he couldn't be sure even of that.

The Bell Dog stood and inspected his work and he motioned for Kem to get up. Then he looked away, off through the woods, as though his attention was partly somewhere else. Kem lost his balance trying to stand; the Bell Dog had to grab his unbroken arm and steady him. They looked at each other, face-to-face.

"I guess I really screwed up this time," Kem said.

"Not your fault," said the Bell Dog.

"It's not?"

The Bell Dog let go. At first Kem thought that he had reverted to his normal, maddening form—stubborn and secretive—but then he shook his head and said, almost kindly, "You just see part of the thing, is all. Not the whole thing. You mean to do good, mostly."

"What thing?" Kem had the feeling that at any moment the Bell Dog was going to lapse into silence again; he felt like he was rushing to get a few more words out before the barrier dropped. "If I don't see the whole thing, why don't you tell me? Why don't you *help* me, for god's sake?"

The Bell Dog looked at him and narrowed his eyes and Kem saw how ridiculous that last question was, addressed to someone who had tracked him for many kills through the wilderness, apparently to splint his broken arm.

Then it occurred to him that he wouldn't have broken the arm in the first place, if the Bell Dog hadn't tripped him. And for that matter, he didn't really know why the Bell Dog had come. He didn't know whose side the Bell Dog or anyone else was on; he didn't know whether there were sides at all, or just Kem against the whole dark and pitiless world. Kem and maybe Davina. Trapped in the web. He felt like crying. He felt like killing someone.

The Bell Dog laid a hand on his shoulder. "Probably should have helped you," he said. "Maybe so. Maybe should have helped other people. Lot of people, before." He shrugged. "Don't know. Always done my job. Helping people, that's somebody else's job. Always thought so."

He shrugged again. Kem could see something like deep concern in the little man's face. He thought it was odd that in all the time had had spent with the Bell Dog he had never gotten the sense of really knowing him—as he knew Sander, for instance. He wondered if that worked both ways—if the Bell Dog had ever really known him, either.

The Bell Dog nodded, a signal that seemed to indicate that the talking was over. "You come with me," he said. "I help you now."

Hope—that lost and precious and formless thing—returned to Kem's breast. He said, "Where? Where are we going?"

"Back there."

The Bell Dog gave a nod, into the morning sun, and Kem understood at once where *back there* meant.

"But . . ." He tried to think of some rational objection, but the whole thing was too vast, too inchoate. "But they'll . . . I mean, they'll *know*. They'll, won't they . . ."

The Bell Dog said, "That's right, most likely. Most likely they know. But it's all right. Most likely, if you come back, they trust you now."

They walked for no more than a kill and then they came to a wide dell with a pond at the center. Beside the pond two horses were loosely tethered. They were the same horses Kem and Tallheron had ridden out on. Kem knew there was no point in asking the Bell Dog about this. Besides, his arm had begun to throb and to swell and he was hungry and exhausted. He knelt beside the pond and drank from the water (it had a slightly rotten taste, like fallen leaves) while the Bell Dog untied the horses and checked their saddles.

The Oasis was waiting. They approached it in fading daylight, riding slowly across a stretch of poor rocky ground where the trees grew so short that you could now and then get a view of the landscape over the tops of them: a shadowed expanse of gray-green trees and the Oasis in the distance like a monster rising from the earth. Then the ground would dip or the trees would rise and you were staring at nothing again, the leaves, the dark undersides of branches, the indigo empty sky.

And something else. One other thing. Kem saw now that there was another element in the picture that he had not noticed because it was smaller and harder to focus upon. But up in the sky, in the moments when the trees cut off his vision of everything else, he thought he saw some subtle motion, a whirling or circling high above. He squinted, but the evening was rushing on and it was too hard to train his eyes on those blurred, incessantly moving forms. It seemed to him, though, that as daylight ebbed and he and the Bell

Dog got closer to the Oasis the forms became more numerous, the circles or spirals narrower.

"Are those ..." His lips stopped moving of their own accord.

The Bell Dog followed his gaze upward, and both of them slowed their horses nearly to a halt.

You could almost make them out, those dark flyers. Kem's mind filled with a vision of great spreading wings, onyx eyes, sharp beaks, long pointed talons.

"Caracaras," said the Bell Dog at last. You could barely see anything now. "Desert eagles."

"Eagles?" said Kem. It was what he had thought, the word he had not spoken.

"Not really eagles," said the Bell Dog. "Carrion eaters. Like vultures, some. Don't see them much here up north."

Maybe you didn't, Kem thought, but the Bell Dog did not seem surprised to see them now. In fact he recognized them pretty readily, despite the fact that it was almost dark and the birds were tiny against the sky and as devoid of color as the Oasis, whose navigation tower Kem could see now over the treetops, tapering into the sky, spiraling sunwise and up while the desert eagles spiraled moonwise and down.

Floodlamps poured hot white light into the woods. Kem might have stopped and held back, out of fear, trying to get his head together, but the Bell Dog was moving along behind him and his horse had found a little trail, a path beaten by previous comings and goings—including Kem's own departure, he guessed—and marked by trampled earth, broken twigs, and piles of manure. As they got closer and closer the Oasis lost all form and became only a place ahead, a region, vast and dark, waiting to receive them. Kem turned and started to say:

"Well listen, thanks for—"

But the Bell Dog was gone. Kem had been riding alone, leading the extra horse, for ... how long now? A guard stood indolently, watching with a frown, at the ramp that led up to the stables—a big man dressed in a dark gray uniform with no insignia—and for a few seconds Kem tried to think of how to play this, what to say, what kind of explanation to give. But the guard behaved as though Kem's arrival was a minor irritation, nothing more; he gestured for Kem to dismount and he said, "Be sure you've got all your personal crap out of the saddle bags."

As Kem complied the man took charge of the horses and Kem got the hell out of his way. He walked slowly around the hull toward the old hatchway he had used as a snipe, an entrance that was never lit (his old comrades made sure of that by snipping the electric wire), which suited Kem in his present state. He thought he would go aboard through the engine flats and use a service ladder to get up to the infirmary. The Bell Dog had made him promise to get his arm properly attended to, and Kem thought that it would be just as well to get cleaned up before he saw Davina. He did not want her to worry, which probably constituted a functional definition of love: that he had almost been killed and had broken his arm and gone without food for over a day and spent the night on a pile of rocks like some fugitive, and he was returning now to this place where some awful fate might be in store for him—but he did not want Davina to worry.

The infirmary was near the Residents' wing. It was an extensive series of compartments, as one would have expected given the nature of the Oasis. Kem had made periodic trips here to be salved and bandaged after the routine minor injuries that were part of life in the engine flats. He was not particularly fond of the place but he had no fear of it. There were small rooms, somewhat removed from the main facility, in which more serious cases were treated, and Kem walked quickly past these without glancing in. He did not want to add anyone else's troubles, even in passing, to the growing list of his own.

The attendants asked no questions. They never did. It was not for them to wonder how his forearm came to be broken and splinted with the limbs of a rowan tree. The principal attendant even kept up a good-natured banter as he made a cast to immobilize Kem's arm and tied it gently in a sling. Kem imagined that with the hopelessly ill all around you— victims of the crying whom, though you might alleviate their suffering for a time, you could never heal—a matter as simple as a broken forearm might be a welcome little diversion. He smiled at the attendant and thanked him: stiff upper lip and all that. He knew that when he left the infirmary, there would be no one to protect him. There would be no one to save him as the Bell Dog had done, or tried to do. And it might be that what the Bell Dog had done was not to save him but simply bring him back, a fugitive brought to justice. Or a beast returned to its pen.

As Kem walked out the way he had come in, this new spirit of perversity, which might itself have been a form of self-punishment, led him to peer left and right into the chambers of the gravely ill. He saw with some disgust and some satisfaction those things that are to be seen in such places, and he thought that there was a certain universality to human suffering—that the faces of these unfortunates, Residents and ordinary crew members alike, were very much like the sad face of Tallheron as Kem remembered it, and that they were also almost indistinguishable from the sick and the maimed and the dying he had seen all his life out on the Grind—and he supposed that in one way this made you feel a bond with those who were suffering, a sense of your common mortality, but in another way it made you feel indifferent. Because in some sense you had seen it all before. You had seen these faces and these recumbent forms a hundred times in a hundred different places. And you would continue to see them, everywhere, all the time, until your own turn came, and you took your place among them.

That's how Kem's thoughts ran, anyway, until he came to a room, one of the last in line, where he came to a halt. And as he stared into the room he decided that he was full of shit, even more so than usual. Because no matter how bad you felt, how sorry for yourself, you had *not* seen it all before.

There is always something new—always one thing more dreadful than anything you have seen—and you just can't imagine what it could be until it lies in front of you. Then you know.

Kem looked into the little room before him and he saw Sander lying flat on his back, his eyes open the way a corpse's eyes are, staring straight up at the ceiling. His body was partly covered by a sheet, but he must have thrashed about because part of the sheet was twisted around his legs. His skinny chest and shoulders and arms were exposed and Kem could see that they boy's skin had lost all its color. It was white, or slightly yellowish. You could see the bones underneath it. Except that his rib cage slightly rose and fell a couple of times, Kem would have thought his friend was dead.

He entered the room feeling ill himself, dizzy, almost nauseated.

"Sander?"

The boy's wide eyes moved a little, back and forth, as though they were tracing out some pattern overhead. Kem thought that the room smelled funny, sour or spoiled somehow, a smell that seemed to fit the color of Sander's flesh. The thought made his stomach turn but then his mind got control of it; he told himself that this was Sander and whatever had changed about him, whatever had gone wrong, he was still the friend Kem remembered and who had cared about Kem when no one else did.

"Sander?" he said again. When the boy did not respond, Kem sat down on the side of his bed, his knee propped up next to the thin white chest, and he reached slowly, somewhat fearfully, and touched his friend on the shoulder. Sander's skin felt oily and cool. Kem rubbed the shoulder a little but this felt awkward, somewhere between the good-natured roughness of a comrade and the gingerly delicacy of a parent toward a small child. Somehow it felt more natural to behave as one might toward a stricken lover; so Kem raised his hand to stroke Sander's bony, sweat-covered brow.

The boy blinked but still seemed to have no idea of what was going on.

"Sander," Kem said, a bit more loudly. "Sander, it's Kem."

The boy twitched a little. Kem adjusted his position on the bed. He was settling in to wait—he was prepared to stay as long as necessary, until Sander came around or until the attendants ran him out—when a cool hand touched his arm and Sander said, "Kem"—in a voice that seemed to have been produced by breath alone, a current of air too weak to stir the vocal cords.

The boy's eyes had sharpened. Still they had a distracted

or unfocused quality, as though they were fixed on something other than Kem. Maybe he was seeing ghosts. Kem didn't know how to act or what to say.

"It is night?" Sander asked him.

Kem was confused but he nodded.

Sander nodded back. "I thought so," he said. The effort of speaking seemed to perk him up rather than tire him. He went on after a moment: "You can tell, even though they won't let you have a clock."

"They won't?"

"They don't want me to know anything."

Kem was inclined to think that Sander was confused, that he had lost his grip on things. "Sander, what's the matter? What happened to you?"

Sander's eyes seemed to strain, and his hand grasped at empty air. Kem took the hand and held it. It felt like nothing—cool and damp and weightless—and there was no strength in it to hold his back. Sander said, "They told me you'd gone. They said . . ."

"Who said?" Kem did not know what Sander meant but it sounded alarming. "Who said what?"

Sander shook his head. He seemed unable to remember, or to concentrate. Something was very badly wrong.

"Sander, listen." Kem squeezed his friend's hand hard, as though he might force some strength into him. But the little bit of strength Kem had to spare must not have been enough; Sander just stared at him in what seemed utter bewilderment.

Then out of nowhere he said, "They missed you at the party."

Kem thought this was a brave attempt at friendly banter. He tried to smile. "Yeah, well. I was kind of busy that night, I guess."

Sander shook his head. "It was morning. It happened in the morning. But they missed you."

There was no way to tell what Sander meant or even whether he knew exactly what he was saying. He did seem at least to know that he was talking to Kem, and Kem was grateful for that. He thought he'd try his question one last time.

"What's wrong, Sander? Have you ... I mean, have they told you ..."

The words would not quite form, though they seemed to crowd into the front of his mind. Sander's eyes had closed again and Kem figured that was just as well. The best thing, probably, was to just let him rest. With some reluctance he let go of Sander's hand, setting it down lightly on the rumpled sheet.

He was standing up when Sander spoke again. Kem didn't catch exactly what he said at first; then he realized it was his name.

"Kem," the boy said again, "Kem—"

"Hey, it's all right, I'm still here."

He sat down again on the bed and now he saw that Sander's eyes were closed because the boy was crying. Tears made narrow channels across both cheekbones and down the sides of the narrow face. For the first time since Kem had known him Sander looked like just a kid, a little boy far away from family and home. But this was his home, and Kem supposed he himself might be as close as Sander came to having a family. Brothers in the Oasis.

"It's all right," he told Sander. As before when he said these words, but even more fervently, he wished that they were true even while he disbelieved them. He said them again anyway.

And after a while Sander said

"I don't feel good, Kem.
I don't feel good
at all."

PETALS FALL

Water spumed from the fountain. On the trading deck between rows of olive trees in their deep sunken planters a submersible pump recirculated warm water, forcing it upward in a thrilling, silvered stem that opened like a flower, became transparent and then insubstantial as it was caught by the evening sun and the dry desert breeze and flung sideways, outward, turning to mist and finally to dampness, distilled to its essence. Then only the light remained—something like candlelight, yellow and warm, a light that seemed to have been sponged across the faces of the children who gathered to play near the fountain and across the traders and farmers and wagon people and a few odd members of the crew who had come, like Kem, to watch them. Kem hung back near the olive trees, and he could see out of one eye the handful of men who did not speak but merely stood apart from one another watching, while out of the other eye he absorbed the rest of the scene. The drama here was a quiet one but it was no less absorbing for that. Now and then a child would be scooped up in the arms of a parent or taken by the hand and led, balking, away. Other children wandered off, bored at last or perhaps moved by a sense of belonging elsewhere. After a while the sun got very low, tangled itself among the upper limbs of the olives, and the mist blowing off the fountain began to feel slightly chilled, a warning of the end of summer or the coming night, and by that time the number of kids had fallen to half a dozen or fewer, little stalwarts, and these were the ones Kem was inclined to worry about. It was too easy for him to imagine his own little sisters here because these kids tended to be about his sisters' age and to resemble them in other ways too: skinny kids with bright, curious, feckless eyes, taking it all in, glancing sometimes over their shoulders as though they might be comparing what they saw here to what they had to go back to. Kem supposed if he were one of these kids he would have been making the same comparison, weighing on one hand the Oasis with all its wonders and its mysteries and on the other the rough, familiar comforts of the wagon and the Grind.

At the same time it was more than possible that some of these kids were making a comparison of a different sort. A few of them might be orphans and others might be runaways, neither status being exactly uncommon out here, what with the crying and the general lousiness of wagon life. For kids like that, no matter how awful or frightening the Oasis might seem, there wouldn't be a whole lot out there to go back to. Kem figured that if he stuck around long enough the sun would set and some snipe would turn the fountain off and all of the kids would go home except maybe one or two. And then he guessed these men around the olive trees would come forward with an offer of some kind, food or drink or whatever—this was a trading deck, after all—and shortly the Oasis would have gained a new citizen, someone not bound like Kem to a well-defined term of labor but to something else, perhaps no less particular. Or so Kem supposed.

But in truth he didn't know (as he almost never knew) whether this was anything more than the work of his mood and his increasingly morbid imagination. As a matter of fact he preferred it that way: he had reached that level of knowl-edge at which he understood that ignorance might not be an

altogether bad thing; it might be a form of innocence after all
and therefore something to try to hang on to. So while a little
bit of sunlight was left—not much, but at least some tinges of
orange among the blackening leaves of the olive trees—he
turned and left the market square and entered the hallways of
the Oasis where it was unnaturally bright, where the day shift
had ended and the night shift had begun and some poor
snipe, way down on Mole's shit list, was crawling up and
down passageways turning the lights on.

They had been back on the Grind for the better part of a
month, having left the Oak Barrens someplace in the past.
Kem thought he must have been hibernating or something at
the time; he could not remember crossing any line either
physical or symbolic, as for instance on a navigational chart.
His broken arm had mended, but gradually, as all things
mend, without milestones. It was late summer, and while the
Oasis rumbled generally south and west, into the desert
wind, the wagons were blowing east, away from it, toward the
Gut and Riley County and the winter camps. Scarcely a day
passed without a cluster of little sails bobbing up on the
western horizon, as though exhuming themselves from that
deathly flatness, and within an hour or so, by peering through
the optical devices up in the tower, you could begin to make
out the details of the wagons themselves—the shapes of their
cabins, how they were rigged out, what kind of wheels they
rolled on—and from such raw information anyone with a
knowledgeable eye, such as Kem's, could have told you many
things about those wagons and the people who lived in them.
This hypothetic watcher (not Kem, but like him) could have
made informed estimations as to number of occupants, contents of cargo bay, relative wealth or poverty (by wagoneer
standards), principal means of sustenance, most recent stopping place, intermediate and final destinations, right on down
to such fine and subtle points as manner of dress, quantity of
stored food (measured in units of time, e.g., five weeks'
worth), and type and efficiency of solar pack. There wouldn't
be much left to know by the time such a penetrating gaze had
been cast, the main question still unanswered and unanswer-

able, temporarily, being that of whether this particular wagon would hoist its pennant or otherwise signal its desire to trade with the Oasis—and the greater uncertainty, of course, of whether the Oasis, having received such a signal, would actually stop.

It was something you could wager on: yes, no, how long, what for, things like that. The gang on duty in the tower would sometimes get a betting pool started, which Kem, no better than the rest of them, would join; but this was perhaps only because he did not want to feel as alone as he often did recently. He was still badly shaken up about Sander and it hadn't helped that the boy, when Kem went back looking for him, was nowhere to be found. Not in the dispensary and not in Crews' Berthing, and the dispensary staff hadn't been too forthcoming either. They knew who Kem was talking about, all right; only they professed not to know exactly what had become of him, and his medical status, of course, was confidential. He had checked out, one guy told Kem, and gone back home—*Home?* Kem asked, genuinely puzzled—while another guy went so far as to claim that Sander, when they last saw him, was doing fine.

Well, anything was possible, as Kem should have been the first to agree. He watched from the navigation deck with a kind of tantalizing dread as a cluster of wagons moved steadily closer across the Grind. Some of the wagons maneuvered to intercept the Oasis while others changed course to pass as far abeam as possible, the way Kem's father always had done. Most of the wagons just stopped. They struck their sails as one might upon sighting an ominous-looking cloud on the horizon and they waited to see what the Oasis was going to do, whether it would blow harmlessly by or whether, like a cyclone, it would choose this piece of barren earth to touch down on. Kem waited with them, his wagon-boy's soul floating out to them, until the Oasis committed itself to one course or the other. Three times so far it had stopped and the other times the wagons dead ahead had been forced to skittle out of its way like panicked sand crabs. Kem would listen for the crunching of wooden exoskeletons (he wasn't sure, though, whether you would even hear anything like that, with all the other noise) but it seemed the wagons were always quick enough, barely.

On this occasion, though, the command to halt came rattling down the voice tube and the snipes far below went about braking and clutching-in and shifting-over, once again diverting the inconceivable energies of the craft into storage systems of varying degrees of wastefulness. Because it was late in the day the sun wings were not deployed; that task would fall to the night shift, a not-unpleasant diversion in the twilight before dawn which probably Mole would want to supervise himself. By the time the ritual of stopping was complete and the shocks were bled and the first ramp was lowered to the Grind, lights were already coming on here and there and you could barely see, in contrast to their brightness, whether many wagons were waiting out there or not, or if anyone had been dispatched to greet them. And only in Kem's imagination (increasingly morbid) could you hear the throbbing of a pump and the splash of water and the squealing of children down on the trading deck. In reality, from way up here in the tower, none of those things would have been perceptible at all.

He was astonished to find Sander at the door. This was the following morning: the boy was braced lightly with one arm against the jamb and one long leg stuck down straight with the other tucked behind it. He was thin enough that the pose was heronlike. He wore plain clothes in his personal style of half a year ago, and Kem was so glad to see him that he made a chaotic rush toward the door with the book he was reading (folktales distantly akin to *Sun Tales and Moon Songs*) flapping open in one hand, only stopping a stride and a couple of heartbeats short of hugging his friend, before a piling-up of little signals—the boy's aloof, cooler-than-thou expression among them—made him stop and stand there dumbly, inexpressive. The book, for an interval weightless, felt heavy again. Sander smiled.

"Good morning, Davina," he called tranquilly across Kem's shoulder into the room. "Good morning, Kem."

"Hi, Sander," Davina said without standing up, but then of

course she wouldn't have known there was anything to stand up for. Kem hadn't told her. He hadn't told her about finding Sander or about how it made him feel, because most of the story (the beginning and the end) would have been missing, but more than that because of a decision he had made, on that trip back to the Oasis with the Bell Dog, to keep Davina out of it. Out of what, he couldn't have said, but that was all the more reason, probably.

Sander looked at Kem as though waiting to see how he was going to handle this: the sudden manifestation of someone lost and worried about and—he must have known—feared dead. At the same time his blithe expression seemed to contain a warning. Just keep moving, pal. Don't look back and don't ask any stupid questions.

"How are you doing?" Kem asked anyway, about as stupid a question as they came.

Sander favored him with a smile, serene and rather too self-satisfied for Kem's taste, though he took this as a healthy sign.

"I thought," the boy said, "you might like to go out."

"Out?"

"For a walk. It's a beautiful day, had you noticed? I bet not, all locked up in here." Sander was about the same height as Kem now and had no trouble peering around him, taking in the cluttered room. His eyes flicked over everything as though checking each item off against some master list. They returned to Kem at last. "I see you're keeping up on your reading."

"Where have you been?" said Kem. "I've been looking all over for you."

"You have? But why?" Sander's expression parted company with his words, though; a darkness came down from his forehead into his eyes. He tossed his head sideways—the long sun-whitened hair whipped like a horse's mane—then back, and he laid a hand, almost weightless, on Kem's shoulder. Their eyes did not meet in that moment, and Kem felt both awkward and gratified, because he sensed that he was being given some acknowledgment, maybe a silent and uniquely Sander-like form of thanks. "Actually," said Sander meanwhile, "I've been staying with Gardner."

Hence, maybe, Kem supposed, the critical appraisal of this modest little room. When he looked eye to eye at Sander again, the boy made a quick sideward motion with his eyes, at last a signal that Kem could read.

"I'll be back in a little while," he told Davina. "I think Sander and I are going for a walk."

It was the first morning of the fourth stop the Oasis had made since leaving the Barrens. It was relatively cool on deck and there were people everywhere, crew members and wagon people and Residents all out for a bit of air and sun while both remained tolerable. Kem thought Sander would be heading down to the trading deck, where the action was, but they took a wrong turn for that.

"Hey"—an anxious thought came to him—"you're not heading back to that guy's place, Gardner's, are you?"

Sander looked back over a shoulder. "What do you have against Gardner?" He waited a couple of seconds but Kem waited him out. "No, of course not. We're going for a *walk*. You said so yourself."

Where it turned out they were going was the ramp leading down from the Oasis, a hundred or so strides from which the main body of wagons was encamped, with others scattered here and there over maybe a kill or so, a patch of dry hardpan as broad as it was long. The whole thing happened so fast—reaching the brow where the ramp was attached, nodding to the stolid and unresponsive guards, signing themselves out, quickstepping down the slanting, cross-ribbed walkway, and finding themselves suddenly down on the warm surface of the Grind, gawking at everything like sightseers— Kem had no time for misgivings or anything else until it was much too late for them. Then they were all over him. He felt something like associational overload and he held back when Sander struck off toward the wagons.

"Wait," Kem said irritably, catching up. "You can't just . . . Listen, are you all right? I've been . . . I mean, seeing you like that in the infirmary, is anything—"

"Oh, that." Sander stopped walking but kept staring ahead, avoiding Kem's eye. "That was nothing. What did you think, I had the crying or something?"

Kem opened his mouth but he could not quite bring

himself to say either *yes*, which was the truth, though he had not quite admitted it to himself before now, or *no*, since he had never been good at lying.

"Well I don't," said Sander. He turned to Kem, his eyes full of stormy, childlike anger. "Are you satisfied? You don't have to worry about catching anything from me. Okay? Now would you please drop it?"

Sander stalked away, toward the wagons, and Kem let him go. He felt wounded, a bit, but at the same time he thought he understood a little of what Sander was feeling—embarrassment, maybe, at having been caught in a moment of helplessness, something like that—and he was glad, truly, to find out that Sander was all right. Assuming of course that Sander *was* all right. How could you really tell?

Anyway, Kem was satisfied for the moment. He allowed his thoughts to stray from Sander (now a dozen paces off, still walking) to the rest of the scene—the wagons, the people, the Grind. He felt once again an odd sense of circularity: this was, he supposed, a kind of homecoming for him, or at least as much of a homecoming as he was likely to make on this particular turn of the wheel. And to be honest it was as close to "home," whatever that meant, as he cared to come. In slow, uncertain steps he began loping after Sander, giving himself time to take it all in.

At first he kept his eyes down on the Grind itself, the thin double tier of life that hung on just above and a little bit farther below it. The earth out here looked like only partly broken-down sandstone, a gritty substance rich in feldspar and little else that you could hardly dignify with the name *soil*, though it allowed a surprising degree of colonization, when you got right down to it. Between the prominent clumps of opuntia, teddybear cholla, one-seed juniper, smoke bush, and mormon tea, grew quieter drifts of short-stemmed grasses and flowering forbs whose seasons had mostly passed, reduced now to desiccated stalks and seedheads, some of which—the *Helianthus* tribe, principally, and a few other composites—might be constructively browsed by savvy wagon folks with enough of an appetite. That was one thing kids were good for. But this was only half the story, the sunny one, and for every finger-height of visible living substance there were whole hidden fathoms of darkness, an underworld where roots dug deep, unknowably deep, through the hard crust of the Grind seeking water and non-salt-poisoned soil and, more poetically, a place to hide, a refuge from the sun's remorseless bounty that gave life and destroyed it with equal lack of restraint. Here and there Kem's practiced eye picked out holes that might have belonged to snakes or burrowing owls or maybe, in the case of one or two larger ones, a skulk of kit foxes. You wouldn't be seeing those creatures in daylight, though. The best you could hope for was a glimpse of some of the insect and just possibly rodent life, both remarkably rich out here, all things considered. Kem ambled among these natives and opportunistic immigrants of the Grind (to one of which communities, he was not sure which, he belonged himself) on a course that zigzagged more or less the way Sander was headed. Wherever that was.

After a while he looked up to get his bearings and found that he had drifted rather far afield, still within the vague boundaries of the wagon encampment but off to one side of it, away from the Oasis. He saw Sander a dozen strides away, talking to a wagon girl a little younger than himself. As Kem watched, Sander looked around at him, just barely making eye contact and then looking away, back at the girl. He repeated this, his eyes moving quickly from Kem to the girl and back again as though stitching the three of them together. Later on, Kem would wonder whether something deeper than chance had led Sander out to this particular no-man's-land. Also whether Sander's glance was meant to be an invitation or a warning or what. But for now he occupied himself wiping his brow in the gathering heat and wishing he had thought to grab a hat; though why should he have? —when Sander hadn't told him where they were going.

Sander was coming closer now and bringing the girl, or maybe the girl had just quietly decided all by herself to tag along with him. They did not look quite connected; it was like they were each of them approaching Kem from a very different place. Not physical places, either. The heat was awful now. Kem guessed that was why he felt dizzy, why the world seemed to have spun very quickly around during one of the times that he blinked the sweat off his eyelids so that here he stood in the same place but suddenly off balance. Sander should have said something by this time but instead by his very silence he seemed to invite Kem's attention to the girl, now moseying up a few strides away from him, in the direction his eye's blind spot would have been if the eyeball hadn't been twitching. There she stopped. Her hair hung down long past her shoulders, touching the place where next year or the one after that her breasts would be. Her eyes seemed less to absorb than to reflect light. Kem entertained briefly the heat-stricken thought that he was dreaming her.

The girl said, "Hi."

Oh my lost fucking soul, or whatever you really think that such words approximate, Kem thought. The girl was his sister. The oldest of the two, and he hadn't recognized her till now (though of course he had, the recognition had made him feel slightly crazy, throbbing up from some psychic underground, the place where his roots grew) because she had changed so much in the last—was it a year?—since he had seen her. Changed in her way as drastically as Sander in his: grown a lot taller, with cheekbones now strikingly evident as though they had emerged out of a dormant state from beneath baby fat, and her eyes that were fixed on him seemed a more definite shade of brown, their irises thin and sharply delineated. Even her manner of dress had changed though the long unadorned frock looked oddly familiar; Kem wondered if this might not have been their mother's, a remembrance their father had hidden away all these years in some secret pocket of the wagon.

"H-hi," was all Kem managed to say. Maybe that was enough. His sister came across the remaining distance between them and hugged him briefly, fervently, and then stepped two considerable paces back. From that distance they resumed taking each other in.

"How's, um," Kem got himself going again, "how's . . . everybody."

Ewinda (she was not without a name, though this was not how she was filed in Kem's mind) looked straight back at him. "Chris died," she said simply enough, adding, "Father's fine. You ought to go see him."

"Chrissie . . ." Kem felt as though some major portion of

his heart had summarily been lopped off. He stepped un-
thinkingly forward, hand moving up to the site of the ext-
raction as though checking for blood, scars, and clue as to
who'd done it. "Wh-what happened?"

Ewinda clearly did not want to talk about this, beyond the
necessary minimum. She shrugged. "It was only a couple of
months after you left. She just got sick and died. I don't
know."

Kem wondered if he ought to be crying or anything, if it
was detestable that he was not. He just could hardly believe
it, was all; it was hard enough to believe that Ewinda was
here, how she'd changed, and she was standing right in front
of him. Little Chris . . . how old could she have been? Eight,
maybe, when it happened?

He said, "I'm sorry." Ewinda shrugged again. It was
getting really awkward, and Kem could now have just about
shot Sander for sticking around, which he figured later was
maybe how his grief was coming out, irrationally like that. "I
mean," trying again, "I'm sorry I wasn't there. To help, I
mean." And thinking further: "To help Dad. With everything."

"He's the one that sold *you*"—spoken with the ease and
simplicity of childhood, a false surface that (Kem remembered)
concealed awful terrifying depths. This memory at last gave
him the shove he needed to go over to his sister and put his
arm around her, allowing her still to face partly away from
him, maintaining her reserve, which she no doubt needed as
much as she needed her big brother's reassuring nearness.
Kem looked at Sander whose expression was as unreadable as
if he'd been a member of some different species, watching
from the safe position of his alienness.

Ewinda said, "Are you going or not?" And when Kem did
not understand she added, "To see Father."

Kem let his arm drop. "I don't know." He didn't want to,
he meant, without being quite sure why. Having been sold by
his father for a set of tools was not the point, actually. It was
more like the final page of a long, complicated, circular story,
that had become the first page of another one. But inasmuch
as even Kem could see that the two stories were connected—
might even both be parts of a longer and stranger story after
all—he said, "You think I should?"

Ewinda only took his hand and led him silently, sister-style, over the battered face of the only world that, up until a year or so ago, Kem had ever known. And then in too little time to get a grip on his thoughts (as he had gotten a grip, for instance, on the crossbow back at Tallheron's place, arming himself) he stood a few strides from the wagon that had been his boyhood home, the means of his family's survival. And there too was the family itself, what was left of it: Kem and Ewinda and (not crawling from under the chassis, as Kem had last seen him, but opening the ratty duck flap and stepping down, each foot placed with a sort of assured deliberation as though he owned the place, this patch of bled-dry dirt he happened to have camped on for a couple of days), of course, their father. What Sander must probably have seen from his slightly safer vantage, out of the path of looks that could maim or blind, ordinary family stuff, was the three of them standing there beside an aged, spoke-wheeled, junk-rigged contraption that looked like somebody's idea of a monster insect—lightweight frame supporting a canvas carapace, masts and sails folded overhead like vestigial wings, up front the bulging geodesic polymer-skinned steering pod like a hundred-faceted, idiotic eye (Kem's father's domain, there), and behind it, dispersed around the open cargo hold, boxes and cooking stuff and a nice-looking set of tools like the just-deposited remnants of what the creature had had for lunch. The tools gave Kem something to look at, a way of accusing his father without bothering to speak.

"So," his father spoke instead, "you've come back around. You look fine."

Kem was willing to concede the first part of this but not the second; to have been looking fine would have meant something to the effect that life aboard the Oasis had turned out to be, as his father had predicted (the words came swimming up to him, out of the hateful past), *not so bad after all. You'll see*. When in fact it had been many times worse than anything his father could have imagined.

Kem stood his ground. His father (in some way, mysteriously, a stranger now) looked shorter than Kem remembered, the muscular arms emerging from a body that seemed too small or weak—you might have said frail—to have given rise to

them. His face looked old, too. Weary. The skin sagged
around his eyes. Hair hung loose, like something shredded,
around ears that seemed to have grown as the rest of the head
shrank. Kem was surprised he hadn't remembered his father
this way. Then he wondered (the question, in occurring,
surprised him) whether his father had actually *been* this way.
Before Kem left, that is. Or whether it was possible that in
only one year this man whom Kem, like any son, had been
inclined to regard as a constant, all-enduring, changeless
feature of the world at large might just possibly have become
a different, older, less innocent or ignorant person in much
the same way that Kem himself had.

Well, the old man's life *had* changed, for sure, with the
death of a daughter and all. And all ... which of course
included Kem, whose absence during the year now ending,
the year the two stories diverged, must have made things
harder in some ways. In obvious physical ways—a pair of
hands no longer available for such chores as rigging the sails,
tending cookfires, gathering food—but also perhaps in other
ways as well, which made Kem feel uncomfortable to contemplate, empty in some inner place he was only now discovering.
He had never wondered if maybe his leaving the wagon,
going off to follow the spiraling path of his own life, had cost
his father something even as it had cost Kem a home, a
family, a sense of belonging someplace, being part of some
reassuring order—that maybe there had been a reciprocal
loss on the other side, the place Kem had been plugged into,
maybe for every spot where his own heart had been wounded
and left to heal as best it could there had been a corresponding
wound in another heart, an older one that didn't heal so fast
anymore.

It took a little while to work his way through all this, and
meanwhile time had not obligingly come to a halt, the wheel
was grinding and Kem's family was behaving as he would
have expected it to, under the circumstances. There was
much standing around and a little awkward talk. Ewinda, a
real trooper, was doing her best but Kem and his father were
pacing around a bit, surveying the territory.

"So this," the old man said, nodding at Sander, "is one of
your crewmates?"

There was nothing particular in his voice except for a certain emphasis on "crewmates?"—but that was enough to make Kem think this was not just a simple question, or if it was a question that it was Kem, not really Sander, that the old man was asking about.

"This is Sander," he said, waving an introduction. "My best friend."

Sander looked to be enjoying this. He stayed right where he was—safely apart from the family circle—but straightened himself up a little, stretching out his limber spine, as though presenting himself for admiration. Or anything else: Sander couldn't have cared. Kem found this quality, which in normal times annoyed the shit out of him, suddenly wholly admirable. He watched his father as his father watched Sander for a second or two, did not say How do you do, and finally got back to looking at Kem.

"What do you do there," his father now wanted to know, "at that Oasis?"

"What do you mean?"

The old man shrugged. "What are your duties—what kind of work."

"Work?" (This was Sander, sounding as though he were about to titter, Kem guessed catching onto a certain flow in the conversation.)

"Oh, you know," said Kem. "A little of everything."

It was truly perverse, he supposed. But here he could equally well and with greater ease have told his father about working in the galley, then down in the engine flats, then up standing watches in the tower. His father might have found that interesting: the equipment, the navigational charts. Instead Kem withheld the simple facts and gave only signals, hints, clues that might have been either misleading or revealing, even Kem wasn't sure about that. Such, he would figure later, is the language of family life. Right now his father was sniffing around after something and Kem, on other counts, was curious too. You might have said it was the first time he and his father had met on a level field, two more-or-less independent adults free to draw their own conclusions.

"Is this your uniform?"—pointing at Kem's off-duty pants and shirt, of the same loose cut as Sander's. To a wagoneer, these clothes must have looked at the very best impractical—dangling sleeves and baggy pant-legs to get tangled in machinery.

Kem ignored this and went right for the heart of things. "Why did Chrissie die? Couldn't you have gotten help or something? Couldn't you have even tried to catch up with the Oasis? They've got doctors there, you know. There's—"

The muscles of his father's face tightened up and the jawbone locked into place and for an instant Kem almost flinched, expecting to be punched at. But it was not only anger that that face was sending out. The eyes dropped a bit and looked even wearier; the lips moved as though trying words out, getting the feel of them, and then, without any nameable emotion at all, Kem's father said, "It happened pretty quick, you know? The fever wasn't bad that first night, and we had some parthenium left from that plant you found, that big one out near the cutback, remember? So we gave her that in some tea. I guess we could have tried other things, I don't know. Maybe I shouldn't have gone to sleep that night. By the time we got up she was so hot she couldn't talk real well, and I didn't know . . . you remember, we had broken down for a while, fallen behind the other wagons. There was no one to ask, no place . . ."

The old man looked aside, down at the Grind, up at Ewinda, sideways at Sander. He did not look back at Kem for a while after that and it came to Kem that in a bizarre, twisty sort of way, he himself, by having been absent, might have contributed to his sister's death. It had always been Kem who had the feeling for what medicine to administer, in what doses, how often, things like that. Even while his father spoke he had been thinking, only half-mindfully, *Echinacea, why didn't you try that?* But Kem was the price his father had paid to get the wagon moving again, and maybe it had turned out that he was only part of the price, the up-front installment.

"I guess you did everything you could," he said.

His father nodded, no doubt figuring that really he had not, that Kem was just saying so. At least to this extent they understood one another. "Well," he said after a little while. "You two want some lunch?"

They stayed for a few hours and what was most amazing

was how little else happened—no words, no gestures or symbolic acts to change the way things stood among them. But Kem figured he was spending some time with his sister whom he had so often consciously missed, and he guessed that even awkwardness and all, he would be glad later to have seen his father again. (To have seen him again *before* . . . isn't that what comes next?) What else was odd was how immediately well Sander and Ewinda struck up an acquaintanceship, chatting quietly or eyeing each other with some sort of cheerful understanding from which both Kem and his father were excluded. Just like Sander, he guessed, to steal the show.

At some point, though it hadn't really gotten late, it was time to go; Kem felt it and Sander was already on his feet, stretching like a cat knowing a door's about to be opened. There were farewells and certain vague promises, if the Oasis was still around tomorrow. . . . But only when Kem was (in his mind at least) on his way, having hugged Ewinda and shaken hands with his dad, parting on better terms than they had the last time around—only then did it occur to Kem that what this had felt like, this whole visit—and this was why it had seemed only half-real, happening at a certain remove from him—was like it had not been a return home at all, or anything of the sort. It was not a return, for one thing, since this particular piece of the Grind was not a place he had ever been before. And more than that it was not "home," not for Kem, if indeed it had ever been, if indeed the word had any meaning. Because if it *did* have a meaning, for Kem personally that is, then "home" had nothing to do with this pitiful little wagon nor with this family that had ceased to seem, during the last year, to belong to him. Kem's home was someplace else. It was looming now in the face of the approaching sunset, gray black against the orange and pink and burgundy of the sky; it was waiting for Kem placidly and without expecting much, only that he return as of course he would return, as he must, because that after all is what "home" was, if anything: the place you returned to.

So he returned to it, leading Sander this time instead of following him. His journey was interrupted only once, and only for a few seconds. He had barely turned his back on the

wagon when a weight seemed to descend on him—a genuine
weight, not just a metaphor, or perhaps really both—and he
felt around him, like a belt, tightening, momentarily warm, a
restraining force that held him in place for a minute or two,
gathered him in, clutched him right around the middle,
near the heart, then for a second time letting go, and Kem
stepped out of his father's arms.

Into a darker embrace. The Oasis got moving again that night
while Kem was on watch—not the safest thing to do, what
with the wagons out there in the darkness, but Kem guessed
the one thing living on the Grind must teach you was that
you had to take care of yourself. You had to be ready for
anything. By first light, the wagon encampment was far
behind and the future lay out along the horizon like a low,
irregular ridgeline, purplish, its outlines obscured by twilight
and haze, seeming at times to recede before them but really
just waiting there, impassive, a great slumbering monster
that might at any minute now awake.

"The border," they said, and Kem had heard this before.
"We're crossing the border"—the same indefinite whispers
coming from everywhere that he had heard a year ago, late in
Fly South Moon, when he had been working down in the
galley and he had wondered, *Border to what?*
    To a place, he learned, called the Province of Industry.
Kem ran his fingers over the lettering on the chart. The
Province was shown as a rayon blue polygon that intruded
into the Grind from the south and west and unlike the
Barrens, whose array of randomly spaced tree-symbols blurred
into the Grind's brown dots along a winding, indefinite
frontier, the borderline of the Province was inscribed crisply
in black lines that joined at right angles, orderly and precise.
It made Kem wonder. He had not known the boundaries of
the world (physical and other) to be so well defined. Even the
Gut, that great natural divide, was said to have changed its
course by dozens of kills over the past century or so. Kem
wanted to see what a straight-line, right-angled border would

look like. He was more intrigued by that, in a way, than by what kind of place the Province was that they were about to cross into.

He would find out soon. The terrain along the high western edge of the Grind was dead smooth with a barely discernible slope up toward the unseen, legendary mountains, and the prevailing local vegetation was nothing to slow down for: poverty weed, buffalo grass, hairy grama, all gone to dry rust-colored seed stalks now. The great plain was playing dead until the rains came back in late winter. The Oasis rumbled south as fast as Kem could recall it ever moving, maybe fifty kills a day. At this rate they would reach the border by the day after tomorrow. Kem began to look forward to it, to getting there, and that, of course, at the Oasis, was a mistake.

The depth of this mistake was made clear to him early in the evening when he was getting ready to go on watch. Davina stood watching while he tucked his shirt in, brushed the hair that had been getting longer lately out of his eyes and generally went about making himself presentable, because you never knew. . . .

"Did you hear that the people in Industry all live in these big underground places?" Davina said. "Like huge tunnels or something?"

Kem said he had not. His face in the mirror looked a tiny bit worried.

"They do. And they keep the air inside cool all year long. And they grow food in these gigantic greenhouses, and they raise jackrabbits. To eat, I mean. For protein."

Her face grew bright, recounting these marvels. Her wide eyes stared hard at the world she was imagining. Kem stepped across the room and touched her shoulder. She took his hand, kissed it, looked up at him with a childish sort of longing. She said, "Wouldn't you love to see it?"

"See what?"

"*Industry,*" she said, as though hurt that he wasn't listening.

Only he was listening all too well. "We're going to see it," he said. "We'll be there in a couple of days."

"No, but really *see* it. Really go there, I mean. Into the

tunnels and all. Wouldn't that be interesting? Don't you think?"

Kem shrugged. "From what I hear, they're pretty choosy about visitors. Kind of like Riley County. Only they have more guns."

"But they let the Captain in. Don't you remember, last year? And all the Investors. They took the horses out there and were gone for a couple of days. They say that's where the Investors come from."

"They do?"

She nodded. "That's why they're so rich. Because Industry's where all the money is."

Kem rubbed Davina's shoulder, absentmindedly, giving this some thought. He had heard stories about Industry himself. But they were different stories. It was hard to put the things together. He said, "Don't they have some kind of religion there? Don't they all believe they're gods, or something? Or they come from another planet?"

"They're rich, is all I heard. Maybe they come from a planet with lots of money."

Kem laughed. He turned to leave, but even in the act of doing so he had a sense that it wasn't going to be that easy.

"I bet this year we could go," said Davina, tossing the words after him. "I bet if you asked Captain Hand . . ."

Kem turned in the doorway. Blood rushed up to fill his neck, his face. "When? Ask him when? Ask him *what?*"

Davina wore ingenuousness the way other girls her age, the kind you met on the Grind, might try on another person's clothing, just to see how it fit. She said, "Ask him at dinner tomorrow night. Up in his quarters. We're invited, Sander said so. We could just tell him we'd like to go to Industry, with everyone else. The worst he can say is no."

Or yes. Kem figured that yes would be worse, if it got him more tangled up (as it must, because that's the way things worked) in the Oasis and its higher-level intrigues. But that was not, actually, what bothered him—the idea of a trip into Industry, gawking at underground temples or pleasure chambers or whatever else they had there. What bothered him was the way Davina had worked it all out. This invitation to dinner. Which no doubt she had pulled some string or other to get, done somebody a favor, promised something, the Goddess knew what.

Kem stood on the navigation deck while the Oasis slept and groaned and shuddered blindly forward during the long hours of night. After things had quieted down, with only the usual sounds of watchstander talk and the beeping of semifunctional equipment and tinny chattering out of the voice tube to distract him, he decided that what was bothering him was the thought of dinner in the Captain's quarters—and especially the thought of Davina being there. Davina in the center of the web. Davina entangled—shit, hustling to entangle herself—in the whole baffling network of conspiracy, betrayal, shifting alliances, the system that once Kem had thought of as a kind of machine, its components smoothly meshing, great wheels rolling toward some definable goal, but which now he saw as more like a net, a maze, a trap. A trap in which the inner darkness itself, the mystery of it, was the bait. You wandered in because you wanted to know what was inside there—just like Kem had wanted to know, looking at the Oasis across the Grind—then *snap*, you found that what was inside was you, and there was no way out.

Now Davina was determined to wander in, and as far as Kem could see there was no way to stop her.

Well, fuck it, then. Kem stomped across the deeply shadowed deck thinking *if that's what she wants, let her have it*, but of course his feelings were more complicated than that. Maybe they had something to do with that trip out with Sander, seeing his father again, hearing about the death of his sister. Or maybe it was Sander himself, pulling himself or being pulled back from the brink. Kem stepped out onto the platform, where ladders wound sunwise and up, moonwise and down, and he stared into the empty sky. He felt like he had stepped back from the brink, himself, at least once—at least that day at Tallheron's farm—and he was in no mood to step near it again. And it seemed to him that the Captain's quarters must be about as close as you could come to the big drop-off, the precipice where all the little winding paths reached their destinations. He did not want to have dinner there. He did not want Davina to have dinner there. The other thing, the horse ride out to Industry—hell, Industry might as well be on the other side of some unpassable river, if you had to go through the Captain's quarters to get there. It might as well be the Underworld.

Behind Kem, footsteps thumped on the steel plates. Kem turned to find the mate of the watch standing behind him, looking over his shoulder into the darkness. This particular mate and Kem had pretty well gotten used to each other; they had been standing watches together for several weeks. Though they had nothing in common and actually did not talk much, beyond the normal minimum, it seemed that they had become friends anyhow, as was perhaps inevitable among people who are together night after night. The mate did not look at Kem but merely said, "Are you listening?"

"Listening to what?"

The mate nodded, as though directing his attention to something. But Kem heard nothing at all: only the muffled throb of engines, the clash of treads. He frowned.

"Can't hear anything, can you?" said the mate. Then, apparently satisfied, he stepped back through the hatch, returning to his watch station. Across his shoulder he said, "That's Industry. That's what it sounds like."

Kem was intrigued despite the mess of his emotions. He followed the mate inside. "Why?" he said.

"Why what? About Industry?" The mate gave a sort of smirk. "The place is dead, is all. There's not a goddamn living thing within a day's ride of it. That's how you know you're getting there."

Kem stepped back out onto the platform, briefly, just to check. Sure enough: there were none of the flutters or chirps or wolf cries, the beating of wings in the dark, the sense of scurrying life-forms, not even the dry whisk of desert air through parched sage leaves. Lifeless, Kem thought. The air tonight was lifeless, and it went way beyond the mere absence of sound, down to some level that made you feel empty in your gut.

He stepped inside, pulling the hatch shut behind him.

"Why?" he asked, a second time.

The mate said, "Beats the shit out of me. I guess they're

THROUGH THE HEART

not much into any kind of, you know, wild stuff, the folks at Industry. They like things . . . orderly."

Kem nodded, dubious, though his watch-mate could not see this. The mate went on:

"You know, they live in these underground places, right? And I guess it's like, they don't want any of your random microorganisms or shit like that contaminating their little biosystems. I guess they figure it'd bring in diseases or something. They're very big on health, I hear. I mean, like doing stuff because it's good for you, you know?"

Kem nodded again. He didn't have the faintest idea what the mate was talking about. His mind was still back somewhere around the *lifeless* part, trying to grasp that. "How did they do it, though? Did they just . . . kill everything off, or what?"

"Shit." (Kem imagined the mate spitting on the deck.) "They'd been doing that for years. Didn't you guys learn any history at those winter camps?" He paused, then must have taken Kem's silence to mean that no, they had not. "It's all a question of priorities, see? It's like, what you think is really important. These guys at Industry, they've never thought a whole lot was important besides themselves. Or their own *souls*, I guess. They've got this, sort of a philosophy or something—"

"A religion?"

"Sort of like that. And it says that, you know, you do a good job here, work hard, keep your dick in your pants, and in the next life we'll give you this *whole planet* to fuck around on. You can be your own little god. So it's like, they spend their whole lives trying to *prove* something, like they know how to really get in there and get a planet under control, they'll make good little goddies, kick ass and take names, spank the kids when they get out of line, like that. Does that make any sense?"

"No," said Kem.

"Yeah, well. That's the point, then, I guess. You either buy the whole thing or you don't. These guys buy it, obviously. That's why they're living at Industry. That's why we're not."

The mate tapped quietly on the log table, apparently satisfied that he had tied the strings of this philosophical knot

together nicely. Kem was not so sure. In any case, the mate
had succeeded in getting Kem's mind off Davina for a while,
and even after the navigation deck had returned to its normal
nighttime silence—a silence that now seemed to have become loud and clangorous—Kem found that, once more, he
was being drawn in, lured by the strangeness, the darkness,
the mystery.

By dawn, when Kem climbed moonwise down the ladder,
certain things had become rather more clear, almost horribly
so. It was light enough to see the plain that stretched away
from the Oasis, out toward the horizon where the Province of
Industry lay perhaps half a day away. This was technically still
the Grind—the chart said so—but Kem would not have
chosen to call it that. He might have called it "the desert" or
something, but surely it did not deserve the same name as
the place where Kem had lived almost all his life. The Grind
possessed (though Kem had never acknowledged it until now)
a certain rough beauty, a vitality, even if the life people lived
there was a brutal one. At least it was life. Here in this
borderland there was no life at all. Or to be strictly precise,
there was life of a monolithic sort. The ground was covered
from one horizon to the next with cheat grass, a dead-looking
weedy interloper you saw now and then out on the *real*
Grind, but only in places where brush fires had raged through,
and only for a couple of seasons, until the native bunchgrasses
and forbs and subshrubs reestablished themselves. Here the
cheat grass—who knew how—had displaced everything, closed
off all the niches, more thoroughly even than the devil's oaks
had reclaimed the old farm country of the north. At least the
oaks had left room for other things, even provided shelter for
some things that couldn't have lived there otherwise. Cheat
grass, as Kem well knew (for they had learned *that*, at least,
at the winter camps), left room for nothing. Its tiny seeds
were nonnutritive, its roots were too spindly to check erosion, its blades too thin to give shade, too short-lived to
conserve moisture or provide even desperation forage, and
above all it was so ruthlessly competitive that it broke all the
rules of cooperation, coexistence, mutual benefit that had

sustained the intricate living systems of the Grind, as far as
Kem knew, forever. At least forever until a little while ago.

Which was all very much, he guessed, as the mate had left
him to expect during the night, only nothing could have had
the same impact as really seeing it. It was the visual equiva-
lent of sticking your head out into the night air and hearing
nothing, not one sound of anything alive. It was stranger than
the Barrens and more frightening, even, than being lost and
adrift on the endless Sea. And they had not even reached the
border to Industry yet.

It was something to think about.

The sky was brownish orange, a color that made you thirsty.
Kem and Davina presented themselves at the door of the
Captain's quarters just as the sun touched down on the
crenellated edge of the world. Kem took Davina's arm, to
keep her from knocking on the door just yet. He needed to
get his bearings.

The sunwise spiral around the tower, ending here at the
top, had been dizzying in more ways than one. This was the
highest place Kem had ever been, the farthest he had come
from the surface of the earth. And it was the only place Kem
had ever stood from where the Oasis looked in any way
diminished. Even from a long way across the Grind, the great
craft dominated the landscape. But from up here—up in the
sky, as it seemed—you saw that the landscape wasn't everything. It wasn't the only world. There was the world of the
sunset, the world where eagles cocked their wings and the
earth turned over. Kem stood for a moment at the entrance to
this other world and he felt a seeping of fear, the loss of his
sense of attachment. He squeezed tighter on Davina's arm.

The door opened. Inside, standing barefoot and very simply
dressed, was the Captain of the Oasis. He held the door
wide, making room for them to enter.

"I am so glad," he said, smiling at Kem, "you have finally
been able to come."

Which was a funny thing to say, Kem thought as he
slipped by (carefully, as though dreading that they might

touch), because it sounded like the Captain had invited him again and again, and Kem had steadfastly declined.

Well, had he? Had there been an invitation, of some unspoken sort? And had Kem understood this all along, recognized the invitation and shunned it?

"I am sorry," the Captain said, closing the door behind them, "we will be a little cramped."

Cramped was about right. The cabin, owing to the narrowing of the tower, was only half a dozen strides across, roughly square in shape but rounded and braced at the corners (for greater structural strength, Kem supposed; even so, you could feel the tower swaying, flexing with the motion of the craft). There was a bunk in one corner, a tiny kitchen in another, a dining table built along one bulkhead. Sweetgrass matting covered the floor. The walls were bare, and all in all the place had a spare, almost monkish character, as though before the greater drama outside those windows—the sky, the endless plains, the restless colors of sunset—one could only stand humble and quiet.

Not that anybody was doing so, from what Kem could see.

"Here you are," the Captain said. He gestured toward a tiny table, where a few glasses and a bottle were set up. "Have a drink if you like."

Almost wagon-style, Kem thought. No frills. The Captain turned away, attending to other guests. Davina released the breath that she had been holding in. She stared at Kem with eyes wide, as though barely able to contain herself. Kem looked around the modest cabin and he thought that this was not exactly what he had expected. It didn't fit. Yet on some other level, a psychologic one, it fit exactly.

"It's Kem, right?"

Kem started. The person addressing him was a youngish man of medium height, in plain clothes like the Captain's, smiling. . . . Oh, I see, it's Gardner. Kem recognized the Investor, Sander's friend and protector, by his brilliant and empty smile. He said hello. Gardner pressed his hand hard, as though he were insisting on something. Davina seemed to have noticed someone across the room; she edged away.

"Kem, I'd like you to meet Stockard." Gardner let go of Kem's hand in order that it might be taken by a happy-looking fellow, a big-brotherly type, whose hair was beginning to gray but whose round face remained boyish, as though he were cheerfully oblivious of where he was and what was going on around him. His handclasp lingered also, as Gardner's had. Kem felt very much as though he were being sized up, measured against some unforgiving scale.

"Well, Kem, I've heard about you," Stockard finally said. Very friendly, like. "We missed you at the party, back in Ripe Berries Moon."

"Yes," said Gardner.

Yes, thought Kem. *They missed you at the party.* The words echoed from down in his memory somewhere. Not for the first time, he wondered exactly what they meant.

"We were hoping," Stockard said, "from what the Captain told us, that you might like to go with us this year."

"To Industry," Gardner explained, adding, "Kem's only been aboard for a few months."

"Thirteen," said Kem.

The two men looked at him.

"Thirteen months. I've only got six years to go. Less than that, actually."

He meant this to be a dark sort of joke—as though six years were nothing, barely a heartbeat. The two men did not get it. They looked at him with their respective kinds of curiosity: Stockard's straight-faced, Gardner's grinning and sly.

Stockard said, "Are you so sure you want to leave us? The Oasis has much to offer, you know. A fine career, for a young man of ambition."

Leave us, Kem thought. As though Stockard and the Oasis were a single organic entity. Well, perhaps Stockard was an Investor, like Gardner, and perhaps that's what being an Investor was all about.

"It's a shame, though," Stockard went on. "You would enjoy Industry, I'm sure. Well, perhaps next year."

"Yeah," said Kem. "I'd kind of like to see it. I've heard a lot of stories." In truth he was thinking about Davina, thinking that the trip out might be nice for her, something to break the monotony. "Is it hard to ... I mean, can anybody go there? Do you need to get permission or something?"

"Not just anybody," said Stockard.

"No," Gardner agreed. Both of them were smiling again. That awful, depersonalized, all-encompassing smile.

"We'd love to have *you*, of course," Stockard hastened to add. "Next year, perhaps. There are certain preparations, you see."

"Yes," said Gardner.

Kem did not smile back. "What about this year?" he said. "Can we go this time around?"

"Well . . ." said Gardner, and he looked at Stockard, deferring to him, it seemed, as one might defer to a bigger kid in the school yard.

"I'm afraid not, Kem." Stockard's manners were impeccable. He laid a rather beefy hand on Kem's shoulder and he said, just-between-us like, "You see, we missed you at the party."

Which was weird enough. That whole conversation, the way those guys acted, would have been enough to satisfy any yearning Kem might have felt for the bizarre and unsettling. But the evening, as the saying went, was still young.

After several more minutes, as sunset approached, Captain Hand loosened the dogs on a pair of hatches, which swung so wide that one of the walls seemed to vanish. The guests flowed out, as though blown by decompression, onto what Kem supposed must technically be a flying bridge: a wide deck bordered by sturdy railings and surrounded by nothing but sky. At the far end, a large night scope stood on a tripod. Nearby were a two-scope optical device, a compass repeater, a voice tube. Other than that—unless you looked behind you and saw the tangle of cables, guy wires, antennas, satellite cups, and other mysterious objects sprouting from the roof of the cabin—you would not have guessed that you were standing in an elevated command post. You would have thought you were in a garden, a roof garden, and an exotic one at that.

Kem stepped warily between the other guests—there were eighteen or twenty in all—and between the big tubs and planters, placed asymmetrically, out of which swelled great-leaved plants like exaggerated drawings in a storybook. The tubs bore handwritten labels: OPLOPANAX HORRIDIS. PSYCHOTRIA. DAMA DA NOITE. TOLOACHE. MAIKOA. Alien words that suited the plants perfectly, as though these huge, improbable-looking things had been summoned forth by incantation. Kem felt tiny, miniaturized, walking between them.

He found Davina at the far side of the deck. She was standing alone, he thought; then he saw that she was engaged in conversation, or just had been, with someone else. The other person stood somewhat apart from her, leaning over the rail, gazing downward. Now Davina noticed Kem (who was hanging back, sizing up the situation) and Kem, at last, recognized Delan.

"Hey," he said.

Delan looked around. Davina held her hand out, beckoning Kem to join them.

"We were waiting for you," she said.

"Mm," said Kem.

Delan said nothing for several moments. He watched with those glass-bright, narrow eyes as Kem stepped to the edge of the deck, the brink, and then he said, "So, Kem. Here you are."

Kem acknowledged this with a short nod.

Delan spread his hands wide. "Here we all are." He smiled at Davina, as though there might possibly be any doubt as to what he meant.

Kem thought you had to hand it to the guy. If Delan's role in all this—*all this* being Kem's life—was that of an arranger, a broker of shady deals, then here you had quite an arrangement. Here you had a galley-boy-turned-snipe and a former stable girl, cleaned up and on their best behavior, ushered into the innermost circle of the Oasis. And all that had been needed was a modest exchange of favors, certain minimal sacrifices—as of, for instance, Kem's old ideas about himself, about what he was capable of. . . .

"I was sorry," said Delan, "to hear about the old Resident. Tallheron, was it? Interesting name. I understand he was a friend of yours."

"Yeah, well." Kem turned his head, feeling bitter. Then he said, "How did you hear about that?"

Delan began one of his slow, elliptic shrugs, but Kem did not wait for it.

"I'm not kidding," he said. "How did you hear?"

Delan was watching him closely now. Kem's sudden agitation must have been obvious, for Delan wore a look of bemused interest—like, wondering how far it would go.

"Or listen," said Kem. "Never mind how. Just tell me *what* you heard. Okay?"

The trouble was, even if you could figure out where you stood with Delan, you could never know for sure where *he* stood—on which side, good or evil, if there were such things; or in more prosaic terms, representing whose interests, what ultimate goal.

The way Kem looked at it, though, there couldn't be too many people who knew what had happened back at Tallheron's farm. Three, to be exact. And two of them were dead. Plus the Bell Dog, who had never gotten the whole story (unless he had been hiding in the trees, watching it happen) because Kem had not told him. So if Delan was sorry to hear about Tallheron, you had to wonder what he possibly could have heard.

Delan shook his head, as though regretful about something. "You might find this interesting," he told Kem, "since you used to work in the engine flats. Or perhaps not. But I just heard this afternoon that the chief engineer was killed."

"I never met him."

"Oh?"

"No." Kem resented this: this blatant, even contemptuous change of subject. As though Kem's question was not even worth responding to. He said, "I mean, I'm sorry to hear about the chief engineer and all. But listen, what I want to know is—"

Delan raised a finger; he cocked his head. What Kem wanted to know would have to wait. A bell was tinkling. Dinner was being served.

Captain Hand presided over the meal with an air of someone filling in for the genuine host, who unfortunately could not be present. He stood about smiling at people and taking a polite interest, not much more, in their conversation. He lifted long skewers of vegetables and meat from the coals of a roasting-bed and laid them out on dinner trays. He chuckled at people's jokes. There was something wistful, even melancholy, in his eyes. Or maybe the wistfulness was in Kem's eyes, projected outward. The bottle on the little table in the cabin was emptied, replaced, emptied again. The guests ate while wandering about, trays and glasses and smoldering jays expertly balanced in their hands.

Maybe Kem was wistful (if he was) because Delan had reminded him of Tallheron. Maybe hearing about Tallheron made him think about death, which made him think about Chrissie, his little sister. So hard to imagine, that she was gone. And all this time he had not known; he had been missing her and Ewinda and hoping they'd be okay, they'd stay away from the Oasis, and all the while it was too late, Chrissie was already dead.

"The end of the journey," Kem heard someone say behind him. He was standing alone, Davina having wandered off (he suspected) to flirt with Gardner, staring out over the deck rail toward the place where the sun had gone down. It seemed to him that he had been here before—not at this particular rail but in this region of his heart.

The voice behind him, barely loud enough to hear, said, "The journey that began so long ago, in another dry land, ends here. It ends tonight."

Kem thought that this was so odd a remark that he turned halfway around to glance at the man who was speaking. He nearly flinched to discover that the man was Captain Hand. And he had been speaking, in that soft and uninflected voice, only to Kem.

"You have been here before, haven't you?" said the Captain—which was also startling, seeing as how Kem had been thinking pretty nearly the same thing only seconds before. "You were here last year, I believe. Shortly after you signed on."

Kem tried to slow his breath, to relax. He could not understand why the Captain of the Oasis would take such an

interest in an unimportant member of the crew. Hand came
another step forward, joining Kem at the rail.

"What do you think"—he nodded outward—of the Province of Industry?"

He spoke with unnatural precision, as though there were
something suggestive or revealing about the place-name itself. Kem shrugged. He was glad to have a reason not to look
at the Captain, to turn away from those discomfiting eyes.

"I don't know," he said. "I guess I really haven't seen much
yet."

"You've seen something. Quite a lot, actually. Most of what
there is to see, you have seen by now."

As usual with Hand, Kem got the idea that this was all
part of some lesson, at the end which there might or might
not be a test. He supposed it was just the Captain's manner.
Still, he wanted to hold his own, to prove something—and
maybe that's what the nature of the test was.

He said, "Then there's not much here, I guess. A whole
lot of goddamned cheat grass."

The bitterness of his own voice surprised him. Hand did
not look around at him, but the corner of his mouth twisted
slightly, as though at the threshold of a smile. Kem breathed
deeply again. He went on:

"Actually I don't guess I like the place. I like the Grind a
lot better. I even liked the Barrens—the, what is it? Carbon
Bank Forest. At least, you know, there was stuff alive there.
It was actually kind of pretty."

The Captain nodded. "But after all"—and he did look
around now, his eyes lay on Kem's easily, almost gently—"this
is the end of the journey, is it not? The journey that is the
oldest story we know, or at least the oldest story in which we
ourselves have played a part. The great sweep of history. Of
civilization. Or at least a certain inbred strain ... *diffusion*
they used to call it, though nowadays one might think of a
different term. *Metastasis*, perhaps. In any case, the end of
the process, whatever one calls it, is right out there, at the
foot of those mountains. What do you think the end is like,
Kem?"

Kem figured this was the test, now. An all-or-nothing
question, designed to measure how well he'd been paying

attention, how much he'd learned. He looked at the Captain and for some reason—or many reasons, an accumulation of things—he felt anger swell up inside him. Anger at this man and his lectures, his tests, his manipulation of helpless people like Kem, like Davina, like everybody on the crew and maybe everybody else, the Residents, even the Investors, people who in some ways were little better than his captives, who lived under his dominion because they had no other choice, it was a hard world, illness and deprivation were everywhere, the Oasis was one of the few havens and it was a false one, an unnatural thing, an abomination—

"I actually don't give much of a shit." The words blew out, like objects picked up and hurled by Kem's internal tempest. "As far as I'm concerned, you can fuck the Province of Industry. Fuck history and civilization and everything else. The end of the journey is right here. Right now. Right in this goddamned garden."

He was scared again even before the words were out of his mouth. His knees felt weak, and he was afraid to look the Captain in the eye. But afraid or not, he kept staring at the Captain because there was no way not to, those pale eyes would not let him go. They remained impassive, as did the rest of Hand's face, even the ghost of a smile that flickered half-visibly at the edges of his mouth.

Then Hand said, "I suppose you're right." He dropped the smile but he did not seem upset. If anything, he looked melancholy again, as Kem thought he might have looked earlier, before deciding that the whole thing was his own imagination. But this did not seem like his imagination; the Captain seemed, just like Kem, to be overtaken by some sadness, some feeling of loss, so deep that you could only guess at the true nature and dimensions of it. "For you," Hand said (the words seemed to come from under water, Kem could barely hear him), "the journey does end here. Be glad of that. Be glad that you are not immune."

That was all. Making no more sense than ever, Hand turned and he walked across the deck, through his private garden, among the shadows of huge leaves, into the night.

• • •

The night was darker than Kem remembered. Darker, that is, than he remembered from last year, when the Oasis had come to a halt and he and Sander had crept into Delan's stateroom and Kem had swallowed a mouthful of diviner's sage. That night had been brilliant, lurid: so bright in Kem's memory that he could still see with nightmarish clarity the pale stallion, the single rider with his staff, the glare of spotlights, the fog of dust.

Tonight was not going to be like that. It was earlier in the moon cycle, for one thing. Petals Fall was so new that it had long set by the time Captain Hand excused himself from his dinner party and set off for the stables, far below, to prepare his mount. Several other guests departed as well—Gardner and Stockard among them, Delan not—but they left by a different route; they went out the cabin door and down the spiral ladder, moonwise and down, the way they had come. Hand took what Kem supposed to be a private shortcut. Only a couple of minutes after their strange conversation, the Captain walked to the center of the flying bridge, between two planting troughs crowded with bamboos, and lifted what seemed to be a quite heavy deckplate. It was a hatch, though you would not have recognized it as such before it was opened. Kem could just make out, in the half light, the uppermost rungs of a ladder, the curving walls of a roughly cylindrical shaft. All was blackness beyond the first fathom or so. Adroitly, Hand scrambled into the shaft and down the ladder. He was soon invisible in the darkness, and for all anyone could see he might as well have dematerialized.

Kem stared into the shaft until a couple of senior mates came over and lowered the hatch cover into place. It closed with a thud. But Kem thought he had seen enough. He thought he knew what this shaft was, where it began and where it led to. He felt like he was finally getting an answer, at least a partial one, to a long-standing question of his own.

"Isn't this exciting?" said Davina, clutching his arm.

He smiled at her, at her girlish enthusiasm.

"Being up here, I mean," she said, "getting to watch everything. Isn't it great?"

Kem agreed that it was. He even did feel a little excited, himself—perhaps he was catching it from Davina—and the feeling intensified when he looked over the rail and noticed the crowd that was gathering on the decks and catwalks and balconies below.

That's where he had been, a year ago. Down there. Among the galley boys on a narrow deck that stank of rot, of mud, of effluent. And here he was, one scant year later, in a garden in the sky, desert wind in his face, breathing air that smelled of something powerfully sweet—this plant with huge, pendulous white blossoms, he guessed—and that was the least, the very least, of all that had changed from last year to this. Some of the changes had been for the good: Davina, to take an immediate example. Some had been horrible. It was hard to draw any conclusions. It was hard for Kem to decide whether his life had improved or whether it had grown irredeemably dark; whether his soul was lost, his heart shriveled, his mind overrun by thoughts and fears of death.

For that had been the prophecy, hadn't it? *Death:* that had been the single syllable that filled his mind, his final conscious thought on that night one year ago. He had imagined that the thought had come from the mind of the stallion, Hand's stallion, but that was not literally true. It could not have been. It had come from somewhere, maybe—other than Kem's imagination, that is—but surely not from the mind of a beast.

Where, then? Was there a future, and could it be read? Was the future anything more than an abstract set of probabilities (Hand would *probably* ride out to Industry without being thrown from his horse; he *might* come back tomorrow); was it in some way real, concrete, apprehensible? Kem had felt a thrill of intimation when he first looked at Davina, or even before that—the first time he'd heard her laugh, way off across the cargo bay. Could he have sensed somehow what was *certainly* going to happen?

Popping sounds—gunshots? firework?—came across the desert, echoing through the night. Davina squeezed Kem's hand, drawing his attention downward. A ramp was being lowered; dust was hurled up in great puffs, like exhalations; the excitement of the mass of people below was a tangible thing, hot, rising in waves like thermal gusts.

Davina laughed in delight. That same laugh.

Kem shivered with dread.

He backed away—"Just a little dizzy . . . so high up here,"
allaying Davina's look of concern—groping behind him for
anything solid, the smooth edge of a planter. The planter
came about waist-high, like the gray-water tanks behind the
galley, but instead of sedges and cattails it was filled with
something more delicate, soft leaves that gave off a pungent scent when Kem brushed them. A familiar smell, which
reassured him; anything familiar was reassuring; but what was
that smell, exactly? It brought back memories, the way smells
do. But not definite memories, just an attenuated blur of
awareness.

Below, people began to cheer. The cheering grew louder.
Even the crowd on the flying bridge joined in; Kem could
hear Davina's voice among the others, always distinct. He
broke off one of the soft leaves and rolled it between his
fingers. The odor sharpened, lanced his nasal membranes. It
was like nothing else but what was it? Without thinking
(actually, thinking of the noise of the crowd, the clapping, feet
stomping in rhythm on the decks of the aged craft) he slipped
the damp, pulpy ball of crushed leaf into his mouth.

And then he remembered.

And then Captain Hand rode out on his huge pale stallion,
the color of moonlight.

And the Kem struggled against a reflex that made him
want to retch.

And then the Captain's horse pranced wildly, crazed by its
sudden freedom, looking as though it might at any moment
toss its rider and bolt away in the darkness.

And then Kem's hand clutched the rim of the planter,
fingers stabbing carelessly into the loamy soil.

And then the Captain reined his stallion in, giving the lie
to any notion of freedom, reasserting the order of the night.

And then the crowd clamored its approval.

And then Kem's fingers came in contact with something
other than dirt, something small, wooden, circular—a ring,
he thought. A counter. Something like that. He pulled it out
of the dirt, rolled his fist around it. A thing to hold on to.

And then Davina said, "Are you okay?"

And then the stallion spun around, defiant of its rider, who

would have held it back if he dared, but the beast was not to
be restrained, Destiny glared from its dark malevolent eye, it
bore its prisoner away with diabolic speed.

And then Kem said, "Yeah, I'm fine."

And then a hundred other hooves beat down the dust of
the Grind and the knights of the Oasis plunged bellowing
into the darkness.

He could not have slept anyway, probably.

He figured that just his conversation with the Captain, just
that, would have kept him awake, as almost all his encounters
with Hand had done. Kept him brooding all night.

But as it was, he had this little kicker. This small mouthful
of diviner's sage, not as much as he'd swallowed the first time
around, a year ago, but even one leaf was plenty. Just as the
pungent smell of the plant had cut through all the other
smells of the Captain's garden, so had the chemicals inside it
been enough to alter the flavor of his whole consciousness, to
spice it like a synthetic stew. It roiled now inside him, filling
his brain, overflowing it, running out into the night and
carrying Kem along with it.

He thought Davina would never go to sleep. He did not
want to worry her so he lay very still but it seemed that every
movement she made, every breath, was almost violently
expressive. The flicker of an eyelid sent waves of energy
bouncing around the room. He could not imagine that she
could be sleeping through all that, but of course she was, she
may have been for an hour or more by the time he decided
he couldn't keep lying there any longer. Maybe when you ate
it fresh the effect was different, drawn out somehow. Kem felt
wide awake and the room, from its one small window, seemed
to be flooded with light.

Anyway, he made it outside, into the hallway, without
betraying himself.

Now he wondered what in the world he intended to do.

Not run into anyone, surely. Though there seemed little
danger of that. The excitement of early evening, the Captain's
departure and all that, had died down long ago; everybody
but the watchstanders had gone to bed.

Kem wandered down passageways that he only half remembered but that his body seemed to recognize, whose windings and changes of level his feet anticipated, so that his movements meshed with the great motion of the craft. He felt himself step forward, his weight shift from foot to foot, his head swivel and duck, and he felt the engines of the Oasis groan and shudder, its windmills whir, its joints flex, and all these things seemed far removed from him and at the same time intimately connected. This was a pleasurable sensation, a surrender of his ego to the oversoul of the great machine.

It was something like the way he had felt in the Barrens. Or the Forest: its other name fit better with the way he remembered the place. He remembered stepping easily from one root mass to another, his footfalls padded by moss, the sound of birds screeching at the dawn, yellow light, dampness in the air. He remembered . . .

Then—*whooosh*—he forgot. Realities ran together, like busted eggs. The forest dissolved and the Oasis congealed around him. Kem drew himself up.

Before him, crisscrossing a narrow compartment, some kind of utility space, ran a large number of pipes. Kem had to bend low to step beneath them. They were painted in contrasting colors, a code Kem faintly recognized: blue for water, green for methane, red for . . . red for what?

Ahead of him stood a ladder. It led upward, terminating in a small round hatch, and everything about the ladder and the corridor and the events of the night and Kem's life thus far seemed to suggest that this ladder had been placed here for him to climb. Kem was not in a mood to argue. The Oasis gave a shudder, releasing a bit of kinetic stress, rolling over in its sleep, who could tell? Kem stepped onto the first rung of the ladder and pulled himself up.

The hatch opened easily, almost sighing open as the tension of its latches was released. Kem squirmed through into what seemed to be a larger and darker compartment. He shut the hatch behind him. He stood up.

Only then did he realize that he was standing abovedecks, out in the desert air. The world was very quiet and very dark, with only the stars for illumination. The stars seemed more distant than usual and highly agitated, and they held Kem's attention for a while. He stared at them, forgetting himself, forgetting the Oasis and all the world around him, only breathing the coolness of the night.

It was no longer summer. And yet it was nothing else in particular. There were no seasons, in particular, besides that. Only summer and a long passage of in-between time, a time of waiting for summer to come again. A time to rest, to reflect on things. To tally your losses and count the things that were left for you, the days and the people and the off chance of happiness, somewhere down the line.

Petals fall, Kem thought. The words felt heavy and poignant. Petals fall. Not the name of a moon any longer, a phrase that meant nothing, that you never thought about. But words that some person, some old native, one of the people who had been here before, had thought up on a night like this and spoken low into the darkness. The thought of this old person, probably imaginary (though Kem knew that), made him sad, as though he had actually known that long-dead elder, known him and mourned him.

"Petals fall," he said. Understanding now. Understanding at last. "Petals—"

"*What the fuck.*"

Kem jumped backwards, his heart lurching with dread.

The voice came again—"*Who the fuck's there?*"—and this time Kem realized that it was just a human voice, after all.

He squinted in the darkness. He could barely make out, by starlight, the jagged contours of furniture, a row of deck chairs facing away from him. Whoever had spoken was clattering around, knocking chairs aside, getting to his feet.

"Hey, I'm sorry," said Kem, "I didn't mean—" He stopped because his words sounded too weird, all hollow and echoey, and anyway he was still feeling pretty shaky. A chair fell sideways. A shadow rose behind it. Kem backed up some more.

"You didn't mean what?" the shadow said. "Didn't mean to scare the shit out of me? Who the fuck is that, anyway?"

The shadow came closer at considerable speed and Kem was afraid he was about to get himself punched. In self-defense, as much as anything, he stammered, "It, it's Kem."

"Kem."

The shadow blurred into focus, two narrow eyes peering out of the darkness.

"Kem."

"Mole?"

"Fucking right." A hand swam up, clapped Kem companionably on the shoulder. "What're you doing, catching up on old times? Old lady cut you off? Hey, listen"—the Mole leaned in closer, the sharp bones of his face coming into view—"no hard feelings about all that, eh? Like, it was nothing personal, right?"

Kem nodded, a little bewildered, though Mole could not see that in the darkness. Or on second thought perhaps he could, the darkness being Mole's native element. "Sure," he said. "Nothing personal. Right."

"Man, you sound fucked up."

Kem nodded again. There was a rustling sound, and Mole seemed to dig around in his clothing, searching one pocket after another.

"Rough night, eh?" he said. "Well, hey. I've had a few rough nights myself. Got just the thing for you."

Mole dragged a chair out of line, motioning for Kem to sit down. Kem was surprised by this, an uncharacteristically sociable gesture, and equally surprised to find that he welcomed it, that he was happy to settle into the chair and happy to see Mole pull up another chair for himself. Maybe in his present state Mole was the only person he could relate to.

Mole struck a match, which cast an almost blinding glare over the scene. Kem could see, before the flame died, the dark shapes of trees, surrounding them in loose, circular formation. It occurred to him—another surprise—that they might possibly be in the middle of the trading deck, the place with the fountain. Talk about your circles, he thought. Your nets, your twisty little mazes . . .

"Take it," said Mole, gasping the words out, waving a jay in Kem's face.

Kem took it almost gratefully, not caring what it was or what it would do to his already overextended consciousness. This morsel of human contact—with Mole, of all people—had aroused a sort of hunger in him. He sucked at the acrid little stub glowing hot between his fingers.

"Hey, shit." Mole slapped his knee, a new thought evidently having occurred to him. "Hey man, sorry about the Bell Dog and all. Guess you guys were pretty tight there."

"What?"

"I mean, like that's life and everything, but shit. Hate to see it. Guy like that."

"What?" said Kem again. "The Bell Dog? What—"

Oh but he felt it coming. He felt the future and the past, both equally real, equally irreversible, felt them pressing in around him like the dark, half-seen shadows of the olive trees.

"Shit, man, you haven't heard? You must've heard, word got out a whole day ago. Didn't you?"

"I heard . . . I mean, something about the chief engineer, is all."

"Blew right up on him," said Mole, shaking his head, handing the jay over. "Pressure built up, I don't know, relief valve jammed or whatever. Could've been an accident. Hard to tell by the time anybody got there. I was asleep, man. Don't believe half of anything, anyway."

Kem was more than spaced-out, more than confused. His brain had overloaded—*pressure built up*—and all he could do was give voice to certain thoughts as they blew by. "But what . . . I mean, you said the chief engineer . . . but I mean, what, the Bell Dog . . ."

Mole shook his head. "Won't be another one like him," he said. "Never. Probably pick some asshole out of the wardroom, career type, kiss Hand's butt as soon as wink at him. The old Bell Dog never kissed butt for anybody. You know that. But hey."

You might find this interesting, Delan had said. Well, fuck Delan, Kem thought. Fuck all of them. He sucked hard at the jay but it had gone out. Everything was damp, the jay and his fingers and his cheeks. *The pressure built up* and Kem was weeping like a little boy.

"Yeah, man," said Mole, "I know exactly how you feel, but look at this."

Kem tried to look but he couldn't see much of anything.

"They gave this to me," Mole rattled on, perhaps to cover the awkward gap in Kem's side of the conversation. "Didn't

know what else to do with it, I guess. Guy pretty much kept
to himself, no friends to speak of. Guess they figured I might
as well have it, sort of his second in command."

Kem saw something bright, a silver gleam, momentarily
brilliant where it caught a ray of starlight. Mole was holding
it out, offering it to him.

"Here," he said, "you ought to have it, more than me.
Maybe you understood the guy. He liked you. Shit, I don't
know what the fuck it is, even."

Kem held out his hand and it closed around something
hard, warm—a metal cylinder. He recognized it all at once
by feel alone, though he had never touched it and only seen
it once.

In a sudden movement—giving Mole a start, for he jerked
back reflexively—Kem swung the piece of metal down to
strike the deck. It hit hard and bounced off. The sound it
made was sharp and tinny at first, but as Kem held the rod
aloft it seemed to soften, to grow smooth without diminishing
in volume. It gained in resonance, took on complex overtones
that swelled in the stillness of the night, and by the time it
faded below audibility—many seconds later, perhaps half a
minute—Mole was digging in his pockets again. He produced
a second match. His hands were shaking.

"Here," he said. "Look. It's got something written on it."

Kem was still holding the little rod aloft, aiming it like a
wizard's wand, remembering the Bell Dog doing the same
thing, remembering the morning he'd done it.

"Look now." Mole leaned closer. The match flared.

The silver rod gleamed white, a mottled white like the
moon's. By the flickering, fast-dying light, it was just possible
to make out the words scratched shallowly, in a childish
script, into its surface. Kem read:

> *To Hóz'q from his loving sister,*
> *May you keep Shimá always*
> *in your heart.*

HARD RAIN

"You don't believe me," Kem said.

"No," said Davina.

Kem could not keep still. He stood in a fighter's pose: knees flexed, weight rolling fluidly from the ball of one foot to the heel of the other, elbows cocked, hands curled into hook-shapes, not quite fists, pawing the air. "Then what's it going to take?" he said.

Outside the little windows of the cabin, gray blotches moved around the sky.

Kem jabbed at a hank of muslin drapery. "First Tallheron." He jabbed again. "Then Sander. Now the Bell Dog." He pivoted with an uppercut. "What's it going to take? Me? You?"

Davina wasn't quite looking at him and wasn't exactly looking the other way. She wasn't staring out the window, either. You couldn't really have said what she was doing; it was as though she were withholding even that degree of

commitment. After a few moments she looked up at Kem and
said:

"Sander isn't dead."

Her voice was like that of a teacher or a nurse. It aggravat-
ed the hell out of Kem. He punched a big hole in the air in
front of him.

"Yeah, well, not because they didn't try. You should have
seen him that night."

Kem became still, remembering how Sander had been
that night. He sensed Davina watching him. He tried to
make his face cloudy, full of ominous disturbance, like the sky
out there, dark like the clouds.

"And there was this thing he said, something funny, *They
didn't get you at the party*, something like that. Or, *They
missed you*. And listen—your friend Gardner and that other
guy, Stockard, they were saying the same thing at the Captain's place. Exactly the same. It was weird."

"You're imagining things."

Kem didn't think so. "Well, look—Tallheron was murdered,
I'm not imagining that, right? And so was the Bell Dog."

"The Bell Dog wasn't murdered. You don't know that. He
was just . . . the boiler or whatever it was blew up, he was just
standing there, you said so yourself."

"*They* said so. But come on—it's too much of a coincidence. I mean, look. The Bell Dog was the only other one
who knew about Tallheron. Just the Bell Dog and me."

Davina shook her head. Like Kem was totally out of his
mind. "That could have been anybody that killed Tallheron.
You don't know who it was. It could have been a robber. It
could have been a bunch of scavengers, some local gang. You
don't know—"

"That wasn't any gang."

"You don't know that. Besides, there's just no *reason*. Why
should anybody want to kill a sick old Resident? I don't get
it."

"He knew something, maybe. Or they were afraid he
might know something."

"Know what?"

Know what: Kem had been through this already, in his
mind. What had Tallheron known? It wasn't an easy question.

A little knowledge ... and Kem knew less than that. Kem knew just about nothing. "See," giving it a shot, "he had this idea ... like about the crying, where the crying comes from. It's hard to explain, but—"

Davina was staring at him. Slowly she shook her head. It was as though she meant, No not just about what Kem was saying but about Kem himself, the very idea of him.

Kem one-two-punched the air. "You just don't believe me, do you?" he said. "You believe *them*."

"Believe who?" The patience was gone from her voice. "I don't believe anybody. You can't, here. But I don't believe there's a *them*, either. I think you're just being paranoid."

"Fuck. Paranoid? Where'd you get that from? Is that one of Gardner's words? *Don't worry about Kem, he's just a little paranoid.* I can hear the asshole now."

He could, too.

Davina lowered her eyes. She said quietly, "You know, if they wanted to get you—even if there was a *them*, which there isn't—they would have gotten you by now. Wouldn't they?"

And Kem had no answer to that because it seemed to be the truth. Only of course what seemed to be the truth was not necessarily the truth, *nothing is the way you think it's going to be here*, so there had to be some reason—why they hadn't gotten around to Kem yet, why they were saving him, jerking him around, whatever they were doing. . . .

"And why in the world," Davina said, maybe figuring she had him on the ropes, "would anybody want to kill the poor Bell Dog? And Sander . . . that's really stretching it, to think somebody would want to kill Sander."

"Maybe they didn't want to kill him. Maybe they just—"

"Kem." Davina's eyes held a warning. Kem guessed that if he kept talking she was going to accuse him of being paranoid again. As though it were even possible to be paranoid in a place like the Oasis, where everything turned out to be so much more awful and convoluted than you ever could have imagined.

"What about those two kids?" he said. "The ones from Riley County. What's happened to them?"

"You tell me."

"Okay. I found them and the Captain took them away in his boat, and *poof*. They've disappeared. What do you think that means?"

"It doesn't mean anything. They could be anywhere. This is a big place, in case you haven't noticed."

Kem felt like striking out again. For an instant, less than a heartbeat, he felt like striking not at the empty air but at Davina, for her snideness. The thought of this—even the very faintest momentary intention of hitting the girl he loved, or thought he loved, or had loved pretty recently, when he was still sure of anything—deflated him. He sat down on the edge of the bed. He stared at the rivets in the deckplates. Davina moved a little closer but did not quite touch him.

"You give me *any reason*," she said quietly, "to think something has happened to those kids—something bad—and then I'll believe you. But right now I just can't. I'm sorry."

She stood up and walked to the door. "I'm late," she said.

"For what?" said Kem.

Davina smoothed her hair down, straightened her dress around those boyish slender hips. She opened the door.

"Where are you going?" said Kem. "Wait—"

Winter was short, as all winters are.

One day in Tall Skies Moon, while the Oasis eased itself down the thousand-kill slope toward Body of God, down to the Sea, Kem went looking for Sander. He hadn't seen his friend for a month or more—hardly at all since that day out on the Grind. Now he wasn't exactly sure where to start looking. Sander's ascent, if that was the word, through the many layers of the Oasis was a puzzling phenomenon, like the life cycle of some peculiar insect; each successive phase was like a whole new incarnation, the outer trappings of the last life shucked off like a used-up husk, with only the innermost being, the essence, remaining constant. Kem figured Gardner's apartment was probably as good a place as any to start with. And come to think of it, *ascent* probably wasn't right, after all. Sander's path more nearly resembled a spiral, a roughly circular movement leading inward, always inward, nearer and nearer to some core. Like a desert eagle, a caracara, flying around and around in tightening circles, waiting for a wounded creature to die. And come to think of it (Kem had time to think, looking for Gardner's place, which he vaguely remembered being around here somewhere), Kem's own progress, if *that* was the word, seemed to follow a similar pattern. Only in his case the spiral seemed to lead downward, into realms of greater darkness. Kem would just as soon have circled the way the Oasis circled, never straying from its track, through the heart of the desert, seven trips around the Grind, then broken off and sailed outward like an object flung away. To where, though? To life, he supposed. His own, grown-up life. The world at large.

He recognized Gardner's place at last by the pictograph on the door. He was about to knock, but on an impulse—perverse, surely—he held his ear close and listened. There was music, scarcely more than a faint pulse, an ancient rhythm that had no relation to the grinding, unrelenting rhythms of actual life. The music paused and resumed, modulated, grew soft and wistful, then high-spirited again—its variations seemed endless, as though defiant of a world that was endlessly the same. Kem started to knock again.

This time the hand stopped of its own accord, in midair.

Laughter, gentle, trilling, like part of the music, floated through the door. It ended, and Kem listened for another minute but the laughter did not come again. Still, he had heard it once. That voice, her voice, had always been distinctive, even through closed doors. In fact, he seemed to have heard it through closed doors more than once, more than a few times. Now as he looked back on things he thought you could make a kind of chart of their relationship, like a snipe's schematic diagram, by tracing out the series of closed doors he had heard that voice, that laughter, through. It would be a diagram like the one on the door, a sort of code, part of a secret alphabet, full of meaning for those who could read it. Kem was reading it now, standing outside Gardner's place reading the handwriting on the wall.

He knocked twice loudly.

Nothing happened for a while and Kem had the odd, dreamlike feeling that maybe there had been a mistake, maybe he was being granted a reprieve. He was ready to turn

and get out of there but then the door swung wide and there
stood Gardner. Gardner looked surprised to see him but only
for an instant; then he broadcast that big smile and waved his
hand—"Come in, come in!"—like they were the best and
oldest of friends. Kem felt like anything in the world except
going in, but it seemed that was the only option available to
him, this time around.

He found Davina sitting on a sofa, as he had pretty much
expected to. Who he had not expected was Captain Hand.
The Captain stood near the door to the balcony, as though
he had been interrupted coming in or going out. His eyes
seemed to acknowledge Kem without changing in any overt
way. Davina, for her part, looked much less surprised to see
him than Gardner had been, even perhaps a little smug, as
though she'd known this would happen all along; as though
she'd *wanted* Kem to find her here. Wanted to show him.

"We were just talking about you," said Gardner, which was
more or less the sort of preposterous lie Kem had anticipated.
He edged his way around the sofa, getting deeper into the
room without getting appreciably closer to Davina or the
Captain. "No, really," said Gardner. "Weren't we?"

Davina smiled—at Gardner, not Kem—and said nothing at
all.

Gardner said, "Can I get you anything? A drink? Davina
was just telling me that you've been to the Bright Land. Must
be a fascinating place. Always wanted to go."

"I didn't go there really. Not all the way." Kem was acutely
conscious of the Captain watching and listening; he kept his
eyes on Davina, who narrowed hers back at him. "I just went
out there in a boat one day. Then I, um, came back."

Gardner nodded, as though this story were very interesting and informative. He looked back and forth between
Davina and Kem. A nice young couple, his expression seemed
to say. What the fuck is going on here, thought Kem.

"Sure," he said, "I'll take something to drink."

Gardner's smile adjusted itself—happy to be of service,
now; it was surprising how many meanings that single expression could convey. But it was surprising too how meaningful
other things could be. Davina's posture on the sofa, for
instance. She sat with one leg—the one nearest Kem—pulled

up and the foot tucked underneath it, displaying a bit of athletic haunch as though to taunt Kem while at the same time reserving the option, should the situation warrant, to kick him out of the way. She held her gaze in what appeared to be an arbitrary direction, across the wide room toward a shelf bearing a few pieces of Gardner's archaic stuff: a black box lying open to display its electronic innards, half a dozen decrepit books, a deck of fortune-telling cards. The music had become sprightly, upbeat, full of tinkly percussion and gushy strings.

Gardner came over with Kem's drink, clear liquid with a mint leaf on top. Kem figured there was no need to say thanks.

"You know, Kem," Captain Hand said unexpectedly, as though he had been waiting for the formalities to be done with, "you needn't be so angry all the time. Your life isn't so bad here, I should say. I should say you've been fairly lucky."

"You would?" Kem tasted the drink: tart, like unripe berries.

The Captain took a couple of steps and opened the balcony door. He nodded his head in the general direction of *out there*, the world outside this opulent apartment. "You see, Kem," he said, "most people don't understand a single thing in their lives. They are, the great majority of them, incapable of achieving insight into anything. And for the most part they don't care. They're content to leave their eyes on the ground in front of them. It's enough for them to do their jobs, keep their shoulders to the wheel. But you're not like that."

"Oh?" Kem said. "What am I like, then?"—which came out sounding smart-ass, though actually he wanted to know. He really wanted to hear what the Captain thought.

Hand smiled as though he perfectly understood. Well, who knew? Maybe he did. "You want to know *why* the wheel is turning," he said. "You want to know which way it's headed. What other wheels it's connected to. Things of that kind."

Kem nodded; he thought that this was true.

"You're a bright young man. Bright and determined. Stubborn, perhaps. And extremely curious. Right away, we noticed that."

We who? Kem thought, wondering if there might be some relation to the *they* that Davina did not believe in.

"So tell me this," Hand said, "as one curious person to another. Have you ever wondered why there are such things as rituals and ceremonies? Why there are traditions? Why, for example, I am addressed as *Captain*, which is a term used long ago on sailing ships? Or why we give names to the moons, instead of just letting them pass? Or why we repeat the same journey, year after year? Have you ever wondered—to put it another way—not just why the wheel is turning, but why a wheel exists in the first place? Have you?"

Kem felt somewhat adrift in the Captain's metaphor. He supposed, yes, that he had wondered something along these lines.

"Do you suppose," the Captain went on, "that it is all part of our war against time? That such things as tradition and ceremony are weapons in that struggle? Perhaps the wheel is a key, a clue, to the secret of timelessness—it turns for the sake of turning, not to go anywhere but just to *go*, just to turn without stopping. What do you think of that?"

Kem shrugged. This sounded vaguely like something a teacher might have said, back at the winter camps—a discussion of the symbols in some old story. He said, "I guess so. But it's a losing game, isn't it? Trying to fight time. You're going to lose in the long run."

"Are you?"

Gardner hovered just outside the line of sight that connected Kem and the Captain. Kem could feel Davina out there too, off to the side. It was like a contest, a sparring bout.

"Even if you are, though," the Captain went on—"even if the struggle is hopeless in the long run, it's still worth carrying on, isn't it? For its own sake? And maybe—*maybe*—it is not so hopeless after all."

Kem did not understand, and said so.

"Well, for example." Hand swept an arm across the expanse of sky framed by the doorway. "Suppose the wheel is not losing energy but gaining it. Suppose with each turn it spins with a bit more force. We might conclude that our wheel was in place with some greater cycle, perhaps the greatest cycle of all. We might conclude that time was not our enemy after all—that we had aligned ourselves in such a way that time was working in our favor."

"Yeah, well," said Kem. "You can suppose anything."

The Captain smiled at him. "Why, yes. You can."

Davina spoke suddenly, irritably: "There's no use talking to him. He'll just argue with you. He's been like this... *forever*. He's got this idea that everybody is against him, he doesn't believe that people are trying to help. He's just paranoid or something."

Kem felt again the violent impulse that had surprised him once before. It slipped away quickly, leaving him saddened. He felt somehow, not even knowing what it meant, that so much had been lost. He looked at Davina and he looked at himself, as best he could, and he wondered what more proof anyone needed that the war with time was a doomed cause. Time was kicking your ass every day and after a while you just wouldn't feel like picking yourself up again.

"Just let him go," said Davina. "*I'll* listen."

But the Captain came a step nearer to Kem. He watched Kem's eyes with a friendly sort of curiosity. "How long," he asked quietly, "would you like to ride the wheel? How long would you like to live here?"

Kem stared back as hard as he could but he could not imagine what sort of test this was, what kind of mind game the Captain was playing now.

The Captain pressed him: "Would you like to live here a hundred years? Two hundred?"

Feeling helpless, Kem looked around the room—for clues, support, anything. His eyes swept over the ancient artifacts, the pieces of broken engines, decayed electronics, works of art so old their cultural codes were unbreakable. Music out of some lost timescape filled his head. He looked finally at Gardner—the glass-bright eyes, the imperishable smile, the sun-cured leathery skin. Gardner looked back at him. His expression was so hard to read that he might as well not have had one.

"Kem," said the Captain, gently, like a father—not Kem's father, but somebody's, some fatherly ideal—"would you like to live here ... indefinitely?"

And Kem said, "I don't think so."

Delan had no idea, either, where Sander might be.

"But you know," he said, "there's no need to worry about
him. Sander will always be fine. He will always find a way to
take care of himself. Or someone to take care of him, if need
be."

Kem wasn't so sure. Nor for that matter was he sure, after
all this time, how far he could trust Delan. He declined an
invitation to enter the small, airless stateroom; then on
second thought, for no particular reason, old time's sake
perhaps, he accepted. They sat down together on the narrow
bunk.

"Why do you stay in this room?" he said. "I mean, you
could find a better place if you wanted to. Couldn't you? You
found *me* a better place."

Delan smiled, shaking his head. "I'm comfortable here,"
he said. "I have everything I need. And it's more ... conven
ient."

To what? Kem wondered. Galley boys' berthing? He said,
"I've just been kind of worried about him, you know, since ..."

"About Sander?" Delan raised his eyebrows—a bit too
knowingly, it seemed to Kem, unless it was all an act.

Kem nodded. "Since last summer. Ripe Berries Moon."

"Ah," said Delan. "The Captain's party. Well. But there's
nothing to worry about, though, is there? I'd say there's
nothing to worry about at all."

Kem shrugged. "I don't know. I'd just like to see him."

"To say good-bye?"

Kem's throat constricted. "What do you mean?"

Delan smiled. "If you'd like to say good-bye to someone,
you might as well say it to me. I'm your friend too. I'll pass it
on to Sander the next time I see him."

He looked away for a moment, at the little shelf barely at
arm's length away where half a dozen books—well-thumbed,
still-living books, unlike the ones in Gardner's place—stood
in a crowded row. Then he turned back.

"I *am* your friend," he said. "No matter what you may

think. I will certainly not, for example, tell anyone that you're leaving."

Kem felt panicky again.

"You don't have to say anything," Delan said soothingly. "It makes absolutely no difference to me. Though I will miss seeing you around."

And Kem, to his own surprise, said, "I guess I'll miss you too."

Then the great day, the secret day, came and the Oasis reached Body of God and Kem slipped out of bed an hour before sunrise. The craft had stopped during the night and Kem had been lying sleepless for hours, biding his time. Now his time had run out and thank the Goddess, he thought, Davina was still asleep or this would be too hard, too painful for him. It was hard enough anyway with only his own thoughts and feelings to deal with. Davina breathed lightly, puffs of air damp and sweet from her lungs lifting a wisp of brown hair that lay across her face, then dropping it, then lifting it. Kem leaned low over her, nearly but just not brushing with his lips her girl-soft skin. She could be so tough on him when she was awake—more and more lately the toughness was all he saw of her—but now she was all gentleness and vulnerability like a child asleep. And in a way, Kem thought, a child is what she was, just as in a way he was a child himself, an innocent, or a stupid kid, whichever way you looked at it. Anyway he was sufficiently stupid to still be in love enough to cry as he left her sleeping there.

At the small hatch leading down behind the engine flats, where he and the Bell Dog had gone a year ago, Sander stood waiting for him. Actually, *waiting* was a matter of conjecture, but what else made sense? The boy sat with his long skinny legs drawn up at the head of the ladder, hugging his knees. He stood up when Kem arrived. He looked sleepy, as though he had been up all night. The first light of day, reflected from the pale salt-flat surface, illuminated his face from below and gave him a strange, ghostly look.

"Delan says you're leaving," he said.

"Shh." Kem looked around, though of course there was no one near, and anyhow the tightness in his stomach did not come from worrying about that.

"Don't worry. They'll never catch you. They probably won't give a shit. Why should they?"

"Thanks," said Kem. "Everybody's telling me not to worry lately. The Captain told me I ought to be happy."

Sander smiled; his eyes brightened a bit. "Well, you should be. You just don't know it."

"Yeah, sure."

They stood there, Kem feeling rather at a loss. For all the time he had spent looking for Sander, now it was hard to know exactly what he had wanted to say to him. "Where have you been?" was what he settled on.

Sander shrugged. He tossed his head, throwing the long hair to one side. Then he seemed to think better of it and said, "I've got a new lover who works in the Residents' wing. It's nice over there. Quiet."

Kem felt a tug of something like irritation, maybe anger, maybe something else. Sander annoyed him, for sure, with his air of worldliness, when here he was only, what, fifteen at most. But on the other hand Kem supposed Sander really *was* worldly, if anybody was. Definitely worldlier than Kem, at least, which may not have been saying much. But Kem was tired of all that, of feeling too old and too young all at once, which had something to do with why he was going, though it was not the whole story.

"I just feel like there's something I've got to do," he said, as though Sander had asked him. "There's somebody I've got to see, there's this thing I've got to give her. Then, I don't know."

Sander said, "Yeah, okay."

Kem said, "Yeah."

Then they were standing there again, looking and not looking at each other. It might have been Kem's imagination but he thought you could see the day getting brighter, the shadows growing more definite across Sander's face. He even had the idea that he ought to let Sander go, let him get safely to bed, lest the sun catch him abroad and Sander—night creature that he was—be seriously hurt.

"Well," he said. "Bye, I guess."

"Yeah."

For an instant Kem thought they were going to embrace; for an instant Kem wanted to do that. Then Sander turned and then, like a good night creature, he vanished.

And then, only then, at last, Kem was really gone.

Gull cries came through the mist all around, as though the air were thick with wings. Kem had the urge to duck his head again and again, but he just kept walking straight down the slope, swirling fog in aftertow, hardly even bothering to look where he was going because there was so little to see and really, anyway, it was hard to think of anything except where he was coming from. You could not see the Oasis, except maybe as a slightly darker region of gray, like you could only see the sunrise as a *direction,* a zone of relative brightness. Kem figured it was good to be going from the one to the other, darkness to light, though he could not have said he felt anything fundamentally but terror.

He came among the pilings and flotsam and shattered sea-craft of the village. Besides the noise of gulls there were no indications of life; you just had to believe that you had not reached some desolate extremity of the earth. Kem slowed down and looked for familiar things, felt inside himself for that just-conscious recognition that makes you relax, that lets you know you're someplace you've been before. If the feeling was there his fear was so much stronger as to drown it out. He kept walking anyway. Even if he was lost he wanted to get as far as he could from the Oasis before the fog burned off. He remembered the two-scope optical device on the flying bridge, incongruous in that exotic garden. He walked a little faster.

Out of the gray haze, a woman's voice:

"You're Hóz'q's friend, aren't you?"

Kem looked around and saw only broken piers, scrap timbers. Then something fluttered at the corner of his eye; a dark face peered over a rotten wall, ten strides off.

"Hi," he called back. "Yeah, I was. I am."

The woman stayed put—sensible caution, thought Kem. She seemed to confer quietly with someone else. At last she said, "Sitiké is waiting for you. Do you know the way?"

"Well, um, actually . . ."

"I'll show you."

When the woman came nearer, Kem was struck by contradictory impressions: how alike she was to the Bell Dog and his sister—the same coloring and body type—but at the same time how distinct. This woman was younger and her eyes lighter and her facial bones finer and more prominent. But you had to really look to notice these things; it was something like the way every patch of the Grind is different from every other, though this does not seem to be the case at a quick or uncaring glance. The woman avoided Kem's eye as though she were embarrassed, and he realized that he had been staring at her.

He said, "Oh, I'm sorry, I . . . So you know Sitiké?"

The woman nodded. She motioned with her head but when Kem just stood there she began walking, striking off in a direction that would not have occurred to him. Her path led straight into the ruins, through the twisting alleys of Body of God.

It was almost like intruding into people's homes. They passed through what must have been—before the spiteful Sea-god rose up and destroyed them—backyards or gardens or other private sanctuaries. Here and there some freak survival, a trellis or grape-arbor or lovingly pruned fruit tree, gave a hint of the former nature of the place. But mostly Kem got the impression of abandonment, decrepitude, old gardens gone wild. Still there was a kind of beauty here, even a certain lushness, that he had not expected, and that he would never have found had he followed his own instincts and kept to the obvious, well-trodden path. He supposed there was a kind of lesson or moral in that, as in so much else, but then he guessed it was only from being around Captain Hand that you found yourself thinking this way, looking at life as something other than itself, other than just a succession of instants, but rather as a kind of mystery, an accumulation of clues and hints that ultimately led to some deeper or grander level of meaning. What a bunch of crap, he thought, glad to be away from it.

Then he noticed a colony of irises, rich violet blue flowers as big as fists, growing all around the edges of what appeared to be, must have been, a crumbled fountain, something like the fountain on the trading deck but built all of marble, with a piece of shattered statuary whose remaining solid parts looked highly voluptuous. And he thought, But it's really true: there really *are* these stupid hokey obvious symbols everywhere, gardens run wild, beauty flowering among the ruins, icons turned to dust . . . and once you start seeing the world that way you just can't stop, the world *is* that way, from then on. Thank you, Captain.

"Here."

The woman stopped and pointed upward. Kem found that he was standing beneath Sitiké's platform, with its patchwork lean-to and its rows of vegetables in makeshift containers. The woman was already leaving him.

"Hey, thanks," he called after her. But evidently a different sort of etiquette applied here, because she just continued walking without looking back.

A ladder ran up to the platform as he remembered from last year. He called hello from the foot of it, but when no one answered he went ahead and started climbing. He was unable to bear the pressure of waiting. When he reached the top he was startled to find Sitiké sitting there, legs crossed, with her back to him, staring out at where the Sea must be, though with the fog you couldn't see it. She didn't move and Kem wondered if she could possibly be sleeping. Then she said, "Come in," still without turning.

Then Kem figured that somehow—maybe because it was just him, arriving alone—she knew.

He came forward slowly. The little silver tuning rod was in his pocket and when he pulled it out it felt impossibly heavy. He stood just behind Sitiké looking down on her. Abruptly she turned. Her eyes went straight to the silver rod, then away. Kem would have preferred to leap over the side of the platform, given the choice, than to keep standing here in silence. But the choice was not given to him. Or rather, he had already made it, or it had been made for him, in the instant that Mole handed him the Bell Dog's only possession of consequence and said, "You ought to have it, more than me."

He could not see Sitiké's face when she began to speak.

"I knew it would happen," she said. Her voice was a monotone but it was full of many things, dark and deep, like the flat Sea. "I saw it coming, far off. Just as clearly as Hóz'q saw *you*."

Kem struggled to absorb these words; they were simple enough but his mind had to stretch to contain them.

He said, "Saw . . . me?"

"Oh yes." She looked up at Kem; her face looked toughened, as though her grief were already months old. "He told me. That night when you were out there, out in the boat, he told me then."

Kem felt dizzy, disoriented, as though he had been spun rapidly about. He had expected to come here and deliver an awful message; instead it was Sitiké with a message to deliver, Sitiké who spoke and Kem who stood and listened.

"Hóz'q said, *That's where he's got to go*. The Bright Land, he was talking about. He said, *Someday he's got to go there. Someday he'll have more questions and that's where he's got to ask them.*"

Sitiké's eyes searched Kem's as though gauging whether he understood, or perhaps (as he feared) whether he was worthy of this message. Well, but the words were the Bell Dog's, weren't they? As with the tuning rod, it was not necessary to understand these peculiar bequests—only to pass them on. Out of a sense that he ought to fulfill his part in the ritual, Kem held out the silver rod to Sitiké. Probably the act deserved more gravity, more ceremony, but things were moving too quickly for that.

She shook her head.

"It is no good to me," she said. "It was no good to him either, I think." And as she gently pushed Kem's hand away, urging the rod back upon him, she added (in what seemed to Kem a distinct echo of another voice, a very different occasion): "Maybe it will be some good to you."

• • •

So they waited out the third quarter of Tall Skies Moon. They watched the captain's gig spurt through the village like a leaping fish and stared until it vanished among a million glinting wave-tops. Then they waited for the circle of the tides to turn in its ancient, stately pace, day upon day, until the high tide coincided with the sunrise. On that morning the captain's gig reappeared, exactly as it had done the year before, to shoot between the pilings. If Kem had entertained any private dread of being captured—search parties combing the village, Hand himself there to receive him as he was carried in manacles over the brow—he learned during that week exactly how important in the scheme of things he really was. The lesson ended with the captain's gig being winched up into its davit, pneumatic shocks pumped up, sun wings retracted, and—a stirring sight—the Oasis like a lumbering monster roused from hibernation grumbling off across the salt flats. For several minutes the ground beneath the village shuddered with its departure, and for an hour after that you could still see the black form, growing gradually less distinct, reaching and crossing the horizon. It took much longer than that, of course, for Kem to believe that everything—his home, his job, Davina, Sander, the whole world that he knew—had really vanished.

He sailed out to the Bright Land that night.

The journey was not long. A man from the village, a fisherman whose name Kem never learned, took him out in his little sailboat, steering only by the north star and the wind. They embarked before midnight, and a couple of hours later Kem eased himself over the gunwales into shallow water and down at last onto a surface that felt firm and gritty beneath his feet. He wore his old snipe's boots and coveralls, with a few other pieces of clothing and miscellaneous belongings stuffed into a bag slung around his neck. For the most part he had left everything behind. The moon gave barely enough light for him to make his way through reeds taller than his head onto marshy ground that in turn yielded to sand, sparsely knitted with dune grass. He turned to wave goodbye

to the fisherman but could not find the sailboat out on the
dark water.

He had the sense of great forms looming above him, but
there was nothing he could see by looking up, only gradations
of darkness. Somewhere a night bird was calling, waiting for
an answer that did not come, calling again. Kem figured that
since sleep was out of the question he would try to save his
energy by sitting still, closing his eyes, feeling the cool Sea
air brushing over his skin and listening to the waves. He was
really *here;* but until he saw the place he could not believe
that. Fantastic towers rose in his mind, filled with marvels
beyond imagining. Visions of them shimmered before him,
becoming stranger and more wonderful as they blurred from
thoughts into dreams. Kem lay on the sandy floor of the
Bright Land, breathing slow and deep.

Yellow sun awoke him. It was hot but the air was still cool, so
that when Kem sat groggily upright he had the odd sensation
of being sunburned on one side of his body while nonetheless
feeling chilled to the bone. Grains of sand adhered to his leg,
his arm, his cheek. His eyes felt strained and watery.

For these few instants the immediate, bodily stimuli of the
new day preoccupied him. Quickly then his awareness spread
outward, first to the dunes and the reedy shore and the
sapphire sky, then to the wind-stunted pines, bald cypress,
and live oaks that marched inland, away from the water, and
almost immediately—for he could not have kept himself from
seeing them any longer—to the great blue-green structures
that leapt out of the trees a hundred strides inland and soared
skyward, immeasurably vast and tall. Staring up, failing to
see the tops of those towers, made him feel for a moment
slightly nauseated. He lowered his head. The feeling passed
and he looked up again because there was no way not to.

The presence of the towers was so overpowering that you
could *hear* them, hear the way they molded the air currents,
the way they muffled certain sounds and amplified others.
They even seemed to create their own miniature climate:
here on the north side of the island, where the fisherman had
made his approach, the vegetation was mostly grasses and

forbs with occasional rangy trees, whereas around the curving
shoreline Kem could see that the trees grew thicker and
taller with a distinct seaward orientation, as though they were
trying to grow out of those monstrous shadows. But the tallest
of the trees was only fifteen heads or so, a magnitude Kem
could relate to the Oasis, and that didn't come anywhere
close to even clearing the bottommost platforms.

Kem had not brought food, figuring he would be too
agitated to eat. Now he discovered that he was famished.
Thirsty, too. It hadn't occurred to him that in the middle of so
much water you could find yourself with nothing to drink; but
here he was. Now as crazy as it seemed there was nothing for
him to do but go right up there and walk in the door, if there
was a door. Either that or go hungry. Kem figured it was a
little silly, at this stage of the game, to worry about playing it
safe. Playing it safe had ceased to be an option, the way he
figured it, since the day his family's wagon broke down. And
for sure he had not come out here to forage for berries and
nuts. He set his eyes on the base of the nearest tower and he
began walking.

The Oasis had not prepared him for this. As bizarre as it
had been, it had not even come close, because the Bright
Land was not just bigger and more exotic; it was *wild*—the
towers rising from tangled, subtropical vegetation, the un-
ceasing easterly wind off the Sea, cries of gulls and great blue
herons, smells of brine and flowers and warm earth—all of it
was exotic and somehow fundamentally untame, uncivilized,
which was very much in contrast to the Oasis where the
presence of other people was inescapable, where every finger-
width was under somebody-or-other's control. Kem made his
way between coastal pines and sand cherries, locusts, paw-
paws, sweet gums, many of them overgrown with wild grapes
and passion fruits, entering finally a glade or hollow carved
out in the shade of old gnarled oaks and of the towers
themselves, where the light was diffuse and greenish and the
silence so immense it seemed to reverberate. The base of the
tower was only a dozen strides off; from this close you could
almost not discern that it was cylindrical, you could barely
see the curve of the great steel wall. Kem approached with a
feeling of awe that felt somehow obligatory, as though it were

being wrung out of him by the place itself. He stood at the foot of the tower and this time he was afraid to look up; he was afraid he *would* vomit. There was no door in sight so he began circling counterclockwise, the direction that was supposed to break enchantments.

The base of the tower plunged straight into the sandy soil with no evident foundation, as though it had been buried there like a gigantic fence post. Though when you looked at it another way, you might have imagined that the soil had actually been piled around the tower, or perhaps accreted naturally. From where Kem stood, you could look at it either way.

About halfway around, he found a ladder.

The ladder, too, seemed half-buried in the earth. From ground level it rose straight up for three heads or more, ending at a hole about as tall as an ordinary-sized person and maybe twice that wide. The hole was dark and empty, from what Kem could see. With a kind of eagerness that was hard to distinguish from dread, he walked to the ladder and heaved himself upward.

The hole, when he got there, turned out to be the mouth of a tunnel. Kem stared into the hollow space, all dark and echoey, and he thought he could see an end of it, a blank wall ten strides or so deep in the body of the tower. He stepped cautiously inward, his soggy work boots striking with resonant thuds on the metal floor.

The wall at the end of the tunnel was composed of a series of narrow steel plates, lapped horizontally like wallboards. Kem's snipe instincts suggested to him that this was some kind of door or hatch, perhaps the entrance to a cargo bay. The system of steel plates looked like something designed to fold up on itself, retracting upward or downward. This in turn suggested that there ought to be a control mechanism. It was hard to see in the faint light drifting in from behind him; Kem moved slowly along what he supposed to be the door, then examined the sidewalls, finally the ceiling and the floor, but found virtually nothing. There were some mesh-covered wells, like cages, recessed in the ceiling, but if these were light fixtures then no switches were in evidence. Other than this, there were only two small metal plates, set into a narrow wall segment and painted with nearly identical symbols—

—which reminded Kem of something. After a few moments he remembered the little pictograph on the door at Gardner's place, evidently a fragment of some symbolic language or alphabet that Davina had been able to read. He supposed then that these symbols must also be decipherable, though he could not imagine how to go about breaking the code. At last, in frustration, he thought of the Bell Dog's tuning rod.

He was wearing the rod now around his neck, on a leather cord, as the Bell Dog had done. He pulled it out carefully, almost reverentially. It flashed silver white in the gloom of the tunnel. Without pausing to deliberate he bent down and struck the rod against the deck. Immediately, as the chime rang out to fill the hollow space around him, he grew chilly with fear and doubt. Was it wise to announce himself this way? Suppose the rod had some significance he wasn't aware of? What if someone came and took it away from him?

These thoughts faded with the sound of the tuning rod, subsiding gradually in the dark. For another minute or more Kem stood very still, listening to the quiet that now seemed heavier than before.

It seemed unthinkable that he might have come all the way here, all the way from being a wagon boy on the Grind to being a pilgrim in this place of legends, yet in the end find himself forced to turn back, returning to whatever drab or desolate fate might be waiting for him.

But it was too early to give up: Kem forced himself to think that. Surely there must be some way, some entrance, if not here then somewhere, it's a big place after all. . . .

He was halfway turned around, gearing himself up for the plucky trooper routine, stiff upper lip and all, when he glanced once more at the two little plates bearing symbols or coded diagrams—

—two spirals almost alike except that they coiled in different directions, the one turning sunwise and the other moonwise, like the narrow stairway that wrapped itself around the navigation tower on the Oasis. Sunwise and up; moonwise and down. Kem stared at the symbols with an odd mix of emotions, regret and bitterness and maybe a trace of homesickness, and out of this arose an impulse to run his fingers over the right-hand member of the pair, the spiral that turned sunwise like an eagle soaring. He touched the plate—coarsely textured paint on cool metal—and as he did so he felt the plate move slightly, as though whatever secured it to the wall panels was coming loose.

A deep loud CLUNK came from behind the wall. Brilliant lights flooded down from their mesh-covered cages. There was a sound of motors engaging, a muffled electric whine, and then as Kem could only stand immobile with surprise the wall at the end of the tunnel began to rise; the plate-on-plate structure folded up like an armor curtain.

Well, thought Kem. That wasn't so hard.

On the other side of the door was a small chamber, more or less cubical, that seemed to float on a blanket of cool white light. Its walls were made of steel mesh, through which you could see another set of walls, a box-within-a-box arrangement, and you could also see thick black cables, heavy beams and cross-braces, sinews of the massive structural system that held the tower aloft. At Kem's first, hesitating step, the floor of the chamber trembled slightly, and there was a just-perceptible dipping or swaying motion. Kem relaxed; he knew all he needed to know. He had been a snipe for too long not to recognize a freight elevator.

The only question now was how to get the thing to move, and this turned out to be what the Bell Dog would have called a happy problem: the kind that solves itself. Kem kept still for a few moments, and the elevator mechanism—responding, he guessed, to the cessation of movement—lowered the door panel back into place, sounded a buzzer twice (probably another sort of code) and then turned on the winch that hoisted the metal box up in its shaft.

Knowledge, however, is not the same thing as understanding, and Kem's ability to figure out how things worked did not mean that he was prepared for what was happening. Not at all. His stomach lurched as the elevator yanked him upward at surprising speed, forcing air with a swooshing noise through the steel mesh and incidentally bringing smells of old, oxidizing metal and eutrophic air and rancid grease into his nostrils. He felt a moment of panic recalling engine-flat horror stories—snipes who had stepped into an unventilated hold, taken a few breaths, and fallen dead, all the oxygen in the place having been chemically removed by the ceaseless process of rust. But the elevator kept moving and Kem kept breathing and it seemed that everything was going to be all right, at least for the next few moments.

Then the buzzer sounded again—just once this time—and the elevator braked, and Kem's stomach knotted again. As quick as that, after all this time, he had reached his destination.

Or so he imagined. All destinations are just resting places, though, as any wagon boy can tell you.

In one way, the place Kem came to when the elevator stopped and a new set of doors rolled open was everything he was looking for, a confirmation of all he had expected and hoped and halfway dreaded, vis à vis the Bright Land. It was gigantic. It was a single room as big as a wagon camp, one of the platforms that Kem had seen from below that spanned the distance from tower to tower, fifty heads or more in the sky. The Oasis could have lain end to end in the space between this tower and the next. Kem guessed he was looking at a five-minute walk, maybe more, to get from one to the other. He wasn't really sure, though, that he wanted to take another step.

The thing was, the place was empty. It was completely barren of anything but its own necessary parts—suspension cables and so forth—and the scale of its emptiness was such that when Kem looked into that bright void, the shining steel, the sun-warmed deck, he felt a surge of hopelessness, of complete futility, as though some process of psychic decompression were turning him inside out. He lowered his eyes to the deck.

The Grind was big too, much bigger than this, but it had never caused Kem to feel so small or so desolate. In fact it had usually done quite the opposite; staring sleepily over the Grind, as the family wagon rattled along, was the most comforting of all his memories. What was the difference, then? Kem glanced up again, across this perfectly engineered netherworld suspended in the sky, and he wondered if the difference might be that the Grind was just the opposite of empty: it was as full as it could possibly be, crowded with all the living things that its complicated structure could support. And when you looked at the Grind—this was another thing, this was important—you got the idea that the place had a *purpose*. Kem couldn't have said what the purpose was, exactly; but you could sense it, just by standing there. Whereas in *this* place, you felt nothing like that at all. You could admire the ingenious design, gawk at the cables as big as water mains, wonder how such a thing could ever have been built, what kind of people had made it—stuff like that—but you couldn't really *feel* anything, except maybe some sense of how tiny and vulnerable you were.

Kem looked ahead of him, across the platform, and behind him into the elevator, and he figured that's what the choice came down to, forward or back. But that was no choice at all. He started to walk.

About halfway across, he got the notion that he wasn't getting anywhere. His feet were moving over the solid, unyielding deck, but there was no way to confirm that he was actually moving forward. The scale of everything was too far removed from human frame of reference; one stride or two or three didn't really count for anything. Plus, the structure was rocking in the wind. It was hard to believe, but Kem was sure it was happening—the entire building flexing easily, silently, back and forth, its great spine rippling with waves of kinetic energy. Kem supposed this amounted to nothing when you considered it in perspective—a tiny fraction of a percent of the structure's size—but compared to the size of

Kem's body the rocking counted for a lot. It nearly heaved him off his feet. By the time he reached the second tower he was physically and philosophically exhausted.

He came to a door like the one that opened to the elevator, except that this one bore three plates instead of two—

—and of course he chose the unfamiliar one, the one that looked somewhat like a pupilless eye. Still he expected nothing, or nothing much.

What he got was this. The door lifted like a curtain, as before, to reveal a cubical chamber. But this time, on the opposite side of the chamber, a second door was opening in synchrony with the first. Kem found himself standing at the entrance to what seemed to be a kind of air lock. He could feel a breeze blowing through, and the new air was much different from the air of the vast empty room. It was *full:* full of dampness, a spicy tang, maybe a hint of noise, like the last echo of some commotion that had just ended. Kem had been tired before but now he felt a renewal of his energy. He ducked through the door before it had opened all the way.

He emerged in a garden. It was an enclosed garden— Kem could see the webwork ceiling high overhead between arching palm leaves. The room that contained it did not seem to be so terribly large as the place he had come from, though in truth he could not see very much of it. His vision was blocked in all directions by leaves and fronds and planters as big as the water tanks of the Oasis.

For several moments he just stood there, inhaling the jumbled aromas of the garden until the odors of steel and oil had been purged from his lungs. Then he climbed a run of stairs that led to an elevated walkway. He hoped to get some perspective on the place, but all he had got was more or less a squirrel's-eye view of the dense green canopy. Within arm's reach, branches sagged under the weight of some purplish and exotic-looking fruit. Kem glanced around, a thief's natural furtive reflex, then leaned over and picked one.

The fruit was soft and heavy and there seemed to be no
elegant way to eat it. It was too fat to take clean bites of; you
just had to thrust your face into it and gnaw your way
through, like a hungry rodent. Juice streamed down Kem's
chin, onto his shirt, spattering the pack that still hung around
his neck. The fruit was almost overpoweringly sweet. Kem
found it delicious.

He walked on. One kind of plant gave place to another; in
some sections different species grew together in lusty tangles.
The walkway turned one way and another, opening onto new
but always artfully limited perspectives. Despite the mystery of
the place, Kem had a sense of well-being here, of being safely
enclosed. He stopped walking and he took a deep slow breath.

A crackle:

then a swishing sound:

and then branches parted next to where Kem was standing
and something large, tan, heavy-looking:

a guy with a machete—

Kem stumbled backward, got tangled in his own feet and
slammed back against the railing.

The guy with the machete landed on the walkway a couple
of strides ahead of him. He let go of the handle of some kind of
pulley-driven contraption, suspended on a long dangling wire—
even in panic and desperation Kem could not help taking note
of the mechanics here—and let out a lungful of air.

"Whup," he seemed to say.

Kem thought very dimly that something was wrong, the
guy was losing his momentum, his element of surprise, not
that Kem was capable of taking advantage of it.

The guy tottered a little. He was extremely large, a head
taller than Kem and lots heavier, more muscular. . . .

"Hey," said Kem, holding his palms out, like look at me
I'm harmless, "I didn't come to do anything. I mean, I'm not
here to steal or anything like that." The big guy just frowned
at him, and he added, not sure whether this was good or bad,
"I'm from the Oasis."

The guy said, "I figured that."

To Kem's amazement, he slipped the machete into a notch
in his belt. It did not look like a very safe arrangement. Then
he held his hand out and said, "My name's Nuri."

Kem squeezed back into the railing, partly out of surprise but also partly because Nuri's hand was so big, you couldn't help but worry. Then he got himself under a little better control and he stuck his own hand out. They shook. Nuri seemed satisfied. He nodded.

He was not that much older than Kem. His skin was a bit darker but not so dark as the Bell Dog's had been. He wore his hair long and tied behind his head, the way the fishermen did at Body of God. But he did not look like a fisherman. His clothes were khaki-colored, utilitarian.

When Nuri seemed not to have anything further to say, Kem ventured, "So, is it all right for me to be here?"

Nuri shrugged. "What did you come here for? Are you looking for work?"

Kem found this ludicrous somehow—the Bright Land wasn't any place that you just *came* to, looking for work—but then he saw the look in Nuri's eye and he thought maybe Nuri found it ludicrous also. They stared at each other, their expressions canny. At length Kem decided to risk a guarded smile. Nuri returned it.

"Or maybe," Nuri said—the words came out slowly, as though he were observing their effect on Kem—"you've come to get the answer to all your questions. Maybe it's something like that."

"Something like that," Kem agreed.

Nuri nodded. He looked aside, down the walkway. "Well, maybe you should find your way around first," he said. "It's easy to get lost here."

"Sure," said Kem.

They set off together, cautiously still, but companionably enough. Kem decided that under the circumstances he could take this as a decent welcome.

For three solid weeks, Nuri was the only living soul Kem saw. They worked together in the garden, whose true dimensions Kem never did exactly grasp, clearing vines that threatened to choke less vigorous species, harvesting fruit of various kinds and loading it onto conveyors that ran through dark hatchways, out of sight, checking pipes and gauges, cleaning filters, adjusting valves. Whether or not Kem had been looking for work he appeared to have found it. And he found that it was work he generally enjoyed, something like being a snipe only more relaxing, not quite as strenuous, and certainly less dangerous.

The trouble was that Nuri was not much for talking. Either that or he was keeping deliberately quiet. Even at night, when the two of them finished working and settled down in the large, well-appointed berthing area that they seemed to have to themselves, Nuri had nothing to say beyond a certain minimal banter—discussions of what to have for dinner, things of that sort—and the pressure of all the things left unspoken, the questions unasked, was building up on Kem.

On the other hand, Kem did not want to blow anything. He was not sure what the terms of his residency here might be—he suspected that he was going through a kind of probation—but he could not think of any better approach than to just wait it out. That, and stay on his good behavior. Keep his shoulder to the wheel, as Hand had said. He wasn't sure what, if anything, the people here might know about him. He didn't even know for sure that there *were* people here, other than Nuri. (There must be, though, mustn't there?) It was not inconceivable, given the dark art of communications, that they had already learned from the Oasis everything there was to know about Kem, including maybe things that he didn't know himself.

Or maybe he was just being paranoid.

He missed Davina more than he had ever missed anyone, including his family, including his poor dead sister Chrissie whom he would never see again.

He missed other stuff too, in varying degrees, and with all the hours of silence here he had a lot of time to think about such things. But he did not miss the Oasis. Every time his thoughts rolled around to that he got a feeling somewhat like an escaped prisoner must get, of having stolen his own life back. He had not learned much about the Bright Land; but so far his life here was not all that bad, and he knew for sure he would never go back. Nothing could make him return to the Oasis.

• • •

One night it started raining and did not stop.

This was not exactly a surprise—it was Hard Rain Moon, the end of winter, the time of floods and violent storms and general havoc among the wagons—but here the rain had a quality Kem had not known before. It was steady, coming down all night and all day with hardly any change in force. The wind that blew from the east off the Sea seemed to be the same wind that brought the rain, and there was no end to either of them, not even an interruption. The sky was darker, too, than the sky over the desert, where the sun often managed to break through for a few hours at a time. Here each day reached a certain level of brightness—the gloomy kind of half light that comes before dawn—and it stayed that way until nightfall, when the sky became black as earth. Nuri and Kem would work in the garden until there was just enough daylight seeping down through the glass and metal webbing for them to find their way back to the berthing space; then they curled up in dim amber puddles of light under reading lamps, numbed by the droning sameness of rain-sounds, turning the pages of old books containing endless descriptions of plants and their cultural requirements and their native habitats, some of which might have been interesting but Kem found that it was impossible to concentrate, the rain was making it hard for him to think.

He was not even sure how much time had gone by, three weeks until the rains began but then how much? Two weeks more? A month? Kem looked across the room at Nuri, each of them sitting alone in his private sphere of lamplight, and—breaking a silence that seemed to have lasted for days—he said:

"How can you stand this? What are we doing here? Are we just going to sit around like this forever?"

Nuri looked up but not at once; his eyes lingered for a last moment or two on the book he was reading. Then he gave Kem an incurious sort of stare, showing no surprise and very little of anything; maybe a hint of amusement. At last he said, "We're waiting."

"Waiting for what?"

"For summer, I guess."

Kem felt like doing something, anything—laughing, hurling his book across the room, smashing the light bulb. Instead he

kept looking at Nuri, who kept looking placidly back. It was
unbearable. Kem guessed that it would be unwise in the
extreme to make any display of temper, but really—he couldn't
sit still anymore. He had come here for *some* reason; he
couldn't say what the reason was but he knew it hadn't been
to sit around like this.

"Can't we go somewhere?" he said. "Like, for a walk or
something?"

Nuri's mouth flicked. Kem thought it was a smile but
there was not much you could tell for sure about Nuri,
including how smart or how cunning he was. With a flat
expression Nuri said, "In the rain?"

"Sure," said Kem. "Why not?"

"Why not," Nuri repeated. He seemed to consider the
question in his ponderous way. Slowly he rose from the chair.
He said, "If that's what you want to do."

Kem thought, So it's as easy as that.

They passed along wide corridors that could have been
anywhere inside the tower, illuminated by lights that clicked
on automatically at their approach, threw their shadows far
against sleek metal bulkheads, then clicked off behind them.
Once Nuri got moving he moved fast, his big arms swinging
and legs pumping. Kem had to hustle to keep up but he was
glad they were not wasting time; this big empty hallway gave
him the creeps, as though it were a haunted place and he was
the ghost that was haunting it.

The corridor ended at a doorway like others Kem had gone
through, complete with a row of pictographs. Kem had gotten
accustomed to these by now, though this time there were
symbols he had not seen before.

They stood there for a few moments and finally Kem
realized that Nuri was staring at him, apparently waiting for
him to decide, to choose one of the plates and press it. But of
course Kem did not know what any of the symbols meant,
and moreover he suspected Nuri knew that. Captain Hand

had been unduly fond of arranging little tests like this and Kem thought that maybe this is where Hand picked up the habit. He looked from the symbols to Nuri. Nuri smiled.

"What do you want to do?" he said.

Kem scowled. *What do you want to do. What did you come here for.* Everything seemed to end in a question; everything was a mind game. He supposed that after a while you would get used to this and it would seem quite natural, a perfectly natural way to behave. It would be like the way you got used to seeing the world as the Captain saw it, as being more than just itself, full of symbols and metaphors and deeper levels of meaning. Soon enough he supposed you would look at yourself that way too; you would get used to thinking of each of your actions, every single choice you made, as being not just a simple action but a move in this big lifelong game. Choosing a pictograph and pushing it would not just be a matter of simple choice, of guessing; it would reveal some hidden thing. If you picked *this* symbol, the line that bent slightly, like a road twisting away into the distance, it would mean something entirely different than if you picked *this* one, the one that looked like a pair of eyes. Picking the eyes would be an obvious sort of thing to do; it would be a way of saying, like, *I want to take a look around* or something, an answer to Nuri's question. It was so obvious that Kem stuck his hand out and pressed the middle plate with a certain spitefulness. He could play the game as well as anyone.

The door panel retracted. Beyond it, in place of an elevator, there was a narrow room like an extension of the corridor. The room had three smaller doors, and one of these swung open while Kem watched.

Through the door came the sound of pouring rain, the smells of brine and ozone, the weird purplish light of a full moon buried in clouds.

Kem hurried through, not waiting for Nuri. He stepped out onto a huge balcony. It might have been an observation deck. It stretched into the darkness as far as Kem could see, running along the edge of one of the giant platforms. What little bit of light there was made its railings glow dully like tarnished silver. Kem edged farther and farther out along it, gasping with the force of the rain and the chill of the night

air. By the time he had taken a dozen strides he was soaked
all the way through, his old blue snipe's coveralls hanging
limp and heavy from his limbs, hair streaming with water in
his eyes. It felt wonderful. He threw back his head and let
water fall into his open mouth. The water tasted sweet. Kem
laughed.

Unexpectedly, he heard laughter coming from behind him.
He turned to see Nuri standing back against the bulkhead,
somewhat sheltered by an overhang but not much drier than
Kem. Nuri seemed to be grinning—it was hard to tell for
sure in the darkness—and Kem got the idea that Nuri was
laughing at him, at the fool he was making of himself. The
thought made him angry, then stubborn.

"Hey, come on," he said. "Isn't this great? I mean, it's only
water."

Nuri walked out to the railing where Kem stood. He said,
"There's no such thing as *only water*."

Kem had no idea what he meant; Nuri was staring out toward
an invisible horizon. Kem followed his eyes, wondered if he was
talking about the Sea. Somehow the idea of the Sea made him
feel funny, uncomfortable—the thought of all the water that there
was in the world, while back on the Grind people like Kem's
family spent most of their time within a day or two—or an injury,
or a broken gearbox—of death from dehydration.

Kem felt restless, agitated. He wanted to move, to walk.
He slid down the railing, even farther from the door they had
come out of. Out here, he might as well have been adrift in
the night sky: the towers were invisible, the earth below was
absolutely dark, there were no referents at all. There were
only the sound and the feel and the taste of rain. He had an
urge to take his soggy clothes off, to romp in the downpour
the way wagon kids did, during the rare storms out on the
Grind. He wished he could have shared this experience—
unlimited rainfall—with someone, someone he had known.
But he could not because he had left everyone behind; every
person and every familiar place was lost in the past. He
looked for Nuri in the darkness but could not find him.

And then, at last, he wondered why. Why he had come to
the Bright Land. He thought he had come because he
needed to, but what sort of need was it? It was not some

life-or-death thing, like the need to eat. It was not like the need for love, for sex, for friendship. Those were deep and genuine needs and yet he had given up all of those things in order to come to this place, and he had never really understood or even asked himself why he was doing it, what it was that he hoped to accomplish. Now he asked himself and there was no satisfying answer.

That's where he's got to go. That was one answer, the Bell Dog's, and though it had seemed to make sense when Sitiké repeated the words, in a voice that contained some trace or memory of her brother's, it did not seem to make sense anymore. *He'll have more questions*, the Bell Dog had said, *and that's where he's got to ask them.*

"What questions?" said Kem, to the wind and the unseen waves and the blackness of the earth below him.

There was no reply; only the relentless ostinato of the rain, the drone of Kem's own thoughts. The Bell Dog could not hear him and could not answer because he was dead. Tallheron was dead, and so was the man who had killed him. Little Chrissie was dead. The two kids from Riley County, the ones whose names Kem had forgotten, they might be dead too. People were dying all over the place; the trail that Kem had followed here was a bloody one. This made him more angry than sad—angry, he guessed, because he wanted all the deaths to make sense, to *mean* something, the way other things meant something. Sentences, symbols, crumbled fountains, lines on a chart, irises blooming in an old garden—all of these things stood for something other than themselves, and it seemed to Kem that death ought to stand for something too. There ought to be a pattern, as there were patterns in a story, the kind of pattern Tallheron had once talked about: how a disease in a story was not a particular disease but *disease*, the idea in its broadest sense, the whole pattern and not the part. When a character died in a story it was like that; it was not just a single death but *death*, it stood for something and there was a reason for it. Death was not pointless, in stories. Kem wanted life to be like that. He wanted life to make sense the way stories made sense. He wanted to understand it, and he wanted to understand why people he had known and loved had died. And that, he guessed, was why he had come to the Bright Land.

He turned and Nuri was standing beside him and that did
not surprise him. In a story, it would have happened that
way. Nuri was looking at him, expressionless as ever, staring,
waiting. Waiting, he had said, for summer. Waiting for an
answer. Waiting for Kem.

Kem felt a surge of some strong feeling, an inner certainty.
He had a sense of liberation, as though he *had* taken his
clothes off and frolicked like a kid in the rain. He clapped
Nuri on one of his big arms. Nuri did not flinch, but it
seemed to Kem that his head cocked slightly, quizzically,
repeating a silent question.

"Don't you want to know?" Kem asked him.

"Know what?"

"What you . . . you know, the first thing you said. When
you first saw me. You asked me why I had come here."

Nuri said nothing at first, and Kem thought for a change
he had gotten the jump on the guy. Then Nuri said, "Tell me."

"Because," Kem said, with a sense of building certainty, "I
like stories. And a lot of stories don't really *end*—it's like they
stop but they leave you full of questions. But this place . . . I
don't know. It just feels like the end of something. The end of
a story. And I want to know what it is."

"Once upon a time," the slender woman said, "people like us
were widely respected. We were revered. We were like a
kind of priesthood. The people trusted us, they wrote books
about us, they gave us money, they gave us awards. We were
the guardians of the mystery. We were the keepers of the last
faith. People *needed* to believe us. They depended on us for
truth, they needed us to answer their questions. They looked
to us for salvation."

It was funny, because Kem had been thinking for some
time that the woman and her colleagues were like priests or
monks or something: they dressed in simple unadorned clothes
and they wore their hair straight and long and they spoke in
quiet, dignified voices. Which was not to say that they all
looked or acted alike—the woman lounging before him in the
canvas-backed chair was more outspoken than most, more

energetic—but you could see a certain commonality among them, something like the commonality that there had been among the mates of the Oasis: members of the same class or order.

"Now," said the woman, "we are penitent. We take full responsibility." She gestured around her. "For everything. For everything that went wrong. For betraying the faith people had in us. For screwing up the world."

Kem followed the woman's gaze as it ran along the high walls of the room. They were sitting in a large airy place— every part of the Bright Land was large and airy, Kem supposed—that seemed to be a kind of museum. He and Nuri came here in the evenings, now, after their work in the garden was done. The walls of the room were lined with shelves which in turn were crowded with instruments: tools, small motors, microscopes, grinding wheels, scales, centrifuges, scanners, oscilloscopes, and a hundred other things Kem had never seen or heard of. It would have been a snipe's paradise, except that none of the instruments seemed to have been used in the lifetime of anyone present. Besides the slender woman, Nuri and half a dozen other people were sitting about the room, and some of them—a couple of the men especially—looked very old indeed.

"Oh, I could tell you stories, all right." The woman flashed Sea-blue eyes at Kem, eyes that seemed full of stories of every kind, eyes that had seen everything. The woman was smiling but her smile was a complicated one; it contained many more things than happiness, and Kem supposed under the circumstances you would expect that. "Some things you wouldn't believe," she said. Around her people nodded and some people murmured in agreement, though elsewhere in the room other conversations were in progress. This wasn't the only one and Kem was by no means the center of attention. The woman seemed to have taken an interest in him, however, and Kem was glad for that. Nuri had told him the woman's name but he had forgotten it.

"We really screwed it up," she said. "Because those people who trusted us, not many of them really understood the things we did. *We*, I mean the people like us, back then, not really *us*, you see? But even though they didn't understand, they trusted us, they supported us, they came to us and they said, here are our problems, here is our money, now you go and conduct your investigations and tell us what you have found. You tell us what we should do. You find the answers. Of course, I'm oversimplifying."

She smiled. Kem thought he liked her. But at the same time there was something a little frightening in her manner. When she said that people like her had screwed up the world, you really believed it.

"We had our critics, of course. But like any good priesthood we excommunicated them. Criticism to us meant disbelief, and disbelief meant heresy. We had no doubts that we were correct, we were the chosen, we were pure. Priesthoods are like that. Or at least I imagine they are. Actually I don't know the first thing about who priests are or what they do. Do you find me arrogant?"

Kem said he did not. In truth he guessed he did, a little bit.

"Well, it goes with the territory. We are all arrogant and we always have been, you might as well know it. We have always been convinced that we are the sole custodians of things like truth and understanding whereas in fact most of us know nothing at all outside the little tiny area of our specialization. We are trained to look through one little window and whatever we see out there we think is all there is. And let me tell you we more often than not couldn't tell shit from shinola unless we happened to be shinologists. But arrogance, that's the least of our sins. The very least. Let me tell you."

Kem was happy for the woman to tell him anything. Whatever she wanted to say, he was eager to hear it.

She waved her hand around, a worldly gesture, very blasé, like one Sander would have made. "Let me tell you the truly reprehensible thing," she said. "Our greatest sin. The people didn't understand us. I've told you that. They had no idea whatsoever what we did. But they believed us. And of course we ourselves, we felt they should believe us, why not? We believed ourselves. After all, we were the only ones who *knew*, you see. We were so very terribly clever that we would make a certain thing, develop a certain process, a certain body of technique, and of course no one but ourselves knew what the hell it was or how it worked, no one had the faintest idea. Very few of *us* even knew. Only the few of us looking out a particular window. But you see, we believed one another. That was the professional thing to do. We did not question one another because we did not question ourselves. We never asked ourselves, *What are the dangers of this, Is this good, Is this bad, What effect might this have on other things, What terrible purposes might this be used for*. Because of course those issues were not within our area of specialization, questions like that fell outside our little window. They were for someone else to answer. They were for *society* to answer, don't you see. Because they are messy questions, they are questions that have no clear answers, they cannot be *objectified*, for heaven's sake, how can we be expected to answer questions like that? We give you this *data*, these *facts*, these *discoveries*, it is up to you to decide what to do with them. But then of course"—the woman made a gypsy motion, snapped her fingers, faked a pirouette— "*then* we would turn around and tell you, You are not qualified to make decisions of this type, you do not understand the issues well enough, these questions are too highly technical for people like you, you do not have the specialized training, you are illiterate, you are innumerate, you are superstitious, you are *technophobic*—we had any number of ways of dealing with people like *you*, the great unwashed, the heretics, the unbelievers. And that, you see, is the reprehensible thing. We had you in a trap. We built the trap and then we put you in it and then we said, No, you have no right to call this a trap or to question your being placed there. We would say, The very fact that you speak in terms of traps, a terribly antiquated concept, proves that you are the sort of person who knows nothing about our *advanced human containment systems* here, but please do not try to understand that, please do not ask me any questions now, here would you please just go study this bible, this textbook, it may help you to see the error of your ways."

The woman paused for breath, as Kem figured she well might. Around the room, other conversations seemed to have tapered off; people seemed to be drawing in a little, caught by the woman's tirade. She swept the room once with her eyes and then returned them to Kem. When she spoke again her voice was lower, as cool as glass.

"Once upon a time," she said, "people fell for crap like that. Once upon a time we dished it up and they ate it. They trusted us. They let us create things like *this*, this place here, they let us build things like your Oasis. They let us do anything we want. And that's why the world is the way it is, because we made it that way. We had the power to do anything, anything at all, and this is what we did. And that's why we are here. Because we are the only people like us who are left. We are the only ones who can remember. And therefore we *must* remember, we must tell our stories again and again and never let them die. We must keep staring out our little windows until the eyes rot in our heads. And then someone else must take our place."

With alarming speed and ferocity, the woman leaned forward, straight at Kem.

"*Never forget*," she said, rapping it out. "Never forget. Never forget."

Then she receded into her chair, easing herself back in its canvas bindings.

"We must never forget," she said more calmly, her eyes narrowed like a cat's, "that we are responsible. For what happened to the world. Once upon a time."

Now his life was very different. Now that he had been admitted, at least peripherally, to the odd but mostly congenial group of men and women who referred to themselves as Penitents, Kem had more or less free run of the Bright Land. He could wander about during his off-hours, in and out of the towers, up to the highest observation decks, down among the trees and the dune grass and the vines, even occasionally out with Nuri in a little sailboat. Nuri was still detailed as a sort of guide for him, a workmate, an instructor, but Kem guessed this might just reflect the closeness of their ages and the fact that Nuri himself seemed to be near the bottom of the ladder here, authoritywise. He still kept quiet, pretty much, but now Kem was not sure what to make of that, whether Nuri was being cautious, letting Kem prove himself, or whether he just didn't know what to say.

More and more, Kem enjoyed his work in the garden. He was learning the names of plants and the way they lived, the things they needed, much as he had learned the names of machines and how to maintain them when he was a snipe. He found that it was a pleasure to care for the plants, to get to know them. Compared to all the other things he had done in his life, the work was reasonably fulfilling; for sure, the life cycle of growing things, their seasonal rhythm, was more pleasant to contemplate than the old routine at the Oasis, that sterile yearly circuit of the Grind. Kem felt lucky to have been assigned to this job, and he wondered what fascinating jobs the more senior Penitents must have. What did the slender woman do, for instance? What little window did she stare out of?

Spring was well along. Soon it was Birds Cry Moon, and Kem had been away from the Oasis for nearly three months. Here at the Bright Land spring was a longer, more definite season than out on the Grind, while it was little more than a quick prelude to summer. Here the constant breeze tempered the heat, and flocks of migratory wildfowl passed in waves, in skeins, in wedges across the pure blue sky.

At night the Penitents came together for dinner, taking turns at the cooking and the cleaning up. These were relaxed and very informal gatherings that sometimes lasted well into the night. There was music, an abundance of food, sometimes drink, always stories. There were plenty of stories to tell; everyone had them. Even Kem: he was surprised that when his own turn came he had something to offer, recollections of growing up on the Grind, tales he had heard long ago around cookfires, legends of the wagon folk. The Penitents enjoyed hearing all of that—these people who lived in the most fantastic place in the world sat rapt with attention while a former wagon boy recounted the humble story of his life.

Kem was not used to this, to grown-ups caring what he had to say, nor to the kind of unassuming fellowship that

existed among the people here. For their part, the Penitents
seemed to take a genuine interest in him, and he found
himself more and more feeling like one of them. Gradually
the relaxed manner of living that seemed the order of the day
here—which at first Kem found irritatingly languorous, mistaking it for laziness or lack of purpose—had its effect on him.
He found himself rising early, enjoying the salt air, the smells
of water and earth, the quality of sunlight on green leaves.
The Oasis, the Grind, the people he had known, all began to
seem inconceivably distant. He began to think about staying
here, of becoming a Penitent himself, of keeping the old
stories alive.

It was easy to imagine spending his life on this island,
among these towers, tending this verdant garden. He was
happy here. He could think of no reason to leave. He said as
much to Nuri one day, as they stood among flats of the new
season's young container stock, and he was puzzled by Nuri's
passing frown.

"What about the crying?" Kem wanted to know. "Does
anybody get the crying here? It's all over the Grind."

Nuri stood for a moment looking at Kem and then he said,
"I don't know. What is the crying?"

Which pretty well answered Kem's question. "They must
have found a cure, then," he said quietly, mostly to himself.
The thought made his heart race. "We used to hear rumors
about a cure—out there, I mean. At the Oasis. I bet they've
really found one here. They must have."

Kem had been wondering about this. He had learned
quite a few things about the Bright Land, but one thing he
had not learned was how Captain Hand plugged into it. It
was hard to figure how two such different things could fit
together. But if there really was a cure for the crying here, if
the Penitents had really found one, then that answered half
of the question—the part about what the Bright Land had
that the Captain wanted. The part that remained unanswered
was what Hand could offer the Bright Land in return.

Kem looked at Nuri and was surprised to see that the big
young man was shaking his head. He was watching Kem with

what seemed to be a tolerant, maybe even sympathetic,
smile. It made Kem feel like a stupid kid, a feeling he hated.

"What?" Kem said. "What's the matter?"

"The Penitents don't believe in cures," Nuri told him (and
Kem noted that he said *the Penitents* as opposed to, for
instance, *we*). "What they'd say is, the notion of a cure
implies that disease is a *thing*, like a machine you could
repair. But it's not, it's only an aspect. It's what they call a
fissure in the *whome*—that's from a story called *Finnegans
Wake*, it means sort of like the ground of being, the primal
body. They say that where the whome is unbroken, sickness
can't exist."

"I don't get it," said Kem, though in truth he caught the
gist of it, he just needed to think it over. "I don't think I
believe it, either. If some carrier brought the crying here,
they'd come down with it. And if they didn't find a cure,
they'd die."

Nuri shrugged. "I just told you what they believe. But
since they *do* believe it, they'd never go looking for a cure.
That just isn't how they operate."

Kem didn't quite accept this, but he didn't tell Nuri that.
He settled down to work and he thought that he really had
come to a place where anything was possible, where the most
incredible stories might turn out to be true.

One night something happened; it was not exactly a party but
it was not quite a ceremony, it seemed to be somewhere in
between them.

It was down on the island, on a sandy stretch of ground
near the water. Birds Cry Moon was on the wane and had not
yet risen when Kem and Nuri went down to join the Penitents at what looked like it was gearing up to be some kind of
big cookout. That's not what it turned out to be but Kem
didn't know that yet. Nuri had told him only that he might
want to change out of his work clothes, he might want to
wear something clean and something warmer; the breeze off
the Sea could be chilly at night. Kem changed into his old
loose-fitting linen suit, the one he had worn at the Oasis
when he wanted to make a good impression. He tried to

remember when he had worn it last. That night at the
Captain's place, out on the flying bridge? It was possible. He
had avoided socializing after that; the linen suit had laid at
the bottom of his clothes bag. He was glad now to have an
occasion to dig it out again.

There were some fires lit when he and Nuri got down from
the tower—broken branches, dried fragments of wood, other
beach debris. Under an old live oak trailing spanish moss,
very atmospheric, four or five women had gotten together
with some musical instruments that looked handmade, harps
and ceramic flutes and various forms of percussion. The music
they were playing sounded old but quite lively, somewhat
reminiscent of the music that always seemed to be playing in
Gardner's place. Kem did not like to be reminded of this but
he found that the presence of music in the air gave the
evening a lighter feeling, a definitely altered mood than there
would have been without it. Also there was the matter of the
lights.

The lighting was very strange. Besides the fires, which did
not amount to much over such a wide area, on such a dark
night, the stretch of sand was illuminated from above by
lights that someone had turned on up in one of the platforms.
Only, the platforms being as high as they were, these lights
were shining down from maybe eighty or ninety heads high—
so far up in the air that you lost the sense of the light
originating in a series of bulbs; it was as though there was this
brilliant glare that was just gushing down out of a hole in the
sky, a light that seemed distant and flat like the light of stars,
only brighter. It did not make anyone look particularly good;
it turned everything about you to black or to white, depending
on how it struck, and it made wrinkles appear to sag way
down on everyone's face. But Kem guessed it was better than
stumbling around in the dark, waiting for the moon to
come up.

He kept thinking they must be about to eat, they must be
waiting for the food to get here. But the food didn't come.
Instead some guys came down with some plants that looked
like they had been yanked right out of the dirt. As a gardener
Kem was offended by this idea, and he didn't like it either
when the guys tossed the plants just like trash onto the

brush-fires. Because the plants were green and moist they made a great deal of smoke. The wind off the Sea kept the smoke down low, blowing it into everyone's mouths and noses and eyes. It was acrid but also peculiarly sweet. After a few breaths of it Kem figured the guys must know what they were doing, the smoldering plants were like an impromptu form of incense.

The music got more vivid after that, and Kem wasn't hungry anymore.

Nuri wandered off somewhere. Kem looked a while for him, but the strange lighting, or something, made it hard to walk; he was halfway stumbling and he figured it would be better if he just sat down and waited. Everyone else was sitting down then, ranging themselves in no particular way across the sandy soil, looking basically like a bunch of people out on a picnic, passing mugs around, scratching where bugs had bitten them, nodding their heads along with the wooden blocks and chimes and a little brass gong that were laying down a pretty interesting rhythm. Kem thought he liked this music better than any he had heard before.

That's when the thing started that was not quite a ceremony. It didn't even have a beginning, exactly. There were a lot of people talking and gradually there were fewer of them and finally there was one. It was the slender woman. Kem remembered then, feeling very clearheaded tonight, that her name was Ursa. The bear. The name of something in the sky.

"So those are the two visions of immortality," she was saying, and everyone was listening because it was so easy to, Ursa had an arresting kind of presence, she spoke and her words seemed to crackle with energy. "The first vision is that of the vampire and the second is that of the alchemist. You find these visions in stories dating all the way back, as far back as we can remember, the collective *we*, I'm talking about."

Kem thought that there was something about her that was familiar to him, something not so much about Ursa herself as about the way she made you feel when she was talking, the effect her eyes had when they fell on you. It might have been Kem's imagination, but they seemed to fall on him more than on the others.

"What these visions have in common," she said, "is the idea of a kind of life essence that confers immunity to aging and to disease and to the usual kinds of bodily harm. In the case of the vampire the life essence is contained in the blood. You can imagine what *we* would have done with that."

There was laughter, moving around Kem quickly like some wave-phenomenon. The laughter died and Ursa started talking again as though they were linked, they were all part of the same collective process, which Kem was starting to find a little weird.

"What *we* would have done is, first we would have denied that this so-called life essence existed. Then we would have isolated it in the laboratory, we'd have done a bunch of analysis to determine its exact chemical nature and get its biophysical activity mapped out. We'd have developed techniques to synthesize it in large quantities. And then with our usual modesty we would have announced that this substance with life-essence-like properties had been *discovered*, only of course we would have given it a different name then. We would have slapped patents all over it and made the fruits of our labors available to anyone, in consideration of certain licensing arrangements to be discussed later. Thus we would have given new hope to all vampirekind."

Quiet laughter again, flowing and receding.

"The *vampire*," said Ursa, her voice getting serious now, "the *legendary* vampire, survives by a transfer of the life essence from one body to another. Life, for the vampire, is a long struggle with one winner and numerous losers. As a matter of fact, in most vampire stories the vampire himself is seen as a loser in the end, his own final victim, and even while he lives he's a pitiful case, a junkie, a prisoner of his own physical needs. The predator in the end becomes the prey, through his hunger he destroys the source of his own sustenance, and hence himself. I'm sure I don't have to spell out where I'm going with this. The vampire story is the archetype of *our* story. But let me come back to that."

Kem was surprised to notice that music was still playing. He would have thought it was perfectly quiet, that nobody was making a sound but the woman who was speaking, but he realized that wasn't the case, and moreover that the music had absolutely no connection with what Ursa was talking about. It was actually quite melodic and quite serene. She continued:

"In the contrasting case of the alchemist, the life essence is seen as a more subtle thing. It's called the fifth essence or *quintessence*, to distinguish it from the four gross aspects of physical matter. The alchemist survives by separating the components of the *prima materia*—which may be of plant or mineral or even animal origin—and then recombining them in a purer, more harmonious form. In this way the life-giving properties of the quintessence are tremendously amplified. From a small quantity of some common raw material, you get this vast amount of finished product. Life for the alchemist is seen as a quest rather than a struggle. There are no losers, and there can be more winners than one, for the *panacea*, if you achieve that, can be used to maintain the lives of more people than just the alchemist. So." She took a breath. "Let's see what we've got. What's the important distinction between the vampire and the alchemist?"

She looked around the way a teacher might look around at her class, but that's not exactly what the look reminded Kem of. What he thought of was the way Captain Hand would look at you after asking one of his questions, the kind he knew perfectly well you were not going to be able to answer. Ursa delivered very much the same look with very much the same degree of confidence, the same rhetorical flourish. Then, just as the Captain would have done, she answered the question herself.

"The vampire is a creature of the physical world alone. He's driven by the needs of the physical body. Whereas the alchemist is a creature of both body and mind—or, if you will, body and spirit. He lives by the power of transcendence while the vampire dies for lack of it. Of course there's more to be said than this. Both stories are long and they both hold a lot of enduring fascination. A final point, though. It is the belief of the Penitents that the great error of the past—*our* great error—consisted of adhering to the vampiric model and not the alchemical. Like the vampire, we became obsessed with that which is gross and physical. Our various disciplines, our whole tradition really, came to be synonymous with the study of physical things, things that can be measured and quantified. Life came to be a struggle, maintained by the transfer of physical substances which we required in ever greater quantity. There were a lot of losers in our long fight to survive—the species that died off one by one, the dirt that once covered the Grind, the snow that used to fall during Tall Skies Moon. But the final loser has been ourselves. I trust that this point does not need to be belabored."

She had finished; even before she turned away and sat down Kem could tell that she was through talking. He could tell because something changed about her, something went out of her eyes.

After that the night rolled on as other nights did. People started to talk again and they started to wander around. A mug arrived in Kem's hand and he drank from it. It was not for a few seconds that he realized that the person who had handed him the mug was Nuri.

Nuri looked at Kem with an unspoken question in his eye. It was probably a telling thing about their relationship, whatever exactly that was, and Kem did not feel any need to hear Nuri's question spoken aloud, just as probably most of Kem's own questions could have been left unarticulated and Nuri would have known exactly what they were.

"I don't know," said Kem. "I'm not sure I get where these Penitents are coming from. They were vampires before and now they're alchemists, is that it?"

Nuri shook his head. He took the mug back and drank from it. Whatever it contained was sweet and thick. Kem figured it would have to pass for dinner.

"Well, what then?" he said. "Neither one?"

"No," said Nuri. "Both."

It was late or it was early. Birds Cry Moon was finally up, it floated in the sky above Kem's shoulder and the narrow blades of the reeds at the edge of the water seemed to bathe in it, to twist languidly in its cool wet light. The ground made sucking noises beneath his feet. Kem had not gone back to the berthing space despite how late or how early it was; he was restless and he was walking beside the water.

A year ago he had walked beside the water, too. A year ago, during Birds Cry Moon, he had walked along the sloping bed of Tuttle Creek, up north in Riley County. He had been alone for a while, then later—about this time of night, he guessed—he had found someone to talk to. He had talked to the skinny girl and her brother while they waited for the sun to come blazing off the water, waited for someone in a little boat to come and carry them away.

Kem wasn't sure why he was thinking about this. The memory was a form of self-inflicted torture, and generally he had learned to push it away, at least to not dwell on it. Tonight—maybe it was the coincidence of dates, the hour of night, the water—he found the memory bursting into his awareness, the look that had been on the girl's face, those eyes so big and unblinking, world-wise and -weary beyond anything that was reasonable for her age.

And Kem thought, She trusted me. The poor skinny kid and her brother, they both had put their faith in him. Kem had told them it would be okay and they had believed it. Why not? He had believed it himself, in a way. In another way he had not, though, and that was the problem.

Never forget. That's what Ursa had said. And something else: *We take full responsibility.* Kem supposed it was time he took responsibility, himself, for the things he had done.

What had he done, though? He didn't know for sure; there was no way to be sure what had happened to those kids, what kind of fate he had delivered them to. Maybe they were just fine. Maybe . . .

While Kem stood there, remembering, arguing with himself, he had been twiddling with something in his pocket. At last he became conscious of it: a small object, round, something his fingers seemed to recognize. He pulled it out and held it up in the moonlight.

It was a little wooden ring. It was the ring he had picked up from the flying bridge, the night Hand rode out on his stallion. The last time he wore this set of clothes. The ring had been half-buried in a wooden planter, his fingers had scraped against it, grabbed it just to have something to hold on to. As he stared at it now, the ring seemed to tingle

electrically in his fingers; he almost feared to hold it, though
he did not understand why. Not right away.

Bit by bit things came back to him. He thought of that
other night, the night of standing by Tuttle Creek, talking,
waiting. The two kids had gotten bored after a while and they
had started playing a childish sort of game, a game played
with wooden counters. Kem had watched them though he
had not known what game it was they were playing: two
colors, light and dark, seemed to war against one another.
Kem could not remember which color had won. Now he was
staring with something like horror at the little wooden ring in
his hand. A dark one: black as blood in the moonlight.

He wondered how the ring had found its way to the flying
bridge, to the Captain's private garden. He wondered what
hand, what small-boned fingers it had fallen out of.

He tried to stop wondering, to stop remembering, but he
could not. The memories flowed out of him like water, like
tears. He remembered the days and weeks after the Oasis
had left Riley County—the run up into the Carbon Bank
Forest, a party he had not attended at the Captain's place,
some kind of annual event, a ritual. He remembered Sander,
so terribly ill afterward. *They missed you at the party*, Sander
had said, and someone else had said the same thing later. He
remembered the trip to the old farmstead, the murder of
Tallheron, the other murder he had committed himself. He
remembered the Bell Dog. And he remembered, finally, the
trip back to the Oasis, and how he had seen the desert eagles
or caracaras, carrion eaters, in the sky,

flying in circles through the air
above the tower.

FROGS RETURN

The Bright Land exploded with life, with potency. Eggs hatched. Trees rained pollen. Flowerheads swelled on grass stalks to be stroked off by the air. It was summer. It was Frogs Return Moon. It was time for Kem to make up his mind.

This is the way he figured it. He figured that the Penitents were a bunch of eccentric but basically well-intentioned folks, doctors or something of that kind, and that they'd discovered a cure for the crying. Captain Hand had gotten wind of this and he'd struck a deal with them. Kem hadn't quite worked out exactly how the deal went, but he was still thinking about it. Naturally a cure for the crying would be worth a lot, it would be worth just about any price you could name, at least from the standpoint of someone who would have died without it.

But the problem was, the way Kem looked at it, Hand wouldn't have wanted to just go out and proclaim that he had this medicine, this pill or potion or whatever it was. Because people would wonder where the medicine came from. They'd start snooping around themselves, and eventually someone would hear some gossip, they'd meet somebody who knew somebody who had once been to the Bright Land, where there was no crying, where there were these bunch of doctors or researchers or whatever they were, and the next thing you knew, Hand would have lost his corner on the market. So he had to find a way to prevent that, a sure-fire way to make himself look like the sole possessor of the secret. He had to keep himself at the center of things, the heart of the maze.

But Hand had found a way, and Kem thought he knew what it was. At least in its broad outlines. It was an idea that had come from an old story, a folktale: the story of the Remedy, the only true medicine, the cure that worked when all others failed. Naturally the story was a horrible one— that's what made it so irresistible. And that's also what made it such an effective cover. You thought about how awful it was, and you didn't even consider that maybe the truth was more awful yet. So Hand had borrowed this story and he had made himself its principal character; he had made a name for himself, cultivated a particular kind of reputation—for brilliance, for mystery, for ruthlessness—because all of those things figured into the legend, they were necessary to make people believe that the horrible story of the Remedy, the only true Remedy, a thing that you had to kill to obtain, was really true.

There was another thing, also—an idea that Kem had had in his head for a while, since the night on the beach. That night seemed to have marked a kind of initiation for him; ever since, he had been treated more and more like a member of the order, a true Penitent. But the thing was, now he was no longer sure he wanted that. His theory about the Captain, with all the lines of thought that led up to it, had given him certain doubts, not about the Captain—he didn't think there was much doubt left there—but about the Penitents themselves.

One day he cornered Nuri, meaning to get some of his doubts resolved. It was early afternoon and they had been working down on the island, clearing out some space for a plot of maize and burdock and sunflower, a triculture plot. Like much of what the Penitents did, this was part of an ongoing project, generations old. The seedlings had been grown in pots up in the tower, but now it was time to plant them out in what the Penitents liked to call the "real world." Kem was inclined to think that nothing in the Bright Land resembled the *real* real world—the world of drought and sickness and deprivation and misery of every imaginable kind. But he supposed the island, where at least there were snakes and bugs and you could get a good case of heat stroke, came closer than the towers, with their boundless clean space and piped-in music and sweet-smelling Sea-cooled air. He and Nuri had been working since sunrise; it was slow work, much stooping and digging in the hot sun. Now they were taking a break.

Kem worded his question carefully, like someone choosing just the proper arrow, threading it into the bow.

"Did you know Captain Hand?" he said. "I mean, when he used to live here?"

This was just a theory, of course. But Kem figured it was the only thing that made sense. Otherwise it was hard to account for how Hand could have worked out such a cozy arrangement. And it was hard to account for certain other things, like the strange quality that Hand shared in common with Ursa, that peculiar energy that seemed to pour from their eyes.

Nuri was a sharp one. Kem had reached this conclusion and he thought you really had to hand it to him: he was very good at keeping his ears open and his mouth shut, a talent that Kem tried with little success to emulate. Now Nuri gave Kem the sort of look a parent might give a bright but particularly irksome child. He took a long sip of his tea and rubbed some pennyroyal lotion down one big arm, a feeble deterrent to mosquitoes. About the time Kem was giving up, threading another question into the bow, Nuri said:

"That was a long time ago."

Aha, thought Kem. The knowledge that he had guessed right, that he was really on the right track, ran through him like electricity. He struggled (and probably failed) to keep his excitement inside. "How long?" he said.

Nuri shrugged.

And that was going to be that, Kem figured. Well, at least it was something.

Then out of nowhere Nuri said, "They told me you would ask about him. About Hand. They told me to let them know, when you did."

"What?" Kem felt the electricity shift into a different channel, changing polarities. "Who did?"

But *who* was not really what he wanted to know. *They* was enough for him. He had always known there was a *they;* he had always been paranoid in that respect, as Davina had pointed out to him. Now he had a pretty good idea who *they* were, exactly. No, he didn't need to know more about that; it was something else.

"They figured you'd get around to it," Nuri said. "Sooner or later. They know you came from there. From the Oasis. I think Hand might have told them himself, a while ago—last year, maybe—that you were coming."

Great, thought Kem. First the Bell Dog and now the Captain. Everybody seemed to be able to read my future; everybody but me.

He said, "I don't get it."

"Yes you do," said Nuri. "Don't you? Where do you think the Penitents come from? What do you think brought them here? They came out of curiosity. Because like you said, this is where the stories come from. The Penitents wanted to know what the stories mean, how the stories end. They have this need, it's like an obsession or something. They need to figure things out." He looked hard right into Kem's eyes and he added, "Just like you."

Just like me, thought Kem. *You are curious,* the Captain had said to him. *We noticed that right away.*

"What about you?" Kem said. "Is that why you came here?"

Nuri shook his head. He said, "I was born here"—and paused, as though about to say more, to further explain himself, but he did not.

This was more than Kem had hoped for. "So you did know Hand?" he said. He was trying to fit the last few pieces in place. "You remember him?"

"I was too young," said Nuri. "But I heard about him. Everybody talked about him. He was very famous."

"Famous how? For stealing the cure, the Remedy?" —This might have been going too far, tipping his hand; but Kem figured he had gotten Nuri talking and there was no use holding back.

Nuri frowned. "You're wrong about all that stuff. I've told you that."

"You haven't been to the Oasis. You don't know what he's doing. If you knew—if *they* knew—you guys would never let him come back here. He comes here every year and he picks up a supply of the stuff, the medicine, whatever it is, and then he goes back out there and you guys have no idea what he's doing, how he operates."

Nuri shook his head. Clearly he disbelieved this. Kem supposed that growing up in this place, where nothing really awful ever happened, and hearing these stories all the time, you would have a peculiar idea about things, a sort of innocence.

"I don't know Hand," Nuri said. "You're right. But maybe you don't know everything about him either. Maybe you shouldn't condemn him so fast. That's what the Penitents would say. We're all guilty, is what they would say. We all have to share the blame for everything that's happened."

"Yeah, well," said Kem, exasperated, "but that's the Penitents. They say this stuff, *we take responsibility* and so forth, and that's cool. It's cool. I understand that. But Hand . . . he's not a Penitent. Not anymore. He really *is* responsible. He *is* doing bad things. It's not the same."

Nuri said, "You're wrong," looking away from him.

"You don't know. I'm telling you, I've been there. I've seen it. I've even—"

"I mean about Hand not being a Penitent. He is a Penitent. That's why he comes here. That's why they let him come. Don't you get it? He's still one of them. He's got his work to do, just like everyone else."

"Yeah, I bet he does." Kem felt somewhat bitter. Here he was practically spilling his guts—he had been about to confess his most terrible secret, right out loud—and Nuri was going on about how he had the Captain figured all wrong.

The Captain was just a regular guy. He's just doing his job. Like hell, Kem thought. "So what *is* Hand's job, then?"

Nuri gave him a slanty-eyed stare, as though sizing him up, deciding whether Kem was worth talking to any further. Then he seemed to figure why not, they had gone this far, and he said:

"The Great Work. That's what they call it."

Despite himself Kem was intrigued by the sound of this. He said, "What's that?"

"I don't know."

Kem felt a certain sense of vindication. "See? That's what I . . ."

Nuri shut him up with a hard look. "I don't know all of it," he said. "But I know some. Have you been to the Barrens?"

Kem nodded.

"So you've seen it? All those trees? Well—how do you think the trees got there? Where do you think they came from?"

That was easy enough. "From here," said Kem.

Nuri waved around them, at the rows of tiny plants. "From this work we're doing now. They call this the Little Work, the work that goes on here on the island. Breeding new plants, special plants, that's part of it. The Great Work is what goes on out there."

Kem followed his eyes across the unimaginable distance from here to the mainland, the Grind, the Carbon Bank Forest.

"So that's the deal," he said.

Nuri raised an eyebrow.

"That's the part I hadn't figured out," Kem told him. "I had it all figured but that. What Hand had to offer. What he's got that the Penitents want." He ran it quickly through his mind, and the way he looked at it, it all added up. Or rather it all canceled out: it added up to zero. Hand came here each year and picked up the Remedy, and at the same time he picked up a new stock of special seedlings, which he then propagated himself up on the flying bridge and distributed along the path of the Oasis. It was all part of some bargain the Penitents had struck—not just with Hand but with themselves, with their own sense of responsibility. They had taken the blame for all that was wrong with the world; now they were trying to make it better. Hand was their Johnny Appleseed. And either they didn't know or they didn't care what he was doing with their Remedy. That wasn't part of the bargain.

"So," said Kem, reflecting on this, feeling a certain degree of disgust but also a certain satisfaction. "You guys are so anxious to get your plants spread around, you're willing to do business with a murderer."

Nuri looked hurt, which was not exactly what Kem had expected. He had expected maybe anger, but not this. Nuri gave him a wounded look for a second or so and then he said, "A murderer? That's impossible."

"Sure it's possible. It's true."

Nuri shook his head with vehemence. "Hand isn't a murderer. He can't be. He's a healer."

"Ha," said Kem, bitterly.

"No, really. That's why he's so famous. That's why people tell stories about him." Nuri squinted his eyes, as though remembering all the stories he had heard, as though seeing them played out in his mind. With distinct fervor he said, "Hand was the greatest healer of all."

They told him he could come back whenever he wanted. They all stood along the shoreline, seeing him off, and they told him he would be welcome back, that he was a Penitent now.

"You are like us," Ursa told him, flashing those eyes, "because you came here for the same reasons that the rest of us did. You wanted to know. You needed to see. And now you've seen." She paused, and then for effect or perhaps because she really meant it she added, "I hope you'll come back."

Kem nodded. He hoped to see her again too. He wished Davina had been a little more like her: serene, self-contained, at ease with who she was. But he supposed that in her own way, Davina had been more like Kem. She had not known who she was or who she wanted to be. She had always been looking for something else; always trying to add one more bit to her store of knowledge. As long as she still retained a scrap of innocence, she had been—just as Kem had been—determined to throw it away.

Kem felt guilty, thinking along these lines. But feeling guilty was what this Penitent thing was all about, right?

"Yeah, thanks," he said. "Well, good-bye, I guess."

He lifted one foot onto the gunwale of the sailboat they had given him. Or was it only a loan? It was a boat he and Nuri had used, now and then—easy to steer, hard to capsize, all important considerations where Kem was concerned. It had a small engine, too, but Kem had some doubts as to how far that would get him, where he was going.

"I'll take good care of it," he told Nuri.

Nuri was standing off to the side. Kem wondered how Nuri felt about all this. Not just Kem's departure: Kem would probably be kidding himself to think that that mattered very much. But all this talk about Kem being a Penitent now; Kem having gotten here the way everybody else did. Because everybody hadn't gotten here that way. Nuri hadn't. He had been born here. What did that make him—a Penitent or not? Or something else? Nuri had always spoken of the Penitents as *them,* always careful to draw some fine distinction. Kem guessed now he would never know quite what the nature of that distinction was. He swung his other foot over the gunwale and stepped down into the boat. It rocked under his weight, sliding away from the pier.

"Here," said Nuri. He stepped forward and tossed Kem his pack, his modest supply of clothing. "You forgot this."

"Hey, thanks, yeah." Kem stuffed the pack down under one of the seats. It seemed a little heavier than he remembered.

"I put in some food," said Nuri.

"Ah." Kem glanced back; the faces were getting smaller. He waved. "Well, thanks, everybody. Be seeing you."

He turned the motor on, to get clear of the island. For some reason he was distinctly aware of Ursa's eyes on him, watching him go. He tried to avoid looking back at her, but in the end the eyes were too much. They yanked his head around.

Ursa was not waving. She was not doing anything in particular. You would scarcely have known she was paying attention. But of course she was. She was, like, presiding over all of this. It was something Kem recognized very clearly, from somewhere.

Then, one last time, from twenty strides out or so, those eyes fell upon him, and they seemed to contain a message, an important message just for Kem. And the message was—

Kem didn't know. He didn't know what he was doing, where he was going, what he hoped to accomplish when he got there.

Or so he thought. But maybe that wasn't true. Maybe on some deeper level he did know. Maybe he knew exactly what he was doing; maybe he could have plotted a course to his destination on a navigation chart. Maybe his whole life was mapped out in his mind—at least the next few weeks of it, which might be all that was left—and furthermore, maybe it had always been that way.

Maybe from the very first time he had seen the Oasis, looming across the Grind, back when he was a little kid, he had known somehow that he would go there, he would go on board and he would climb to the very top of the tallest tower. And when he had first glimpsed the Bright Land, floating like a cloud, like a dream across the water—or even before that, when he had just *heard* about the Bright Land, sitting around the cookfire one night listening to his old man, or somebody, tell a story—maybe way back then he had known, he had begun making plans. Maybe everything he had done and everything he was going to do was something he had been planning all along, his whole life.

Or maybe not.

Kem still doubted it; he still doubted that the future was that much under his control; there seemed to be too many factors, too many other people, too many wills stronger than his own.

This thought led him back to Ursa, and somehow it also led him further back, all the way to Captain Hand. Then the past flipped over and became the future, the dark realm which may or may not be knowable, and finally both past and future collapsed into the present: a mixed-up kid in a sailboat who hadn't eaten anything since dinner the night before.

Kem reached down under the seat, wondering what kind of food Nuri had packed for him. He pulled out the pack, untied its drawstrings. And maybe, if he knew all that other stuff, he should have known already what he was going to find.

Maybe he should have known from the look on Nuri's face, or rather the lack of any particular look, the quietness of manner, the absence of expression. Maybe he should have known from the way Nuri said *they* instead of *we*. But Kem had not known; he was totally surprised and then he felt the beginning of some other feeling, a thing he also should have anticipated. He lowered the pack to the deck of the sailboat, and now at least he knew a couple of things that maybe he should have known a long time ago, including why the pack had been so heavy: quaking in his hand like something alive, gleaming dully, was a small and black and dangerous-looking gun.

The Gut lay open like a gigantic bleeding wound. Only what was coming out of it was not blood; it was the precious soil of the Grind, what was left of it—flushed away by spring storms and then dumped into the swollen river, which was stained rust red with it. Kem supposed the process had been going on for quite some time, because all the way up from the Bright Land he had sailed between islands that looked suspiciously like river waste: they were scarcely higher than the waterline and they seemed to be composed at least partly of debris, rotting tree trunks, sticks of lumber, sheets of plastic, bottles, bloated and discolored objects that could have been anything—all the stuff that the Gut had swallowed and digested and excreted over the years.

You would not have thought it would be a pretty sight, and yet it was. The marshy islands were like tiny paradises, havens for egrets and wild irises, plume poppies, blue herons, swamp orchids, sea turtles, orchids, sweetgrass, alligators—things Kem had never seen except in picture books, and other things he had never seen at all. He was tempted to draw the journey out, to spend a day or two meandering through those islands, a world of flowers rising from the effluence of the Gut, but he was in sort of a hurry and besides, the whole thing was too laden with symbolism for his taste. The bottom of the Gut was like the end of a story whose moral is a bit too obvious, so heavy-handed that even if you agree with it you walk away feeling dissatisfied, you think the story should have ended another way. Kem felt dissatisfied in that way now. He was eager to make his way up the Gut, back up to where the raw stuff of these islands had come from. He wanted to get back to a place or a time from which this ending did not seem to be so inevitable, so foreordained.

As soon as his boat entered the river he got a sense of what kind of journey it was going to be. The Gut was wide here, vastly wide, you would not have known it was a river, that the two banks a couple of kills or more apart were not just other islands, slightly larger than most; except that on those banks you could see the first signs of human presence. While the islands, despite being basically shit-piles, were serene and beautiful places, the river banks were just filthy; they were stripped down to the bare soil and planted in furrows with struggling crops, grazed to the ground and churned to mud and offal by livestock, adorned with stick shanties and patchwork lean-tos and collapsing barns and topless silos and all the other doomed and half-rotten but curiously imperishable works of humankind. It was a fascinating spectacle. It was hard for Kem to believe, as he sailed up the river, tacking diagonally across the current, running up close to one bank and then another, that there were so many people left alive, that so many people managed to survive here despite the obvious hardships, despite the fact that the Gut was prone to flood and the soil to wash away, disease was everywhere, gangs of outlaws roamed the land, kids were stolen and sold, crops failed, insects devoured the harvest, summer was unbearable—and yet despite all that, people lived. They had more kids. The kids grew up with big ideas, crazy hopes, ridiculous notions of what the world might hold for them. And then when they found out what the world really held it usually turned out to be just having *more* kids, making a mess of your life, building yourself a wagon or a shanty or a stupid tent which the first storm would turn to a pile of trash, then falling dead of the crying before your kids were old enough to put their own clothes on. Kem looked at the banks of the Gut and that's what he saw there. That's what he thought about, and he wondered why the fuck anybody even bothered. Why should you struggle to stay alive if that's all life had in store for you?

Then he heard a popping noise, once, twice, three times, and he realized like someone waking from a dream that he was being shot at. Some guy over on the shore was firing a gun at him—lazy shots, several seconds between them, as though it were all the same whether he hit Kem or his boat or missed them, it really didn't matter. But it mattered pretty much to Kem. Before he even had a chance to think about it he had the little gun in his hand, the one Nuri had given him, and although he had never even held much less fired a gun before, he found himself squeezing the trigger, once, twice, three times, and he thought, Take that, you fucker. Then he threw the tiller over and he got the hell away from there.

And after that—in the evening, as the merciless sun was going down, and he was trying to figure out how he could keep sailing all night, how he could avoid having to haul in anywhere along these dangerous riverbanks—Kem thought he had discovered something, the answer to why people even bothered to stay alive. Not that he had really been confused about that. He had just never thought about it before.

You stayed alive, the way he figured it, because you couldn't bear the thought that fuckers like that would outlive you. You stayed alive because it sometimes seemed that you might have gotten a glimpse, once or twice, of something other than this, something besides the mud and the broken-down shacks and the dying children. You stayed alive because at any given moment you felt like there was just one last thing you needed to do, one more place you needed to go, one person you wanted to say good-bye to. You stayed alive because you wanted to hear the end of the story.

He sailed for how long—a week? Longer than that? It must have been longer; the scenery changed and the air felt a little cooler at night, and gradually Kem felt less afraid, less convinced that if he stopped, if he dared to close his eyes, he was going to be killed. He found that the river was shallow enough in places that you could just drop anchor, or throw a line around the ghostly pale trunk of a drowned cottonwood. From time to time he even passed a fellow river-traveler, someone like himself in a small boat or a whole family in a large one, or now and then a bigger operation still, a barge loaded with timber or sacks of grain or something bulky covered with tarps, guys standing fore and aft with high-powered firearms which they waved at Kem, who waved back at them. There was a certain wary camaraderie among the river people that after a while he came to appreciate: you had enough in common to be out here, plying the waters, but you were not willing to concede any more than that. It was as close a thing as Kem had ever encountered to perfectly reciprocal respect.

Then he came to a region that looked strangely familiar. Or not quite that—a part of the world where he knew he had been before, because he recognized certain unmistakable landmarks, crumbled monuments, old buildings still essentially intact where he had come with his family, where he had gone to winter school; but everything looked completely different now. He had never seen the world from this side, from the water looking inward, though he had stood many times on the *other* side, staring out at the Gut and the opposite bank, wondering where the water was going and what kind of world there was there. He knew so much now. He had this insane wish, a desire he understood fully well was impossible to go ashore and hunt down his younger self, the long-gone innocent Kem, and tell him about all the things he'd learned, the wonders he had seen, the strange and incredible places he had been to. But that was crazy. Time only went one way and you couldn't sail upstream on *that* river.

Two days beyond the last of the crumbled cities, at a trading post planted on stilts, sticking out over the river, he sold the sailboat.

The negotiation was quick, the deal seemed almost fair, or least fair enough for Kem's purposes. He came out of it with a

pocketful of money, some of which he spent right away for
new clothing, the kind of stuff wagon kids wore, and for food
and a compass and a map and a larger pack to carry it all in.
Then he left the trading post and set out across the Grind. It
was getting pretty late in the season to be traveling on foot,
but Kem figured he was young and had a right to be foolish
now and then; and besides, he didn't have very far to go now,
and on foot was the way he wanted to arrive there.

At Riley County, they didn't blink. They took one look at
Kem and their eyes seemed to say, Another one. Another kid
from off the wagons. Where do they all come from, those
eyes wondered.

"Here is a list," said the smiling officious woman. "Here is
a list of places you can go, places where you can obtain
clothing and shelter. And here is where a school is located. If
you are under eighteen, you are entitled to free schooling.
But I don't suppose you are, are you?"

"Yes, I am," said Kem. "I'm only seventeen."

The woman looked at him with the same smile. She did
not believe him, but only her eyes said that. The smile was
the same as Kem remembered though it seemed to have
grown more wistful, more worn-out. She had been smiling
too long; she had smiled at too many kids, too many thirteen-
year-olds who looked twenty and seventeen-year-olds who
smiled back at her like the toothy grinning head of Death.

"Well, good luck," she told Kem anyway. "I hope you will
find a home here."

But her eyes said that she knew that he would not.

Which was cool. Which was exactly how Kem wanted it. He
wanted to blend into the twilit gray fringes of this place, just
like the other kids who came drifting in every day off the
Grind. He wanted to find a nice quiet shelter and a clean bed
and get a good night's sleep, the first night's sleep he had
gotten in a long time, almost two years, that was not haunted
by thoughts of having been singled out for some uniquely
horrible fate; the first night in all that time during which he

could lie there knowing he was just like everybody else, he was just a kid without a home and without a destination.

At the shelter, in his nice clean bed, he lay awake most of the night. Then he slept fitfully, shaken by weird dreams, dreams in which blue eyes cut through him like knives, without pain, laying his heart open so that he could see inside it.

"Horses?" the guy said. He looked at Kem as though Kem had just offered to tell him the secret of the universe: like, What, a kid like you?

"That's right," said Kem. "I want to buy some horses."

"You want to buy some horses."

Kem just stood there. He knew what he looked like and he could imagine what the guy was thinking. But he didn't feel like flashing around his wad of money; that would have made it too easy, and he was somewhat enjoying the way things were playing out. The guy looked him over from top to bottom and then you could see his brain click over; he was deciding to humor the kid, to play along.

"All right," he said. "How many horses would you like?"

Kem had an answer for that, and it was the last answer he had. It was as far as he had gone either in his mind or in any other place, his heart, his map, his money-pocket.

The answer was, "Four."

"Four?" said the guy. His eyebrows went up; he was curious despite himself. "Four horses? What's a kid like you want with four horses?"

"I don't want anything," said Kem, which was actually almost true. "I just need four horses, all right?"

The guy seemed to be enjoying this. It was a slow day, the middle of a long slow summer. He opened his arms, expansive like. "Well, now that's going to cost you a bit of money."

"How much?"

"How much," the guy winked at Kem, "are you prepared to pay?"

"Let's see the horses first."

The guy led Kem swaggering back into the stables, past the younger and sounder animals up near the front, back to the lame and the ailing and the rheumy-eyed old beasts cooped up two to a stall in the rear, standing in their own manure. They looked dolefully at Kem and he looked back at them with the closest thing to genuine sadness he had felt since . . . well, for a while now. Then he looked at the beaming horse trader.

"Now here are some fine mounts for you," the guy was saying. "Here are some horses that will do you proud."

Kem thought for a moment of reaching down into his pack and whipping out the black pistol; he imagined waving it at the guy, imagined the oily little eyes bulging with fright out of the guy's skull. The guy deserved that, Kem thought. The guy deserved to be robbed, just for treating helpless animals this way.

Then another thought came to him. His lip curled up, ironically; he had a change of heart.

"They look fine," he said. "How much do you want for them?"

He paid the guy half of what he was asking, and in a little while he was leading four old horses out to freedom, out for a last wild ride.

They rode for days, Kem and the horses. As far as he knew the horses had no names. He had not asked about their names, and maybe the guy wouldn't even have known. Kem assigned provisional names to them, but only in his mind. They were names he did not want to say out loud. To speak them aloud would be to divulge a secret he was keeping from himself.

Kem hoped it hadn't been a mistake. Of course, this whole farfetched and hopeless enterprise was surely a mistake, but he hoped buying these horses hadn't been. The old animals needed to rest pretty frequently, and even between rest stops they did not make very good time, and Kem had been running late to begin with. Frogs Return Moon was near the end of its wane; soon it would be Ripe Berries. The Oasis had left Riley County a couple of weeks ahead of Kem—some kids at the shelter had told him that.

It was funny, he thought. How easy it had been. But Riley

County had been easy the year before, too, and Kem figured it was because he had found the perfect disguise. He looked exactly like a real kid.

The horses and Kem rode as fast as they could, given their ages and the burdens they carried, north through the upper reaches of the Grind, across the frontier, into the Barrens, the Carbon Bank Forest.

Kem remembered how last year the trees had seemed to comfort him, to make him feel safe, and he saw that this year was not going to be like that. This year he felt more anxious than ever as the dense foliage swallowed the horizon, taking away from him all sense of motion, of progress. If not for the compass, he wouldn't have known which way he was heading. If not for the map—a crude thing, compared to the detailed charts on the navigation deck—he wouldn't have had any idea where his destination lay.

Last year he had looked down at the forest from twenty-seven heads high. This year he rode in fear that he might accidentally stumble out into the open and someone twenty-seven heads high—or higher, someone with a two-scope optical device—would see him coming.

But what then? What did he have to worry about, really? He was just a lost kid. He was just a runaway, making his way back home.

Then he caught up with the Oasis.

It did not exactly happen without warning. A day before, one of the old horses had blundered out of the forest and into the broad swath of flattened-out woodland that the Oasis had left in its wake. The horse had gotten spooked, starting making a lot of noise, and Kem had pulled the gun out and gone to investigate. He was afraid the poor animal had run afoul of a bear or something, or stumbled and broken a leg, but when he saw what the horse had found he felt about the same way the horse did.

It was a pretty horrible sight. It looked like a road cut through the woods by some diabolic power. And in fact, as Kem reflected, that's more or less exactly what it was. He had to do a bit of coaxing to get the horses to follow this

frightening trail; but they were good animals. In the end,
they did what he told them.

Ah well, he thought. Another trust betrayed.

They rode up the wide and frightening path for almost two
days. Near sunset on the second day Kem spotted a dark gray
tower far ahead. he decided to play it safe, for once. He led
the horses into the woods. Then he climbed a tree to get a
better vantage.

The Oasis had stopped. He was pretty sure of that, though
it was far away and its sun wings were still retracted. Kem
watched it for several minutes and he did not see any
movement. No sounds of crashing trees or grinding engines
came over the distance. The only sounds he heard were birds
and the whir of wind, and the only thing that moved was the
sun going down.

When he got back to the horses, he realized that he had
forgotten to buy any rope to tie them up with. Well, he
would just have to make do. He and the horses would have to
come to an understanding.

"Now listen, guys," he said. "I'm going to leave you here,
okay? So you've got to stay put and wait for me. All right?
Understand? I'll only be a couple of hours. I hope so,
anyway."

He might have felt foolish under other circumstances,
talking to a bunch of dumb animals. But under these particular circumstances, with the sun going down on what might
turn out to be the last day of his life, a brisk wind whipping
up, owls hooting like they knew something Kem didn't, the
sound of his own voice was pretty welcome. It was about the
only safe and comfortable thing left to him.

"You'll be okay," he told the horses. He wished the horses
would tell him the same thing back. "Just wait here until
tomorrow morning. If I'm not back . . . well, what the fuck.
That's the end of the story, I guess. You guys can probably get
along okay without me."

Which was probably, he figured, sad but true.

He waited a couple of hours; waited until the sun was good
and down and the night was as dark as it was going to get. It

seemed like about a month had gone by. Kem figured that was long enough.

He walked out into the middle of the wasted strip of forest. He could see lights ahead, where the Oasis squatted in the path of its own devastation. He could see stars too, big and bright overhead, and that was about all he could see. There was no moon, so he couldn't tell which part of the cycle it was—the end of Frogs Return or the beginning of Ripe Berries. If it was not Ripe Berries yet, he might have gotten here in time. Not that it was going to matter, probably. Except of course to Kem.

The last thing he did was change his clothes. He dropped his old snipe's uniform onto the ground, where it was immediately invisible, midnight blue against the black of the soil, the deep green of crushed leaves, the brown of limbs still bleeding sap. He held up the shirt and pants of unbleached, loose-fitting linen. They glowed spectrally in the dark. As he slipped them on he checked for his various talismans: the little wooden ring in one pocket, the black pistol in another. Then he took the silver tuning rod and tucked it under his belt.

He felt like an outlaw. He felt like a ghost. He felt like a lost and frightened kid.

The Oasis lay at the end of the road. Or to put it another way, the road ended—as Kem had known it would, always—at the Oasis.

He slipped around to the small side hatchway, the one used by the snipes, the one where the light was always out. That was easy.

It was a little harder to actually open that door and it was harder still to take the couple of steps necessary to climb up and through it.

Kem stood alone in a narrow hallway, deep in the engine flats. He could not see very well, but he felt acutely the presence of great bodies of metal, engines lying restively in their hollows until the hour, not long off now, when they would be summoned back to life. The air was full of the smell of burnt oil, electricity, the muted throb of a backup genera-

tor, the clunk of distant footsteps. Through his legs Kem felt
the flywheels, aimlessly spinning, their wasted energy trembling up his spine as though it belonged there; as though the
ungovernable quaking was Kem's own; as though he and the
Oasis had been separated unnaturally but now they were
rejoined.

Nothing had changed. It felt to Kem as though no time at
all had passed, or very little: a single turn of the wheel.
Walking down the dark narrow hall was surprisingly easy,
effortless, a swim through an element that welcomed him.
His feet knew the way. He merely followed them. He forgot
with most of his mind that he was in danger, that he was in
dread, that he was almost done with the part of the journey
that maps could be drawn to. A few more steps, a few more,
and he was in uncharted territory.

He entered the steering box. He remembered when the
place had seemed immense to him—four or five heads high,
as wide as the Oasis—but that was before he had seen the
Bright Land. Now he moved quickly to the middle of the
space, ducking under the cables out of unthinking bodily
habit. There was nothing furtive in his actions; he moved
with a sense of purpose, of inevitability, of convergence.

The steering box had the peculiar stillness of motion in
abeyance, its machinery turned on but not in operation, its
cables locked into place under extreme tension. High overhead, the wide mouth of the shaft opened to darkness. At its
center, near the top, there was a faint dimensionless glow,
like the eerie luster of moonlight. But tonight, if Kem had
figured it right, there would be no moon. Tonight was the
space between one moon and the next, the breath between
seasons. Yesterday the crops were still being tended; at dawn
tomorrow the harvest would begin. Tonight was a time of
transition, an end of waiting. Everything, Kem thought,
staring upward, is going to come down to tonight.

And he pulled out the Bell Dog's tuning rod. It flashed in
the darkness. He brought it down like a tiny sword, striking
it sharply against a metal engine casing; then he raised it
toward the opening above him. The chime resonated for
several seconds, more, half a minute, slowly fading to silence.

For a full minute Kem heard nothing at all—then the

gratifying crescendo of an unseen servomotor running overhead. A shadow began to drop. It was a basket. Kem climbed
in. He jiggled the cable. The basket began to climb again.

That's it, Kem thought. From now on everything is new,
everything is made-up.

The basket kept on forever, higher and higher, passing the
catwalk where Kem and the Bell Dog had stopped before,
the deck where Girl's Berthing was, where he had met
Davina. It climbed past several decks more; then at last it
stopped at a narrow landing, not much bigger than a catwalk.
From there a ladder led up, straight up, into the yellowish
puddle that was like moonlight, but it could not have been
moonlight. From here you could see the shape of the end of
the shaft, a hole leading out that was perfectly round.

Kem gripped the ladder, swung his weight onto it. The
basket bounced crazily, then its motor engaged and it began
to descend again. Startled, Kem almost lost his balance; the
great abyss opened under his feet; he felt as though gravity
were sucking at him, the earth trying to reclaim him. He
squeezed his eyes shut, took a deep breath. Then he forced
himself to look upward.

There was a sound from there. Kem could barely hear it; it
was so subtle that it was less noise than pure feeling: a
rhythm, a rising and falling of voices. As he looked up he
thought he saw the light change slightly, as though a shadow
had moved across it. But the change came again; the light
was flickering. Kem took a step up the ladder. One more, one
more.

A hatch swung open beside him.

He barely registered dark eyes, burly arms, panels of
glowing lights—he was yanked roughly through the hatchway,
into a well-lit room. The person who had grabbed him struck
him hard in the face, and the lights flashed more brilliantly
behind Kem's eyes. Then they went dark, then Kem was on
his ass on the deck of a small compartment.

The lights flickered back on, blurry with tears. A big,
thick-shouldered guy in an unmarked gray uniform stood over
him, his legs straddling Kem's, his fist cocked ready to slug
him again.

"Thank you," another voice said. Kem could not locate the

source of this voice; the man's body filled most of his vision.
"That won't be necessary, I don't think," the voice went on.
"You can leave him with me. I'll take care of it from here."

There was no mistaking that mellow, cultivated voice for
anything else. It belonged to Delan.

The burly guy gave Kem one last malevolent look, then
swung his leg over and stepped away from him.

Across the room, Delan stood half-propped against a bank
of glowing lights, electrical readouts. He did not quite look at
Kem but threw him a sort of rapid, cautionary glance.

"Look here," he said to the other guy. He pointed to the
hatch still open to the dark shaft, the hatch Kem had been
yanked through. "Why don't you just take a look, see if there
are any more of them."

The big guy seemed to consider this. He moved to the
hatch and stuck his head out. His motions were ponderous,
as though the bulk of his body made it hard to move. He
reminded Kem of another guy in a gray uniform, the one who
had killed Tallheron. The one who lay rotting with Kem's
arrow through his chest.

Kem's eye flicked over to Delan and back to the man in
the hatchway. He thought then of the pistol stuffed into his
pocket.

There was a moment when he could have pulled it out—a
moment when he almost did. He let the moment tick by. The
man in the gray uniform brought his head back into the room
and his eyes fell upon Kem as though he knew by thuggish
instinct that Kem was up to something.

"Watch your fucking self," he said, which on the whole
Kem figured was pretty good advice. Then the man told
Delan: "It's too dark to see, I'm going in. You call if you need
help."

Then he was gone. Delan closed the hatch behind him.
He leaned over to Kem, held a hand out; Kem allowed
himself to be eased up into a chair. It occurred to him, a
triumph of irrelevancy, that this was probably the squirrel
cage. Delan had offered long ago to show him the place, back
when Kem was a galley boy. Now things had come all the way
around.

"Well," Delan said.

The surprise was still in his eyes and in his voice. But surprise was not all. It seemed to Kem that Delan was also pleased; after a couple of moments he gave Kem a wide and apparently honest smile.

"So," he said. "You have come back."

Kem said he guessed he had.

"Mm," said Delan. "I wonder if that is a smart thing to have done."

Kem wondered too. His head felt like if had been broken open and then slammed shut.

"We shall see," said Delan, quietly, like he was talking to himself. "We shall see."

For a few moments, Kem's thoughts drifted back to the weapon in his pocket. He found that the urge to draw it had passed. Partly it was a matter of instinct—Delan was not the sort of person you pulled a gun on. Partly too it was this: if Delan had been planning to hurt him, to turn him over to the guards or anything, he could have done so already.

What does he want, though? Kem wondered.

Delan said, "Why *have* you come back, Kem?"

And of course Kem had no answer for that. Or rather, the only answer he had would have taken too long; it would have been a pretty long story.

"Have you come back for the party?" Delan's eyes were almost merry. "I bet you have."

The party—the words seemed to crawl through Kem's ears and down his spine. His head gave a painful throb, forcing a groan out of him.

"You just had to find out," said Delan, shaking his head. "Didn't you? You couldn't keep yourself away. You had to see for yourself."

It was exactly like something Ursa would have said. And Kem thought, No, you've got it all wrong—but then he thought that was okay; it was fine to let Delan think that, to let him think he had come back out of a kid's stupid curiosity.

"Well, you shall see, my boy," Delan told him. "You certainly shall."

Kem shifted miserably. Delan was tormenting him in a manner, and for a reason, he did not understand. He would not have gone along with it except that as far as he could tell he had no option. Wrong as Delan was about his motives, he was right about one thing: the Captain's party was what Kem had come for. Nothing could have kept him away from it.

Delan turned thoughtfully, opened a drawer. He pulled out a little box.

"Here," he said. He opened the box and held it out to Kem. "Here, take this."

The box was full of diviner's sage. Kem eyed it warily. "Um, I don't," his voice came out sluggish, like something long unused, "I don't want, I mean—"

Delan shook his head. "I am trying to help you," he said, like a kindly uncle or something. "I have always tried to help you, though I know you have found it difficult to believe that. You have always doubted that I am your friend."

Kem thought he was right about that. He said, "No, it's just, I've taken this stuff before."

"Of course you have. But it's not the way you think. You see, they're going to give you something, there at the party. Something that will make you sick."

Kem felt sick already. Sick with fear; sick with disgust.

Delan went on: "This will help with the sickness. It will make the sickness not matter so much. And other things. And don't mistake me—the sickness is not a serious thing. It is just a side effect. It will pass, and then you won't have to worry about being sick again. You won't have to worry . . . for a very long time."

Kem was very much afraid that he knew what Delan was talking about.

"Eat," said Delan, wagging a hand at the box of diviner's sage, smiling benignly. "Eat and enjoy."

And Kem—because he was afraid, and because he was sick already, and because Delan told him to—grabbed a fingerful of desiccated leaves and shoved it into his mouth. His mouth filled with spit; his gag reflex kicked in. He struggled to masticate, to swallow. The leaves scored his throat like caustic grit.

"Is it the Remedy?" he said, half-choking.

"What?" Delan stared as though he had not heard him, or else as though he had heard him perfectly well.

"At the party," said Kem. "What they're going to give me. Is it that?"

Delan frowned, and after a couple of silent heartbeats he said, "Why, yes, Kem. As a matter of fact, it is."

Kem was led, like a crazed or half-lame animal, out of the squirrel cage by a different door than the one he entered. Delan pointed him now this way, now that, along a narrow, winding passage. Sunwise, thought Kem. Sunwise and up.

It felt to him as though he must be flying. Some part of him was flying, anyway, though not the part that used to be his body. That part had disappeared. There were no lights in this part of the Oasis; only tiny portholes through which deck lights and starlight and some other, less steady light seemed to leak, to ooze.

At one place the passage ended in a head-high hatch, tightly dogged, and to the right a stair rose almost vertically. Delan nudged Kem forward, pressing him up against the stair, but for a few moments, or maybe it was an hour, Kem stood stiffened-up-like, staring at the closed hatchway. He had this idea, this crazy certainty: he was sure that if he concentrated really hard, he could see right through this hatch like it was a window. Or maybe he could just *know*, just flash onto what was behind it. Delan gave him a shove, and in that instant Kem saw it. He remembered.

He remembered a little deck, not much wider than a ledge. He remembered a pair of davits, steel cables running down from them. He remembered the captain's gig. He remembered the figure in white, scrambling over a rail, down a ladder.

"I've—" He wanted to tell Delan something; he wanted to let him know. "I've seen—"

Delan shushed him. "There are guards," he said. "We don't want to alarm them, do we? We don't want anybody to get hurt."

He grabbed Kem by the belt of his linen pants—grabbed him hard—and forced him up the stairway. Kem started climbing. For a squirrel, Delan was pretty strong.

The stair took them up to a hatch near the navigation

deck. Kem felt an impulse to dash in there, to seek refuge among the old unreliable machines, the log-table, the charts. It was like a bizarre form of nostalgia. Delan was starting to act impatient. Kem smelled something odd, something that frightened him. Sunwise and up: they went sunwise and up again. A bunch of thuggish types were milling around, doubles and triples of the guy that had slugged him. They looked angry, very angry at Kem personally. One of them, standing near, looked him right straight through the eye.

"You don't matter," said Kem. "You're not part of this."

The guy looked startled. Delan hustled Kem along, murmuring something—It's all right, he's just—and Kem felt very cool. He felt he understood everything, he had seen it all. Even this door; he knew this door was the one to the Captain's quarters.

"Has it started yet?" Delan asked somebody.

The other person said Yes, or said No. Kem was not really listening; he was listening to someone else, something, laughter...

"Well, Kem."

Delan's face blurred in and out of focus. Too close to him, or something. Kem shoved outward, forcing him away.

"It's all right," Delan said, to Kem or to somebody else. "I'm leaving now. You're on your own."

The end. Kem thought, this is the end. The end of the road, the end of the story. And he thought that what was important was not what happened now, whether the ending was happy or sad; it was just that he had made it here.

Only where he was, was not that easy to say. At the Captain's place—he knew that. But even though it was still the Captain's place, a place he had been before, everything was different now, it had been transformed, the way a stage is transformed into a different place, a story-land. A rose garden, say. A haunted forest. A windblown island.

What had the Captain's place been changed into? Kem bumped his way inward, moving by touch as much as anything, by memory; there were no lights, or rather no lights of an ordinary kind. There was only that strange dull glow, that flickering. It came through the windows on one side, the side where a door opened out to the flying bridge. Kem saw no people at all as he crossed the darkened stateroom. The door was closed; he pushed it open. And then he saw.

He saw what the Captain's place had become.

It was not part of the Oasis anymore. Or anyway that's what you were supposed to make believe. You were supposed to make believe that the flying bridge, with its exotic plants tumbling from big containers, was really a garden, really connected to the earth. A wild place. A place like the Bright Land, the island, where the old gnarled pine trees grew. Only wilder than that. Only much more strange.

To help you make believe, someone had spread dirt across the deck. The dirt seemed to have come from the planters, because plants lay heaped up in stacks here and there, four stacks, like points of a compass, and somebody had set fire to them. The plants were green and didn't burn well, but they were smoldering, producing small flames and great drifts of smoke, and that's what was making the light Kem had seen, the dull flickering. That's what was making the smell that had frightened him, too. It was the smell of all those exotic things—oplopanax horridis, dama da noite, psychotria, maikoa— that had been growing here on Kem's last visit, if "visit" was the word. Now those things were torn up, dying, smoldering; or rather certain ones of them were, a selection. Smoke, bitter-scented, hung in the air like a hellish cloud.

It seemed to Kem that he had figured something wrong, that he had made a miscalculation. But it was too late now; there was no time to go back and figure it right. It was hard enough going forward, feeling his way; it was hard enough just trying to breathe. He moved across the flying bridge and now at last he saw the people, the other people who were there with him. Here on this stage, this make-believe wild place. This miniature Underworld.

There were not many people, and for an instant, as he hovered there, Kem felt like he knew every one of them. They had not seen him yet, hanging back in the smoke, away from the fires, and he had a chance to move his eyes from one of them to the next.

There was Gardner, the Investor. Next to him was Stockard,

his friend, the man with the round boyish face. They were standing by themselves, murmuring together. They seemed to be watching something, but Kem could not see what. Whatever they were watching was on the other side of a planter, lost in the smoke.

Then there was Sander. Sander was almost naked; he wore only a small cloth wrap, the size of a towel. He had cut his hair—or somebody had. It had been chopped off crudely; the remnants of it stood in shocks about his head. Kem thought that Sander looked terrible. Then Sander turned and gazed right toward where Kem was standing. His eyes did not change, Kem could not tell whether Sander had recognized him or whether he was too wasted even to react if he had. Slowly Sander's hand came up, it came to rest on somebody's shoulder. The other person turned around.

The other person was Davina. Davina was beautiful. She was perfect. She was wearing a pale dress that seemed to float around her, as weightless as the smoky air. She looked hard at Kem for several seconds without moving or changing expression in any way, and Kem felt that there was some problem with his heart; it seemed to have stopped for an instant but now it had started again and it was out of control, it was beating so hard he was sure his chest was being bruised, his ribs were straining with the effort of trying to contain it.

When Davina's eyes locked on his, Kem had a feeling of elevated awareness, of supreme mental clarity. He felt sure, a moment before she did so, that she was going to begin walking toward him. She started walking. He felt sure he was going to hear her laughter, that trilling musical sound, and as she came near to him she smiled, her eyes opened wide. She tilted her head back. She laughed. And then Kem felt sure she was going to slip into his arms, to rest against his chest like a little girl, like a lost lover. She took a step closer; her eyes blazed. And then she seemed to grow dizzy. She took a bad step, lost her balance. She fell, and Kem lunged forward to catch her.

In his arms, she languished like someone half-asleep, like someone badly ill. The dead weight of her body made Kem stagger. He lowered her to the deck, right down onto the dirt that was spread out there. Her eyes rolled crazily, toward Kem and away from him.

What the fuck's wrong with her, Kem heard himself say. As soon as the words came out he realized that what was wrong with her was wrong with him too. It must be something in the smoke. Not the diviner's sage, though he could feel that too—it lay across his mind like a piece of glass, a solid transparency—but this feeling was different. If anything, the diviner's sage seemed to be giving him what clearness of mind he still had. He wondered if that was what Delan had meant. He wondered if this was another thing Delan had done to help him; and again, whether *help* was the right word.

A hand touched Kem's shoulder. Sander was looking down at him. His face had grown much older—not just the way you would have expected, eyes that had seen too much, an expression too jaded for its years. There were those things, but there was something else. Sander's skin looked tougher than it ought to have been, much too tough and leathery for a fifteen-year-old boy. It was like Gardner's skin, like Stockard's: like something carefully, artfully preserved.

"What's the matter with her?" said Kem. His voice was working better now. Anger, a familiar sensation, made him feel closer to normal. "What's the matter with *you?*"

Sander shook his head. It was not a dismissal, not a refusal to talk. Nor was it a warning. It was something else. It was a summation of things, like one of Sander's encompassing remarks. Sander had always been notable for his economy— Kem remembered when the boy's entire philosophy was contained in the words, *Do whatever you want to.* Now he had grown more economical yet. Everything he had to say, everything he needed to explain to Kem, fit tidily into a single shrug.

"Damn you," said Kem. "Damn this place. Damn—"

"Hello, Kem," a courtly voice said behind him.

Kem shivered. He had dreaded to hear this voice and yet he had known he must hear it. He had known this, and he had known he must once more, one final time, look up and meet those eyes. For a few moments he avoided doing so. He reached into his pocket and he touched the little counter, fingered it like a charm. Never forget, he told himself. Never forget. Never forget.

He stood up and he met the eyes of Captain Hand. The Captain smiled. He was immaculate as ever in his plain white uniform. Uncontaminated. His expression was gentle; the eyes might almost have been sad, softened by regret. He said, "I was hoping you'd come."

Just like that. Just like Kem's sudden reappearance was no more than a pleasant surprise, nothing much out of the ordinary. Like Kem had been in the neighborhood and just decided to drop by. Just stopped in to have a little chat. Couple of drinks, a puff of dama da noite—well, Kem could make believe that. The way he felt, he could make believe anything.

"Who'd you send this year?" he said to the Captain. "Who'd you sent to Riley County to get the kids?"

Hand raised an eyebrow, like he didn't have any idea . . . then he dropped it. He looked at Kem more critically, then he glanced down at where Davina lay, half-conscious, her eyes rolling, limbs stretched out in the dirt.

The Captain said: "Her."

"Bullshit." Kem felt like punching him. But the diviner's sage was still working, still propping open the window in his mind. He got a pretty vivid mental picture of what Hand would do if he tried something like that. He looked at the Captain and the Captain nodded, knowing like. Kem turned to Sander. "That's bullshit, isn't it? That he sent Davina. Isn't it?"

Sander shrugged again. The language of shrugs was more expressive than Kem might have thought; this one contained a distinct note of ambivalence, a reluctance to answer.

Damn, thought Kem.

"She wanted to go," said the Captain. "She wanted to earn her invitation to this . . . important gathering. And now you're here, too, Kem. That's very nice. It's so nice that you two can be here together."

Then Gardner, ever attentive to the needs of party-goers, came out of the smoke and he gave them a bleary-eyed grin. "Won't you join us?" he asked Kem. "Over here—maybe it'll help you get into the spirit."

Kem wanted perversely to continue his talk with the Captain; but Hand had turned aside, he had shifted his attention. Kem had been dismissed. He looked down at Davina, who now appeared to have passed out. Well, she's better off like that, he thought. But it made him feel disconnected. He looked over at Sander, but Sander was already moving away, following the direction of Gardner's arm. He glanced back at Kem, and for an instant Kem thought he recognized something in the boy's expression, a familiar hint of conspiracy. Kem hoped that's what it was. He went after Sander, with Gardner behind them. And they came to what Kem supposed was the heart of the party.

It was at the open center of the deck, near the voice tube and the compass repeater. The four piles of smoldering plants lay evenly spaced around it, so that no matter which way the breeze shifted you were downwind of one of them. Overhead, through the haze, you could see stars, like distant, grimy lights. And once or twice Kem thought he glimpsed something else up there, blinking out the stars, shadows moving around in the sky. But probably that was his imagination; or maybe it was the diviner's sage, working its way deeper into his mind.

Around this open space, on the dirt that covered the flying bridge, sat half a dozen people, most of them the same general type as Gardner and Stockard, prosperous looking, their ages indeterminate. Investors, Kem supposed. But two of them were just kids. The kids looked awfully young to Kem; they looked as young as Sander had been, back when Kem first met him. Skinny, sharp-eyed, feckless-looking kids, trying to act older and braver than they could carry off. Actually they looked to Kem very small and very helpless; and they looked also as though they knew this, as though they were starting to get a little scared because they knew something was coming down but of course they didn't know what.

Nobody was paying much attention to them. The Investor types were lounging around with big clay mugs in their hands making a show of enjoying themselves. One of the kids—a pale-skinned girl—was sitting by herself, and Sander went over and sat beside her. The girl smiled nervously at him. He took her hand, pulling her closer. She hesitated; he whispered something close to her ear; she turned to look at him as though he was totally insane.

The other kid, a black-haired and slightly older-looking boy, was busy checking out something, some type of contraption in the middle of the deck. Kem drifted a little closer and he saw that what the boy was looking at was a low table covered with small instruments, laboratory equipment or something like that. It was the same sort of stuff that had filled the big room like a museum back at the Bright Land: a centrifuge, a power cell, various tubes and pipettes and beakers in little racks. Kem's insides felt shrunken, twisted around. He sidled up next to the boy and he said:

"Hey."

The boy looked quickly around. His face was mean looking, a face that would have scared Kem a little had they been more like the same age. As it was, it struck Kem as fairly sad that a kid whose first shave was maybe three years off and whose nose was covered with freckles should feel compelled to look as though he were ready to pull a knife and slice your guts out. Kem couldn't think of much to say to a kid like that, but he wanted to talk, he wanted to do or say or learn something. So he said:

"My name's Kem."

The boy lifted his head back a little, like the first half of a nod. Real cool, like.

Kem said, "So what do you think of the Oasis?"

The kid said, "It's great." He said this as though daring Kem to disagree.

"Yeah, it is, I guess," said Kem. "Kind of. Where are you staying?"

"I don't know." The kid shrugged. He seemed to be deciding that Kem was okay, it was okay to talk to him. "We've been sleeping at some guy's place. Lots of shit all over, I guess he's got a lot of money or something, he hasn't tried anything, or any shit like that."

"Is she your girlfriend?" Kem gestured with his head—the girl seemed to have gotten into some tight conversation with Sander. They were leaning close together so that nobody else could hear and it made them look very kidlike.

"We're just friends," said the boy. "We just met a little while ago, back there at . . ."

His voice trailed off; he was looking at something over Kem's shoulder. Kem followed his eyes.

It was Captain Hand. He had come to the edge of the circle, and on his arm, leaning hard on him and looking quite sick, was Davina. He urged her another couple of steps forward. Into the circle.

"Here, now," he said. "You must participate. If you are going to be here then you must take part, that is very important."

Davina nodded though Kem was pretty sure she couldn't have understood; especially seeing as how he understood so precious little himself.

"Well," said Hand. "I suppose we ought to get started. Things always take longer than you expect."

That seemed an odd remark to begin with, but that didn't matter. Kem saw that. Whatever anyone said or didn't say, the wheel had rolled around to its foreordained position, things that had been only vague ideas in Kem's mind until now were about to become real, they were about to become inevitable, the story was about to come to an end. Around the deck people began to rise, to move inward, drawing the circle tighter and tighter.

Kem glanced at the boy he'd been talking to just a few seconds ago, and he saw that the kid was starting to look a little more scared. He had backed a few steps away from Kem and away from Hand, but that only brought him closer to a couple of people, Investors, who were standing back in the shadows. One of these people grabbed the boy from behind, pulled his arms back. The boy cried out in surprise, in anger. The cry changed quickly to one of pain; the second Investor came forward and struck the kid hard on the side of the face. The sound it made might as well have been a cannon going off. Kem's mind, already revved to a state of high energy by fear and by diviner's sage and by the alkaloids in the smoke, kicked over to another level altogether, a sort of hover-state, skimming along the surface of events but unable to penetrate them, unable to feel or to react properly. The Investor hit the boy again, and again, and again, and the boy lost his tough-kid look and started to cry. He wailed loudly, out of control, like a child. But of course that's what he was, a child: tears and blood ran down over his freckles.

Kem looked away. He saw the girl, standing next to Sander, huge-eyed with what Kem guessed would be disbelief. She looked at Sander, stared at him imploringly, as though begging him to tell her it wasn't for real, it was only make-believe. Or maybe hoping that Sander, somehow, like a storybook hero, was going to rescue her. Sander took her arm and lifted it very slowly, ceremoniously almost. When it was all the way up he turned and offered the arm, offered the girl herself, to Gardner. Gardner grabbed her and yanked her over to him, and before she could scream or kick or resist in any way he had clamped his arms around her like a cruel parody of a lover's hug. She only came up to his chest; he lifted her a little and pressed his mouth on hers. She writhed in his grasp but Gardner was the athletic type. The girl was helpless. Kem glared angrily at Sander, who stood looking on with an absolutely inscrutable expression. You'd have thought, Kem reflected bitterly, that he'd at least show a fucking smidgen of remorse.

Sander must have felt the pressure of Kem's growing anger, because he turned to Kem and for a second or two returned his stare. Kem came close to hurling himself across the deck at his old friend, taking him down the way he had once taken a guy down on the beach at Riley County. What stopped him was not his better judgment—that was long gone, out the window—but something in Sander's eye, a warning, a message, something. . . .

"Watch him," said Captain Hand. He nodded toward Kem. Stockard and another Investor moved up a little, but they did not come very close to him and their presence did not feel particularly threatening. They had been told to watch Kem and that is what they did, very closely. Kem glared at them, just to check, but they did not respond in kind. Stockard's round face may actually have brightened up a little.

"Now," said Hand. "From this point you all may feel certain things—twinges of pain, flashes of strong emotion. You must try not to let these things bother you overmuch.

They are simply side effects of the process we are about to undertake, and in any case they will be over soon."

He made a slight beckoning motion. The two guys holding the boy dragged him over to where Hand was standing. Hand gestured again; they forced him down into the dirt. The boy stared up, his eyes as small and bright as those of a cornered, terrified animal. He kicked, he twisted his body one way and another, but the guys had no trouble holding him down; they did not even seem to work very hard at it.

"What we are trying to do here," Hand said, "is to activate a very small organ. A gland."

He might have been saying this for Kem's benefit, or for Kem's and Davina's. He looked from one of them to the other, they were the only ones, Kem guessed, who hadn't seen this before.

"The gland is ordinarily dormant," Hand went on. He looked down at the boy as though the kid were nothing but a laboratory specimen. "But it does become active in some people, under certain circumstances, and early adolescence is a particularly susceptible time."

As he spoke he leaned down to the little table, where all the equipment was. He picked up a latex hose, a flask, a suction bulb. "Pain often triggers the activity of the gland," he said. His voice had become clinical, detached. "So does sex. So do the early stages of death, or near-death. We do not know the precisely optimal conditions."

He turned around, looked at Davina, looked at Kem. "This is not an exact science. At our present stage of knowledge, it is more like a craft. Or if you will, an art."

"It's a fucking fake," said Kem.

Hand looked at him placidly. He shook his head. "Oh, no. The fact that we do not fully understand it does not mean that the phenomenon is not real. But you will realize that very shortly. You will see." He turned around, pointed down at the boy. "Him first. We'll start with him. Stockard, would you like ... ?"

The round-faced Investor stepped forward. He reached down to the lab table and picked up a knife. Kem guessed this was it, this was the moment—he went tense all over his body, coiling like a snake—but the knife looked wrong, it was

small and hooked and Stockard was holding it too lightly. As
the two guys held the writhing boy more or less in place,
Stockard bent over him and began slicing up his clothes. It
was like skinning an animal, the clothing came away in long
strips. The boy screamed, he continued to struggle, and this
caused him to get cut in several places. But none of the cuts
were too bad, and for all Kem knew this might have all been
part of the craft, the art: a little more blood, a little more
pain.

And now, he supposed, the sex part. Stockard looked down
at the skinny naked body, a pitiful sight, with undisguised
relish. Kem did not think he could bear to watch but he
found it difficult to turn away. Stockard was down on his
knees when a slight movement at one side caught Kem's
attention.

It was the girl. She was still tight in Gardner's grasp but
he was no longer embracing or kissing her. She was just
standing there and tears were rolling down her cheeks, but
she did not actually seem to be crying. She was not even
looking at the boy and Stockard, though of course Gardner
was, everybody was. She was looking instead at Sander, and
even though Sander refused to look back at her Kem got the
distinct idea that something did not add up here, there was
some other drama, a shadow-play, going on.

"Now," said Hand. "Certain feelings may began to occur. A
sharpening of the senses. Arousal. Pain. These experiences
will not be your own—they will be his." Hand pointed; he
meant the poor kid now being slammed around in the dirt
with Stockard on top of him. Hand said: "The gland we are
trying to activate is closely associated with the phenomenon
of transpersonal awareness. This is yet another thing we don't
understand. We are forced to work around our own ignorance. You have been exposed to a number of substances
tonight which should serve to augment your receptivity. That
is so that we will know when the moment has come to begin
the process. Precise timing is, of course, essential."

"The *process*," said Kem, spitting the word out. "A fucking
con job, is what it is." He took a step forward, glancing left
and right, but it seemed that the people around him, the
Investors, were not going to interfere. They looked unruffled;

hey must have been taking their cue from Hand. Kem said,
'I know you've got a real medicine, somewhere. I know
where you got it from. You're just *doing* this, you're just
putting on a show."

Hand watched him, as though waiting to see how far he
was prepared to carry this.

"*Kem*"—from Davina, standing behind him. "Kem stop it,
you'll just—"

He turned on her, and his expression must have been
pretty alarming. Her eyes got wider; she backed a step away.

Kem looked back at Hand and he said, "I know you're
lying. I've *been* to the Bright Land, I *know* that's where the
real medicine comes from. This is just a bunch of crap you've
knocked together out of old stories. You get everybody high
on this, this stuff you're burning, whatever it is, and you
convince them that you're really doing something. Like you're
his magician or something, this great doctor. But all you're
doing is murdering a couple of little kids. And your friends
are getting their rocks off. You're really sick. This is really
disgusting."

Hand heard him out with a look of not much more than
polite interest. Nobody made a move except for Stockard,
who heaved himself up and down, moaning with pleasure.
The boy whimpered beneath him. Sander drifted a little
closer to them, as though to get a better look.

"You're partly right," Captain Hand said, unexpectedly.
He nodded at Kem, like one colleague acknowledging the
helpful remarks of another. "Actually, the process was developed
in the Bright Land. That was necessary, that is the only place
with adequate research facilities." He narrowed his eyes,
seeming to reflect on that. "But you're wrong about the rest
of it. The Bright Land is not the source of the Remedy. It is
the source of—"

He stopped, as though his mind were suddenly drawn
elsewhere. His expression grew thoughtful; he raised his
fingers to his temple, rested them lightly there. His brow
furrowed as though deep in contemplation; then furrowed
more as though in pain, in serious pain. Agony. He bent over.

Kem thought this might be carrying it a little far, but
then—

"*Oh—*" Davina cried out behind him. Other people around
the circle made other noises, little cries of alarm or fear or
Kem couldn't tell, they might have been pleasure, ecstasy,
something was definitely happening here and it seemed that
only he was immune from it.

Only he and Sander.

Sander slipped up fast and silent as a cat behind Stockard.
As he moved, he reached into his little cloth wrap and drew a
knife out of it, and before Kem understood what was happening his friend had buried the knife deep between Stockard's
shoulder blades. Stockard arched his back, letting out one
final moan as though he were having a volcanic orgasm; then
his body shuddered and fell limp and heavy and still. The kid
scooted out from under him. He knelt there with eyes that
were crazed, almost delirious.

That broke the spell, whatever odd thing had been happening that everyone had shared.

Hand was the first to come fully to his senses. He pointed
at Sander and he said, "Kill him." He was very calm about it.

Gardner let go of the girl and he fell into a dangerous
looking crouch. Sander had left the knife in Stockard's back
and he stood there looking like he expected to die, like he
really didn't care one way or the other.

Or maybe that's not what the look meant. Maybe it was
something entirely different, a weird sort of confidence.
Gardner was still in his crouch, moving forward, when the
little girl came running up behind him, jumped onto his
back. It was a hopeless act, of course, an act of desperation
and Gardner reached up to pull her off, to toss her away. His
hand got up to neck level and stopped there. His eyes
stretched out, he clutched at his throat. There was a bubbling
noise; blood gushed onto his hand and his arm and then
Gardner toppled forward. He twisted in the dirt, his trachea
spuming red foam. The girl stood back from him. She looked
at Sander. Sander looked at Kem.

"I hope you've got a gun," he said.

Kem did have a gun. He yanked it out of his belt and he
leveled it at Captain Hand.

"Don't move," he said. "Don't do anything."

Sander sighed in relief. "Delan said you'd have a gun."

Kem figured he could be amazed by all this later. Right now there were certain obvious problems to take care of. He wondered if he had enough bullets to take care of them. He glared around at the remaining Investors, who had sense enough to stay right where they were standing. Kem turned back to face the Captain.

Hand might have been caught off balance for a moment, he might have been vulnerable, but by the time Kem got his brain working that was all over. The Captain was staring at him with absolutely no expression. Certainly no fear.

"Well," he said. "You've really lived up to our expectations. Our expectations were high to begin with, and yet you continue to surprise us."

"Us," Kem repeated. "You always say *us*. Who's this fucking *us*? There's pretty much just you, the way I see it."

Hand shook his head. "There are many more of us than just me. Many Penitents. As you, Kem, ought to know by now. You have been to the Bright Land, after all. You are one of us, yourself."

"No."

"No?" Hand cocked his head. "That's not what I hear. What I hear is—"

"*Stop.*" Kem stared down the gun-sights. "I don't *care* what you hear. I don't want to know. I know enough. I don't want to listen to you anymore."

Hand looked saddened by this, regretful. He shrugged. "There is one more thing—"

"Shut up."

"One more thing you *should* know," the Captain went on, as though Kem's words meant nothing, as though the gun was a toy. "You ought to know why. You know a good deal about what and how, you've been quite clever about that. But you ought to know why."

Kem glanced around him. He saw Sander, Davina. The girl, the boy. He saw the bodies of Gardner and Stockard, like deflated things; the dirt that covered the deck soaked up their oozing blood. He saw the other Investors, shady figures in the background, faces obscured by the haze. And in the middle of it all, the death scene, the violent awful tableau, he

saw Captain Hand, seeming very much unbothered by any of
it, including Kem's gun. Especially Kem's gun.

As though he sensed a change of momentum, Hand spoke
to him quietly and rapidly. "You have wasted an important
opportunity," he said. "A *vital* opportunity. You might at least
want to understand what you have done."

"I know what I've done," Kem said. "I've saved two kids'
lives. I've broken up your little party."

Hand shook his head. "Not *my* party." He jerked his head
toward Sander, then around the circle of Investors. "His.
Theirs. Many other people's. Not mine."

Despite himself, Kem had let Hand recapture his attention. He had allowed those eyes to take control of him. Damn
him, he thought.

But he listened. And the Captain said: "They have been
exposed to the crying. They depend on this"—gesturing
toward the table—"they need this to survive. But not I. And
not you either, as far as I know."

"You're lying," said Kem.

"No," said Sander, out of nowhere.

"No," repeated the Captain.

Kem looked from one of them to the other. The Captain
looked regretful; Sander looked impossibly old and sad.

The Captain said: "You are incompletely informed. There
is only one Remedy. There is only one way we know to
prepare it. Without it, without the Remedy, things would
have gone much further than they have. As things stand,
there is a kind of equilibrium. There is a balance between life
and death, between humanity and the rest of the world. Or if
you prefer, between mortals and the Goddess. And that is
why, Kem. Why the wheel turns. Why we perform this
ceremony year after year. So that the balance may be
maintained. So that life can go on."

"That's fucking ridiculous." Kem lowered his gun a little.
The Captain made him so angry, he hardly felt like shooting
him. He wanted to argue for a while. There was no hurry, he
figured. The night would be long and moonless. He could
finish this at any time. He said, "Even if it's true about the
Remedy—"

"It is," Sander said quietly. "Delan says so."

"But even if it *is*," Kem persisted, still staring at Hand, "people aren't going to die off, just because you're not there to save them. There're too many people for that. The crying isn't going to get all of them. I've lived on the Grind, I've seen it. I've seen people that've had their whole families wiped out. But they're still alive. So you can forget your stupid Remedy. It just doesn't make that much difference, in the long run."

But of course it did, he knew it did. If Sander was infected, the Remedy made all the difference there was.

He raised the gun again. But Hand merely shook his head, like a parent who has tried and tried to teach you something but it just isn't getting through.

Hand said, "I don't mean the Remedy. I don't mean that all the people would die. Of course they wouldn't. That's not what I'm talking about."

What, then, thought Kem.

Hand gave him a sad smile. "You're very bright, and you've learned a great deal in a rather short time. That is why we have always welcomed you. That's why we value having you among us. But you haven't learned everything, even you must realize that. For instance, *Why is there a wheel?* Do you remember that, that question you didn't understand? *Why is there an Oasis?* Tell me."

"Sure," said Kem, bluffing. He pointed to the Investors. "There's a wheel so they can make money. They gave you the money to set this operation up, and you go around selling your Remedy to anyone who can afford it. You split the profits."

"You assume, then," said Hand, "that the business of the Oasis is to dispense the Remedy. But quite the opposite is true. Listen to me: *The purpose of the Oasis is to spread the crying.*"

Kem thought about squeezing the trigger right now; he did not want to hear this. But at the same time, of course, he did. The Captain had him trapped, helpless, using only the weapon of his words.

"Oh yes," Hand said. "The Remedy is incidental. Its only purpose is to protect *us*, to ensure that our activities proceed without interruption. Because as you have said yourself,

there is no chance at all that people will be killed off. As long
as there is any habitat at all, humanity will proliferate. The
sequence of events that brought us *here* will continue. Given
the chance, people will pick right up where they left off, and
eventually there will be nothing left at all. No Oasis, no
Grind, no seasons, no grand cycle. Nothing. The great story
will come to an end. And that, Kem, is why there is a wheel.
That is why there is a cycle. The wheel turns in order that it
may continue turning. The cycle of death and life exists so
that the story, the oldest and longest story we know, may go
on without end. And that is why we call this the Great Work.
That is the cause we serve. You and I, all the Penitents. Do
you see?"

Kem did see. He had wanted to see and now he did. He
whispered, "Never forget."

"What?" Hand did not seem to have heard him.

"*Never forget*. Somebody told me that."

"Who?" said the Captain. "Who told you?"

Kem thought that for once Hand really seemed curious.
Why, though? He thought about Ursa saying those words,
remembered her standing at the waterfront, seeing him off.
He remembered the look in her eye, his last memory of
her—a look that seemed to contain a message, a look he did
not understand.

Now he looked at the Captain, the curious expression on
the Captain's face, almost a look of innocence. Or perhaps of
youth, simplicity. A childish kind of look. He tried to imagine
the Captain as a child, and he was very surprised to find that
he could. He could see him, a little boy with blond hair. He
could see Ursa, too. The two of them together.

He said, "I have a message for you, I think."

"What message?" said the Captain. "From whom?"

Hand looked more surprised and more genuinely puzzled
than Kem had ever seen him. He stared at Kem in much the
way Kem had so often stared at the Captain—looking for
meaning in a pair of silent eyes.

Kem said, "Do you miss her very much?"

Hand narrowed his eyes. Then slowly he smiled. His facial
muscles softened. His eyes relaxed their hold on Kem; Kem

could feel their power dissipate as though it were a physical thing, as real and forceful as the heat of the sun.

"Yes," said Hand. "Sometimes. Sometimes I—"

Kem shot him through the heart.

They hit the Barrens running. The captain's gig had barely touched the earth when Davina and the two kids scrambled out and took off as fast as they could go, making for the safety of the trees, the adolescent forest. Only Kem hung back a few moments, and only to say good-bye to Sander.

"You can still come," he said. "Really. We've got enough horses. We'll figure something out."

He did not need the look Sander gave him to understand that this wasn't true; there was nothing they could work out because there was no treatment for the crying, no Remedy but one. Anyway that wasn't what Kem had really been trying to say. He was trying to tell Sander that he would miss him, he loved him, Sander was his best and only friend, things that he would never actually say in real words. Fortunately real words were not the language Sander spoke nor the language he understood.

"Get out of here," Sander told him. "Before they figure out about this boat thing."

"It's called a gig," said Kem. "Anyway, who? Who's left to figure it out?"

"Get out of here," said Sander.

In the first faint light of day, his face looked almost boyish again. Almost hopeful. Kem did not want to be around to see that change.

"Well, all right," he said. "I hope you know what you're doing. And Delan. Who'll take over here, now? Who's next in command?"

"Somebody. Or nobody." Sander tilted his head back, gave Kem a cocky, imperishable smile. "Who knows?"

"Yeah," said Kem. "Who knows."

That was it. Kem heard the winch engaging as he tucked himself into the shadows.

The horses were right where he left them. Right where he told them to stay.

"Good girls," he said, patting them, hustling everybody aboard. "And good boys. Good horses."

It was getting light. It was Ripe Berries Moon. It was a new day.

"Where are we going?" Davina asked him.

The horses ambled through the woods, heedless of time, of the need to stick to their course. "Riley County," said Kem. "Have you ever been there?"

Davina shook her head. "But what if they send somebody after us? What if we get the crying? What—"

"Damn it." Kem reined in, looked at her seriously. "Let's just finish this, all right?"

She blinked at him; she looked confused, worried.

"That's another damned story," Kem said. "Let's finish this one first."

Then a screeching startled him, a sound that came suddenly out of the sky. Kem flinched—but the birds that danced through the treetops were not desert eagles;
they were birds of the forest;
they were birds of the north.
They were ravens.

I miss you, Matthew

ABOUT THE AUTHOR

RICHARD GRANT is the author of three previous novels, *Saraband of Lost Time* (winner of the Philip K. Dick Special Award), *Rumors of Spring*, and *Views from the Oldest House*. He has recently completed *Ravens*, a novel about an aging motorcycle gang, and is currently doing research for a book about Deadheads in the afterlife. He lives in Maine, where he is an advisor to the state arts commission.